BANISHED PRINCE TO DESERT BOSS

HEIDI RICE

HIRED BY THE FORBIDDEN ITALIAN

CATHY WILLIAMS

MILLS & BOON

First Published in Great Britain 2022
by Mills & Boon, an imprint of HarperCollins*Publishers* Ltd,
1 London Bridge Street, London, SE1 9GF

www.harpercollins.co.uk

HarperCollins*Publishers*
1st Floor, Watermarque Building,
Ringsend Road, Dublin 4, Ireland

Banished Prince to Desert Boss © 2022 Heidi Rice

Hired by the Forbidden Italian © 2022 Cathy Williams

ISBN: 978-0-263-30078-9

04/22

MIX
Paper from
responsible sources
FSC™ C007454

This book is produced from independently certified FSC™ paper
to ensure responsible forest management.
For more information visit www.harpercollins.co.uk/green.

Printed and Bound in Spain using 100% Renewable Electricity
at CPI Black Print, Barcelona

BANISHED PRINCE
TO DESERT BOSS

HEIDI RICE

MILLS & BOON

This book is dedicated to my mum,
who reads my books and tells me she loves them,
even though there's no golf or bowls in them
(and there never will be).

CHAPTER ONE

A COMBINATION OF nerves, heat exhaustion and tightly leashed fury tied Jamilla Omar Roussel's stomach into knots as she watched the Zafari royal jet, its red and gold insignia glinting in the sunshine, land on the desert airstrip.

She glanced surreptitiously at her watch for about the ten thousandth time that afternoon.

You're an hour late, you—

She cut off the name she wanted to call Dane Jones— the jet's illustrious passenger, and the man she was here to greet officially on behalf of her employer, Sheikh Karim Jamal Amari Khan—before it could properly register, let alone spill out of her mouth.

She would not stoop to the same level as the Manhattan playboy being flown in to replace her employer by calling him names.

Jones was Karim Khan's half-brother, the result of King Abdullah's rocky marriage to his fourth wife, American socialite Kitty Jones. And even if Jones didn't use his father's surname or his royal title and had never even visited his homeland since his parents' divorce at the age of five, he was the only person Zafar's rather traditional ruling council would accept to represent the country in Karim's absence. The important trade mission to Europe had been in the offing for two years and was due to start next week, but Karim and Orla had decided to remain in their home in Ireland with their three-year-old son Hasan to await the birth of their twins when Orla had been diagnosed with gestational hypertension two days ago. Karim had refused point-blank to leave his family to embark on the tour alone and as many of the dates and events could not be rearranged at such short notice, calling on his half-brother to step in had been the only way to avoid cancelling the tour altogether.

Anxious concern for her friend Orla tightened the knots in Jamilla's stomach...

You can do this, Milla. You have to.

At the age of only twenty-four she had just become the Zafari royal family's chief diplomatic aide. She spoke six languages fluently—plus the four local dialects. She had a master's degree in political science from the neighbouring University of Narabia and in the last few years had worked her way up from being the Queen's personal assistant at the palace to Karim and Orla's right-hand woman in affairs of the Zafari state... Orla's pregnancy scare had handed Jamilla a sudden promotion which she would never have expected, or wanted in these circumstances, but which was still an opportunity to consolidate her position in the royal court. And finally offer her a chance to travel to countries outside the kingdom.

An exciting, challenging opportunity she absolutely refused to fail at.

And not just because it would give her career an impressive boost if she could pull this off—and turn a Manhattan playboy into a royal prince—but because Karim and Orla and Zafar were counting on her.

She dabbed her brow with her now sodden tissue while blinking furiously to keep the sweat—which had gone from a trickle to a flood ten minutes ago—out of her eyes. As the luxury jet taxied to a stop, she reviewed the detailed itinerary for the coming week of preparations in Zafar, which she had finalised late last night and had planned to brief the stand-in head of state on during the two-hour drive back to the Palace of the Kings. A cloud rose from the runway, covering her and the delegation of officials standing next to her to greet their new temporary head of state too in a spray of fine grit.

Their exceptionally *late* new temporary head of state.

Jamilla gritted her teeth against the wave of misery, and pressed sweaty palms to the tailored knee-length grey pencil skirt she'd donned that morning, but which now felt like a damp straitjacket. She'd opted for a modern professional look over traditional garb. Unfortunately, when choosing not to wear the full, flowing dark desert robes intended to maintain a woman's modesty as much as regulate her body heat, Jamilla hadn't factored in the practical aspects of wearing a fitted designer suit and four-inch heels for any length of time in the afternoon sun.

She straightened her spine, swallowed down the increasingly persistent nausea and ignored the low-grade headache gripping her skull. Once she had greeted the American billionaire and introduced him to the long line of dignitaries, she would forego the briefing and take the opportunity to relax in the front seat of the air-conditioned limo while they travelled back to the Palace.

She was far too frazzled now to think clearly—and she probably looked an absolute state, not at all the first impression she had intended to make. While she had planned to hit the ground running today—as they had only eight days before flying to Europe to begin their royal tour—it would make more sense to ease Jones in slowly. Tomorrow would be soon enough to arrange their first proper briefing—and give Jamilla the chance to set the right tone for their future working relationship.

She lifted an arm, heavy with fatigue, to shield her eyes

from the brutal sunshine as the ground crew wheeled the jet's metal stairs into place and the door opened.

The elderly ruling council member who had travelled to New York to accompany Dane Jones back to the kingdom on Karim's orders appeared first, followed by his staff, the cabin crew, the pilot and the co-pilot. As they all exited the aircraft, then either climbed into cars to head back to the Palace or joined the welcoming committee, the jet's door remained open for two... Three... Curse it, four more minutes.

What is he waiting for? An even bigger entrance? Hasn't he delayed us all enough already?

Jamilla was ready to weep, the sweat stains on her suit now probably visible from space, when a tall, broad figure appeared in the plane's doorway.

Finally.

He made his way down the aircraft stairs.

She blinked, wiped her brow again, her heart jumping into her throat as something warm and solid wedged itself between her damp thighs.

Goodness.

She pushed a breath out, drew in another.

She'd seen photos of Dane Jones in the celebrity magazines and websites she checked each month—purely for professional purposes. She needed to know who was who in the VIP world, as the Khans enjoyed hosting events in the kingdom. Although Karim's half-brother had never accepted any of the invitations Jamilla had extended to him, she knew he was an exceptionally handsome man. Not really surprising, given that he was Karim's blood relation.

But as he stepped onto the desert floor, a leather bag slung over his shoulder, her gaze absorbed every breathtaking detail. The fluid, almost predatory gait, the worn jeans hanging loosely on narrow hips, the black T-shirt moulded to defined pecs, the chiselled cheekbones, the heavy stubble covering a hard jaw and the wavy hair—a burnished bronze streaked with sun-bleached gold—long enough to curl around his ears, topped by a baseball cap with a New York Yankees logo.

She swallowed past the lump of something raw and unfamiliar in her throat.

Okay.

She sucked in another crucial breath, beginning to feel light-headed—which had to be the heat, surely. As Dane Jones strode towards her, he lifted his head to reveal dark aviator sunglasses. His head dipped, his gaze cruising the length of her body, and no doubt taking in the sodden power suit. She felt the searing perusal everywhere as the temperature shot up another few thousand degrees.

'Hey,' he said, his voice a husky rasp, as if he'd just woken up. Maybe he had.

They'd been informed the delegation from Zafar had been forced to wake him up at his penthouse apartment when he hadn't shown up at the airport for the flight.

Probably far too busy sleeping off a hangover with one of his many girlfriends.

Jamilla cut off the thought, which had conjured up an unhelpful image of the man in front of her stark naked.

'Dane Jones,' he added by way of introduction, while she stood there speechless. Why couldn't she talk right now? 'If you're the welcoming committee, let's go. It's like a damn oven out here.'

'Your… Your Highness,' she began, finally managing to ease a word out of her bone-dry throat. 'I am Jamilla Omar Roussel…' She began the spiel she'd rehearsed. 'I've been assigned as your top diplomatic aide and advisor during your tenure as Zafar's head of state for the European tour and trade mission. Let me introduce you to…' She lifted her arm to indicate the line of dignitaries who had been waiting in the hot sun for far too long and looked stiff with expectation. Before she could remember any of their names, her mind a fuzzy mess, though, he interrupted her.

'Your what, now?' he asked.

'Excuse me?' She dropped her leaden arm.

'What did you just call me?' he asked, a muscle ticking in the stubble on his jawline.

'Your Highness… Your Highness,' she replied.

He sighed, pulling off the cap, and swept his fingers through the mass of wavy hair. 'Yeah, I thought so. Don't.'

'Don't what, Your Highness?' she said, having lost the thread of the conversation, her mind turning to mush under the wave of displeasure rolling off him.

'Don't call me that,' he said, then muttered something under his breath that she felt sure was not polite. 'I'm a US citizen. I answer to my name; that's it. So call me Dane, or Jones, or don't call me anything at all…'

'But, Your Highness, you are a direct blood descendant of the house of Al Amari Khan and second in line to the Zafar throne after Crown Prince Hasan…' she began, the hot weight jammed between her legs joined by a flare of heat in her cheeks.

'Yeah, I get that—' he interrupted her again '—or I wouldn't have had to fly eight thousand miles to this godforsaken…' He cut off the words, but she heard the sentiment and the snap of temper. And her own temper—which had been ruthlessly controlled—snapped back.

Why was he so annoyed? What he had been asked to do was an honour of the highest order. And Zafar wasn't godforsaken. Quite the contrary; it was blessed. Especially since Karim had gained the throne five years ago and begun a bold quest to turn the country back into a constitutional monarchy after his father's disastrous rule, and bring its depleted infrastructure into the twenty-first century.

'I'm doing this for my brother and his wife, end of.' He cut into her thoughts, the snap of anger slicing through her composure. 'He asked me, so I came,' he added, not sounding at all happy about it. 'At considerable expense and inconvenience to me and my business. I had to move a ton of stuff around and bump two major openings into the summer. Here's hoping when we're through, Karim and his cute wife will have two more healthy kids to add to their brood, so I'll be so far down the line of succession no one will ever ask me to do something like this again. But I'm not happy about it. I'm not royal, and I could not give a damn about this country or its future. My life is in New York. So calling me Your Highness is just gonna piss me off more. Okay? So don't do it. Because you won't like me much when I'm pissed.'

'I don't like you much now.'

Did I just say that out loud?

Shock came first, swiftly followed by horror. As her caustic comment echoed across the desert floor, shooting past Dane Jones's tall, indomitable frame and the stunned dignitaries, then echoed around the gleaming jet, the line of chauffeur-driven limos, the grey airport building and boomed out over the inhospitable terrain towards the Palace of the Kings two hours' drive away and probably as far as the Kholadi tribal lands two hundred miles to the north and the neighbouring kingdom of Narabia six hundred miles to the east.

A curse word her mother would have soundly slapped her for even knowing let alone thinking crossed Jamilla's fevered brain—she bit into her lip to stop it bursting out into the fetid, febrile air too.

'I beg your pardon, Your Highness,' she managed, wanting to die on the spot. Or at the very least melt into the puddle which had been forming at her feet.

He didn't say anything. But she could feel that hot,

searing gaze on every inch of her skin, making her heart pound hard enough to be heard in Narabia too. The nausea turned the giant knots in her stomach into enormous hanks of rope.

She couldn't believe it. She'd torpedoed the career opportunity of a lifetime—less than two minutes after meeting him. He would have her replaced. Of course he would. He was a king—or, rather, a king's brother—and she was supposed to be guiding him through this assignment with tact and diplomacy, not telling him what she actually thought of him.

She waited for the axe to fall, busy reconfiguring her once stunning resumé in her head, aware of the horrified looks being sent her way by the ruling council members and the other dignitaries. But, just as a wave of panic threatened to engulf her whole body, Dane Jones yanked off his sunglasses, revealing the most piercing blue eyes she had ever seen in her life. A spark twinkled in the deep cerulean blue, the tanned skin around his eyes crinkled as his gaze narrowed and she got the impression he was seeing her properly for the first time.

Then he threw back his head and roared with laughter.

Dane Jones's belly hurt he was laughing so hard.

Damn, but the look on the woman's face had been priceless as her snapped comment cut through the desert air as if she'd used a megaphone. That look—seriously horrified—had almost been worth getting woken up at dawn and forced to fly to this sand hole in the desert. Her previously pinched lips relaxed to form a perfect O and her eyes—a stunning shade of amber he'd only just noticed—widened to the size of dinner plates to consume her whole face.

He scrubbed the heel of his hand under his eyelids, actual tears running down his cheeks as the barks of laughter subsided to dull chuckles.

Okay, man, get a grip. It ain't that hilarious.

The truth was he was just exhausted and on edge, and super pissed that he was, one, having to do this thing for a whole month. And, two, being forced to set foot in a country he had promised never to return to in his lifetime.

The minute the jet had touched down, the weight he'd spent years expelling from his stomach had dropped right back into it again. And started to roll around.

Added to all that, he'd had barely any sleep—last night's inaugural event in the new club he'd opened in a rehabbed pickle factory under the High Line hadn't finished until five in the morning. He'd been woken up an hour later in his loft apartment in the Meatpacking District by the stiff now standing ten feet away staring at them both disapprovingly.

He rubbed his hand across his stomach as he finally got a grip, his abdominal muscles sore now.

'Please excuse me, Your Highness…' she began again.

'No excuse necessary. I was being a horse's ass,' he said.

Her shoulders collapsed with relief. Did she think he was going to get her fired over one snarky—and mostly justifiable—comment?

The last of his laughter died. Yeah, probably. Wasn't that exactly the way his father had always treated his subordinates? Even though his brilliant brother had been in charge for five years, he and his pretty little Irish wife couldn't achieve miracles. No doubt the palace staff were still intimidated by his father's autocratic legacy.

With the panicked look gone, Jamilla Roussel's face relaxed, making him more aware of the smudged makeup under those compelling amber eyes and the sheen of perspiration making her soft brown skin glow.

She looked almost as shattered as he felt.

'But I'm not kidding about the Your Highness stuff,' he added. 'That's gotta stop.'

She nodded. 'Absolutely, Mr Jones,' she said, finally getting the message. 'If that is what you prefer.'

'Call me Dane,' he said, not sure why he was goading her but suddenly keen to establish a working relationship with her. He was stuck with this assignment for the next four weeks—he'd given Karim his word, and as his brother had never asked him for a damn thing before now he knew he couldn't wheedle his way out of this promise, like he had so many others in the past.

'I'm not sure I should be so familiar, Your...' she began, then caught herself '... Mr Jones.'

She really was stunning, he decided. High cheekbones, wide eyes the colour of rare gems, ebony hair, the curling tendrils hanging down from a ruthless knot which only accentuated her gravity-defying bone structure—and the lean curves beneath the tailored suit that he'd noticed straight off because, hey, he was a guy.

'Jamilla, you just told me how much you don't like me,' he said, enjoying the way her brows shot up her forehead at the reminder. 'I think we can safely say over-familiarity isn't gonna be a problem between us.'

Although, even as he said it, he could feel the fizz working through his veins—which was weird. And also not at all welcome.

He was a guy who always appreciated a good- looking woman, and this woman was certainly that, but he didn't appreciate rules and regulations and being told what to do—and that was literally this woman's job. And he also never dated women he was in a working relationship with. Firstly because it was *so* not cool, but more importantly because it could lead to serious complications when the relationship turned sour, which always happened sooner for him than for the women he hooked up with.

But the fizz was still there, annoyingly. And making its presence felt, especially when she sighed, and he saw her decide to give it to him straight. What was it about those little glimpses of the woman behind the mask of etiquette and appropriate behaviour that appealed to him so much?

'I just don't feel comfortable using your first name under the circumstances, Mr Jones,' she said. 'Not only are you my employer's brother but you're of royal blood and…'

'Okay, hold up.' He held up his hand, the comment making his temper spike. 'Let's figure out a compromise,' he said, forced to appreciate the irony. She had to be the first woman who had ever struggled to use his given name. Ever since he'd hit puberty, women usually wanted to get way too familiar with him, way too fast.

'How about you call me Jones and drop the Mr, which makes me feel prehistoric?' And he was more than jaded enough already at the thought of the next few weeks— and having to pretend to be someone and something he was not, for the benefit of an institution, and a country, he despised.

She studied him and he could see she didn't like it, but he could also see her suck up her disapproval. That she was so transparent didn't help with the fizz one little bit.

She nodded. 'Okay, if you insist.'

'I insist,' he said, getting an added buzz out of the fact he could insist and she would have to obey him.

Okay, that was kind of kinky. And not in a good way. Since when had he been into dominance and submission?

What made it even hotter, though, was the knowledge that he doubted any guy could get this woman to submit. Not unless she wanted to.

She lifted her arm again and directed him towards the

line of stiffs waiting patiently in the sun. 'Can I introduce you to the rest of the ruling council and the King's household staff, most of whom…?'

'No, thanks,' he said, cutting her off before she could launch into another speech.

Just one look at those guys in their official garb made him shudder, bringing back the few unpleasant memories he had of his old man, and made him a lot more aware of how hot it was in the sun, and how much he just wanted to get the rest of this day over with ASAP.

'I'm sorry?' she began, clearly confused by his refusal to follow the protocol. Yup, they were definitely going to need to work on that.

'I'm dripping sweat here and shattered and I'm not in the mood.' He glanced over at the men, most of whom had to be well into their seventies. 'And they look shattered too. How about we reschedule the introductions for tomorrow, somewhere cool?'

'But…' She seemed totally nonplussed for a moment. And it occurred to him she wasn't a particularly spontaneous person. Why did that just make pulling the rug out from under her more appealing?

'But nothing,' he said, channelling the dominant again just for the hell of it. Maybe he could have some fun with this mess after all. 'I'm the guy in charge here, right? For the next little while.'

She nodded slowly, forced to concede the point. Her wary expression had him swallowing down a chuckle—and a new surge of heat.

Yup, that's right, Jamilla. I'm playing this game by my own rules. Not yours, not theirs and sure as hell not the ones set down by my bastard of a father.

'Then I hereby decree we all get into the fleet of limos over there, whack up the air-con and crash out before we pass out.'

Her jaw tensed but a trickle of sweat worked its way down the side of her face, in direct counterpoint to the mutinous look turning those amber eyes to a rich gold.

She wanted to refuse the direct order. The fire in her expression was somehow even more gorgeous than the slight overbite, the defiant pout on her full lips or those stunning golden eyes, but it was pretty obvious she was as hot and exhausted as the rest of them. Sweat stains the size of Brooklyn did not lie. Plus she'd just admitted he was the boss.

She dipped her head in deference to his wishes, but he could see it was an effort from the stiffness in her neck. And a very nice neck it was too, dark springy tendrils clinging to the sweat accentuating the slender line.

'As you wish, Your... Mr Jones,' she said.

'Just Jones,' he corrected her again.

She gave another stiff nod, then spoke briefly to the assistant behind her, before leading him over to the biggest limo in the line. The red and gold flags attached to the hood waved in the hot desert wind.

'Your Highness.' A young man in traditional robes opened the car door then bowed so low Dane was astonished he didn't fall over.

'Thanks, buddy,' he said, holding onto his irritation.

How did Karim deal with this level of deference twenty-four-seven? Because it was already starting to drive him nuts.

He threw his bag into the car then slid into the wonderfully cool interior.

'I'll ride up front so you can rest, Mr Jones,' his new top aide said briskly as she leant into the car but didn't meet his gaze. 'The drive will take approximately two hours. There are refreshments in the bar in front of you. Is there anything else you require?'

Something wholly inappropriate popped into his head, the fizz of awareness becoming a definite buzz.

Down, boy.

He scowled, no longer amused by the unbidden reaction. Because it was just one more inconvenience in a whole host of them.

'It's Jones. Just Jones,' he barked, his voice harsher than he had intended. 'No mister required, remember, Jamilla? And no, I don't require a thing except not to be disturbed until we get there.'

'As you wish,' she said, in that far too obedient voice which he was now sure was totally passive aggressive.

But it wasn't until the young man had closed the door and he'd relaxed into the cold leather, ready to sleep for a week, that it occurred to him she'd avoided calling him Jones again by not calling him anything at all. Thus getting the last laugh.

Touché, Jamilla. You got me... For now.

A wry smile twisted his lips at the thought of their battle of wills.

At least it would distract him from the foggy exhaustion, the prickle of irritation—and the heavy weight in his stomach caused by the ghosts he was going to be forced to confront in two hours and counting.

CHAPTER TWO

'Ms Roussel, His Highness has gone missing…'

Jamilla tapped the stop button on the treadmill in the palace's gym and waited for the machine to power down, taking in the panicked expression on Hakim's face.

Picking up her towel, she mopped the sweat off her neck. 'What did you say, Hakim?' she asked, fairly sure she couldn't possibly have heard the young valet correctly.

Hakim had been assigned to take care of their new head of state, and she had asked him to check on him at precisely six o'clock this morning. Of course, Hakim wasn't supposed to wake Dane Jones if he was still sleeping—he had looked wiped out when they'd arrived at the palace yesterday evening. So wiped out he hadn't even made any sarcastic comments before he'd skulked off to his suite.

But Jamilla had wanted to know as soon as he woke, so she could prepare their schedule accordingly. Thanks to his decision yesterday not to do any official duties, they had a lot to cram into the next week before the tour began.

'His Highness—he is not in his rooms,' Hakim repeated.

'Are you absolutely sure? Perhaps he was in the bathroom?' This was Hakim's first assignment as a valet; he was eager and smart and conscientious, but he was probably as unprepared for dealing with Dane Jones's unconventional behaviour as the rest of them. She'd already

figured out her exciting new challenge was going to be
a nightmare—which was why she had decided to hit the
palace gym for a vigorous two-mile run on the treadmill
this morning before facing him.

The man instinctively seemed to know how to provoke
her. Running off any excess aggravation before she had
to deal with him again had seemed like a good solution—
she did not want a recurrence of that weird melting sensation that had assailed her yesterday—or the insult that
had slipped out without warning.

That said, she really hadn't expected him to start causing problems so soon.

'I checked everywhere, Ms Roussel,' Hakim said, his
voice rising with panic. 'I had the staff help me search
the palace. We couldn't find him anywhere. He has left.'

'He… What?'

*Where could he have gone? And how? We're in the
middle of a desert!*

'What about his security detail? Surely they must know
where he is?'

Hakim shook his head. 'They said they are not aware;
they are only assigned to him when he leaves his suite,
and no one had informed them he was awake yet.'

She stepped off the treadmill, her knees wobbling—
and not from her workout. 'Okay, Hakim, don't panic…'

*Because I'm doing more than enough of that for both
of us.*

Had he gone back to Manhattan without telling anyone? Was that even possible?

He'd seemed odd yesterday when they'd driven into
the palace courtyard. He'd been stiff and silent, his movements lacking the panther-like grace and relaxed confidence she'd noticed at the airstrip. He hadn't even goaded
her, just told her he needed to crash and left. But she'd

noticed the muscle in his jaw ticking overtime, and the haunted look in his eyes.

She'd assumed the strained, empty expression was fatigue. Now she wasn't so sure.

She shot towards the gym's shower units, barking orders over her shoulder en route.

'Get Saed to check with the palace guards. Then contact the garage and see if he's taken one of the palace cars.' Every vehicle had a GPS tracker, so there was that. Could he have headed back to the airstrip? Surely not. He couldn't have taken the jet without someone knowing.

Think, Jamilla, think.

'Perhaps he's taken one of the all-terrain vehicles.' Surely that had to be it. If he'd left the palace, maybe he'd just gone for a drive to the nearest town to meet the local people... *Five miles away? Through the desert? Alone?*

Did he have any idea how dangerous the desert could be? How tough the terrain was to navigate? Of course he didn't; he lived a pampered, pointless existence in Manhattan.

And why would he want to meet people he'd already made it clear he had no desire to represent?

'Yes, Ms Roussel,' Hakim said, turning to rush off.

'Wait!'

The young man skidded to a stop. 'Yes, Ms Roussel.'

'Do you know if His Highness can ride a horse?' Was it possible—could he have taken one of Karim's prized Arabians for a ride?

Even the thought of it had her stomach dropping to the floor and her throat contracting. Her breathing accelerated past panic to hyperventilating.

Hakim stared at her. 'Um...'

'It's okay, forget I asked that,' she said, and let Hakim rush off.

What were the chances Dane Jones could ride a horse

well enough to handle one of Karim's highly strung thoroughbreds? The Arabians could only be ridden safely by people like herself, who had been riding almost before they could walk. And the desert terrain was even more treacherous on horseback.

But, as she showered and changed, the panic refused to subside. Because she already suspected just how arrogant and reckless their new head of state was.

After getting dressed, she dashed down to the palace stables, just to put her mind at ease while they waited for news. She reassured herself every step of the way that even Jones couldn't be *that* arrogant or *that* reckless—to risk breaking his neck in the middle of nowhere, just to spite her. She was being ridiculous.

Ten minutes later, though, she discovered her gut instinct had been correct.

Dane Jones was even more arrogant and reckless than she could possibly have imagined. And she still had no clue where he'd gone.

Dane let out a rebel yell, the shout lost in the rush of wind and the surge of adrenaline as the horse's muscles worked in fluid motion beneath him and he shot up the rocky dune chasing the red light of the dawn.

He gave the stallion its head, let the animal fly and felt as if he were flying too, away from the energy- sapping fury of being forced to spend a night in the palace again after twenty-five years. He'd had to get out of there, get away. He'd have to go back soon enough and endure another week of the place, to get the job done he'd promised his brother he would do. But at least this dawn ride to the Halu Oasis would make it a little more bearable, a little less draining—bringing back one of the few good memories from his early childhood in Zafar.

As they crested the rocky ridge, Dane squeezed his

knees and tugged on the reins. The horse lifted its head and slowed—so expertly trained it only needed the suggestion of an instruction once it had conceded who was boss.

Dane smiled as he patted the horse's neck.

It had been touch and go there for a while, after they'd left the palace, Azzam testing to see if Dane had the skill and strength to handle him. But they'd figured it out in the end and Dane had enjoyed every minute of it. Nothing like a head-to-head with a one-thousand-pound stallion with an attitude problem to clear out the cobwebs after a virtually sleepless night.

The pulse of adrenaline hit hard.

Of course, not all his restlessness had been down to the overflow of memories from his childhood, he thought ruefully, remembering the dream which had woken him up in a sweaty mess before dawn—featuring wide amber eyes sparking with challenge and the musty scent of girl sweat.

Yeah, not going there, remember?

He ignored the awareness rushing over his skin and concentrated on the twinge in his thigh muscles as the stallion picked its way down the slope towards the water as sure-footed as a cat. It had been a while since he'd been on a horse—probably at least six months since he'd been able to take a break and visit the farm he owned in Upstate New York where he kept his own stables. He'd pay for this ride tomorrow for sure, but as his gaze landed on the cluster of palm trees, the small corral, the sparkle of iridescent blue water bubbling from the fissure in the red rocks, he knew every single ache and pain would be worth it.

Calm settled over him at last. He could remember the feel of his brother's arms around him as he cradled Dane's small body against his bony chest and they rode out to this place—an oasis in more ways than one during the turmoil of their childhoods—to catch the dawn together a million summers ago. He could even hear the ten-year-old Karim—an expert horseman even then—speaking to him in Zafari, patient words of reassurance and encouragement and distraction to stop him crying, back when Dane had been fluent in the language too.

He let out a half laugh, amused by his own sentimentality.

Damn, if Karim knew how much that long-ago memory still meant to him, and how much he'd missed those summer rides, this single spot, once he and his mom had been kicked out of Zafar for good, his brother would probably cough up a lung laughing.

After jumping down from the horse, he pressed his face into the stallion's neck, clung to it for a moment, feeling grounded again for the first time since he'd agreed to this fiasco. He stroked the sleek coat, took in a lungful of the pungent scent of horse sweat and grinned. 'Good boy, Azzam.'

The horse snorted and whinnied, acknowledging the compliment as if it were his due. The animal really was magnificent. No surprise there, though. Karim had always been a connoisseur of prime horseflesh.

He led the stallion into the corral, glad to see the place was still kept well stocked. The burble from the waterfall was almost musical in the desert quiet as the morning sunshine made its presence felt. The water beckoned, cool and clear, a translucent turquoise he'd never seen anywhere else, as he filled up the horse's water pouch. A swim would be the perfect way to wash off the layer of sweat and grit he'd accumulated during the hard ride, before he had to head back. But he unsaddled the horse first, took off its bridle, rubbed it down, cleaned its hooves, then fed and watered it—just the way his big brother had taught him a lifetime ago.

Jamilla drove along the rocky ridge, following the trail she'd managed to pick up just outside the palace grounds nearly an hour ago. Her skills as a tracker were rusty, but it hadn't been that hard to follow the trail of turned rocks, crushed plants, the occasional hoof print, given that the horse and rider had clearly been moving at speed. Once she'd realised how fast Dane Jones was travelling on Karim's prize stallion she'd had several anxiety attacks. Had the horse bolted? It must have. It was a miracle she hadn't found the man's broken body already. She'd contacted the palace guards on the satellite phone she had in her pack, told them to meet her with an ambulance at the trail head just in case, once she'd figured out the horse seemed to be heading towards the Halu Oasis.

Her head lifted as the scent of fresh water hit her nostrils. The Jeep topped the last rise and Jamilla scanned what she could see of the pool and its surrounds from the dune. She spotted Karim's stallion Azzam, unsaddled, standing sedately in the shaded corral eating from a feed bag as she drove up to the fence. But there was no sign of the man.

She jumped out of the Jeep. As she rounded the small shelter she noticed someone had filled the trough with water for the stallion and taken off his saddle and bridle.

Dane. Not dead then. Safe. By some miracle.

The anxiety finally released its stranglehold on her throat. Fury replaced the panic. By an incredible stroke of luck he'd survived the ride, while sending her and the whole of the palace staff into an uproar. She had helicopters out scouring the area, three all-terrain vehicles heading in opposite directions from hers, just in case the trail she'd found wasn't his.

She heard the splash of water and headed through the grove of desert scrub and palm trees, determined to find him and give him a piece of her mind. She didn't care if he was Zafar's head of state for the next month, she didn't care if he was Karim's half-brother and second in line to the throne, she didn't even care any more that she was effectively his subordinate. She wanted to murder him with her bare hands—for putting himself and Azzam in danger, for wasting everyone's time, and for scaring the life out of her.

Of all the arrogant, reckless, thoughtless...

But as she stepped from the cover of the palms and reached the pool's edge, the heated diatribe in her head cut off and heat exploded into her cheeks.

A man stood not twenty feet away, with his back to her under the fall of water from the rocks.

A completely naked man, the muscles of his spine, his long legs and impossibly broad shoulders glistening in the sunshine as the water pounded down.

He moved, reaching up to slick back his hair and tilt his face into the deluge. Her avid gaze skimmed over him, taking in every stunning detail. The red and black tattoo that covered his right shoulder and most of his upper arm, another scrawled across the bottom of his back, just above the tight, hard, perfectly formed muscles of his glutes. Sensation—hot, fluid, devastating—flared across her sweaty skin like wildfire under her short robe, heating the burning in her cheeks and flowing like hot lava to lodge between her thighs.

The fury she wanted to feel was replaced by shock. And stunned arousal.

She shouldn't spy on him. He was still a prince and not someone she needed to know intimately, in any way.

So look away then.

But she couldn't stop her hungry gaze from devouring every inch of his bronzed skin. The lighter patch across his buttocks, the ink old and new, the small scars on his back, his shoulder, that suggested a life not quite as pampered as she'd assumed.

She was utterly spellbound.

She'd never seen a naked man before in the flesh. And certainly not one in his prime. She'd seen pictures in textbooks, of course she had. She was twenty-four years old and she'd always been curious about sex. Excited about finding the right guy—once she'd established her career—to experiment with. She'd had kisses, even a bit more than that while studying in Narabia; she wasn't a prude. And she didn't feel the need to wait for marriage, as so many young women her age did in Zafar. Her mother had eloped with a French diplomat as a nineteen-year-old, having rejected the arranged marriage her parents had wanted. While that hasty marriage had ended up being a disaster, Farah Omar had always had a forthright view of sex, which she'd passed on to her daughter.

Jamilla had told herself she just hadn't found the right guy yet—to go the whole way with. But neither had she felt the yearning to search for him... Until now.

She swallowed heavily, the insistent throbbing between her legs beginning to ache. She had never expected to feel something so raw and real and... Insistent.

Except Dane Jones is not the right guy. Not even close. You don't even like him.

Despite her best efforts, though, her gaze remained riveted to his physique as he turned and strolled back towards her, his head bent to avoid stepping on the sharper rocks on the pool bed.

Her gaze dipped past the ripple of muscle and sinew, glittering in the sunlight, to locate another tattoo scrawled across his hip flexor, before zeroing in on the long column of his sex nestled in dark hair. Her throat dried to parchment and moisture flooded her core. Her knees shook and her eyes felt as if they were about to bug right out of her head.

And everything flew out of her head, bar one singular, astonishing and terrifying thought.

He's absolutely beautiful.

Dane's head lifted, alerted by the sound of a gasp so loud he could hear it above the splashing waterfall. He stopped, spotting the striking young woman standing on the bank. She wore a voluminous thigh-length robe which covered her head and gathered around her waist in the hot desert breeze, doing nothing to disguise her athletic build and the shape of high full breasts. His gaze took in the jeans and boots which completed the arresting picture.

She was stunning. He was stark naked and she was staring straight at his... The swell of arousal hit hard.

Who was she? What was she doing here? And did she like what she saw, because he sure as hell did. Maybe they could...?

But then her head lifted, their gazes met, and he recognised those amber eyes—dazed with shocked awareness.

Hell, it's just Jamilla. My royal babysitter.

Irritation and something which felt vaguely like disappointment joined the shot of heat which refused to die.

Damn, did Little Miss Protocol follow me here?

He kept walking, satisfied when her gaze jerked away from his junk at last, and began to study the bushes to her left as if her life depended on it.

'How about you throw me my shorts?' he said, vindicated by the fierce flush on her cheeks.

If you didn't want to see it, honey, you shouldn't have looked.

'You're staring right at them,' he added, because she seemed to be frozen in place.

She cleared her throat. 'Um... Yes.' Jolted out of her trance, she scrambled to find his boxers among the pile of clothing he'd left on the bush. She threw them towards him, then turned her back on him. 'I apologise for...for...' She seemed at a loss for words, and because he was having difficulty controlling his reaction to her heated stare he decided to help her out.

'For checking out my junk?'

Her head swung round, then swung straight back again

when she caught him still tugging on his shorts. But he'd spotted the flash of temper and it was almost as enjoyable as the now nuclear blush.

'I—I didn't expect… I mean, I—I didn't mean to…' she stammered, struggling to explain.

Sure you did. A blush that radioactive doesn't lie.

'It's okay, Jamilla. You're not the first woman to see me naked,' he said, unable to resist the chance for some payback. After all, he was struggling to control an inconvenient erection, and she was the cause. 'Luckily, I'm not a shy guy.'

'Well, that's fairly obvious,' she murmured.

He laughed. He couldn't help it. Her hissed comment was almost as hot as the sight of her standing on the bank like a young Valkyrie checking him out.

He leant past her to grab his T-shirt, felt her stiffen and shift away.

'Relax,' he said. 'You're not my type.'

But, even as he said it, he captured a lungful of her musky scent—fresh and spicy, overlaid with a tinge of salty sweat—and knew it was a lie.

The truth was he'd never considered himself to even have a type. All he required of hook-ups was that they be available, uncomplicated and into him. If that was a type, this woman was the opposite of all his main requirements. But there was something about her that got to him. Maybe it was the fierce intelligence he sensed behind the veneer of deference, maybe it was those compelling hints of temper he seemed able to trigger despite her best efforts to keep them hidden, maybe it was just that she was insanely gorgeous in an artless, unstudied, vaguely uptight way. Maybe it was the challenge she represented— or maybe it was a combination of all those things. But whatever the hell it was about her that made him want to tease and provoke her and see the flash of gold light up her eyes—he didn't like it. Because he preferred his sex life to be simple. And Jamilla Roussel had complication written all over her.

Perhaps this was just the result of not having any woman in his bed for months—an enforced drought brought about by the success of his business, and the fact he'd become jaded with the whole dating scene in recent years. Given his current circumstances, he wasn't going to be able to remedy that situation for at least another four weeks.

Awesome!

'That's very good news,' she said, protesting way too much as the wind whipped the scarf off her head, revealing her long dark hair, ruthlessly tied into a bunch. 'It would be completely inappropriate and make our working relationship untenable. I have a...'

Her prim statement faded away as the rush of blood heading south gathered pace. He rubbed his T-shirt across his pecs, his gaze snagging on her slender neck.

What would she taste like in the soft hollow beneath her earlobe? Sweet? Spicy? Even a little sour? How would she react if he nuzzled the smooth skin? Would she giggle? Gasp? Moan?

Not gonna happen. Not your type, buddy, remember?

He tugged the damp T-shirt over his head, grabbed his jeans, trying to control the new blast of heat.

'How did you find me?' he demanded, interrupting whatever she'd been saying about their working relationship. Not that they had one. Not one that was working at any rate.

'Can I turn around?' she asked, sounding a little more sure of herself again. 'Are you decent?'

'*Decent?*' He chuckled. 'No one's ever accused me of that.'

She huffed. 'I meant are you fully clothed, Mr Jones?'

Again with the mister.

He shrugged. 'Sure.' She turned to face him and he noticed the blush had become less explosive. Shame, the colour added a becoming glow to her tawny skin. 'You really oughta call me Dane, seeing as you've seen more of me now than some women I've slept with.'

The blush reignited. And her brows crinkled into a cute frown. 'Okay, *Dane*,' she murmured, and he gave himself a mental high five—knowing he'd just scored a major victory in their battle of wills.

'In answer to your question, I followed your trail in one of the palace Jeeps, which wasn't that difficult as you were obviously going so fast,' she said. 'I was extremely worried about your safety after I heard you'd taken Azzam for a ride.'

'Uh-huh,' he said, impressed she'd managed to track him, and also weirdly touched by the genuine concern in her tone.

No one had ever been worried about his safety before. Not even his mom. Not *ever* his mom.

'Well, I survived,' he said, annoyed now by the pulse of reaction caused by her worried frown.

'You don't seem to understand, the Arabians are very temperamental, Dane. Azzam in particular needs a really experienced rider. You could have been thrown.' The schoolmarm tone was back. And while a part of him found that haughty attitude a major turn-on—*go, figure*—another part of him found it super annoying.

'Not only that, but you're very lucky to have stumbled upon this oasis.' She huffed and crossed her arms over her chest, which plumped up her spectacular breasts.

Terrific.

'Uh-huh,' he said again, as it occurred to him she hadn't just underestimated his ability to control Azzam. She'd also assumed he was dumb as a post.

'The desert can be an extremely unforgiving environment for the unwary, Dane,' she added, condescension dripping from every word now, her frown becoming a lot less cute. 'Or the unprepared.'

Clearly, they were going to have to get a few things straight before they went any further.

'I didn't luck onto this oasis,' he said, letting his irritation show—as the buzz of arousal flowing south started to piss him off.

What was it about her that got him hot and mad at the same time? Because that was just perverse.

'I knew exactly where I was going. In fact, I could probably find this place blindfolded if I had to, because it's the only place in this whole godforsaken country that doesn't give me nightmares. And FYI, I've been riding since I was three years old—and Azzam is a smart horse—smart enough to figure out real quick who's the boss.'

She blinked and dropped her arms—the hissy stance gone. But something else had replaced it, something he liked even less. Why was she looking at him with that strange emotion in her eyes? As if he'd revealed something he hadn't intended?

'*You,* on the other hand…?' he said, determined to push back against it.

Satisfaction surged when the blush went radioactive again.

'I see. I'm sorry for the misunderstanding.' But then she looked at him as if she did understand.

He should have won that round, so why did he feel as if he hadn't? Quite.

'Are you ready to return to the palace?' she asked.

Not ever.

'Sure.' He wasn't a quitter, not any more.

But when they got back to the corral and he saddled

his horse, he soon discovered they had another problem. One that didn't improve his mood one little bit.

'I can call on the satellite phone and have one of the palace mechanics pick me up,' Jamilla said, already reaching for her pack. She should have checked the Jeep was properly equipped before she'd left the palace, but she'd been frantic. And now the vehicle had a flat tyre and no spare.

'How long will that take?' he asked.

'Not long,' she said, feeling like a fool.

She'd miscalculated, badly. Dane Jones wasn't the pampered playboy she'd assumed. The scars and the haunted look when he spoke of his memories of Zafar, suggested a very different reality. Why hadn't she researched his past properly? She had assumed he would have no memory of his homeland. He'd left when he was still a young boy and never returned. Because he was his father's second child, the product of the King's disastrous fourth marriage, and Karim had been the Crown Prince, by all accounts Sheikh Abdullah had not maintained contact with the boy or his mother after the divorce. But from the darkness in Dane Jones's gaze, the flash of turmoil, and the memory of his reaction yesterday when they had arrived at the Palace of the Kings—surly and tense—she could see now Jones's past association with Zafar might well be more traumatic than she had assumed.

She knew from intimate conversations with Orla, who had become a friend as well as her employer over the last five years, that Karim's childhood had been blighted by Abdullah's violence towards his mother. What if Dane had experienced something similar? Compassion welled in her throat. She needed to speak to Saed and maybe Ameera—who had attended King Abdullah's wives at the Palace.

If she was going to do her job properly, she needed to understand where Dane Jones was coming from. She had to earn his trust. She had assumed he was arrogant, but it appeared she was the arrogant one who had not done her job properly.

'How long?' he demanded again.

'An hour, maybe two,' she replied. It would serve her right for driving out here without doing the proper research about Dane Jones's ability in the saddle.

The thought brought with it an unbidden image of him walking from the water with all the grace and strength of a sea god, gloriously naked, and not at all pleased to see her standing there like a ninny, gaping at him.

Getting stranded at the oasis would serve her right for that piece of unconscionable voyeurism too.

She found the satellite phone at last, the heat burning the back of her neck as well as her cheeks.

'Figures,' he grunted and strode off to saddle his horse.

After she finished calling through the problem to the palace garage and letting them know to call off the search party, Jamilla watched as Dane grabbed the pommel of his saddle and mounted the powerful black stallion in one fluid move.

Azzam snorted indignantly, then reared.

Jamilla braced for Dane to fall off, panic shooting through her. But he controlled the horse effortlessly with light touches on the reins, his commands calm and steady but firm, his body at one with the huge animal, utterly unfazed by the stallion's fit of pique.

The man, like the horse, looked magnificent—every inch the desert prince despite the jeans and baseball cap, even if he didn't think of himself as one.

Jamilla's breath released, the shame washing over her again. Whatever happened next, this man deserved her respect. He had returned to a country that held few happy memories for him at his brother's request. And while she had originally resented the need to have him lead this diplomatic mission, they were both stuck with this situation.

The horse settled down quickly, Dane's easy mastery making Jamilla feel like even more of a clueless idiot. His expert horsemanship also amplified the pulse in her abdomen, which hadn't left her since she'd first spotted him in the water.

Another fitting penance for your hubris.

She vowed never to underestimate him again. Or the catastrophic effect he seemed to have on her hormones.

'Have you called in the breakdown?' he asked.

She nodded, a little perturbed when he trotted towards her on the horse. Leaning forward, he extended his hand. 'Come on,' he beckoned. 'We can double up. I'm not leaving you alone out here for hours in the middle of the day.'

She stepped back instinctively, disturbed as much by his gruff chivalry as she was at the thought of sharing a saddle with him all the way back to the palace.

'It's okay, there's water here and shade. I can easily...'

'Jamilla, that's an order,' he said, but then his lips twisted in a mocking smile, the challenge in his eyes unmistakable. 'I promise not to bite. And I'm sure you've got a ton of things we need to be doing today.'

It was a dare. Plain and simple. A dare she had to take or he'd know how the sight of him naked was still playing havoc with her senses.

'Okay, thanks,' she murmured, not feeling remotely thankful.

She clasped his forearm. A zap of electricity shot through her as he gripped her arm and the calluses on his palm rubbed her skin. He yanked her up behind him with an effortless strength which had the weight in her stomach plummeting further south.

She sank into the saddle, jammed up against him, her thighs cupping his muscular butt and the scent of fresh water, musty horse and salty male sweat suffocating her. She eased back, trying to create some distance between her chest and his back. Maybe if she could just…

'You're gonna need to hold on, Jamilla,' he said, interrupting her desperate thoughts. Resting one large hand on her knee, he gave it a condescending pat. 'Or this trip will take even longer. And I've got a feeling neither one of us wants that.'

True.

She let go of the saddle and banded her arms around his waist, pressing her face into his back. Her nipples swelled into stiff peaks on contact—because, of course they did.

Please don't let him be able to feel them.

He pressed his heels into the horse's flanks and flicked the reins over its neck. 'Let's go, boy.'

The stallion launched into a gallop, forcing Jamilla to tighten her grip and cling to his strong, powerful body.

She ground her teeth together and squeezed her eyes shut, her body acutely aware of every flex and bulge of his as they flew towards the dunes.

Then she prayed, as she'd never prayed before, that she would survive the next hour of pure, unadulterated—and totally deserved—torture.

CHAPTER THREE

'JAMILLA, ARE YOU BUSY? I have something for you to see.'

Jamilla looked up from her laptop to see Saed Khouri, the head of the royal household, standing at the door to her office with a file folder under his arm.

Of course I'm busy. The tour starts tomorrow. And I'm not sure Dane Jones will ever be comfortable as a royal representative.

She cut off the unhelpful panicked thought and took a breath before closing her laptop.

'Of course, come in, Saed.' She glanced at her watch. Ten o'clock already; she should try to clock off before midnight. The royal entourage was scheduled to leave for Rome at nine in the morning—and she wanted to be as fresh as she could be.

She needed to be able to keep her wits about her at all times if she was going to be travelling so closely with Dane.

That said, she and Dane had somehow managed to create a stable working relationship in the last seven days. Ever since their torturous ride back from the oasis he had even been cooperative…mostly.

It was obvious he found the whole concept of monarchy a challenge. But she'd learned to live with the tension between them, tried to forget what she'd seen at the oasis, and had managed to maintain a professional—or professional enough—demeanour ever since. And so had he.

While she'd briefed him extensively on the punishing schedule they had committed to over the next three weeks, he'd sat patiently without much comment. She suspected it was because he was bored, but she had considered it a major boon he had managed to refrain from any sarcastic remarks.

It seemed they'd both returned from the oasis with a greater respect for each other and she was certainly a great deal more aware of her dangerous attraction to him—and the pressing need to control it. She had decided work was the perfect solution to the problem.

With that in mind, she'd worked tirelessly during the time she had away from him—while he was dealing with his own business concerns—to refine those events that were flexible over the next three weeks during their whistle-stop tour of key EU countries where Zafar was looking to increase its trading links.

Originally planned for Karim and Orla—who had a great deal more experience of the role required of Zafar's royal ambassadors—the European tour had included events which would not play to Dane's strengths or interests. So, liaising with all the relevant authorities, Jamilla had managed to modify some elements of the itinerary she thought might be particularly challenging for him—the day-long visit to an all-girls academy in Barcelona, for example, which had fitted perfectly with Orla's passion for female education, had been reduced to two hours. Forcing Dane Jones to spend a whole day with a group of pubescent girls had seemed like a recipe for disaster; she could just imagine every one of them developing an inappropriate crush on him.

Her face heated. After all, he seemed to have that effect on a lot of women.

With some careful juggling, she'd also managed to factor in a two-day stopover in County Kildare to visit Karim and Orla after their first week in Italy, sure that a chat with his brother couldn't help but bolster Dane's confidence.

Not that Dane Jones seemed lacking in confidence, generally speaking. Quite the opposite. But she couldn't seem to dismiss the shadows in his eyes when he had first arrived at the palace, and when he'd spoken of his past experience of Zafar at the oasis. They hadn't talked of the oasis since, and she could only be grateful for that too. Because she was very much afraid she had the vision of him naked coming out of that pool tattooed on her retinas for all eternity—and, along with all the work she was doing, it wasn't helping with her sleep deprivation.

The duties Dane would be carrying out, though, were going to be exceptionally challenging for him—not least because he had no knowledge whatsoever of Zafar's people and culture as it was now. So, as well as all the briefings—and her own efforts to tailor the schedule better for Dane—Jamilla had also arranged a series of visits with him to local clinics and schools, the nearby marketplace and a string of businesses, ostensibly to give him some hands-on training in royal protocol, but also to introduce him to his countrymen and women and the modern desert kingdom he would be representing.

She'd congratulated herself on the hands-on approach; at least he hadn't seemed bored—she'd also discovered he understood a great deal more Zafari than he'd let on, even if he said he didn't speak the language. Underneath the bored, jaded cynic, Dane was a people person—unconventional, yes, but also compelling, a man who could be very charismatic if he wanted to be—which had to explain why his nightclub empire was such a success. She planned to build on those strengths as much as she could, while at the same time ensuring she didn't make the mistake of falling under his spell herself.

Luckily, so far, he seemed determined not to turn his killer charm on her, which could only be a good thing.

'Come in, Saed. What's on your mind?' she asked as the head of household continued to hover by the door.

She and Saed had not always seen eye to eye. He'd struggled to accept a woman in the new role of chief diplomatic aide, but while he was a traditionalist, she knew he was also extremely good at his job. She'd spoken to him about Dane's childhood in the palace, but Saed had said he had no information he could share. As it was over twenty-five years ago, she had understood. Similarly Ameera— the Queen's principal lady-in-waiting—had told her she knew nothing about King Abdullah's marriage to Kitty Jones as the American socialite had brought her own employees to the palace with her and had spent most of the five-year marriage out of the kingdom—jetting back to America and Europe and only taking her son with her to the US after the divorce. Which had seemed strange and rather sad to Jamilla—why hadn't Dane's mother taken her young son with her when she'd travelled? But Jamilla hadn't been able to glean any more information and had decided not to pursue it further.

Now she and Dane seemed to have established a workable relationship, perhaps it would be best for her not to risk disturbing it by probing into his past.

Saed nodded and walked into the room, placing the file folder on the desk. It was older than she had assumed, faded and crammed with what looked like correspondence.

'After our conversation about His Highness, I decided to look back through His Majesty King Abdullah's personal effects,' Saed said. 'I was sure I had seen something there that might be of interest… This evening I found the file I was looking for.'

'Oh, I see.' She studied the folder, her curiosity piqued. 'What's in here?' she asked, pulling the folder towards her and flipping it open, but before Saed answered she could see what the correspondence was. The address on the first letter—which simply said *The King, Zafar Palace*—was written in a child's hand with a New York postmark. She flipped the letter over and found a return address also written in a child's hand.

Dane Amari Khan
Centil Parc West
USA
The World

So he hadn't always refused to use his father's name.

'They are letters—many letters,' Saed said. 'From the young Prince to his father, written over a period of six years, after he left Zafar with his mother.'

Jamilla swallowed past the raw spot forming in her throat. Every one of the letters, she noted, was unopened.

'Do you know if King Abdullah received them?' Surely he couldn't have. If he had, wouldn't he have opened them? Or at least had his staff open them?

'They were with his personal effects, so I believe he must have,' Saed said, his voice low with concern.

She realised from the grave look on Saed's face that the austere head of household must have realised the implication too. King Abdullah had made a point of not opening his second son's letters. Of filing them away and ignoring them. But he had kept them too, making the decision not to open them seem even more callous and vindictive.

She sighed and ran her thumb over the painstakingly

written address on the first letter, from a child who had probably only recently learned how to write.

Perhaps she should have expected this. She knew King Abdullah had been a difficult and controlling man. He had abused at least one of his wives, Karim's mother, Cassandra Wainwright, and been violent towards Karim when he was a teenager and he had returned to Zafar during the summers, having him whipped whenever he defied his father. But why did this feel even more cruel and neglectful?

She flicked through the letters, noticed the handwriting becoming more fluid, more cursive as Dane became older, the return address changing frequently, but also becoming more accurate and better spelt. Each envelope, though, remained sealed.

Nausea joined the sadness pressing on her chest, the strange feeling of connection unbidden, but there nonetheless. She knew what it was like to be rejected by your father, after all.

'Do you wish to open them?' Saed asked. 'Perhaps, if you read them, you would get the picture you seek of His Highness's relationship with his father.'

Probably, but she knew she couldn't open them or read them, however curious she was about the content. She had no right.

She shook her head. 'Thanks for these, Saed. I think the right thing to do is probably to return them to Dane.'

She hated to be the one to do that. Hated that his father's behaviour probably wouldn't dispose him to think well of the Zafari monarchy, the legacy he was here to represent or her either, by association. Discovering that his father had never opened the letters he'd sent him would also risk undoing all her efforts in the past week to get him more invested in the country and the culture that was his birthright.

But what else could she do? Surely the little boy who had written to his father so diligently over so many years, and probably waited just as diligently for a reply, had a right to know the truth.

CHAPTER FOUR

DANE STEPPED OUT of the chauffeur-driven limo at Zafar's airstrip to find Jamilla waiting at the bottom of the aeroplane steps. Awareness shot through him as he took in her athletic frame in the fitted pant suit, the colourful headscarf whipping around her face.

Her gaze fixed on his and he felt the reaction everywhere, damn her.

She was a beautiful woman, no doubt about it. But why couldn't he get a grip on his reaction to her? Why couldn't he get those amber eyes, those sleek curves out of his dreams? They'd been working together pretty closely in the last week and he'd made sure to keep things professional, but his awareness of her had only become more intense. And it was starting to make him surly, which he knew wasn't fair. He'd seen the adjustments she'd made to the tour itinerary, knew she'd worked her butt off to help him out. And he appreciated it. But why did she have to look so hot in her tailored suits and pristine hair and make-up?

Still off-limits, buddy.

'Hi Dane, did Hakim forget to provide your uniform this morning?' she asked.

'I told Hakim to put it in my luggage,' he said. Or, rather, snapped.

He drew in a breath but resisted the urge to apologise

when she stiffened at his tone. Yeah, maybe it wasn't her fault she affected him in this way, but the clothes were an issue. After spending some time in the last few days getting fitted for what he had assumed would be something more formal to wear to the balls they had scheduled, Hakim had laid out a made-to-measure Zafari dress uniform this morning for him to travel in—complete with gold epaulettes, brass buttons and a row of ribbons he hadn't earned—and he wasn't happy. Why the heck did he have to dress like a soldier when he had never served in the Zafari army—and certainly was not its honorary commander-in-chief like his brother?

'We need to talk about what I'm wearing and when. Because I'm not comfortable in that outfit.'

'I see,' she said carefully, which only pissed him off more. While their working relationship had been less tense in the last few days, he missed the spitfire he'd glimpsed in the early days. Maybe it was just that his temper wanted company. But he didn't like wearing masks and he wasn't comfortable with her wearing one either.

He followed her up the steps and into the jet, far too aware of how her fitted pants accentuated her trim butt.

Look away from the booty.

As they entered the main cabin area—the air crew doing that dipping bow as he passed, which he hated—he caught a whiff of Jamilla's scent, reminding him of the return journey from the oasis. The memory of that ride was still waking him up at night—hot and sweaty and ready to explode.

'What is the problem with the uniform?' she asked as they sat, her face a picture of puzzled concern.

'Are you kidding me?' he asked. 'I'm not wearing it; I'd feel like a phoney.' Or, worse, he'd look like his father.

'But the uniform of the commander-in-chief is a cere-

monial one worn by the head of state, an honour bestowed
on the Kings of Zafar for generations.'

'I'm not the King,' he cut in bluntly.

'Perhaps we could compromise,' she offered.

'How?' he said, not feeling flexible, the light flush
on her cheeks reminding him of how she'd looked while
checking out his…

Not going there, Jones, remember?

'Would you be prepared to wear the uniform for the
state balls and banquets you have to attend at least? Such
as the one being given at the Ambassador's residence in
Paris?'

He supposed he could live with that, but her concerted
efforts to placate him were only making him feel more
taciturn and surly. He knew it was her job to make sure he
was appropriately attired, but he didn't like being treated
as if he were some unruly kid who needed to be managed.
Especially by her.

'You would not look out of place,' she said, the patient
tone not helping with his irritation. 'Everyone there will
be wearing tuxedos or uniforms and traditional ceremonial wear.'

'Uh-huh… What are you going to be wearing?'

She blinked again, the flush brightening. 'I have a suit
to wear to the event.'

'Like the one you're wearing now?'

'Um…yes. I will be working in the background. I'm
not actually attending the ball as a guest but as part of
the royal entourage.'

She looked flustered, which gave him an idea—an idea
which would no doubt shock her, but he decided to go
with it—because it was already taking the edge off his
bad mood. 'I'm not going to that ball on my own, Jamilla.
End of. And I'm sure as hell not going to it in that uniform

without you right there beside me in something equally OTT.' He thought for a minute. 'Like a ball gown.'

'I don't understand,' she said, the stunned look starting to amuse him. She was cute when she was caught outside her comfort zone. Who knew?

'Okay, I'll spell it out for you. If you want me to go to the ball in that outfit, you're going as my date.' He had never seen her in anything other than those severe pant suits or the jeans she'd worn at the oasis. What was wrong with wanting to see her in a dress, something sleek and sexy to match her colouring and those amber eyes? It would probably increase his torture but he didn't care, because this wasn't just about the clothes any more, he realised. He didn't want her in the background; he wanted her beside him, especially for the big state occasions.

He knew how to work a crowd but he was not comfortable in the role of head of state, and he was even less comfortable representing Zafar. He didn't want to screw up this assignment. And not just because he'd made a promise to his brother.

In the last week, after touring the country to get him into the role of fake King, he'd met a lot of people. Smart, hard-working, loyal citizens who looked up to the Zafari monarchy.

He wanted to get this right, for them as well as his brother and Orla, but that still wasn't going to make him a natural at this job. Having Jamilla there—smiling whenever he did something right and making quick constructive comments when he messed up—would provide some much-needed backup.

Plus she fascinated him and entertained him, despite the awareness he didn't seem able to shake.

'But I can't go as your date. It wouldn't be appropriate,' she said, looking horrified now.

'Take it or leave it,' he said. 'Those are my terms. Either that or I'll wear what I'm comfortable in.' Truth was, he had a couple of tuxedos which he could have flown over, but she didn't need to know that.

She simply stared—probably assuming he was planning to turn up at the Zafari ambassador's residence in Paris wearing ripped jeans and a T. He had to hold back a wry smile, but then she chewed on her bottom lip, which sent an uncomfortable shot of adrenaline to his groin.

Eventually she huffed, 'I suppose I could speak to their Majesties when we arrive in County Kildare. If they are okay with the break in protocol, I might be able to borrow something from Orla to accompany you to the ambassador's ball in Paris. If you're sure that's what you want?'

'Positive,' he said, the surge of triumph enhancing the surge of awareness.

Who knew? Calling her bluff was almost as hot as watching her bite into that full bottom lip.

He'd be playing with fire; he knew that. He'd seen the way she stared at him when she thought he wasn't looking. He could still remember the longing in her eyes when he'd caught her sizing him up naked at the oasis. And he could still feel her nipples poking him in the back like a couple of torpedoes ready to launch as they rode back to the palace.

The memories of that ride had woken him up hard and ready every night since. But as he relaxed into his seat and she headed off to speak to the crew before take-off, the usual spike of irritation didn't come.

Maybe this trip didn't have to be such a chore after all. He'd tried ignoring his attraction to Jamilla and it hadn't worked. Sure, keeping her close was going to be pure torture, but torture was better than boredom.

Not only that, but challenging her, provoking her and coaxing out that rebellious streak she kept hidden under the veneer of protocol might help control the brutal twist of inadequacy and the dark thoughts that had haunted him ever since he had returned to Zafar.

So playing with fire it is.

Jamilla looked at the tiny boats on the Mediterranean Sea far below them as the jet banked to head towards the Italian mainland. They had less than twenty minutes before the plane landed in Rome. After six days of diplomatic engagements in Italy they would be heading to Ireland and the Calhoun Stud.

She shuddered at the thought of the conversation she would need to have with Orla before they got there—to request the massive break in protocol she'd agreed with Dane to get him to wear an appropriate outfit so she could attend the ambassador's ball in Paris as his 'date'.

Jamilla's cheeks heated. She knew her employer. Orla wouldn't question the request, would totally sanction the break in protocol—she wasn't much of a stickler for that stuff anyway—and would be more than happy to lend Jamilla a ball gown she could have altered.

Because Orla totally trusted her. And would believe her when she said Dane had insisted she accompany him.

She glanced from her position by the jet's door to the seated area past the galley. Dane Jones was staring out of the window while talking on his phone to one of his management team in Manhattan. Her heartbeat bumped into her throat and the inappropriate thrill shot through her bloodstream again. The same inappropriate thrill which had made its presence felt when Dane had suggested their compromise.

The problem was, Jamilla wasn't sure if she trusted herself any more.

It was true, she hadn't suggested attending the ball with Dane, would never even have thought of it. And she suspected the reason he had suggested it was two-fold.

Firstly, he probably did prefer to have her with him—she'd noticed he seemed more conscientious about the role he was being asked to play when she was close by. He certainly seemed to have lost at least some of his animosity towards the Zafari monarchy since meeting some of his countrymen. And she was good at her job. She would be able to steer him discreetly if he needed it. And she would make a better wing woman if she were by his side.

But, much more disturbingly, she suspected he enjoyed provoking her and pushing her out of her comfort zone. No doubt it was a natural inclination for him, using his reckless charm to undermine a woman's defences... He had no real intention of seducing her. It was simply a game to him—a game being played for his own amusement to distract him from the rigours of representing Zafar.

The problem was it wasn't a game to her. Because she had so little experience of men—especially men like Dane Jones who oozed sexual confidence from every pore—she found it next to impossible to keep a lid on the inappropriate thrill when he showed her the slightest bit of attention. Which would be mortifying if it weren't so pathetic.

She sighed.

Thank goodness she had six days of state engagements in Italy and Ireland before they would travel to Paris and she would have to wear the gown. It would give her time to get the thrill under control. Hopefully.

She gripped the file folder she'd just retrieved from her briefcase. The folder she'd been intending to give to Dane when they boarded the plane four hours ago. But then he'd blindsided her with his Devil's bargain over the Paris ball and she'd chickened out.

How cowardly, and stupid, not to have given him the letters days ago. Why had she waited so long?

Because you want him to like you.

Dane ended the call and slipped his phone into his back pocket.

She steeled herself against the agonising pulse of regret and tightened her hold on the folder to walk towards his seat.

'Dane?' she asked, her breath backing up in her lungs, the inappropriate thrill sizzling when his gaze locked on hers. 'Could I speak to you for a minute?'

He frowned. 'Sure, as long as it's not another briefing about the schedule.'

She pushed out a strained laugh. 'No, it's...' She paused, sat in the seat opposite him and placed the folder on the table between them. A pulse of sadness played havoc with the zing of attraction. 'Saed found these with your father's personal effects. I thought you should have them back.' She pushed the faded folder across the table, regret sinking into her stomach like a stone. He would know for sure now, how callous his father had really been, and how indifferent he had been towards his second son. And he would surely hate her for enlightening him.

Dane frowned at the file of paperwork.

Weird. Why did Jamilla look so devastated?

It reminded him of the disturbing way she'd looked at him at the oasis after he'd let slip a little too much information about his childhood in Zafar.

'What's this?' he asked.

She didn't reply as he opened the file.

The frown deepened as he recognised the yellowing letter on top of the pile. The Manhattan postmark and the terrible handwriting threw him back to a time and a place he didn't want to return to.

He lifted the letter, saw all the others stacked underneath. So many others.

But then he noticed something about the envelope in his hand. It was still sealed.

Well… *Damn.*

'That son of a…' he hissed, then forced a wry laugh to his lips, ignoring the brutal tug in his chest—anger, pain, inadequacy—as the tiny flicker of hope he hadn't even realised was still there, after all this time, finally guttered and died.

So you got the letters, you bastard.

'I'm so sorry, Dane.'

He raised his gaze to find Jamilla watching him, compassion giving her amber eyes a soft glow.

The tug in his chest became a yank. 'What for?'

'For your father's appalling neglect. He was not a good King, this much I always knew, but he was also not a good man. Or a good father. Please do not be too sad.'

'Sad?' His lips quirked again; he couldn't help it. Was she actually serious? The sympathy and understanding in her expression was starting to unnerve him, reminding him of the kid he'd once been, scribbling those letters in the childish belief that his father would read them…and want to rescue him.

A guy who had never rescued anyone.

'Why would I be sad?' he asked, flicking the old letter back onto the pile with the disdain it deserved.

She seemed surprised. Good, he didn't need her pity. That kid was long gone. And good riddance.

'Because…' she glanced at the letters '…he didn't answer the letters you wrote to him. You must have wondered why. After all those years.'

He shrugged. 'Not really.' Maybe he had once, but that kid had been a sap. 'She made me write them.'

'She?'

'My mom,' he said. Maybe it wasn't the whole truth, but it was true enough. 'She figured she'd be able to leverage more money out of him by having me beg him for it. She used up the divorce settlement pretty quick. But...' He looked back at the pile, thought of how Kitty Jones had made him take a break from running wild around the neighbourhood with his pals to write the letters once a month, without fail. It had been his mom's only rule— the only thing she'd insisted on.

She didn't care if he went to school, who he hung out with, where he was most nights or what he was doing, as long as he wasn't in her way. She'd told him often enough what a burden he was, how he'd ruined her figure and it had taken her years to get it back, how much he cost to feed and what a bastard his old man was. But once a month she would grab some stationery and insist he sit down and write those damn letters, the wheedling note in her voice one she only used when she wanted something.

'Make it sound good, baby. Tell him how we're struggling, how bad it looks when you're a Prince of Zafar and I can't even afford to feed you properly.'

He could still remember her standing over him in her boudoir, wearing one of her silk dressing robes, smelling of stale weed and her signature scent—a heavy rose perfume that went for two grand a pop—while puffing on one of the cigarettes she had shipped by the truckload from Paris, marching up and down like a drill sergeant. And the ever-diminishing balloon of hope as he'd written words he had finally figured out his father would never respond to.

Dumb, he thought. To think he'd once tried to kid himself the guy had never received them.

'I guess it backfired on her.' He shut the file, determined to shut out the feelings churning in his gut, and forced a brittle smile to his lips. 'It's actually kind of funny when you think about it. She went to all that trouble to make me write the damn things, but he never even bothered to read them. I guess he won that round in their war of attrition.' The war he'd been stuck in the middle of. Until he wasn't any more… Until his mom had told him…

He cut off the thought, shoved the collection of old letters towards her. 'Take them.'

She looked shocked by the command before she masked it. 'Um…okay.'

For a split second he imagined her as a kid. Winsome and cute. She'd probably been so well-behaved, so smart and hard-working, that dark hair in neat braids, those luminous eyes full of intelligence and purpose. He hated to think what she'd have made of him as a kid. He'd been a little bastard; even his mom hadn't been able to control him once he hit double digits—which was when she'd lost her temper and blurted out the truth, and he'd stopped writing those damn letters. And refused to believe in anyone any more.

Jamilla gathered up the file, still looking unsure. 'What do you want me to do with them?'

He shrugged. 'Throw them in the trash? Burn them? Hurl them off a cliff. I don't care. Do whatever you want with them. They don't mean anything to me. They never did.'

But as she walked away from him with the letters clasped to her bosom, he forced himself to ignore the stabbing pain where that dying flicker of hope had been, which was calling him a liar.

CHAPTER FIVE

'So HOW DOES it feel to be properly acknowledged as a royal Prince of Zafar after being thrown out of the kingdom as a boy by your father, King Abdullah?'

Dane squinted at the young female journalist in the front row. The bulbs flashed and the cameras whirred around him as he ground his teeth to stop himself from giving her a reaction to the probing question. But inside the anger built under his breastbone and all he could think about were those damn letters Jamilla had tried to return to him three days ago.

And how they confirmed what he already knew. He shouldn't be here, posing as a prince. When he was a fake. A phoney.

Jamilla tensed beside him on the dais set up for this press conference at the exclusive six-star hotel in Rome where the royal party was based. A press conference he'd only agreed to on the grounds he wouldn't have to talk about this garbage.

'His Highness is not here to answer questions about his family's personal...' she began. But he held up his hand, cutting off her intervention. The question was out there now, no point in avoiding it or it would look as if he gave a damn—when he didn't.

'It feels great.' He realised his mistake as soon as he closed his mouth.

The press horde rose to their feet, firing out personal questions like piranhas who had just been chucked a hunk of fresh rib-eye.

'How do you feel about your father now?'

'Is it correct you returned to Zafar nine days ago for the first time in twenty-five years?'

'Why don't you use your father's name?'

'Are you planning to open any nightclubs in the desert?'

Most of the questions he couldn't hear, but the ones he did catch made fury twist and burn in his gut.

He had never courted publicity or used his royal credentials and this was why.

But then Jamilla leapt to her feet beside him, throwing her hands up in a quelling motion. 'I repeat, His Highness is not going to answer questions of a personal nature concerning him or his family,' she shouted above the horde, her voice firm, her stance furious on his behalf. 'He is here to represent the kingdom of Zafar on an important European trade tour. If you wish to ask him about his role here today, please do so.' She repeated the instruction in Italian then French and was finally able to lower her voice as the journalists started to sit back down and the barrage of questions was reduced to the odd shouted comment.

'Thank you,' she finally finished.

She pushed an errant strand of hair behind her ear, then brushed her fitted pants over her butt and planted it back on the seat. But the reaction that shot through him surprised him. Because it felt like more than just lust.

When was the last time anyone had protected him with such passion?

Disturbing emotion rippled beneath the heat.

This was their third day of engagements. And it was Jamilla Roussel's job to keep this press conference on the subject of the trade tour. She wasn't protecting him or defending his right to privacy, not really; she was simply making sure this tour did what it was supposed to do—promote Zafar's interests in Europe. And in this instance the country's new olive trade with Italy, the bumper olive harvest this year one of the big successes of Karim's agricultural revolution in the kingdom.

He forced himself to look away from her neck, the soft skin where her pulse pounded against her collarbone, the flush of exertion on her cheeks. He cast his gaze back over the piranhas and forced a smile to his lips which probably looked as brittle and unamused as he felt. Then he murmured, 'So, anyone got a question about olives?'

The ripple of laughter defused the tension in the room but did nothing for the tension in his gut as it occurred to him he had some kind of state banquet to handle after this—with Jamilla seated right next to him, no doubt wafting that sultry scent over him—before he could finally cut loose and shove the unpleasant emotions from his childhood back into the box marked 'ancient history'.

Great.

'Signorina Roussel, can I speak with you?'

Jamilla opened the door of her suite to find the man who was heading up Dane's security detail in Italy standing in the hallway. 'Hi, Enzo, what's the problem?' she said, anxiety squeezing her chest.

She'd left Dane an hour ago, outside the door to the hotel's luxury six-star penthouse suite. With three bedrooms, a giant terrace overlooking the Via Veneto and a full staff to cater to his every whim, Jamilla had hoped he would settle in for the night.

It had been an exhausting three days since they'd touched down at Rome-Fiumicino's International Airport. A string of formal introductions on their first day to the City's officials and a host of national and European dignitaries had been followed by a half-day trip to a factory in Genoa. Dane had been the guest of honour at a soccer match yesterday in Bari's magnificent stadium—and today, after a tour of Florence, she'd had to guide him through the hour-long press conference back at the hotel.

Karim and Orla and their whirlwind romance had captured a lot of media attention ever since their engagement five years ago, but she'd hoped the last-minute change of personalities would have made the press hordes less voracious. No such luck. Dane had always been something of an enigma in the story of Zafar's royal family, so his sudden appearance representing the monarchy had created a lot of speculation. She'd been careful to brief the journalists beforehand on the need to steer clear of any too personal questions. But that hadn't stopped them.

He'd handled himself well, after she'd intervened. But when they'd been whisked to a state dinner afterwards she'd been all too aware of his growing anger with the public scrutiny. And she'd regretted even more their conversation on the plane about the letters.

Why hadn't she simply kept them to herself? Even though he had seemed uninterested in them, unmoved, she'd sensed…something else beneath the cynicism.

And the details he'd let slip about his mother had only disturbed her more.

Perhaps it was her projecting—probably—but she'd been only too happy when he'd insisted they leave the banquet as soon as all the toasts were done.

He'd been brusque and uncommunicative when they'd arrived back at the hotel. But she hadn't blamed him. Royal duties were much harder and more draining than they looked and, despite his heritage, Dane Jones had no experience of the work involved.

She was utterly exhausted now too—both mentally and physically—and they had another three full days of events before they left for Kildare on Monday morning.

She'd already shrugged off her suit. She had a hot bath infused with her favourite bath salts waiting for her in the en suite bathroom. It was close to eleven and after spending the last twenty minutes finalising the schedule for tomorrow she was more than ready to spend the next twenty de-stressing before going to bed. She wanted to get up early tomorrow so she could get a run in and absorb at least some of the sights of the Eternal City—which she'd barely glimpsed from the back of their limo—before clocking back on at eight o'clock in preparation for their next official engagement at one.

Keeping a firm grip on her panic and exhaustion, she ushered Enzo into the room. If there was something Dane needed she was here to supply it.

'Um… I am very sorry, *signorina*, but His Highness is insisting on leaving the hotel without his security detail.'

'But he can't do that.' She blinked. 'It's for his own safety.'

And where was he even going? He'd looked almost as shattered as she felt twenty minutes ago.

'*Sì, signorina*, we explained this to him, but he insists. I thought it best to contact you. He has arranged to have a motorbike delivered; it will be impossible to protect him if he does not want us there.'

'Right…' She'd known keeping him corralled in the hotel would be a challenge. Reassuring him, convincing him not to put his own life in danger, was all part of her job. 'Okay, don't worry, I've got this.' She ushered Enzo out of the suite so she could get dressed again. 'I'll come straight up, just make sure he doesn't leave until I get there.'

'I will do my best, *signorina*,' Enzo murmured, sounding doubtful, which was not helping with her anxiety attack.

She got dressed in double-quick time, throwing on

jeans and a T-shirt, a light sweater and a pair of boots. It wasn't how she wanted to present herself. Appearances were important and she'd already managed to put a huge dent in her professional relationship with Dane. But she didn't have time to reapply her make-up or have one of her power suits pressed.

She shot upstairs to the penthouse suite and rapped on the door.

Enzo answered with a mobile phone to his ear.

'Please tell me he's still here,' she gasped.

'He took the emergency stairs. I am coordinating a security detail to track him from the lobby…'

'Okay, great,' she said, cutting him off; maybe she could stop Dane if she caught up with him before he left the premises. 'You do that, and text me the details,' she said as she ran down the corridor, shoved open the fire exit door and raced down the concrete stairs—sending up a silent thank you that she'd opted for casual attire. She would have broken an ankle trying to pursue the man in four-inch heels.

Leaning over the metal railings, she spotted his wavy bronze hair two floors below. 'Dane, wait, can I speak to you?' she shouted.

His scowling face appeared briefly in the stairwell. 'I'm off the clock. Go back to bed, Jamilla.'

But you're never off the clock as the Zafari head of state.

She accelerated, flying down the steps. She finally caught up with him heading towards the basement level. So much for the security team waiting in the lobby.

'Please, Dane, you can't leave the building,' she said, struggling to catch her breath as she skidded to a stop in front of him, blocking his path into the hotel's underground garage. 'Not without your bodyguards.'

'Jamilla, get the hell out of my way.'

Large hands gripped her upper arms and he lifted her aside—with devastating ease.

But as he went to push open the heavy exit door she scrambled to wedge herself in front of him and pressed shaky palms to his chest.

The muscles flexed under the black T-shirt he wore with black jeans. And biker boots. Adrenaline shot through her, and into some unexpected parts of her body.

'Please, Dane, you can't go out alone. There are press out there. And possible threats.'

'What threats?' His brows drew into a sceptical frown. 'I've been stuck in here for three nights straight now.'

'Just…threats. You're a Prince of Zafar in Rome on an official visit!' she exclaimed, getting frantic now. Not least because of the adrenaline rush which seemed to have got lodged in her abdomen. The scent of him—clean laundry detergent and pine soap—and the flex of solid muscle beneath her palms did not help calm her racing heartbeat.

'Not right now I'm not,' he growled. 'I can handle myself just fine. And to hell with the press. If they want to chase me down, good luck to them.'

Grasping her arms again, he moved her to one side and shoved open the door. She had to ram her shoulder against the metal slab to stop it hitting her in the face.

A gleaming black motorcycle stood in a bay by the door. He fished a key out of the front pocket of his jeans.

Her mouth dropped open in horror as he swung a leg over the seat, fitted the key into the ignition, then lifted a helmet out of the saddlebag.

'You can't ride that—it's not safe!'

He simply stared at her for several long seconds, making the blush ignite her cheeks.

'Who made you my mom, Jamilla?' He clicked the key into the on position. 'Hell,' he muttered. 'Even my mom never gave this much of a damn!'

She didn't have time to contemplate the pang of tenderness at the snarled comment, when he kicked the ignition pedal and the engine roared to life.

She shot across the space, grasped his biceps as he lifted the helmet. The bare skin seemed to sizzle against her fingertips.

'Don't go,' she pleaded, knowing she was concerned for more than just professional reasons. 'It's not safe. And I'll lose my job. I'm responsible for you, for your safety,' she added, getting more frantic by the moment.

She knew Karim and Orla would never blame her if something happened to Dane. But she would blame herself.

To her astonishment he paused. He stared at her, still brooding, that edge of fury she had sensed earlier, first when she'd shown him the letters, then at the press conference this afternoon, emanating off him. But then he thrust the helmet towards her. 'Put it on and climb aboard. If you're so worried you can come with me. But, either way, I'm outta here.'

'But I can't take your helmet!' she said, trying to shove it back.

He glared at her, his hands fixed to the handlebars as he revved the engine. 'Either put it on or stay here. Your choice.'

She slung the helmet on, clipped the strap and then hopped aboard the bike with more speed than skill. If she was with him, maybe she could alert Security to where they were. And talk some sense into him.

Once she was on board the rumble of the powerful engine sent shockwaves through her thighs. Her whole body was far too aware of his, with the memory of their torturous ride back from the oasis, as the bike kicked forward.

'Hold on,' he shouted.

She had less than a second to wrap her arms around

his torso and cling on for dear life before they were shooting out of the parking garage and heading into the Roman night. And the shot of adrenaline wedged in her throat plummeted into her abdomen and hit critical mass.

Damn, the last thing he needed right now was Jamilla's toned curves—curves he'd been obsessing over way too much already—pressed against him. *Again.*

But as Dane wound down the tree-lined thoroughfare of the Via Veneto—putting his foot on the gas to zip past a lumbering delivery truck—the warm night breeze whipped his hair back and sent goosebumps rioting over his skin and he figured the additional torture was a small price to pay. To be free, at least for a little while, from the claustrophobic feeling of his past closing in around him.

A past he'd spent twenty-five years escaping from.

Damn his father and Zafar and all the pomp and circumstance he was going to have to endure for another two plus weeks yet to repay a debt to his brother. A debt his brother probably didn't even realise Dane owed.

Tonight he needed to be himself again. Not the public face of a monarchy that had spit him out as a kid. Tonight, he needed to be the guy who had worked his butt off to get away from that feeling of failure—and built his own business empire with no help whatsoever from the people who had made him a pawn in their disastrous marriage.

Veering off the main drag, he headed down a hill into a cobbled side street. He leant on the horn to scatter the tourists ambling in front of the bike like headless chickens.

He was forced to slow the bike to a crawl as they entered a piazza, inching past the stacked outdoor tables of pavement pizzerias, gelaterias and cafés filled now with tourists and locals alike, drinking strong coffee, sipping Limoncellos and Negronis or tucking into the luxury ice cream the area was famous for while soaking up the night-time energy to prepare for another long day in the sun. The pungent scent of tobacco smoke and frying garlic filled the air along with the exhaust fumes no doubt staining the laundry hanging above their heads, strung between the rows of neoclassical terraces.

He'd been to Rome before a bunch of times, knew his way around. But he could still remember Jamilla's wide-eyed wonder when they'd taken the limo past some of the city sights in the last few days, en route to their official engagements, and how she'd mentioned she'd never been to Europe before. He'd been kind of surprised, given her role in the royal household.

He made a spur-of–the-moment decision to take a right, heading through the labyrinth of alleyways towards the Piazza di Trevi. As they hit the square—still busy despite the clock being only a few minutes shy of midnight—her body jolted with surprise behind him.

Tourists milled around, mostly couples, but aboard the bike they had a clear view of the blue-green water lit from beneath, the triumphal arch and Corinthian columns of the Palazzo Poli providing an impressive backdrop for the famous fountain.

Water from the city's ancient source tumbled over marble. Neptune looked pretty pleased with himself in the centre of it all, lording it naked over the Tritons and what Dane figured were a couple of Vestal Virgins on either side of him.

He stopped the bike, a wry smile teasing his lips when Jamilla's arms loosened. He glanced over his shoulder and caught the same wide-eyed wonder in those striking amber depths he'd noticed a couple of times in the last few days. It sent a shiver through his body he didn't need and the smile died. How could she have that veneer of innocence when she was so smart and ambitious? Why did her artless enthusiasm seem like a direct challenge to his own jaded view of the world?

'It's so beautiful,' she murmured, like a kid in a candy store instead of the woman in a power suit and heels who'd handled the press so efficiently that afternoon. 'Thank you.'

Her gratitude poked at the tangle of emotion in his gut—the glimpse of the wonder-struck girl beneath the capable woman enchanting him in a way he didn't like.

He shrugged, trying to shake the feeling. 'No big deal; it was on my way.'

'Where are we going?'

'A place I opened on the Tiber a couple of years back. Thought I'd do an incognito spot check.'

'You own a nightclub in Italy?' she asked, the inquisitive frown reminding him of the woman and eliminating the girl, which only annoyed him more. Couldn't she forget about her job for one damn night?

'I own several.'

'But do you think that's wise—visiting it tonight when we have a full schedule of official engagements tomorrow? Also the press might be expecting you to…'

'Jamilla, if you want to hop off here and catch a cab back to the hotel to get a good night's sleep you can.' Why the hell had he invited her along anyway?

She shut her mouth and shook her head, the oversized helmet doing nothing to stop her direct gaze reminding him of the stubborn streak he'd seen a couple of times already.

'Then there are rules for tonight,' he said, deciding it was past time he set his own agenda here. This was his night, his escape and if she was going to tag along she needed to know that.

'What rules?' she asked, falling neatly into his trap.

'No talking about tomorrow's timetable or itinerary,

or about your job or mine. If there's a problem with the press I'll handle it. And if you get tired I'll call a cab. But until that happens you're just a woman cutting loose and experiencing Rome for the first time. With me. So you do what I say, when I say it. You got that?'

'But…' Her eyes widened to saucer size and he could see what she was thinking as clear as day. That she couldn't trust him not to do something outrageous. Which, of course, just made him want to do something outrageous.

What was it about this woman that made him want to push her out of her comfort zone?

He'd been a fully-fledged bad boy as a kid. Running with the wrong crowd, dabbling in liquor and drugs, sleeping with women twice his age when he was still in his teens, getting on the wrong side of the juvenile courts a time or two—mostly just to infuriate his mom—and chucking away what little childhood he'd had left far too soon. But these days that tough, unruly kid was an astute and successful businessman who spent much more time working than hooking up, and had been clean and sober for over a decade. Why she should bring that reckless, impulsive boy back he had no idea, but he couldn't deny the adrenaline pumping through his system.

'But how do I know you won't ask me to do something…something dangerous?' she managed.

'You don't,' he said, playing Devil's advocate as the adrenaline rush he'd once been addicted to continued to power through his veins. 'You're just gonna have to trust me,' he added, knowing he couldn't even trust himself any more.

Tough.

She'd insisted on coming along for this ride, so she got to live with the consequences.

She chewed on her bottom lip, sending the visceral spurt of heat south.

'For once you're just gonna have to relax and enjoy the ride,' he added. 'You think you can manage that?'

He watched her debate the question, then figure out she didn't have much of a choice. It was his way or the highway and she was way too dedicated to her job to risk leaving him to his own devices. But then he saw excitement flicker in her eyes and his pulse jumped.

Sweet.

A part of her *wanted* to take a walk on the wild side with him. Even if she would never admit it to herself.

When she nodded he revved the bike's engine and felt her arms grip his waist, her full breasts plump up against his back. But this time, when the adrenaline rush hit hard, he smiled.

He finally had Jamilla Roussel where he wanted her. Time to stop letting her push his buttons and start pushing every one of hers.

CHAPTER SIX

Do not freak out. You're still doing your job. Sort of. You had to agree to his ultimatum. Sort of.

Jamilla repeated the mantra in her head, but it did nothing for the surge of exhilaration making her body hum and her heart bump against her ribs as she clung to the man in front of her and absorbed the incredible sights and sounds around her.

Up close, Rome was even more enchanting. But was that because of the wonderfully lived-in grandeur of the Baroque buildings that pressed in on them, the edgy energy of the nightlife spilling onto the city's streets even at midnight, the staggering beauty of the Trevi Fountain—a sight she'd imagined but never thought she'd actually see—and the other sights he'd already treated her to? Or was it the feel of Dane Jones's strong, powerful body, his clean musky smell, or the thought of spending a night out with a man—a hot, exciting, charismatic and dangerous man like him—for the first time in her life?

But you're not dating him; you're trying to keep him safe. And out of trouble. Sort of.

She swallowed down the twin tides of anxiety and excitement as the bike rumbled through the narrow streets and out onto the banks of the Tiber. He accelerated past the snarl of late-night traffic, across a bridge and down a tree-lined boulevard on the opposite bank. The wind caught her hair beneath the helmet and brushed her cheeks like a caress.

She tightened her grip, felt his abs ripple beneath her palms and buried her face against his back. The clean scent of pine and bergamot only added to the riot of sensation churning in her abdomen.

Despite being so far outside her comfort zone she was practically on Mars, she couldn't seem to control the intoxicating adrenaline.

One night. Would it really be so wrong to let go of the responsible, dedicated, diplomatic aide for one night?

A part of her knew this had to be the romantic, irrational side of her nature she had inherited from her mother—which she had ruthlessly controlled ever since she was a little girl, watching her mother become distraught over a man who had never loved her. Her mother had depended on François Xavier Roussel, not just for love but also for validation and self-respect. And he had denied all three —simply because he could. Jamilla didn't want to give any man that power, certainly not a man like Dane Jones, who was about as dependable as an unexploded bomb... But surely letting go for just one night didn't have to be bad? If she understood the risks.

Even so, as they arrived at a towering brick building on the waterfront—the neon sign announcing it as Jones Roma, the deep bass beat of a rap song pounding through the night air and the neoclassical arches on the upper floors pulsating with a rainbow of coloured lights—her heartbeat became ever more erratic.

Crowds of glamorous people stood outside as Dane parked the bike beside the river, waiting to gain entry to the exclusive venue. The women wore shimmering designer cocktail dresses and gravity-defying heels, their hairstyles and make-up like works of art. The men wore tailored suits and polished shoes, their hair perfectly styled too.

She climbed off the bike, her legs shaky, as Dane looped the bike's anchor chain around a tree, then took the helmet from her and stuffed it back in the saddlebag.

'Dane, I don't think we fit the dress code,' she said, staring down at her jeans and sweater combo. And imagining her face devoid of make-up and her now completely windblown hair.

Nerves tangled with the adrenaline and confusion, creating a volatile cocktail. Who was she kidding? She came from a desert kingdom which had only recently become culturally more liberal, following the end of King Abdullah's reign. They had nightclubs now in Zafar's capital city and youth culture was no longer suppressed, but even in university in Narabia she'd been dedicated to her studies and since then she'd been focused on her career.

She didn't do instant gratification or all-night clubbing. Especially when she had to be up first thing in the morning. But somehow—during the space of one wild ride—they'd leapt from her world into his, a world she had no clue how to negotiate.

Instead of giving her anxiety the attention it deserved, he simply sent her that criminally tempting smile. 'You quitting already, Jamilla?'

'It's not… I'm not…' Outrage surged through the nerves. 'This isn't about me quitting; it's just…' She lifted her arms. 'Look at me; I'm not even wearing any make-up. There's clearly a dress code.' She threw her hand out to indicate the people milling around across the street, ready to party the night away. 'And neither one of us is appropriately attired.'

He chuckled, the low rich sound somehow igniting the fire in her belly.

'Appropriately attired!' He laughed some more, clearly

at her expense. 'Give me a break. It's a club, Jamilla, not a diplomatic reception. You wear what you wanna wear. And no one's gonna be watching you, except me.'

He grasped her hand, and dodging a honking moped dragged her across the street. He strolled up to the main entrance as if he owned the place... Well, to be fair, he did.

The people standing in line outside shouted and gesticulated in outraged Italian, making Jamilla want to curl up and die on the spot. But Dane ignored the furore and spoke in surprisingly competent Italian to the doorman.

The bouncer released the rope instantly to usher them inside.

'You didn't tell them who you are, did you?' she asked. 'Because if he informs the press they'll...'

'Shut up, Jamilla,' he said over his shoulder.

She pursed her lips, trying not to panic even more. But as he dragged her down a shadowy hallway the panic receded, to be replaced by something that felt uncomfortably like awe.

The club's shadowy interior vibrated with sound, the noise and energy becoming louder as they got deeper into the darkness. The music began to throb in her bones as Dane cut through the crowd of hot gyrating bodies pulsing as one with the beat. The smell of sweat and abandon filled Jamilla's senses as the cramped corridor opened out into a huge cathedral-like space.

She craned her neck to take in the three tiers of pillared balconies that wrapped around the building. The majestic vaulted ceiling above them was open to the summer night, but did nothing to cool a dance floor alive with light and dry ice. People danced on platforms, in alcoves, arms high, bodies fluid; she could feel the shocked wonder squeeze her ribs as Dane spun her around, holding her steady as the crowd jostled. Someone pushed past them, nudging them so close together she could smell him—the salty aroma of sweat and the spicy, addictive scent of his cologne.

She stiffened, the last vestiges of that sensible woman clinging on for dear life. 'It's hot in here,' she shouted inanely, desperately trying to make small talk, to drag herself back onto solid ground.

'That's easily remedied,' he said, then grasped the hem of her sweater and pulled it up and over her head. He had tied it around her waist before she had a chance to gauge how exposed she felt in nothing more than a T-shirt and jeans—with none of her usual armour in place. She became brutally aware of the night air, which cooled her overheated skin but did nothing to stop the heat pulsing in her breasts as his hard chest brushed against the aching tips.

'Better?' he shouted, the mocking grin daring her to protest.

Clamping down on the moment of panic, she nodded, refusing to give him the satisfaction of seeing her freak out. And no longer able to deny desert sensations coursing through her body.

He lifted her wrists, draped her arms over his broad shoulders, then placed his hands on her hips and tugged her into the lee of his body. She could feel him everywhere as he gyrated his hips, instinctively picking up the bass beat and letting it flow through his body and into hers. His palms caressed her waist, the anonymity of the darkness, the press of the crowd, the searing intimacy that cocooned them both terrifying and liberating in equal measure.

Holding onto his shoulders, she reached up on tiptoes. 'I can't dance; I don't know how,' she shouted into his ear, ashamed, embarrassed and yet still so alive. The yearning more intense now than it had ever been.

He pressed his thigh between her legs, ran callused palms under the hem of her T-shirt, sending sensation shimmering again over the bare skin of her back to join the electrical pulse in her nipples. He leaned down to press his lips to her ear. 'Then hold on tight.'

A part of her wanted to draw away. She'd never allowed herself to let go before, not entirely. But something about the night, the music, the wild feeling of abandon that had been intoxicating on the bike overwhelmed her now.

She moved with him, capturing the deep pulse of the music in the ebb and flow of her heartbeat—slow, seductive, unbearably arousing—fitting her curves into the hard line of his body, rejoicing when she felt his shudder of response.

She was playing with fire, she knew that, but just this once she refused to be careful and cautious, refused to extinguish the flames and instead let them sizzle and spark, flare and ignite.

This was just one night. One night free of responsibility, of propriety. He wasn't a prince and she wasn't a diplomatic aide. For the first time ever she was just a woman, with a devilishly attractive man. And all they were doing was dancing.

So instead of going with her first instinct—to run away from the shimmer of excitement and yearning, to scramble out of the devious well of desire he seemed intent on building around them—she threaded her fingernails into the short hair of his nape and let herself jump off the edge and into the abyss.

CHAPTER SEVEN

'Wow, I never knew dancing could be so…fun!' Jamilla gripped the rail on the private balcony overlooking the Tiber as the night air cooled her heated skin, the buzz of excitement still pumping through her blood as she struggled to get her breath back.

How long had they been dancing? Hours it seemed as she noticed the purple light of dawn creeping across the dark blue sky that hovered over the cityscape.

But when she should have been panicked, concerned—after all, she had to be up and working in only a few more hours—all she felt was…energised.

She hadn't been familiar with any of the music but had adored every throb and flow of the beat, delighted in the guitar riffs which seemed to go on for ever, revelled in the siren song of voices, the cut and thrust of the wall of sound and scents cocooning them.

'You're a natural.'

She turned, the deep voice behind her rumbling through her torso and adding to the barrage of sensations still charging through her body. She'd never felt more alive, more powerful, more beautiful in her life.

It's an illusion, Milla, get a grip.

But even though her conscious mind was telling her to calm down, she couldn't control the intoxicating feeling of freedom and belonging still making her skin sparkle and zing.

Dane stood behind her, leaning against the wall. Sweat dripped down his temple but the rest of his face was cast into shadow. She could still feel the imprint of his body, the sensation of being forged in fire and sound.

Euphoria flooded through her, buoyed by the floaty feeling of exhaustion.

'You're a good teacher,' she managed, her voice rough with an emotion she didn't recognise but seemed powerless to stop.

He laughed, the sound wry but somehow lacking the cynical edge that had disconcerted her so much in the past. He stepped forward and those harsh, handsome features, that strong athletic build became gilded by moonlight. Her breathing, already ragged, thickened.

'You can't teach someone how to dance,' he said, the rueful tilt of his lips mesmerising her. Why had she never noticed before how beautiful his lips were, the sensual line only made more perfect by the rough stubble that had appeared during the night?

'Not that kind of dancing anyway,' he continued, the bergamot of his aftershave and the aroma of fresh sweat which had tantalised her on the dance floor combined with the muddy scent of river water and the potent perfume of the jasmine which clung to the wall behind him.

'In a club, after dark,' he added, his words dropping like bombs into the hum of exhaustion which had propelled them out onto the balcony after the final track had been played and the crowd began to disperse. 'It's all about gut instinct, letting go, feeling the beat. And not giving a damn what anyone else is thinking or doing.' He lifted a hand, as if in slow motion, and cupped her cheek.

Her breathing stopped abruptly, the feel of his palm in that moment—rough, sure, uninhibited—somehow more

intimate than having his body pressed to hers for hours.
Because now they were truly alone in the quiet dawn as
the city woke up to a new day. The music had died, the
stillness only interrupted by the hum of traffic and the
thundering of her own heartbeat.

His thumb trailed across her lips and she opened them
instinctively. She dragged in a desperate breath, unable
to draw away from the purpose in that pure blue gaze or
the devastating feel of his fingers sifting through her hair
as he cradled her head.

His movements were slow, deliberate, giving her the
chance to pull away. But she couldn't obey the scream inside her own head telling her to stop him, couldn't control
the fierce tug of yearning, the longing which had built to
a crescendo as they'd danced.

'Who the hell knew you had it in you,' he murmured,
more to himself than her, 'to be so wild?'

Her breath shuddered out and she flattened shaky
palms against his abdomen, felt the muscles jump and
tense beneath his T-shirt. But instead of pushing him
back, instead of telling him no, her fingers fisted on the
damp cotton and she tilted her head back as his mouth—
so beautiful, so sensual, so demanding—found hers at last.

She tastes as sweet and refreshing as she looks. Better.

Dane thrust his tongue into the recesses of Jamilla's
mouth, devouring the seductive taste of her surrender. He
wanted more—needed more. His other hand rose to grip
her head, the driving need exploding deep in his gut as
her mouth opened on a startled sob.

The need had been building for hours, every time
she moved against him, every time her breasts brushed
his chest, every time her hips rolled to bump against his
thighs, every time her arms lifted and she threw her head
back—her hair flowing, the ebony curls bouncing, cut

loose from that damn ponytail hours ago—and raised her face to his.

She'd been stiff at first on the dance floor, scared, he guessed, to try something new and wholly inappropriate, but as soon as he had taken off her sweater and challenged her, something fundamental had shifted and changed. And then, as the night drew on, the crowd around them getting more rowdy, more in tune with the music, he'd watched her give herself over to the night. And to him... And he'd been mesmerised.

She'd always been stunning, but tonight she had become an enchantress, a queen, powerful and vulnerable at one and the same time, drawing him into her realm and making him want her.

Well, he was through watching, through waiting.

He lapped up her sighs, savouring the sultry taste of her passion, so potent, so intoxicating, so addictive. He angled her head to go deeper and feast on every last drop.

She shivered, her hands running under the hem of his T-shirt, touching the taut skin of his abs, making him shiver too.

Who was surrendering to whom here?

The last threads of his control stretched tight as need fired into his gut in fierce, furious waves, the throbbing weight in his pants painful. He walked her back until they hit the wall, cushioned in flowers. She trembled as he pressed the hard, heavy ridge into the soft cradle of her sex. She didn't resist, becoming more pliant, more delirious as he grasped her thigh, drew her leg up to hook it round his waist. He kept his lips on her neck as he pressed the painful ridge into the heart of her, rubbing the spot he knew would bring her some relief. Her head dropped back against the wall of flowers, releasing a puff of perfume from the blooms, the noise of traffic drowned out by her sobs of arousal.

He worked the spot through their clothing, nuzzling the sensitive skin under her chin, revelling in her response, his own breathing coming out in staggered gasps.

'Uh... Oh, God,' she whispered. 'I can't...'

'Shh... Just let it happen.' He kept rubbing while devouring her neck, feeling the frantic pulse of her heartbeat, ignoring his own pain to concentrate on her pleasure. He needed her to explode for him, needed her to go over, needed to make her surrender complete.

At last she tensed and her gasping cry of pleasure rang in his ears.

He dropped his forehead to hers, yanking himself back from that brutal edge, letting her body dissolve into his, the pain more than worth the stark joy of triumph.

He cradled her cheeks, looked into those beautiful amber eyes, dazed with afterglow. An afterglow he'd earned.

He tried to even his breathing, resisted the urge to yank down her jeans and panties, unzip himself and bury the brutal erection deep inside the tight warmth of her body so he could ease the pain too.

Not the time, not the place.

He pressed a kiss on her forehead, not trusting himself to take her mouth again—until they got back to the hotel room.

'That was even better than watching you dance,' he murmured, trying to find humour in the situation.

Didn't mean a thing that he'd just behaved like a lunatic, determined to get her off on the balcony of his own club. She'd got what she needed and so had he—or as much as he could get while they were in a public place bathed in the red glow of morning sunlight. Just a natural, elemental reaction to spending five solid hours dancing with her. No more, no less.

But even as he fought to drag himself back from the

edge, shock shadowed her eyes and she drew her leg off his hip to break the intimate connection.

Her chin dropped, her gaze darting away, and the vivid blush—that he had found so attractive in the past—spread like wildfire, darkening her skin, and only annoying him more.

'Hey.' He tucked a knuckle under her chin, lifted her face, and saw panic and shame. 'What's wrong?'

She stiffened, then lifted her arm to scrape her hair behind her ear. 'That…that shouldn't have happened,' she said, her voice a whisper. 'I'm… I'm so ashamed.'

'Are you serious right now?' he demanded as the turmoil in his gut turned to fury.

She finally looked him in the eye, and he could see she was deadly serious. The fury became sharp and jagged.

'All I can do is apologise. Profusely.' She glanced down and her cheeks ignited again, probably because she could see the prominent ridge in his pants. 'I behaved appallingly. And unprofessionally.'

He ground his teeth together until his jaw ached, controlling the urge to shout at her. To tell her what he thought of her apology. But beneath it was that dumb kneejerk agony of rejection, of yearning, that reminded him of that mixed-up kid who had searched for acceptance, for affection, in sex. And never found it.

'You're not the only one out here,' he managed around the anger which was threatening to choke him now. But which he couldn't let her see. Because then she'd have got to him. And no woman got to him. Not any more. Because he wasn't that dumb reckless kid any more, the one who would take any scraps he was offered, any way he could get them. He didn't need that any more, not from anyone and certainly not from some uptight diplomatic aide who felt ashamed of having come apart in his arms.

Her gaze darted back to his. 'Yes, but I was the only

one who…who…' She stuttered to a stop, obviously so mortified now by what they'd done, what she'd let him do, she couldn't even say it. So he said it for it.

'The only one who got off?' he asked.

Her throat flexed and he imagined her swallowing the bowling ball he could feel lodged in his own gut.

'Well…yes,' she said, the flush of embarrassment and regret making her cheeks glow.

'Don't get too cut up about it,' he said, forcing a cavalier smile to his lips that he didn't remotely feel. 'I'm a big boy. I'll survive.' He tried to unlock his jaw to make the smile more convincing. 'And you can shove the apology. Because those little sounds you made when you came were really hot. And I'll be sure to remember them next time you're busting my butt about the schedule,' he added, giving in to the desire to make her suffer as much as he was suffering.

If she thought she could just forget about this, just pack it away into a neat little box marked 'big mistake' and go back to where they'd been, she had another thing coming. Because no way was that happening. He knew now who she was when she let her hair down, literally. When she let herself just be. He had smelt the sultry scent of her arousal, heard the sobs of her surrender, tasted those bee-stung lips. He'd done that, no one else. And now he knew she wanted him, the same way he wanted her.

And there was no way either one of them was going to be able to forget that.

'Please don't…' she began, but before she could complete the thought a glint of light from the street opposite caught his eye. He wrapped his arm around her waist and thrust her behind him.

'Damn…' He searched the embankment, above the line of traffic.

'What…?'

'Stay back,' he said, but he'd already seen the flash again as the photographer's telescopic lens caught the dawn light. He cursed loudly. 'We should head back,' he said, glad of the distraction.

'What did you see?'

'Nothing,' he said. Because what was the point in telling her? She was freaking out enough already.

And so was he.

CHAPTER EIGHT

JAMILLA WOKE SLOWLY, her mind fuzzy from sleep, her body aching from the rampant dream of...*him.*

She could hear a loud rhythmic buzzing in her head.

The memories from last night—the dangerous freedom of the dance floor, Dane's marauding lips, the scent of sweat and arousal and night-blooming jasmine, the fire exploding in her core—returned in a terrifying rush of sensation, propelling her out of that blank space between dreams and reality. She shot upright so fast she almost fell out of the deluxe king-size bed in her suite.

Oh, no.

She raked shaking fingers through her cloud of bed hair.

What had she done? It was almost as if Dane Jones had cast a spell on her with that glorious night ride through the sights and sounds of the city, the endless intimacy of the dance, the stunning dawn kiss when his hunger, his passion had driven her to heights she had never even known existed. But then it had all crashed and burned, the seductive night giving way to the stark reality of dawn.

Except this isn't his fault—it's yours.

The shame descended, like a black cloud covering the sun.

She'd crossed so far over the invisible line between

them—a line she was fairly sure she would never be able to uncross.

They'd returned from the club in silence. The ride through the dawn, past the Trevi Fountain, round the Spanish Steps, along the Via Veneto should have been enchanting, but as she'd sheltered behind him on the motorbike, her cheek pressed against the tensed muscles of his spine, all she could see was the fury on his face after their kiss.

She'd angered him, she could see that—with her shame, her regret—because she suspected he didn't understand propriety, appropriate behaviour, didn't care about the strictures by which she had always lived her life. That his devil-may-care pursuit of pleasure—*her* pleasure—only made him more intoxicating, more mesmerising, just made the position she'd put herself in now all the more dangerous.

The loud buzzing began again and she jumped.

Her phone was ringing.

Fumbling for it on the nightstand, she glanced at the screen. Orla was calling her, and it was already half past eleven in the morning!

She blinked at the endless string of missed call alerts from the different media contacts she had been dealing with for weeks.

But the panic about the job ahead of her this morning didn't come, because the job was the least of her worries now.

Guilt swelled in her chest. She let the phone ring a few more times, gathering herself for the awkward conversation she was going to be forced to have with a woman she had always respected. A woman who she considered a friend. A woman who had trusted her. A woman she had failed miserably last night. Just the way she'd failed the monarchy, the country and the mission that Karim and Orla had assigned her.

Just as she had failed herself.

She sucked in a tight breath round the ache in her chest. Lifting the phone, she clicked the answer button with trembling fingers.

'Jamilla, are you okay?' Orla jumped in before she could say anything. She sounded concerned, even a little frantic. The guilt grew into a boulder under Jamilla's breastbone.

'Yes. I'm so sorry, I overslept.'

Orla gave a small laugh—both relieved and rueful. 'Well, I suppose that's to be expected.'

'It is?' Jamilla asked, confused now as well as heartsick.

'Yes, listen, Jamilla. I just called to check you're okay and to let you know that Dane texted Karim early this morning. And Karim and I have had a long conference call with Jed and Alicia,' she continued, mentioning their press secretary Jed Allingham and Alicia Van Dusen, the top media consultant who Jamilla had been liaising with on the tour. 'To find the best way forward before the news broke.'

News? What news?

'We all think we should cancel the rest of the week's engagements in Italy. Jed feels the press intrusion will be brutal, so it makes sense for you and Dane to fly to County Kildare today so you can take the next five days to regroup while we figure out how best to play this. The tour isn't as important as both of you.'

Dane had texted the King? This morning? *When* this morning?

Shock came first, swiftly followed by nausea. Had he told Karim about what they'd done?

'I just wanted to talk to you, Jamilla, to make absolutely sure you're really okay.' Orla's voice dropped, concern etched in every single syllable.

Jamilla's mortification increased ten-fold. Orla was being so considerate, so thoughtful, and she didn't deserve it. But another part of her was still hopelessly wary and confused. Why had Dane texted Karim? Had he boasted about what had happened? Had the whole night been a trap to destroy her credibility?

The thought horrified her.

He'd been angry with her last night, angry with her reaction to his kiss, and she still didn't really understand why. But she would never have guessed he was the kind of man to brag about his conquests. Or to deliberately try to destroy her reputation. But how much did she really know about him?

The sick feeling of dread became lodged in her gut.

'The young woman on that balcony seemed so different from the woman I know you to be,' Orla added. Jamilla's pulse rate hit the stratosphere. How did Orla know so much? 'But I just want you to know that doesn't have to be a bad thing. And you'll be finding no judgement here.'

'Dane told Karim about last night?' The words were propelled out of her mouth on a breath of stunned horror.

He had told the King about her kissing him like a wild woman, giving herself up to the moment? Mortification engulfed her.

Was she still asleep? Still dreaming? Because this was a nightmare.

'Oh, Jamilla, I'm so sorry,' Orla said, her voice regretful now as well as full of compassion. 'I'm guessing you haven't seen today's headlines. Dane didn't give us any details, all the text said was that there might be a problem as he'd seen a photographer last night, taking pictures of the two of you. Karim hasn't managed to get in touch with him since. Anyway, we tried through several channels to have the photos contained but unfortunately they're all over the press and the internet.'

'*Ph...photos?* Photos of what?' She had to slap her hand over her mouth, the nausea barrelling up her throat. But behind it was also a strange sense of relief that Dane hadn't tried to destroy her. That in his own blunt way he had been trying to protect her.

'Of you and Dane last night, on the balcony of his club in Rome,' Orla said calmly. But not nearly calmly enough to stop Jamilla's whole body shaking. 'Kissing each other as if your lives depended on it.'

A swearword Jamilla had never spoken in her entire life shot out of her mouth.

'There are photos of us? Together? Kissing?' she hissed, worn out with the barrage of emotions after so little sleep. She couldn't seem to put any of it into perspective any more. 'In the media?' she said, trying to make it all seem real when it still felt like a terrible dream.

Even if Dane had tried to protect her, her reckless behaviour, her monumental lack of judgement was now out there, displayed for all the world to see.

'I'm afraid so. I'm sorry, Jamilla. I know what a private person you are. And this is beyond intrusive. I feel absolutely terrible for you both, that you should be put in this position. And especially as a result of your work for Zafar—and Karim and me.'

Jamilla registered the compassion still thickening Orla's voice, and the regret. But it made no sense. Why should Orla or Karim feel responsible when she was the one who had destroyed everything? Panic rose up her throat now to join forces with the nausea.

'I will resign, effective immediately, of course,' she managed to get out as the weight in her stomach reached catastrophic proportions.

'Resign?' Orla sounded genuinely shocked. 'Jamilla,

don't be silly. Why should you resign? It's not your fault some sneaky gobshite climbed up a tree and took pictures of you both in a private moment to sell to the highest bidder.'

'Yes, but…'

I was the one who kissed Dane Jones as if my life depended on it. Because in that moment it felt as if it did.

'But nothing,' Orla interrupted, cutting off the words Jamilla was trying to get up the guts to actually enunciate. 'I'll not have you feeling guilty for the behaviour of the tabloid press. That man had no right to…'

'But I did kiss him,' she managed to get out, the guilt only made worse somehow by Orla's unwavering support. 'I disgraced myself and my role as a representative of the Zafari monarchy. I threw myself at him, I lost control and behaved like a…a…' She stuttered to a stop. She couldn't even say the word.

'Jamilla, it was just a kiss,' Orla said so gently Jamilla's eyes stung.

'It was more than a kiss,' Jamilla said as she scrubbed away the tear that leaked out, the tightness in her chest making it hard to breathe.

Orla gave a soft laugh. 'Well, yes, it looked like a bit more than a kiss. But seriously, Milla,' she added, using the nickname Jamilla had always felt cemented their friendship. 'It was after hours. You're entitled to a private life. And Dane kissed you right back, and I'll be betting he initiated it. Because I'm guessing the man has a mite more experience in these matters than you do. And he's also a total ride,' she added, using the Irish vernacular for hot. 'Although don't tell Karim I said that—he's a bit sensitive about me noticing how hot his brother is, even if it is in a purely observational capacity.'

Was Orla joking now? Jamilla sniffed loudly, trying to hold onto the sobs that were starting to crush her ribs and see the funny side, although she was finding it hard to locate anything at all amusing about the whole situation.

'But I've ruined everything,' she said, giving in to misery again. 'You're going to have to cancel the tour. Can't you see I can't be trusted any more? To do my job. To make sensible decisions. I've ruined everything.'

'Jamilla, no, you haven't. We're not suggesting cancelling the tour, just the rest of the engagements in Italy so the story has a chance to calm down,' Orla said, putting on the firm voice she used with her young son whenever he was tired or cranky. 'You've always set such a high standard for decorum. But you're human. And nobody would even know this had happened if it wasn't for that horrible paparazzo.'

'But I'd know,' Jamilla said. And Dane knew.

'Well, yes, you would. And I think we should definitely have a girl talk once you're here to discuss what's actually going on with my brother-in-law. But that's a personal matter. When it comes to the professional aspects of your role, I wanted you to know that Karim and I still trust you implicitly to do the job you've been asked to do. The real question is do you want to continue working so closely alongside Dane? Now that there appears to be a personal aspect to your relationship with him— and, unfortunately, thanks to that bastard photographer, the press will no doubt be focusing on it during the rest of the tour—we'd totally understand if you would prefer to be reassigned.' Orla sighed. 'I'll admit I don't know Dane that well; he's something of an enigma. Karim acknowledges that he's always had, shall we say, an *effect* on women. Karim doesn't believe he's an untrustworthy person or that he would ever exploit a woman, but they're brothers. I don't want Dane taking advantage of you, however inadvertently...' She added carefully, 'Or for you to feel pressured in any way.'

The memory of the devastating orgasm, the way she'd let go without a thought to the consequences and the argument between them that had followed chose that precise moment to flow through her head in vivid Technicolor. Shame washed over her all over again.

But he didn't take advantage of me. If anything, I took advantage of him.

Dane hadn't wanted her to go with him. He'd only agreed to take her along last night because she'd insisted. And while she'd been telling herself it was so she could keep an eye on him, make sure he didn't go AWOL, she could see now the reality had been different. She'd somehow persuaded herself she was doing her job, when her motivations hadn't been nearly that simple. Or altruistic. She'd seen the frustration on his face, the need to escape, and a part of her had wanted to soothe him, like some wild beast who needed to be tamed. Which just made it all the more humiliating—and ironic—that as soon as she'd climbed aboard his bike the opposite had happened.

He'd tempted her wild side out of hiding, but it really hadn't taken that much of an effort. Because that wild side had always been there, just waiting to burst free. And what made it even worse was that she could see clearly now, she had feelings for him—perhaps triggered by the conversation they'd had about his father's letters, perhaps before that, when he'd spoken about Zafar at the oasis. She'd realised how hard it was for him to take on the role he'd committed to, and secretly she'd admired that. Not only that, but she'd somehow convinced herself they had a connection, because of her difficult relationship with her own father.

Maybe François Xavier Roussel had never been as callous as King Abdullah, but he had abandoned her mother without a backward glance, and ultimately abandoned her too. Somehow, subconsciously she'd been looking for his approval ever since. So much so that she had completely repressed her natural urges, eventually becoming like a pressure cooker, ready to blow at the first sign of temptation. Perhaps she needed to address that reaction because it had surely intensified her attraction to a man she barely knew.

'I wasn't pressured to do anything I didn't want to do,' she managed in answer to Orla's last question.

She'd made choices, bad choices maybe, but they had been her choices. Not Dane's.

'Okay, well, that's good.' Orla breathed out as if she'd been holding her breath, and Jamilla felt a wave of love for her employer. Her friend. 'And so how do you feel about continuing with the tour, as Dane's diplomatic advisor? Karim said Dane made it clear in his text he didn't have a problem with continuing. Which suggests you're doing a great job with putting him at his ease in the role.' She laughed again. 'In a professional capacity, of course.' Her voice sobered. 'But if you want to return to Zafar, we can assign someone else. No questions asked.'

But I don't want to leave him. He needs me.

The thought came out of left field. She swallowed, gripping the phone, and stared out of the large mullioned windows of the suite. She pulled her legs up in the bed to hug her knees one-handed as she tried to subdue the emotion in her chest.

A part of her knew she ought to accept Orla's offer. Spending time with Dane was dangerous in so many ways. She had become emotionally invested in him in more ways than one.

But another part of her didn't want to give up. However misguided her emotions, however dangerous the desire that had blindsided her, she needed to find a way past it.

Because she could see now her fall from grace last night wasn't just about Dane. It was also rooted in that confused, desperately obedient little girl who had tried so hard to make her father care for her and had never understood why he had chosen to live in France with the children he'd had with his mistress instead of her and her mother.

Dane had given her the male attention she'd always craved for one wild night. And she'd lapped it up. She had to get that into perspective.

'I don't want to be reassigned,' she said. 'I'd like to continue with the tour. And see it through.' She couldn't quit. She'd started this job and she needed to finish it, if for no other reason than to prove to herself she could.

'Okay, grand. I hoped you'd say that,' Orla said, sounding a lot more confident than Jamilla felt.

The confidence will come, if you keep the professional distance with Dane you lost so catastrophically last night.

But as they finished the call and spoke of next steps, including the arrangements for Dane and her to travel to Ireland that afternoon, Jamilla could feel the pressure in her chest increasing at the thought of the weeks ahead, working closely with Dane while trying to keep her wayward emotions, and the reckless desire, under wraps.

Once she'd ended her conversation with Orla she received a call from Enzo, alerting her to the fact the press had been camping out at the hotel, ready to waylay her and Dane.

She switched off her phone and headed for the shower. She turned the dial from hot to frigid in an attempt to wake up and wash away the last of the panic and confusion still working its way through her system.

Strangely, though, as her tired body responded to the needle-sharp spray, the thought of reorganising the rest of the tour and running the press gauntlet didn't feel anywhere near as daunting as facing Dane again.

CHAPTER NINE

'WHERE THE HELL have you been, Dane?' Karim shouted over the helicopter noise as Dane jumped from the large black Puma onto the field in County Kildare.

The King of Zafar looked remarkably at home on the back pasture of the Calhoun stud farm wearing worn jeans and a T-shirt and with his arms full of his toddler son, Hasan. But the little boy's wide smile of welcome when he spotted Dane was in direct counterpoint to his father's accusatory frown.

Figures.

'We were expecting you here four days ago,' Karim added as the chopper Dane had co-piloted from the roof-top of his London club for the journey to Ireland finally powered down enough to make speech less of an effort.

'Good to see you too, bro,' Dane murmured, keeping the forced couldn't-give-a-damn smile he'd been working on for four days firmly in place. Ever since his night in Rome with Jamilla…and that kiss.

The kiss he hadn't been able to forget, no matter how hard he'd tried. And he'd tried. A lot.

She'd been silent, they both had, on the ride back to the hotel that night. He'd alerted Karim to the possibility of the photos, then crashed. The next day he'd caught the headlines and been mad as hell about them. But after ducking out the back of the hotel and taking a ride through

Rome to the Colosseum to clear his head, he'd been ready to confront Jamilla about what had happened and what to do next.

The tabloid headlines were bad news, sure. But, the way he saw it, they weren't anywhere near as big a problem as the chemistry they'd ignited on the balcony of his club. Or the emotions churning in his gut at the way she'd freaked out about it.

But when he'd arrived at her suite that afternoon he'd been told she'd already left for Kildare. Apparently, she'd arranged to have him travel separately to Ireland, to avoid the paparazzi getting another shot of them both together and pouring more fuel on the media bonfire before their time out. Or at least that was what the young assistant she'd had waiting for him in his suite had told him. Which sounded smart and reasonable.

He wasn't buying it for a second.

The truth was, she hadn't wanted to see him in the flesh again until she got herself back under control, hadn't wanted to deal with the fallout from that kiss and the sweet sexy climax he'd treated her to. She was running scared. Of him, of the heat between them, just as much as those tabloid headlines. She'd probably figured that by engineering the next meeting between them in Kildare—with Karim and Orla and little Hasan acting as chaperones—he'd be happy to just pretend it had never happened.

Yeah, well, he'd tried that, deciding to give her some space until he was good and ready to see her again too. So, instead of taking the Zafari royal jet which was fuelled and waiting at Rome-Fiumicino, he'd packed a bag, switched off his phone and headed off on the bike to wind his way up through Florence, Genoa, Milan, then across the Alps into France to clear his head. He'd finally switched on his phone again when he'd got to London to pick up his company chopper to County Kildare.

There had been a ton of messages from Karim, the press secretary, his own PA in Manhattan—who had probably been hounded by his brother's staff to find out where the hell he was. The only person who hadn't messaged him in those four days was the woman who the last time he'd seen her had been flushed and wary and showing the first signs of beard burn from his kiss.

I rest my case.

He swept his hair back and ignored his brother to grin at his nephew. 'Hey there, little buddy,' he said, giving the kid a poke in the stomach which elicited the expected belly laugh.

'Unca Dane!' the little boy shouted and stretched out chubby arms.

He scooped Hasan out of his father's arms, ignoring the emotion that hit him at the realisation that his nephew had remembered him. The boy began chattering to him in that language only toddlers understood—providing a handy distraction from Karim's questioning frown—as they headed towards the house. But, weirdly, when he was forced to put the boy down so the kid's nanny could take him in to have his supper, the ripple of emotion turned into a pang.

He wasn't a family guy—he had decided years ago he never wanted to be a father himself. The fallout from his night with Jamilla—and the emotion wedged in his gut at the thought of seeing her again, and finally having it out with her, whatever the hell *it* was—had obviously done an even bigger number on him than he thought.

Something he liked even less than the snarky question his brother shot at him once the boy and his nanny were out of earshot.

'Why didn't you answer any of my messages?' Karim

demanded. 'And where the hell *have* you been? Because that was a genuine question, *bro*,' he added, stressing the word bro in that sarcastic, self-righteous way he had that had always got on Dane's nerves.

He owed his brother a lot, for letting him tag along during his early years in the kingdom, when his brother had visited in the summer—and for keeping tabs on him as a teenager during his exile in Manhattan, when no one else had given a damn about him. Certainly not his mother or their father. But that didn't give Karim the right to boss him about.

'I didn't answer the messages because I switched off my phone,' he replied, struggling to keep his temper under control. 'And where I was is none of your damn business.'

'Well, that was remarkably irresponsible, even for you,' Karim shot straight back. 'And actually it is my business. If you recall, we have a royal trade tour which has just had to be completely rescheduled because you chose to play fast and loose with our chief diplomatic aide.'

His temper exploded like a bomb at Karim's accusation. Words he'd been expecting ever since he'd contacted Karim to give him a heads-up about the photographer. But right beneath the anger was the sting of guilt, thanks to an image that had been bugging him ever since that night. The shadow of shame and humiliation in Jamilla's wide amber eyes, and the reddening mark on the soft skin of her chin.

He shoved his brother back against the garden wall, his arm coming up instinctively to press against Karim's throat. 'You son of a...' he hissed, the forced smile forgotten as he let the anger boil over to cover the sharp sting of guilt. 'I'm not a kid any more, screwing anything that moves.'

And so desperate for affection I figured I could find it in indiscriminate sex.

He swallowed down the humiliating thought, let the fury build to disguise the hole in his gut he thought he'd sealed up a long time ago. 'I kissed her, she kissed me. Got it? She's a grown woman who gets to make her own decisions. I didn't force her. And it's not my fault some sneak took a photo and decided to splash it all over the front pages of the gossip mags. The French leg doesn't start till tomorrow and I'm here now, aren't I?'

'Dane, chill out,' Karim murmured, lifting his palms in a universal sign of surrender, his brother's expression registering shock not judgement. 'I apologise; that was out of order.'

Dane dropped his arm, stepped back, feeling shaky now and tense, and embarrassed by the outburst and the fury still pitching and rolling in his stomach.

'I know you didn't force her,' Karim continued, still staring at him as if he had lost his mind.

Dane raked his fingers through his hair. Hell, maybe he had.

'Jamilla has told us as much, but even if she hadn't, I know that's not the kind of man you are.' Karim placed a hand on his shoulder, squeezed.

Dane shrugged, humiliated now, not just by his outburst but by the knowledge of how much Karim's confidence in him still meant.

Karim had always believed in him, even when he didn't deserve it. That was why his brother had loaned him the money to buy his first stake. He'd paid that investment back with interest a long time ago. So why the hell should he think he'd failed him somehow? Or still care so much about what he thought of him?

'All right, thanks, apology accepted,' he murmured, feeling surly now as well as unbearably tense. 'I said I'd continue with the tour and I will,' he added tightly. 'I just needed some time to clear my head. Okay?'

'Of course,' Karim replied.

Dane looked away, not quite able to meet his brother's searching gaze. He didn't want to see the questions there—questions he couldn't even answer himself.

He'd overreacted to Karim's offhand comment, that much was obvious. And Karim was probably wondering why.

Yeah...good luck with that one, bro.

As he struggled to calm his breathing and douse the last sparks of his temper, his gaze landed on the majestic eight-bedroom Georgian manor house where Karim and his family had been living for the last few months. And where Jamilla had been too for the last four days— no doubt rearranging the tour dates and waiting for the world's press to move on.

The collection of brightly coloured toys discarded on the front lawn alongside a small slide and a little orange pedal car, the lovingly tended vines that clung to the red bricks, currently spotted with spring blooms, the sparkling clean windows which looked out over the lush green fields and the racing stables and the gallops beyond all seemed to mock him now as unfamiliar and inexplicable emotions still refused to settle in his gut.

Karim had restored the Calhoun family's ancestral mansion to its former glory for his wife after their marriage five years ago. His brother's family used the place on and off during the racing season when Orla was managing the stud—or awaiting the birth of their kids.

He'd visited them here several times in the past. Mostly as a compromise, because he'd refused to accept any of the invitations they'd sent him to visit them in Zafar. He'd never had a problem with being here, until now.

But this wasn't just a house any more, however grand, it was a home, he realised. And yet another place where he would never truly belong.

Why did that bother him, though, when it never had in the past?

Then he spotted two figures walking across the fields from the stable yard, chatting. He recognised his sister-in-law from her slow, uncomfortable gait and the silhouette of her rather impressive belly. The other woman, her dark hair falling in loose waves past her shoulders, her taller, slimmer figure dressed in a white blouse and dark jeans, should have been harder to recognise from this distance.

Except she wasn't. Because his body reacted instantly to that graceful physique, those slender curves.

Jamilla.

Her name whispered across his consciousness as all his senses shot straight back into the danger zone.

So that answered one question, at least.

Taking a four-day solo bike tour through the back roads of Italy and France, camping out and taking full advantage of the freedom of the road, hadn't controlled the hunger or the impact of that night one little bit—if anything, it had made it worse.

Her head rose, almost as if she'd sensed him standing there watching her, and she stopped dead.

All of a sudden her movements looked a lot less graceful, a lot less relaxed. The emotions in his guts fired up to go with the heady kick to his senses. Her stance reminded him of a young doe he'd caught in his truck's headlamps one night while heading to his farm in Upstate New York. He'd slammed on the brakes to avoid hitting the beautiful creature and she'd bounded back into the forest before he'd had a chance to really appreciate her.

He kept his gaze locked on the beautiful creature in front of him this time as he set off across the fields towards her. He could see as he got closer that her desire to bolt was even stronger than the young doe's.

But she didn't move. She stood her ground and waited

for him to reach her and Orla, her arms wrapped around her midriff, though, as if bracing herself for the inevitable confrontation.

Smart woman. Because there's no way I'm letting you run away from me—or this thing between us—again.

This woman had got under his skin in a way no other woman ever had. And he still didn't know why exactly. The heady need swelled in his groin at the flicker of awareness in her eyes as he approached.

And the confidence which had eluded him for days returned in a rush.

Maybe the answer to their problem wasn't all that complicated after all. Perhaps it was simply time they both stopped running from the inevitable.

'So I see Dane finally turned up,' Orla murmured beside Jamilla.

But Jamilla could hardly hear her friend's comment above the thundering in her ears.

He looked…magnificent, his bronze hair lightened by the sun, his skin tanned a darker brown. The white T-shirt showed off the defined contours of his pectoral muscles, while the frown on his face and the purposeful stride suggested he had a lot to talk about.

Her reprieve was over.

She'd been preparing for this confrontation for four days. She'd gone through every possible permutation of how she was going to tell him—succinctly and without any flicker of the emotion currently turning her insides to mush—that they needed to put the events of that night behind them, go back to how they had been before she'd climbed aboard his bike and become a wild woman. She couldn't afford to lose herself again, and she needed his help to ensure the rest of the tour went off without a hitch.

That kiss had been a mistake—a massive mistake that neither one of them wanted to repeat, surely.

But what had all seemed so simple, so obvious—while she'd stared at the ceiling above her bed late at night or spent hours deflecting the endless press enquiries with well-rehearsed platitudes about Rome's eternal beauty and its ability to make anyone lose their mind, or took on the titanic task of rearranging the tour commitments so she would be spending as little time as possible in Dane's company—suddenly seemed a lot less simple or obvious.

'He looks like he's got rather a lot to say to you,' Orla added while he was still out of earshot. 'Do you need me to stay?'

'No,' Jamilla said as forcefully as she could manage with the panic starting to choke her.

She'd been enough of a coward already. If she hadn't taken the opportunity to leave Rome ahead of him she could have had this situation done and dusted by now, instead of having it turn into a lump of radioactive waste in her stomach over four restless days and sleepless nights while he'd done his disappearing act. Getting their working relationship back on track was her only priority. And that meant standing her ground and not freaking out.

Reaching them at last, Dane nodded at his sister-in-law but his gaze barely left Jamilla's. 'Hey, Orla, you're looking...' a smile curved his lips which didn't quite make it to his eyes '...enormous.'

Orla let out a half laugh, doing her best to defuse the tension. 'Gee, thanks, bro,' she muttered. 'Now I feel like even more of an elephant.'

He leaned past Jamilla and gave his sister-in-law a brotherly peck on the cheek. 'If it's any consolation, the elephant look suits you, sis.'

'You rat,' she said, giving him a slap on the arm, but then she laughed, the amusement more genuine this time.

The pretty flush of pleasure on her face at Dane's compliment made Jamilla realise this man could charm any woman if he put his mind to it.

But the reckless twinkle in his blue eyes hardened to steel as his gaze landed back on her.

'Hey, Orla,' he said, never breaking eye contact with Jamilla. 'How about you leave Jamilla and me alone for a minute? We've got a lot to discuss.'

Jamilla's blush intensified at the direct, assessing look and the heat in it he was making no attempt to hide.

She'd told Orla all about the kiss, what had led up to it and how ashamed she was of the way she'd behaved. Orla, being Orla, had continued to shrug off all Jamilla's guilt and angst and *mea culpa*s. Orla had also made it clear that whatever Jamilla wanted to do about Dane, and that kiss, going forward, she and Karim would not judge her. Orla had even told Jamilla quite a lot about her own courtship with Dane's brother, which had turned out to be not nearly as straightforward or picture perfect as Jamilla had always assumed. The news that Orla had effectively been 'contracted' as Karim's fiancée before they'd fallen in love for real had been nothing short of mind-blowing.

But, despite the confidences Orla had shared, Jamilla didn't believe her situation with Dane was remotely similar. Orla hadn't been in a working relationship with Karim, not really, despite that contract. And it was obvious the two of them were made for each other. Unlike herself and Dane.

Jamilla had been deeply touched by Orla's support. But she hadn't been able to get up the guts to tell her friend she wasn't quite as worldly wise or pragmatic when it came to intimate relationships as Orla had clearly assumed. And that she had absolutely no prior experience of having been—quite literally—swept off her feet by her desire for a man.

A desire that had burned every night since and was burning now. Along with her indignation at Dane's high-handed decision to have this conversation as soon as he arrived.

I mean, seriously, could he have made this situation any more inappropriate with his demand for privacy?

'I can leave you guys alone,' Orla said. 'If that's okay with Jamilla?' she added, sending Jamilla a pointed look that clearly stated: *Whatever you want to do now, you have my support.*

Gratitude came first, followed by the twist of cowardice.

If only she could say, *No, I don't want to have this conversation. It's too much, he's too much. Just being this close to him makes me want to do stupid things again.*

But she banked the spurt of panic, attempted to swallow it whole, along with a wave of mortification.

I'm not afraid of him or how he makes me feel, she added to herself, and tried to make herself believe it.

The nerves in her belly became more volatile and persistent. But she forced herself not to leap at the lifeline Orla offered. This was her mess to clean up. No one else's.

'Yes, it's fine, Orla,' she said.

Orla gave her and Dane one last look, then nodded slowly. 'Okay, I should go and help get Hasan fed and in bed,' she said. 'We'll see you both for dinner at eight?'

'Great, thanks,' Dane said, still not taking his eyes from Jamilla's flaming face.

And then Orla was gone. And it was just the two of them.

Jamilla sucked in an unsteady breath when he didn't say anything, just continued to stare at her, the temper still sparking in his eyes she'd noticed the last time she'd seen him. When he'd bid her a perfunctory goodbye in the hotel's garage. Before she'd raced up to her suite, and tried without success to dismiss the buzz on her lips, the sting on her cheeks, the deep throbbing ache at her core.

She struggled to recall the speech she'd been working on for four days. The forthright, apologetic speech about decorum and mistakes and professionalism and appropriate behaviour. But she couldn't remember a single word of it.

And something else entirely burst past her lips. 'Where have you been? The Paris ball is six days away. We're travelling tomorrow and I haven't had a chance to brief you on the media strategy we've worked out. *Or* the changes to the itinerary.'

He tilted his head to one side, that heated gaze narrowing on her flushed face. His temper flared like a firecracker. He restrained it, but only just, before he spoke in a deep husky voice which seemed to reverberate in her abdomen.

'Where were *you* the morning after?' he said, not bothering to answer a single one of her perfectly reasonable questions.

'I… I needed to get to Kildare and you weren't there. You'd gone off on another joyride, if you recall.'

'Joyride?' He laughed, the sound doing nothing to quell the heated glow in her abdomen. 'Is that what we're calling it?'

'What else would you call it?'

'Nuts? Dangerous? Wild? Exciting?' he murmured, and she realised he was referring to the ride they had taken together. The one she didn't want to talk about, but now somehow was. The fact that it was making the glow in her stomach jiggle and jive could not be good. 'But joyful?' he said. 'Nah, I don't think so. If it was joyful, I wouldn't have been left with an ache I couldn't satisfy. And you wouldn't have high-tailed it out of there the next morning as if your butt was on fire.'

The blush hit the top of her head and the soles of her feet simultaneously. 'I… I apologised for that ache.'

Fury flared again in those true-blue eyes and she knew she'd hit a nerve. Again.

'And I told you I didn't want your apology,' he ground out.

'What *do* you want then?' she blurted out, and realised her mistake immediately when he reached out and skimmed his thumb down her cheek. Before she could stop herself, she leaned into the caress.

She yanked herself back, but it was already too late because he'd noticed.

He dropped his hand, buried it in the pocket of his jeans, but she could still feel his touch and the brutal hunger ready to drive her to do stupid things.

'What do *I* want?' he said as if he were seriously considering the question. 'I want you to stop lying to yourself and me. And I want you to stop running.'

'I wasn't the one who disappeared for four days,' she countered, drowning now and willing to throw anything at him to escape the incontrovertible truth that there was going to be no going back to the way they had been. He had seen who she really was that night—reckless, impulsive and pathetically needy—and he wasn't going to let that girl hide behind the appropriate, the polite, the professional again.

A part of her hated him for demolishing all her defences so easily. But she hated herself more—for giving him that power. For letting him see behind the façade she had built so carefully, and which had protected her for so long. Until now.

'Fair point,' he said with a nonchalance that scared her.

How could her emotions be so raw and his be so calm, so controlled?

'Can't you just forget about that kiss?' she asked, hearing the pleading note and hating herself even more.

'Nope, I can't forget it,' he said with an acceptance that only pushed her closer to the edge. But then he added, 'Can you?'

'Of course I can,' she said, but she already knew she was lying.

And she had an awful suspicion he knew she was lying too.

CHAPTER TEN

'BY THE WAY, Jamilla, we must pick a gown for you to wear at the Paris ball before you leave,' Orla suggested as she tucked into the delicately marinated chicken which was one of the few things she could eat without upsetting her stomach. 'We can have it altered for you when you get there.'

Jamilla blinked and stared at her friend. Then her gaze shot to Dane, only to find him watching her—like a hawk. Or, rather, a wolf.

Oh, no. She'd mentioned borrowing a gown to attend the ball a week ago without telling Orla about her bargain with Dane. But she had no intention of accompanying him to the lavish event now. Not after their kiss, and the media furore she'd just spent four days trying to get under control.

'I don't think that will be necessary now,' she said, concentrating on cutting the steak she'd been served, which she had been struggling to eat since she'd sat down at the large dining table.

She'd debated not coming down to supper at all, after the way her 'meeting' with Dane had ended earlier. But she'd forced herself to put in an appearance. She didn't want to give him any more ammunition. Didn't want him to think she was running scared. Even if she was. But now she wished she'd chickened out. Because anything would be better than the tangle of nerves playing tag with the few bites of steak she'd actually managed to swallow.

'Are you sure?' Orla said, unaware of the real reason Jamilla had agreed to attend the ball with Dane. 'I think it's a great idea to have you take a more visible role. You've spent months co-ordinating the tour and no one's more knowledgeable than you about the trade mission. I think you'll be a major asset when it comes to meeting with the ministers and dignitaries that are due to attend.'

'I've briefed Dane extensively,' she murmured, giving Orla a pointed look. 'I'm sure he'll do an excellent job of representing the kingdom,' she finished.

After his four-day disappearing act and his insistence on talking about everything *but* the job they had to do that afternoon, she wasn't convinced any more that he was remotely committed to their goal. But, right now, she didn't care.

One thing she did know—she absolutely couldn't go to the ball on his arm. It would only reawaken the frenzied publicity about their kiss, which she'd been trying to crush. Not to mention her hyperactive hormones, which appeared to be incapable of distancing themselves from the events of that night too.

'While your sudden confidence in me is appreciated, Jamilla,' Dane said, his gaze fixed on her face with the intensity of a laser beam, sarcasm dripping off every word, 'I doubt I'll be able to do as good a job schmoozing those stiffs as you.'

The blush she'd been managing to suppress—ever since she'd arrived in the salon for their meal and seen him shaved and showered, wearing a fresh pair of dark jeans and a cashmere sweater that clung to his chest like a second skin—bloomed across her cheeks like a mushroom cloud.

She'd never been a blusher. Now she couldn't seem to stop blushing.

'But if you're too scared to accompany me the way we agreed…?' he added, the implication unmistakable.

She slammed down her knife and fork, forgetting their audience, forgetting everything but the man across from her, his challenging gaze calling her a coward. *Again*.

'I'm not scared of you,' she hissed, the stress finally releasing its stranglehold on her throat.

'Sure you are—you're terrified of admitting you still want me,' he said.

She blinked, so incensed now she could barely breathe. How dare he say that in front of Orla, in front of Karim? But it wasn't the thought of her employers that was making the temper start to choke her, it was that smug expression on his face and the way it made her feel. Angry, on edge and impossibly aroused.

'I don't still want you,' she insisted.

'Yeah, you do,' he said. 'Or you wouldn't have all but melted into a puddle at my feet an hour ago when I touched you.'

Karim cleared his throat loudly, sending his brother a baleful look and yanking Jamilla back to reality.

Jamilla's blush became fiery. 'I'm so sorry, Your Majesty,' she mumbled, wishing she could melt into the floor and disappear. 'I forgot myself.'

She'd been sparring with Dane like a surly teenager—at the dinner table, in front of the King and Queen. The sort of mouthy, opiniated teenager she'd never been.

Dane, of course, didn't look remotely apologetic or even concerned. If anything, he looked even more smug. And even more gorgeous. *Drat the man*. Did appearances, propriety, appropriate behaviour mean nothing to him?

'There's no need to address me by my title here, Jamilla,' Karim murmured. 'And please don't apologise.' He sighed. 'My brother tends to have that effect on everyone.'

'Thanks, bro,' Dane said, clearly not bothered by the observation in the least. He was still watching her, his lips curving on one side into a cynical grin. A grin that was as good as calling her a liar. 'What you guys don't know, because I guess she didn't tell you, is that we had a deal, Jamilla and I. A deal she's now too scared of a little press attention to follow through on.'

'It won't be a small amount of press…' she began, but he simply lifted his hand, silencing her. And sending her temper through the roof.

'The deal was I'd wear the dress uniform of the Zafari head of state if she agreed to back me up at the ball. But, hey, it's no skin off my nose. I'd much rather wear something that doesn't make me look like a phoney. And I'm sure I can wing it with the trade ambassadors if I have to. It's pretty clear Jamilla's scared she won't be able to resist me if she comes to the ball as my date.'

Indignation poured through her like molten lava at his goading words, turning the longing in her chest into a hot lump of outrage. It plunged deep into her abdomen like a comet—making her so mad she was surprised she didn't leap across the table and wring his neck.

He'd made her look like an unprofessional fool in front of people who she respected—people who mattered to her. He had insisted on bringing up their intimate relationship *again*, when she'd done everything in her power to deflect and deny and mitigate the fallout from that night. The way it needed to be deflected and denied and mitigated.

'You arrogant jerk…' She sucked in a breath past the stick of gelignite now lodged under her breastbone and all but choking her. 'I'll have no trouble at all resisting you.'

'Prove it,' he murmured.

Her temper snapped like a dry twig. 'Fine… I will.'

She turned to Orla, who was watching them both with undisguised interest. 'If you're still happy for me to borrow one of your gowns, I'd be more than happy to take a more visible role at the ball. And schmooze the trade ministers to within an inch of their lives.' She shot her searing gaze back to Dane. 'But that means you have to wear the uniform.'

The curve of his lips became a devastating smile. 'Happy to,' he said and tucked back into his steak, but the smug smile had kicked up several notches.

And suddenly she knew she'd just handed him the outcome he'd wanted all along.

Jamilla, you fool.

CHAPTER ELEVEN

'YOUR HIGHNESS, MS ROUSSEL is ready to accompany you.'

Dane turned in the ornate antechamber of the Zafari embassy in Paris at the hushed comment from his valet Hakim. His breath clogged in his lungs. And the heat which was never far away when he was near his chief diplomatic aide flared.

Damn.

His gaze roamed over the exquisite and intricately beaded gown of raw red silk, the demure but somehow erotic neckline which exposed just a hint of cleavage. The whisper-thin gauzy material that floated over the silk did nothing to disguise Jamilla's high breasts, her slender waist, the flare of her hips and her mile-long legs.

At last his gaze rose to her face. The tumble of glossy black curls had been corralled by a jewelled tiara, adding the final regal touch to the dramatic display. Her wide amber eyes, made to look even bigger by expertly applied eyeliner and the golden glitter on her lids, flashed with a rare fire.

The flush of colour only made her look more incredible. More stunning.

And every inch a queen.

The tiara's jewels glinted in the light of the antechamber's chandelier as she stepped forward. Her gaze flitted over him, the flash of a desire she couldn't hide only making the temper in her eyes more arousing.

He adored the bold fury on her face, he realised, even if it was directed at him.

He strode towards her, the sound of the ceremonial sword on his hip clinking, and for the first time let the feeling of power and majesty flow through him unchecked.

When he had first looked at himself in the mirror ten minutes ago—decked out in the ceremonial uniform of Zafar's head of state—he had felt like an imposter, the sight of the ornate and imposing outfit reminding him uncomfortably of his father. Arrogant, cold, untouchable.

It had not been a good moment.

But as he'd continued to stare at his reflection, instead of seeing the man who had ruled Zafar for so long with an iron fist, the man he barely remembered, he began to see his brother Karim. A good man, a good brother and as much a part of his past, a part of who he was, as the man who had never wanted him. Karim, who had not only stood by him as a boy but had stood up for his people, his country, and taken on so much. A true king.

And the uniform which he'd considered a foolish costume had become something more—a symbol of family, of heritage, of legacy. A royal legacy he had never felt a part of, but he could see now—thanks in no small part to the work of the stunning woman standing in front of him, frowning—he could honour for at least one night, if he let that feral, unloved kid go.

He took Jamilla's hand in his and bent at the waist to bring her fingers to his lips. He felt her jolt of shock and glanced up to see her eyes darken to a rich gold as he kissed her knuckles.

'You look like a queen,' he said as he straightened,

not bothering to hide the husky desire in his voice. 'It suits you.'

The colour in her cheeks heightened, making the smooth skin glow. Her throat flexed as she swallowed heavily. 'Except I'm not a queen. You, on the other hand…' she murmured, repeating the line he'd once fed her at the oasis as she sent him a pointed look and he saw the awareness she couldn't hide shadow her eyes.

He let out a rough chuckle, stupidly pleased by her obvious appreciation despite her attempts to maintain her temper. He wasn't a king, not even close. But tonight, for once, he refused to be an outcast. He planned to play the role he'd been assigned to the hilt. Not just to stick it to the man who had rejected him all those years ago, but also to turn the residual flash of temper in those rich amber eyes to something more enjoyable.

He wanted her; she knew that. And he was through playing nice—they'd had six full days in Paris, dancing around each other, the changes she'd made to the schedule conveniently keeping her clear of him most of the time. But he'd bided his time, knowing that tonight she wouldn't be able to avoid him. And now he had her where he wanted her, he intended to use every weapon in his arsenal to hear those soft sobs again and make her soar.

He forced himself to bank the hunger which had been building for over a week, recalling that he had several hours of industrial strength schmoozing to get through first.

He offered his elbow and after a brief hesitation she placed trembling fingertips on his forearm. She looked unsure but determined. The flames in his gut turned into a bonfire.

He loved that she was so transparent, but what he loved more was that she had finally lost the façade of propriety, no longer able to deny the energy sparking between them like an electrical force field.

He led her out of the antechamber onto the mezzanine level, heard her breathing accelerate as the lavish ballroom came into view.

A footman bowed and the ripple of conversation, the tinkle of champagne flutes and the ambient music below them fell silent.

'*Son altesse le Prince Dane Jones de Zafar, et Mademoiselle Jamilla Omar Roussel.*' The usher announced them in French, then English, then Zafari.

The hushed expectation of the crowd was broken by a spontaneous round of applause as bulbs flashed and the ripple of welcome became a roar.

The whispers rose to a crescendo as the eyes of the crowd devoured the spectacle they made—defiant, proud and, in Jamilla's case, hot as hell.

He could imagine the gossip columns going nuts tomorrow, devoting every column inch to the beautiful woman on his arm, but tonight she was his.

As they made their way down the wide sweeping staircase he leaned towards Jamilla, the lungful of her scent making the heat in his abdomen flare, and whispered in her ear, 'Time to knock 'em dead, Your Fake Majesty.'

The throaty laugh that burst out of her mouth, breaking the tension he could feel radiating off her, made him feel like a real prince for the first time in his life.

'Absolutely, Zafar is keen to participate on the world stage in a meaningful way. We have initiatives in place to ensure that our climate goals are met while we expand our agricultural output,' Jamilla said to the German MEP who had been quizzing her for the last ten minutes.

'I'd love to see what those initiatives are,' the older woman said, but then she smiled. 'I must say, I'm impressed, Ms Roussel, after the…' She paused, then coughed slightly, sending Jamilla an apologetic look. 'After the publicity in Rome about the tour I had assumed the title of Chief Diplomatic Aide was a euphemism for something else entirely. I apologise.'

Jamilla's cheeks burned. The woman had said what she knew a lot of other people at the ball were probably thinking. It had bothered her greatly, especially when she'd put on the borrowed gown for the first time and seen how it lifted her breasts and clung to her curves, making her recall the blurred paparazzi shots of her and Dane wrapped around each other. In that moment she had felt like a courtesan, not a queen.

She was used to standing back, to being invisible at events like this. She was there to support and advise, not to take a visible role.

She had wanted to hate Dane for putting her in this position and turning the tour into even more of a media circus than it was already. But as the evening had worn on and she'd found herself talking to a series of diplomats and politicians, civil servants and their spouses, using her linguistic skills and her vast knowledge of Zafar's new agricultural and cultural programmes, she had begun to gain confidence. Not least because, much to her astonishment, rather than belittling her or talking over her, Dane had remained by her side for the first portion of the evening and had been surprisingly encouraging and supportive.

Of course, having him there and being aware of every shift of his body, every waft of his scent, every look he sent her—full of heat and approval—had also kept her on edge, the bomb in her stomach which had begun ticking as soon as she'd laid eyes on him in the honorary uniform now ready to explode. But she didn't resent it any more. Or not as much.

They were doing a good job together. The speculation

about their personal relationship had only enhanced the tour's visibility—and she could do damage limitation tomorrow when she returned to her backroom role.

'Thank you, I think,' she said, giving a half laugh.

She caught sight of Dane about fifteen feet away through the crowd, more at ease now. He'd lost the sword when they'd gone into dinner, just as she had lost her tiara, but he still looked tall and indomitable and commanding and every inch a prince as he spoke to a group that included Zafar's French ambassador, an EU trade minister and a high-ranking British civil servant. She had no idea what he was saying to them, probably not any of the talking points she'd spent months working on, but she suspected, whatever it was, it was going to increase Zafar's profile exponentially.

The man was a born networker—charismatic, ridiculously gorgeous but also with that cool, edgy confidence and don't-give-a-damn attitude which made people gravitate towards him and hang on his every word.

'He is an exceptional ambassador for his country,' the MEP all but purred beside her. 'I am surprised the King has not called on his services before. On *both* your services; you make a very attractive couple,' the woman added.

Jamilla felt the heat in her cheeks flare. 'We're not a couple,' she said.

And Karim has called on my services; in fact I've been doing this job for years.

She bit down on her resentment. The woman had no reason to know who she was, because she had always been invisible before. 'I'm just here to support His Highness for the duration of the tour,' she added when the woman simply smiled as if they shared a particularly juicy secret.

'Your blush—and those photos—tell a different story,'

the MEP said, the confidential smile kind rather than judgemental.

'That was… That was just a moment of madness,' she said, regurgitating the line she'd been trying to sell for over a week to explain her lapse of judgement. But she wasn't sure she was convincing anyone any more. Not even herself. 'Rome is a very romantic city, it was late and we got a little carried away.'

'Pourquoi mentir, ma chérie, alors qu'il est évident pour tout le monde que vous couchez avec lui?'

She stiffened and swung round at the rude comment, the deep French accent laced with amused contempt.

Why lie, my dear, when it is obvious to everyone you are sleeping with him?

A slim man of medium height in a dress uniform with some medals clipped to the breast, his handsome face lined with age and his chestnut hair grown white at the temples, stood behind her. His gaze raked over her and the amused contempt turned to a grudging, but much more disturbing, respect.

'Jamilla,' he said, switching to English as the German politician excused herself discreetly. 'You look as…' he paused to let his gaze roam over her again, making her feel both exposed and unseen '…as beautiful as your mother.'

Jamilla's frantic heartbeat hit her tonsils, the wrenching pain of memory exploding in her skull, of the last time she had seen this man, and he had tugged her small arms from around his waist and told her in stern French she needed to stop making such a fuss, that he would come and visit her, but only if she had learned to behave herself.

A tidal wave of confused, and confusing, emotions—shock, desperation, hope, fear, humiliation—blindsided her, but beneath it all was the sickening undertow of worthlessness which had dogged her throughout her childhood.

And the word she had whispered like a prayer each night before she fell asleep, as she'd kissed the faded, creased photograph she'd kept hidden under her pillow for years after that hideous day, spilled out of her mouth again.

'Papa…?'

'Could I give you my card, Your Highness?' the snooty British bureaucrat asked him. 'I think the Minister for Media and Culture would love to invite you to London.'

'Sure.' Dane took the card, knowing he had no intention of adding another date to the tour, but Jamilla could figure out how to tell the guy. He tucked the card into his back pocket and bid the man goodbye, then strode off before he could get waylaid again.

Where was she? They'd been at this charm offensive for hours. Through six courses of cordon bleu cuisine in the banqueting hall next door after the initial reception, then back in the ballroom for another go-round of tedious small talk. Surely they could leave now. He was tired of schmoozing, tired of being on his best behaviour, and he wanted to get back to that heated look in her eyes. The one she'd been busy trying to bank all evening.

Luckily, at six three he was taller than most of the people in the room. His gaze swept over the heads of the exclusive crowd, the music from a French marching band getting on his last nerve, then zeroed in on her like an Exocet missile.

Wait a minute. Something's not right.

He could feel the tension radiating off Jamilla even from across the ballroom.

He strode towards her, pushing his way through the crowd, ignoring the offered greetings, the obsequious bows. Then she turned and he could see her expression.

Concern pumped and twisted in the pit of his stomach.

She looks…devastated.

Then he noticed the guy standing in front of her, an older man in a uniform. The man was talking to her but she looked stricken and she wasn't talking back. Which was even more wrong. Because if there was one thing Jamilla knew how to do it was talk, even when she was freaking out. He ought to know.

At last he got close enough to catch the end of what the guy was saying.

'Don't be embarrassed, my dear. Your mother knew the value of using sex to get what she wanted. And I'm sure Prince Dane appreciates it.'

The words slammed into him, insulting, contemptuous and just plain wrong. But beneath it was a spike of guilt, propelling his temper from zero to ninety in five seconds flat.

Reaching them, he didn't think, didn't stop to consider their audience or their mission. He grabbed the jerk by the lapels of his fancy jacket, yanked him up to his toes and shoved his nose into the guy's face. 'What the hell did you just say to her, you son of a…?'

'Dane, please, it's okay,' Jamilla said, grasping his forearm, but her fingers were shaking and her skin had become ashen.

'No, it's not okay,' he shouted, shoving the guy away from him. The man sent him an outraged look, brushed off his uniform, but then, noticing their growing audience, he disappeared into the crowd. Dane wanted to chase after the guy, but he couldn't leave Jamilla.

'No one gets to talk to you like that.' He held her waist, felt the convulsive shudder and saw the devastation in her eyes she couldn't disguise. 'No one.'

She flinched, bowed her head, the colour flooding back into her cheeks, probably because lights were flickering on around them as people held up their phones to record the scene.

To hell with them. If they wanted to splash this all over social media they could. He wasn't letting her go until he'd banished the distress from her eyes.

'Let's get out of here,' he said, and she nodded.

He put his arm around her waist and led her through the crowd, shielding her from the camera phones, ignoring the shouted intrusive questions from the scattering of press still at the event. Their security joined them, providing a phalanx of protection, holding the onlookers back as he headed up the stairs to the mezzanine.

Why hadn't she called that old bastard out herself? Where was the strong woman he knew her to be? The strong, smart woman who had the guts of a lion and who, even when she was freaking out about propriety and appearances and all the stuff she'd made it her job to manage, could still cut through him with a single look?

By the time they had reached the floor where their suites were located—and he had dismissed the security detail—she looked fragile and broken. And she was still shaking.

Alone at last, he led her into the sitting room of his suite. She drew away from his hold and walked to the large multi-paned window, wrapping her arms around her waist as if she were trying to contain the pain. He forced himself not to follow her as she stood staring out at the carpet of lights which was the Marais at night.

He crossed his arms over his chest, his heart still thundering in his ears. He wanted to punch something, but more than that he wanted to hold her—until the shudders of reaction still coursing through her body went away. But the urge to comfort her scared him almost as much as seeing her so broken. When had his obsession with her become more than just sexual, more than just a physical need?

After several painful moments she stopped trembling and turned towards him. She'd composed herself and put the mask he hadn't seen for a while back on. But he could see the effort it was costing her to keep it in place.

'I'm sorry I got you involved in that,' she said, her voice firm but her eyes filled with shadows. His temper sparked. She hadn't involved him; he'd involved himself. Whatever the heck had just happened, the only person who wasn't to blame was her.

But he suppressed the knee-jerk reaction to point that out to her because she looked as if a strong breath would knock her down.

'You should return to the reception...' she continued in that firm, *too* firm, voice. 'I will work on a response for the press for this incident...'

'To hell with the press,' he said, cutting her off. Because there was only so much of that hollow, haunted look he could stand. 'Who *was* that guy?' he demanded, suddenly wanting to know. Why did that guy have the power to devastate her?

She blinked slowly, then her lips lifted in a smile that didn't come close to touching the agony in her eyes. 'That was Lieutenant-Colonel François Xavier Roussel, formerly of the French army, now a retired diplomat,' she said. 'I should have realised he might have been included on the ambassador's guest list and been better prepared.'

'Roussel?' he said, his eyes narrowing as he ignored her latest attempt to take the blame for that bastard's smutty comments. 'Is he related to you?'

She drew in a ragged breath, but her gaze finally connected with his—and he could see the woman he'd come to desire finally flicker back to life.

'He's my father.'

Jamilla watched fury cross Dane's face like a thundercloud, before he swore profusely. 'That bastard is your old man?'

She flinched but, strangely, the violent reaction and the outrage darkening his expression released her from the dazed fog which had sucked her in ever since she had turned in the ballroom to see the man whose respect she had once longed for, with that disdain on his face she had never forgotten and in some small corner of her heart had always believed she deserved.

Dane had charged in, looking every inch the conquering warrior he was born to be, and had protected her against that man and that look and that feeling which had always lurked inside her—that she was worthless. That somehow she was to blame for her father's neglect, and her mother's sadness after he had left them and refused to return.

'Why would he talk to you like that about your sex life?' Dane said, his outrage gathering pace. 'Like some kind of creepy pervert?'

A brittle laugh burst from her, Dane's confusion almost as compelling as his outrage. The pain in her ribs released and she sucked in her first full breath in over twenty minutes, making her body feel buoyant. And free.

In his own fierce, formidable, reckless, impulsive and completely inappropriate way, Dane had given her this— the freedom to finally know, *really* know, she had never been to blame for the bad, selfish, dishonourable choices her father had made, or the way her mother had faded and eventually died because of them.

'What's so damn funny?' he said, but his gaze had softened and she could see the relief in his eyes too.

She covered her mouth, another chuckle bubbling out on the wave of release and euphoria. Maybe the laugh was a little manic, a little desperate, and she was going to have regrets about the scene downstairs tomorrow morning—when she was doing major damage limitation with the press, *again*. But all she could see right now was the horrified shock in her father's eyes as Dane had hauled him up to his toes. All she could think about was the ludicrous irony—that her father had accused her of being a whore when she'd never slept with any man, let alone Dane—and all she could feel was gratitude that Dane had been there to protect her when she hadn't been able to protect herself.

'Honestly?' she replied. 'The absolute shock on his face when you told him what a jerk he was.'

'Yeah? Well, he earned it.' His lips twisted in a sensual smile which only made his harshly handsome features more gorgeous.

Adrenaline pumped through her system, chased by the familiar wave of heat. But this time, instead of trying to deny it or contain it, she stepped forward and lifted up on her tiptoes to cup his cheek. 'Thank you, Dane, for coming to my rescue.'

He frowned, but his hands landed on her hips and caressed through the whisper of silk. The flare of desire in his gaze made her heart do a giddy little two-step and heat surged.

'Be careful, Jamilla,' he murmured, the tone husky with warning, the twinkle of amusement gone. 'I've wanted to finish what we started ever since Rome.' His gaze drifted down to her lips and the desire swelled and glowed at her core, releasing a rush of moisture and making the giddy two-step turn into hard, heavy thuds that pounded in her sex and echoed in her chest. 'Hell, long before that, if I'm honest.' He sighed. 'And I'm not great with deferred gratification. So you need to back off, unless you want to finish this too.'

She should have been terrified by the hot purpose in his eyes, and the solid ridge in his trousers pressing against her belly. And the tense line of his jaw, telling her how much it was costing him not to take what she was offering.

But the elemental desire to mate was nothing compared to the surge of longing, of need, in her heart. Maybe he didn't do deferred gratification, but he'd done it for her.

'I… I want to finish what we started in Rome too,' she said, her words guttering out on a husky breath as she wound her arms around his neck and pressed her curves against him, cradling the hard ridge against her belly and making the melting spot between her thighs burn.

His hands rose up her torso—rough, callused, desperate, but somehow still restrained—to lift the heavy fall of hair from her neck and cradle her head. He raised her chin to study her with an intensity that stole her breath. The surge of hunger was nothing compared to the chaotic clamour of her heartbeat as she saw the passion she had long denied reflected in the deep blue depths of his irises.

'Just to be clear, I'm no one's knight in shining armour. If that's what you're looking for, I'm not that guy.'

But you are. You were my knight tonight. The first person ever to stand up for that little girl who thought she didn't deserve her father's love.

She tried to clamp down on the fanciful, romantic notion, but it whispered through her heart regardless. Poignant, powerful, needy, but also somehow so right.

'You need to be sure?' he finished. 'Because sex is all I've got to offer.'

It wasn't true.

She'd seen him with his brother, his nephew, his sister-in-law, had known the struggle to fulfil the role they'd asked of him was much harder than he had ever let on. But he'd done it because he loved them.

And she knew all about the little boy who had written so many letters to a father who had never been worthy of him.

He had so much more to offer than he realised. But

she also knew it would be foolish to believe the person he would offer it to would be her.

'I am sure,' she said, emotion clogging her throat as her pulse jumped, giddy with anticipation.

There would be a price tomorrow—that she would pay, and he would not. There was a reason she hadn't taken this step before, with another man. But she would pay that price willingly, so she didn't have to step back again. She wanted to test her newfound freedom and finally let that girl go for good—the one who had always been so cautious, so careful, looking for acceptance and approval where there was none.

Tonight she would revel in the heat, the power of just grabbing what she wanted with both hands and not thinking, not feeling, not even caring about the consequences.

He swore softly, then bent to lift her into his arms.

Her heart leapt as she clung to his neck and the weight in her chest sank deep into her abdomen and throbbed—insistent, painful, but so real, so raw, so vivid.

As he strode into the bedroom with her in his arms she knew she was fully alive, fully seen, fully herself for the first time in her life.

She revelled in the heady excitement as he dragged off her dress, the whisper of silk against her over-sensitised skin turning the flickering flames into an inferno, and ignored the visceral tug of fear caused by the possessive light in his eyes.

CHAPTER TWELVE

WHOA.

Dane had to stop from swallowing his own tongue as the silk gown gathered in a pool at Jamilla's feet. She stood proud in a couple of tantalising wisps of purple lace, but he could still see the beguiling flush of awareness, the shudder of a response as his gaze roamed over her curves.

The heat in his guts clamoured for release, insistent and barely controlled. The erection turned to iron.

He forced himself to take a breath, to stem the need to rip off the lace, to devour every gorgeous inch, plunge deep inside her and claim her as his.

Chill out. Control it. You're not an untried kid any more.

He couldn't keep her, didn't want to own her in anything other than a carnal sense. And this one night would have to be enough. Because, in some distant part of his heart, he already knew she'd come to mean more to him… to know him better…than any other woman ever had, or could. And that scared him.

But if they only had one night he wanted it to be good, for both of them. Even if he couldn't keep her, he never wanted her to forget him.

He traced a fingertip over the swell of her breast, watched the dark nipple tighten.

'Take off the bra,' he demanded, knowing he couldn't risk doing it himself or he might tear it from her.

The flush deepened, her eyes dark with desire, but also wary. Reaching behind her, she hesitated, then the loud snap of the hook releasing echoed around the room and the lace dropped from her arms.

The heat became painful as he devoured the sight of her high, firm breasts. Lush and full and begging for his attention.

Her arms folded over the swollen flesh, and his gaze snapped to hers. He saw the wariness, the need, mixed together. And it only made the ache in his pants—to claim her, to brand her—stronger and more volatile.

'What's the problem?' he forced himself to ask. Because beneath the desire in those enchanting amber eyes he could see something else. Not fear, exactly, but definitely something he would never have expected from her…vulnerability.

'I… I want to see you naked too,' she said, her hesitation only making the heat spread.

His wry laugh came out on a gruff rumble. 'Sure,' he said. It took him less than ten seconds to slip off his shoes, tug off the uniform jacket, the shirt, then rip open his trousers and kick them off with his shorts.

Her gaze dipped, shock flickered, but perversely that look only made the heat pound harder in his sex. He knew he wasn't a small guy—women had commented on it before. But something about the brutal flush made him want to reassure her. To reassure himself. That the need was something he could control, even though the effort to hold back was tougher now than it had ever been. And it reminded him of that frantic feral kid who had believed sex could fill all the empty spaces inside him.

He stepped closer, trapped himself against her belly

and clasped her chin to lift her face to his. 'It's okay,' he said, his voice rough. 'We can take this slow.'

He watched her throat, that long slender neck contract as she swallowed heavily, felt his own throat dry up at the mix of timidity and determination in her gaze.

'Thank you,' she said. 'I would appreciate that.'

His lips quirked, her weirdly polite response breaking some of the tension.

Stepping back, he took her hands in his, drew her arms away from her magnificent breasts. Her breath hitched but she made no move to cover herself again.

Leaning down, he captured one plump peak between his lips, licked and nipped, then flicked his tongue across the turgid tip.

She gasped, shuddered and thrust her fingers into his hair, caressing his scalp, her panting urging him on. He moved from one breast to the other, then reached down to slide searching fingers under the lace that covered her sex.

His breath stuttered, his own need like a comet, building and burning in his groin when he found her soaking wet.

He circled and stroked the plump nub, holding her neck with his other hand, lifting her chin to suckle the pounding pulse beneath her ear, which he had waited an eternity to exploit again. She moaned. He pushed one finger inside her, still circling, still stroking with his thumb, the sound of her sobs like a siren call to his senses as she gripped him. The thrill of seeing her shatter for him again made the need in his gut turn to burning pain.

He had to have her—now—or he would be lost for ever, the driving hunger threatening to reveal the needy boy all over again.

Jamilla cried out, the orgasm slamming into her like a freight train, so hard, so relentless, so unstoppable.

This was so much more than before. The stunning sensations exploded through her nerve-endings on a never-ending wave, but right behind it was a terrifying vulnerability.

As the orgasm finally released its stranglehold on her body, fear gripped her heart.

She tried to think, tried to pull away, pull back, to protect herself. But all she felt was raw and desperate need as he scooped her trembling body into his arms. She clung to his neck, still shivering, still shaken, every part of her limp and exposed as he cradled her shattered body as if she were precious, important.

He laid her on the bed, climbed over her, the huge erection brushing her thigh as he lifted her wrists above her head, pinned her hands to the bed. His startlingly blue eyes stared down at her, his breathing as ragged and raw as her own, the longing fierce and unfettered.

For a brief terrifying moment the brutal feeling of connection gripped her, but then he took her hips in his hands, angled her pelvis and placed the head of his erection at her entrance.

He pressed in slowly but surely, so large, so demanding, stretching the unbearably tight sheath, then thrust through the final barrier.

He grunted as the pinch of pain made her wince.

He swore, his gaze flying back to hers, the harsh look ripping away that delirious moment of connection—to replace it with accusation, and horrified shock.

She should have told him, she realised, about her virginity. It hadn't really occurred to her that he would want to know. It had felt private, maybe even a little embarrassing.

But it was already too late to do anything about it because he was lodged deep inside her, the pulsing ache building again, despite the pain.

'Are you a virgin?' he demanded.

She wanted to hide from that accusing look, and the shame she suddenly felt. She hadn't meant to trick him, but somehow it felt as if she had.

She opened her mouth to reply, when he said, 'Don't lie.'

Her throat contracted and she was forced to nod.

He swore again, his fingers tightening on her hips, his whole body stiffening, but instead of pulling out, rolling away in disgust, as she had almost expected, he remained lodged inside her. She could feel him deep inside her body, stretching her unbearably, the pulse of him matching the thready, throbbing beat of her heart. Her laboured breathing and his sounded deafening in the room as her chest heaved with the weight suddenly crushing her ribs.

What had she done? Why did he look so stricken, so unhappy?

He dropped his head, his hair brushing her cheek. 'Damn,' he said, the word full of a shame she didn't understand.

She lifted a trembling hand to his cheek, felt the muscle twitch and tighten beneath her palm. 'What's wrong?' she asked.

His head rose at last, his gaze meeting hers. 'Everything,' he said, his expression so bleak it made the weight grow into a boulder, threatening to cut off her air supply.

'I've got to move,' he said before she could ask what he meant. 'Am I hurting you? Can you take more of me?'

She wasn't sure she could, the stretched feeling already overwhelming, but she nodded anyway, shocked when the tug of pleasure pulsed deep in her abdomen as he pulled out then pressed back.

She held on, her fingers digging into his shoulders, aware of his struggle to hold on, to hold back. His hips circled, rocked, establishing a slow, steady rhythm. Each

new plunge forced her to take a little more. But the pleasure built regardless, despite the echo of pain. She concentrated on it as it spread, consuming the frantic jump
of her heartbeat, lifting the unbearable weight as the relentless sensations battered her.

The wave threatened, tumbling towards her, faster and
harder now.

His movements became less sure, less steady, more
frantic, more furious, but it didn't matter any more. The
soreness was consumed by euphoria as the wave barrelled
through her. Huge, wild, untamed, the hot pleasure pummelled her body as he grew larger still.

He yanked himself free just as she flew over the top
of that high wide ledge, leaving her alone in her ecstasy.

The sticky heat of his seed pumped onto her belly as
he collapsed into her arms.

What have I done?

Dane rolled away from the woman beside him, her
tantalising scent invading his senses, the overwhelming
climax still pulsing in his groin leaving him bruised and
battered.

But probably not as bruised and battered as the woman
he'd just pounded into like a mad man. No wonder she'd
looked so wary when she'd seen him naked and fully
aroused.

She should have told him she was a virgin. But, even
as he wanted to be mad at her, a small voice inside him
was shouting, *Don't kid yourself, man. No way would that
have stopped you.*

He forced himself to move, get off the bed and walk
into the bathroom, aware of the shakiness in his legs, the
weightless feeling of unreality in his stomach, the brutal
tug of afterglow doing nothing to diminish the black hole
forming in his chest.

What the hell did you expect, you dumb son of a...?

He cut off the angry, pointless recriminations as he washed away the evidence of her innocence. And recalled the brave, determined look in her eyes before he'd plunged into her.

He'd taken something he couldn't give back. She should have told him. But did that really matter? Because he wasn't even sure he wanted to give it back, the need still like a wild thing inside him, the echo of that titanic orgasm holding his heart in a vice. And the consequences of what he'd done—of what they'd done—pushed at that empty space inside him that for one moment had been filled.

Everything was so messed up in his head. But something he never would have expected had reared its head when he'd torn through that slight barrier and realised the truth.

His honour. And hers. An honour he knew he had to defend. Or he would be nothing again.

He threw the washcloth, now stained with her virginity, into the trash. After wrapping a towel around his hips, he grabbed another washcloth off the vanity. He rinsed it through with warm water. A strange acceptance settled over him as he walked back into the bedroom.

No way was he running from this situation. Or her. Or his father would have been right to discard him all those years ago.

He'd always found it easy to shirk commitment; the desire to protect and possess was a totally new phenomenon for him. But it was still there nonetheless.

He caught Jamilla bent over by the bed with the sheet wrapped tightly around her naked body.

She shot upright, the torn purple lace he'd ripped away before plunging inside her clutched in her fist. 'I... I should go back to my own suite,' she said, a vivid blush spreading like wildfire over her collarbone and up her neck. 'Before anyone finds out I'm here,' she added.

He frowned, not appreciating the guilty flush or the panic in her eyes.

Her hair fell in artless disarray—the dark corkscrew curls mussed from their lovemaking bouncing as she swung around, searching for the rest of her clothing.

He struggled to keep his anger at bay. She was trying to run from him again, the way she had in Rome.

Yeah, that wasn't happening. They'd done what they'd done and now they needed to face the consequences. Consequences she had to be well aware of.

'It's a bit late for that, don't you think?' he murmured, his lips twisting into a smile that didn't have a heck of a lot of humour in it.

They had a big problem, for sure. He hadn't even had the sense to use a condom. But he'd be damned if he was going to try and dodge this conversation.

'No, no, I don't think so,' she said, becoming frantic as she scooped up her bra, bent to pick up the red silk dress pooled on the floor. She held the clothing to her chest, still clutching the sheet in a death grip.

The evidence of her innocence, and the thought that he was most likely the first guy—the *only* guy—to see her naked sent another surge of possessiveness through him, which he made no attempt to control this time.

'If I leave now I can take the back stairs to my own suite,' she carried on, talking as if she were the diplomatic aide again, instead of the woman who had climaxed in his arms. 'And if there are any questions tomorrow we can just stonewall.' He strode towards her as she dipped her head to look for her shoes. 'I can work out a press release to explain the scene with my father. And no one will know for sure what happened after we left the event together. They certainly won't be able to prove...'

He snagged her wrist, halting the frantic qualifications and her attempts to gather up her clothing. Her head rose and her gaze locked on his. And what he saw—panic, guilt, shame—had anger mixing with a cocktail of other emotions in his gut. Protectiveness, possessiveness, for sure, but also a cast-iron determination he never would have expected, to own this situation.

No way was he letting her just pretend this hadn't happened. Because he refused to be ashamed of who he was and what they'd done.

He'd spent so much of his childhood being pushed aside, had become convinced he had no right to his heritage, but he'd be damned if he was going to let her push him aside too.

'Yeah, but *we'll* know,' he said softly, to control the spiky fury churning in his gut. And the spurt of desire as her pulse pummelled his thumb. 'You should have told me you were a virgin, Jamilla. But you didn't and now it's too late. You want to hide this from the press, go ahead, I don't care about that, but you're not sneaking out of this suite tonight.'

Her mouth dropped open, the shock on her face somehow even more devastating than the scent of her—sultry and spicy and hot as hell—and a tangle of emotions he didn't understand in his gut.

'But…' Jamilla stammered, her whole face exploding with the heat still pulsing in her sex. 'You can't be serious, Dane. If I stay tonight, even if we can keep it secret from the media, everyone here will know.'

'So what?' he murmured, the tight smile on his lips defied by the intensity in his eyes. 'You ashamed of me? Of what we just did?'

'No, of course not…' She stared back at him, her knuckles whitening as she held the sheet to her breasts, to

cover skin still alive with sensation. Her breathing accelerated. Was he joking? But he didn't look as if he were joking? He looked deadly serious. 'I just... I didn't expect...'

'What did you think? That I'd kick you out once I'd
taken your virginity? How much of a bastard do you think
I am?'

'No...no... That's not... I never meant to imply you
have no honour...' she began frantically, realising she had
insulted him when that had never been her intention. But
then the furrows on his forehead relaxed.

'Good to know,' he said, seeming to take her denial
at face value.

'I could resign my position,' she offered, the brutal leap
of her heart at his determination not to deny their liaison
only scaring her more.

She had been completely convinced when she had
decided to take this step, this leap...that this encounter
would be a one-night deal.

But even as she had accepted that reality, and had been
prepared for the emotional fallout afterwards, a foolish
bubble of hope she hadn't even been aware of until this
moment had formed.

'You *could* resign,' he said, letting go of her wrist to
thrust impatient fingers through his hair. 'But as I've got
no intention of letting you out of my sight until we know
for sure you're not pregnant, I don't see the point.'

Pregnant?

The word detonated in her chest like a bomb, destroy-
ing the bubble of hope along with every ounce of her
courage.

'But I'm... I can't be pregnant. You...you didn't...' Hot
blood flooded into her cheeks. 'Inside me, you didn't...'
she finished weakly, not even able to say the relevant
words, feeling like a gauche, artless schoolgirl instead

of the focused, capable career woman she had worked so hard to become.

'Are you using contraceptives?' he asked bluntly.

She shook her head, unable to say the words, the guilt as sharp as the feeling of inadequacy she'd once thought she could bury by jumping into his bed.

'Then there's still a chance. Even if I didn't ejaculate inside you,' he said, saying the words she'd been too embarrassed to say.

'I'm so sorry,' she said, realising this was why he felt honour-bound to make this more than one night. Perhaps he wasn't planning to propose, but she knew enough about him now, and his complex relationship with his father and his heritage, to be convinced he would never abandon her to handle this situation alone. 'I didn't think. I should have asked you to wear a condom.'

'Hey,' he murmured, tucking a knuckle under her chin. He lifted her face back to his. 'We were both carried away in the moment, Jamilla,' he said, his willingness to own the situation only making the tidal wave of shame toss and turn in her stomach.

He cradled her face, brushed his thumb over her lips in a gesture so intimate her breath released in a rush. 'We both should have had that conversation, and we didn't.'

She found herself brutally close to tears, needing to lean on his strength—if just for a moment.

How could he be so pragmatic about this? Shouldn't he be furious that she had put him, put them both, into this untenable position?

'I can take a test in the next few days to be sure,' she said, her voice almost as shaky as she felt.

He dropped his hand from her face to rest it on her waist. 'Where are you in your cycle?'

She swallowed at the blunt question, and the colour flared to her hairline.

Seriously, Jamilla? You slept with this man, had several mind-blowing orgasms, had him buried so deep inside you, you could feel him everywhere, and yet you've got a problem talking about your menstrual cycle with him?

'About midway through,' she managed. Then realised the significance of the timing. *Oh, God*, she could be ovulating. What if she actually did get pregnant…? He'd pulled out, but…

Before she had a chance to go into full-on panic mode, his hand squeezed her hip, drawing her back from the edge. 'Stop freaking out.'

She nodded, humbled—but also terrified—by his willingness to take charge, because it opened up that agonising yearning inside her, which had always longed for a man to protect her and care for her. She shouldn't need Dane's care or attention, shouldn't want it, because all it did was make her weak.

But, even so, it took a massive effort to step away from his touch.

She turned from his probing, intense gaze, her fist still clutching her torn underwear and the red silk dress she had worn without any intention of trapping a prince. Or so she'd wanted to think. But, right now, the situation—and his reaction to it—was making her feel brutally exposed.

To think she'd once believed *he* was the reckless one.

'I'm still sorry that I didn't tell you about my virginity,' she murmured as she gazed out of the window at the Parisian night. 'Or even think about contraception.' The Eiffel Tower looked resplendent in its majesty, a mile or so away, rising like a tribute to the city's golden age. She could even make out the dark ribbon of the Seine, winding its way through the carpet of lights. The magnificent view only made her feel more insignificant—and overwhelmed by everything that had happened in the last hour. The last few weeks, in fact. She'd been impulsive and reckless tonight, had let that foolish, fanciful girl free who had yearned so much for male approval. And now look where she was. She didn't feel like herself any more. Or at least not the woman she'd wanted to be.

She forced herself to face Dane, brutally aware of the insistent arousal as she took in the ink on his shoulder blade and scrawled line across his hip flexor, the ridged abs, the defined muscles of his chest, the small raised scars she'd glimpsed once before at the waterfall. So much about him had surprised her, shocked her even, but why hadn't she figured out until this moment that she found every aspect of him intriguing, captivating and utterly magnificent, even more magnificent than the view behind her?

She sucked in a careful breath, scared even more of what these feelings might mean. Was she confusing sexual desire with intimacy? Was this rush of feeling for Dane simply a by-product of the emotional upheaval caused by the encounter with her father? It had to be, but how did she stop it from getting worse?

'I don't want you to feel trapped into making this encounter more than it is,' she said, desperately trying to wrest back the control—and perspective—she had thrown away so carelessly.

He stepped towards her. 'I'll be the judge of that,' he murmured with a purpose that only frightened her more. 'We've got another seven days of this tour, right?' he asked. She nodded. 'Rather than source you a pregnancy test, which is bound to get out to the damn press, why don't we just get it done when we return to Zafar, if you haven't had your period already?'

'Okay,' she said, her lip trembling all of a sudden.

'Hey, stop it,' he said, taking a firm grip on her chin, to peer into her eyes. 'I'm not that bad a catch, am I?'

She sniffed loudly, not really appreciating what she was sure—was hoping—had to be a joke. She held the deluge back, terrified all over again by the treacherous feeling of connection pressing on her chest.

'I can't… We can't be a couple, not even if I get pregnant; that would be insane,' she said, suddenly terrified he might feel he had to propose, and that, given the turmoil of confused and confusing emotions currently churning in her stomach, she might not have the strength to reject him. Which would be wrong in every respect.

Her parents' marriage had ultimately been one of convenience—for her father. From everything her mother had said about the events leading up to it, Jamilla could see he'd been pressured into marriage after he had seduced her mother. And in the end he had offered her his hand to protect his career in the diplomatic service as much as anything else. He had pretended to be in love. Had pretended to care for her mother. Had got her pregnant and then eventually abandoned them both, to return to the woman he really loved. She couldn't bear to be put in the same situation with Dane because he felt somehow beholden to her.

He raised a quizzical brow but didn't respond.

'I really think it would be best if I return to my own suite,' she said, but as she went to walk past him towards the en suite bathroom he grasped her upper arm.

'Nope,' he said.

Her foolish heart bounced up to become jammed in her throat. 'I don't think…'

'I told you already, I'm not letting you out of my sight,' he said, cutting into her frantic denials. 'How sore are you?' he added, the curt concern in his voice derailing her emotions all over again.

'More tender than sore, which is good considering how large…' She stopped abruptly when she realised what she'd almost blurted out.

Instead of looking offended, though, he let out a deep chuckle.

Her flush burned. 'I didn't mean to imply…' she began again. But it only made the wry chuckle turn into a laugh.

'Sure you did,' he said, his eyes bright with amusement at her expense. 'But it's okay. You're cute when you're flustered.'

Cute? She wasn't sure whether to be flattered or appalled at his comment but, before she had a chance to figure it out or get a hold on the last scrap of her already vastly diminished dignity, he turned her around to face the bathroom door and gave her a soft pat on the butt. 'Go grab a shower and when you're ready you can take the bed,' he said, letting her go. 'There's clean T-shirts in the dresser if you need something to sleep in. I'll see you tomorrow for breakfast in the sitting room.'

'But where will you sleep?' she asked, feeling stupidly bereft at the thought of spending the night alone in his bed.

Not that she was ready for more sex—she hadn't lied about being more than a little tender, in places she'd never been tender before.

'There's another bedroom on the other side of the sitting room. I think it's probably best if I crash in there until we head to Spain.' The hot assessing gaze skimmed over her burning skin, setting off a whole new set of bonfires en route. 'Your tender places are gonna need a chance to recover. And I need to source condoms without alerting the media.'

It wasn't until she was under the needle-sharp spray of the power shower ten minutes later, while every one of her erogenous zones throbbed in unison, that her nuclear blush finally began to subside. And it wasn't until she lay alone in his big bed, a good half-hour later, the soft cotton of the T-shirt she had found in his dresser cocooning her in the addictive scent of his laundry soap, that it occurred to her she hadn't corrected his high-handed assumption they were now an item for the duration of the tour. And would be sleeping together again.

As she snuggled into the luxury linen sheets and tried to turn off her racing brain, she promised herself she would correct him first thing tomorrow morning.

CHAPTER THIRTEEN

'SO WHAT'S THE deal with your old man?' Dane watched Jamilla's reaction intently as he dropped the question into their conversation over the lavish breakfast of crêpes and fruit and strong French coffee he'd ordered from the embassy kitchens.

Jamilla had been all business again as soon as she'd appeared from his bedroom that morning, or at least she'd tried to be all business, not that easy when she was wrapped in the suite's complimentary bath robe, her sleep-mussed curls riotous around her head and her fresh dewy skin devoid of her usual perfectly applied make-up.

He'd let her direct the conversation towards strategies for handling any press fallout from last night's events while their breakfast was delivered. And there would be fallout, because he'd already had to field a call from Karim, who had demanded to know what was going on.

He figured he didn't owe Karim an explanation of his sex life. So he hadn't enlightened him on the situation with Jamilla and how the night had ended.

He guessed the smart move last night would have been to help her sneak back to her own rooms. He still wasn't entirely sure why he hadn't, the urge to stand up for her, to get her to stay, not making a whole lot of sense. But he refused to second-guess it now, as he watched her push her uneaten crêpes around her plate. He clamped down on his annoyance at her attitude this morning.

If she wanted to keep their liaison secret from the press, even from Karim and Orla, he didn't have a problem with that, but he'd be damned if he'd pretend last night had never happened.

Maybe it was because of her virginity, perhaps it was about the possibility of a pregnancy, or maybe it was that spike of guilt when he'd figured out the truth about her inexperience—the desire to prove he wasn't a man like his father, who exploited women because he could—but, whatever it was, he wasn't about to change his mind. Plus he'd already figured out that keeping a lid on this chemistry, which had sparked between them the first time he'd met her, was going to be impossible to contain now so he didn't see the point of even trying.

They had a press conference scheduled for later. Jamilla had already worked out a strategy for avoiding any intimate questions about their relationship. But he wanted to know why she'd shut down the way she had in front of her father.

His curiosity about her reaction was about more than just their dance with the media, though, especially when she stiffened and her gaze flicked away.

'It's not… There's not really a deal,' she said, making him even more sure there was a story and it was one he wanted to know about. Because he never wanted to see that look on her face again— stricken and shattered. 'To be honest, I hardly know him,' she continued. 'He left Zafar for good when I was six and never returned. But he wasn't around much before that. He lived mostly in Paris, even before my parents got divorced.'

'Wait a minute. So last night was the first time you'd seen him since you were a kid?'

She nodded and her gaze met his, then darted away

again. But what he saw there—shame, embarrassment, guilt—had last night's anger building again.

The citrussy, buttery pancakes curdled in his stomach. The urge to throttle her father with his bare hands wasn't helped by the memory of the look in the bastard's eyes last night, when Dane had confronted him—arrogance and contempt—before he'd scuttled off into the crowd like the cockroach he was.

What kind of man wouldn't be proud to have Jamilla as a daughter?

He placed his knife and fork on his plate and struggled to even out his breathing, to stop the fury from taking hold again, his reaction only making him feel more exposed.

'It's probably best if we simply refuse to answer any questions about that incident,' she offered, placing her own utensils on her plate, next to the breakfast she hadn't eaten.

He already knew, from talking to Karim, the media were going to be all over her old man's appearance—not talking about it would only fuel the speculation. But, instead of correcting her, he went with instinct and placed his hand over the fist she had placed on the table.

Her gaze jerked to his. The naked emotion in her expression was quickly masked, but it still kicked him in the gut.

'He's a jerk, Jamilla. You deserved a better father.'

Her lips quivered slightly, the sheen of moisture in her gaze crucifying him even more. Because he knew her old man wasn't the only guy who didn't deserve her. He'd pounced on her last night, taken what he wanted... And after a sleepless night thinking about her response to him, that livewire connection, he knew his desire to keep her close for the next little while wasn't just about the possibility of pregnancy.

'I suppose we both did,' she said, so softly he almost didn't catch it.

'I guess,' he said, although he wasn't so sure. He'd been wild as a kid. Wild and untamed and unrestrained, and more than happy to use sex for comfort and validation as a teenager. Maybe most of the women he'd slept with back then had been a lot older than him, but he'd always been the one to walk away unscathed. And, however good they were together, he'd eventually do the same to Jamilla, assuming she wasn't carrying his baby right now. And if she was he would be unlikely to stick around for very long. Just long enough to give her and the child the protection of his name, and his wealth.

There was a knock on the door of the suite. He lifted his hand from hers, ignoring the strange tug in his chest as he stood to answer it.

The connection they shared could only be a sexual one. Maybe they'd both had crummy fathers, but while her daddy issues had created a brave, hard-working woman who'd held onto her innocence for far too long, his had created a guy who couldn't commit to anyone—while the only thing he'd been able to commit to was his business. That was his reality. He'd come to terms with it a long time ago. No point regretting it now, when it was too late to change who that boy had become.

'That'll be Hakim,' he said. 'I asked him to speak to your assistant in confidence and have her pack up your luggage and move it into this suite for the duration of our stay.'

Wait—what?

Jamilla was still struggling to deal with the catastrophic effect of Dane's consoling touch as she listened to him answer the door. Luckily the suite had an entry hall, so Hakim and her assistant Kesia couldn't see her wearing nothing but a bathrobe and one of Dane's T-shirts as they delivered her luggage and left. Even so, she felt compromised and exposed when Dane strode back into the room carrying one of her suitcases. Her instinctive shiver of awareness at the figure he cut in jeans and a T-shirt, the day-old stubble on his jaw only making him look more rugged, wasn't helping.

'Your assistant said your outfit for today is in here,' he said.

'I can't stay here another night,' she said with as much authority as she could muster as he placed the suitcase in front of her.

He straightened, the devastatingly assured movement making every one of her pulse points throb painfully. 'Why not?' he asked, as if he really didn't know.

'Because what if the press find out?'

'They won't. The staff know what happens in the embassy between us is strictly private,' he said.

'But it's not appropriate,' she sputtered. 'I work for you.'

'No, you don't,' he murmured. He stepped closer and cupped her cheek, then brushed his thumb across her lips, his gaze hot and intense and yet somehow also tender. Her heart melted, scaring her even more. 'You work for my brother,' he said. 'And he doesn't get to tell either one of us what to do in private.'

She ducked her head, scared to look at him. Scared of his certainty, his conviction. And the fierce possessiveness in his eyes.

'I can't…' She hesitated, attempted to swallow the bundle of anxiety wedged in her throat. 'I can't sleep with you again.'

'Do you mean you can't — or you don't want to?'

Her head jerked up, the riot of emotions painful in their intensity at the bold, unequivocal question. The longing worked its way up her torso and squeezed around her heart, the wave of need so strong she knew he had to be able to see it.

'You don't have to be a good girl any more, Jamilla,' he added, that deep husky voice coaxing the girl she'd tried so hard to control back out of hiding. 'Not for Karim, not for your bastard of a father. And certainly not for me.' He stroked her cheek, then let his hand fall. 'You're allowed to take what you want.' He pressed his hands into the back pockets of his jeans but his eyes remained fixed on her face, and she had the strangest sense he wasn't as sure or certain as he appeared. 'If you don't want me, I'll back off,' he said. 'But if you do... I say we enjoy this thing while it lasts. Or at least until we know for sure you're not pregnant.'

She heard the qualification. He wasn't offering anything permanent. Even if she were pregnant, she would be an obligation, nothing more. An obligation she had no intention of becoming. But the fierce longing was impossible to ignore.

Could she do it? Could she take him up on his offer? Let that bad girl loose for a little while longer, without regrets? And was there really any point trying to deny this urge any longer?

It would be a risk. A massive risk. Not just professionally—if the press found out the truth—but also personally. And a part of her was terrified she might be considering what he was offering her for all the wrong reasons. But another part of her—that reckless, impulsive part she'd rediscovered last night—pushed back against the fear. Until it turned into something insistent and impossible to ignore.

What would it be like to live in this moment without regrets? To, for once, leap before she looked? To do what felt good, instead of what felt sensible? She'd lived her

whole life by rules—strict rules of decorum and denial—
that she'd set for herself. And why? So she would be respected, admired, appreciated and be above reproach.

But most of all, deep down, so the man who had deserted her would know she was worthy to be his daughter. And now she finally understood, after last night, the
dream she'd secretly been striving towards without even
realising it would never come true.

Her father would never acknowledge her, never love
her, no matter how faultless and perfect she was. So why
was she still holding on for his approval? Hadn't she
earned the chance to finally be herself? Truly herself?
To tell Dane what she wanted, without regret? She'd always believed she'd remained a virgin for so long because the opportunity simply hadn't arisen to discover the
sexual side of her being, but she knew now she'd simply
been waiting. And, anyway, she wasn't a virgin any more.

'I do want you,' she said.

His lips quirked, the gleam in his eyes making her heart
hammer against her chest wall. 'Then I say we go for it.'

She nodded. 'Oh…okay.'

He reached forward and clasped her around the waist.
She grasped his shoulders, the weight in her chest lifting
to butt against her tonsils as he lifted her into his arms.

When he let her down again, they were both grinning
at each other like a couple of carefree kids with a naughty
secret. The sort of carefree kids she suspected neither of
them had ever been.

He clasped her cheeks, lifted her face to his and slanted
his lips across hers, capturing the sob of need.

The kiss was deep, demanding, uncompromising, stak-
ing a claim to more than just her body, as his hands found
the tie to the bathrobe and roamed beneath to clasp her
around the waist, capture her bottom and lift her against
the heavy ridge in his jeans.

He tore his mouth away first. 'How do you feel about being a little late for our presser?' he said, nuzzling her neck in the spot he'd found last night that he knew would drive her wild.

She pushed the fear aside to concentrate on the now.

'We can't be late, but we could be quick,' she gasped, her hands gripping his T-shirt and pulling it out of his jeans, the knowledge that he was all hers, at least for a little while, so intoxicating it hurt.

CHAPTER FOURTEEN

'HOW ARE YOU, Jamilla? In the pictures I saw of the Serrano Academy visit yesterday you looked radiant. But I just wanted to check in with you.'

'Honestly, I'm good, Orla,' Jamilla said, aware of her skin flushing. Thank goodness the Queen hadn't called her on a video app. 'Just a minute,' she said before covering the mouthpiece.

She hurried across the sitting room to the suite's bedroom door. Could Orla hear Dane taking a shower in the en suite bathroom? The thought only mortified her more. She closed the door carefully, aware of the strange feeling of unreality.

Orla was a friend, a good friend, and she'd been nothing but supportive, but Jamilla still wasn't used to being the focus of so much media attention. And she was becoming more and more concerned about the endless speculation in the media about her and Dane's relationship—it refused to die, and had only become more intense since they'd arrived in Spain for the last leg of the tour—despite her endless denials.

What was even more concerning, though, was how the media attention was starting to mess up her own perceptions.

She had seen the pictures taken yesterday too, had cringed at the string of increasingly lurid headlines.

The Prince and the Political Aide
Love on Tour?
How a Billionaire Nightclub Magnate was Seduced
into Becoming a Prince!

The articles accompanying those headlines had been equally ludicrous—full of barely concealed innuendo about her role in Dane's supposed transformation. But it was the photograph which Orla had just described which had stopped her breath ten minutes ago, when she'd been checking the media coverage of yesterday's assignments while waiting for Dane to appear.

The photographer had captured her and Dane in a rare and revealing private moment during yesterday's tour of a girls' school in Barcelona. She could still see the secretive little smile on her lips, the vivid blush on her cheeks and the incandescent light in her eyes as Dane leant close to her while a line of teenage girls stood behind them both.

She could still remember exactly what he'd whispered to her in that moment, his voice wry and wicked, to make the spontaneous smile appear.

'I always thought good girls were overrated. Who knew?'

She had been expecting Orla's call ever since the ball in Paris, when the press furore over the showdown between her father and Dane had hit the headlines.

Dane had fielded all the questions that day—refusing point-blank to answer any personal questions, but it hadn't deterred the media in the least.

He'd been calm, confident, supremely arrogant, every inch a prince. And she'd sat there like a dummy, tongue-tied and embarrassed, but also pathetically grateful for his sturdy presence as the questions were fired at them like missiles.

Her father had, of course, given an exclusive interview

about her failings as a daughter to a highbrow French publication the next day—which had immediately been recycled and extensively quoted in every gossip rag, celebrity blog and tabloid magazine—only making the press attention worse once they'd arrived in Spain.

She hated that she had become the story in the past week. But what disturbed her more was how much she had come to rely on Dane's support, his protection. When they'd arrived at Madrid-Barajas Airport and he'd shielded her from the waiting paparazzi to usher her safely into the limo. At the state banquet the following night, when he'd stayed by her side throughout. During the tour of a fruit market in Seville, when he'd included her in every photo op, much to the joy of the press. And of course at the girls' academy yesterday, the day after they'd arrived in Barcelona.

But much more disturbing than that was how she'd come to rely on him when they weren't under media scrutiny. In the evenings, when they sneaked back to his suite and he slammed the door shut, to take her in his arms and make fast, furious love to her. Or during those late-night meals, while she tried to discuss the itinerary for the next day and he distracted her all too easily, before devouring her all over again.

How had she come to revel in every touch—both tender and voracious? How had she found it so easy to let her mind drift on the tide of endorphins without having to engage with the truth…? How had she become so addicted to falling asleep in his arms, and waking up with him wrapped around her, usually hard and ready for more sleepy lovemaking before they showered and changed and sat down for breakfast to prepare for another day?

How had she been able to let herself forget—for six glorious days and nights—about the reckoning that awaited her when she returned to Zafar, and the tour—and this not-so-secret affair—was over?

'Are you sure, Jamilla?' She could hear Orla's concern from the other side of the continent. 'You looked so...' her friend's voice drifted into silence '...happy,' she managed at last.

'I'm so sorry, Orla. I feel as if I've let you and Karim down. That I've let Zafar down. The tour has become about whether or not we're in a relationship when it was never supposed to be.' The words came tumbling out as the shame Jamilla had been keeping so carefully at bay tightened her stomach into a knot.

She should never have agreed to stay with Dane after their night together in Paris. But, even before that, she'd lost perspective. She'd become entranced by him, ever since she'd seen the pain in his eyes when he'd spoken of his father, and she'd allowed her heart to believe there was a connection between them.

'Jamilla, what on earth are you talking about?' Orla interrupted her panicked confession. 'The tour has been a massive success. To be honest, your obvious...' she paused '...affection for one another has given the whole enterprise much more attention than we could ever have dreamt of. But, frankly, that's what concerns me. The intrusion has been immense, and I know you're not used to that sort of media focus.'

'Honestly, Orla, that's not a problem. And Dane has been wonderful,' Jamilla said quickly. Yes, she'd found the intrusion hard, because she simply wasn't used to the spotlight. But wasn't that the price she deserved to pay, for agreeing to spend her nights in Dane's suite? For leaping into this affair like a woman possessed. For allowing her pleasure to take precedent over her common sense, and her dedication to her job. They had been lucky that the publicity had actually worked in their favour. But it wasn't the thought of how unprofessional she'd allowed herself to become that terrified her now.

'I've noticed how attentive Dane has been too,' Orla said. 'And that's really why I called to check on you,' her friend added.

Jamilla frowned, confused. Where was this leading?

'Jamilla, in the pictures I saw yesterday…' Orla paused again. 'You don't need to tell me if there is anything between you, but you look…' She sighed. 'You look like a woman who has fallen in love.'

The words dropped into Jamilla's consciousness like a stone. And all the things she had avoided admitting, avoided even thinking about in the last week, perhaps even longer than that, coalesced in her stomach like an unexploded bomb. All the things she had come to rely on, to relish, to revel in.

Not just Dane's touch, but those long looks at her over the breakfast table. Those wry smiles of approval whenever they were working together. The attentive way he listened to her, as if everything she said mattered. The quiet times at night, after they had made love, when he held her close and she heard his heart slow. Even the moments when they argued about the itinerary—him trying to shorten every assignment so they could return to the suite sooner rather than later. The memory of their first kiss, as the Roman dawn spread across the horizon. Their wild ride on the bike. The sight of him charging across the ballroom to lift her father to his toes. The fierce compassion in his voice when he'd told her she deserved better than François Xavier Roussel.

Even that silly comment about good girls, designed to make her laugh, which had also lifted her heart. And made it pound so hard against her ribcage she'd been unable to control the tell-tale smile which had spread across her cheeks and made her eyes shine.

What if this *was* more than just infatuation? An endorphin rush she couldn't control? What if it was far worse than that? What if Orla were right, and she had lost her heart to this forceful, fascinating and completely unavailable man?

'I... I don't think that's true.' She forced the denial out, desperately trying to believe it. 'It's just that Dane's quite overwhelming,' she said, then realised what she'd let slip.

It was official, she was actually losing her mind. She hadn't meant to tell Orla that.

'So you are sleeping together,' Orla said, with a gentle acceptance of Jamilla's subterfuge which only made her feel worse about the deception.

'Yes, but that's really all it is,' she said quickly, trying to convince herself as much as Orla. 'It's just... I've never had a lover before and...'

'Jamilla, I had no idea he was your first lover.' Concern thickened Orla's voice and Jamilla wished desperately she hadn't blurted out the truth, suddenly realising it only made her sound more vulnerable and immature. 'I love Dane like a brother,' Orla added. 'But he and Karim both had difficult childhoods and I'm not sure he's very reliable...'

'Honestly, Orla, it's not a big deal,' Jamilla asserted, interrupting her friend, the comment about Dane's childhood making her heart stutter at the thought of the young boy who had been neglected by both his parents.

At least she'd always had her mother. But she'd come to realise over the last few weeks—not just from what she'd found out about Dane's past but also from the way he seemed able to so easily separate his emotions from the intimacy they'd shared—that he had spent a lot of his life protecting himself from rejection. So much so that she already suspected he would never open himself to more.

How could she have forgotten that so easily, allowed

herself to dream, the way her mother had? It was foolish—beyond foolish—it was positively self-destructive.

'All I'm trying to say is,' she continued, 'this affair is about sex and endorphins. And I'm totally good with that. I watched my mother spend her life invested in a love that wasn't real. I'd never be foolish enough to do the same. Even if I wanted to be with him long-term, which I don't, Dane isn't the man for me.' But even as she said it she could feel the panic wrapping around her heart like an anaconda.

Was she her mother's daughter after all? Needy, desperate, wanting more than she could ever have from a man who couldn't—or wouldn't—give it to her?

She ended the call with Orla, having reassured her friend and employer that her affair with Dane Jones was never meant to last. But as she switched off her phone and placed it on the table with trembling fingers she knew she would have a much bigger task convincing herself.

'Even if I wanted to be with him long-term, which I don't, Dane isn't the man for me.'

Listening to Jamilla's words as she spoke on the phone reverberated in Dane's skull. He stood with his shoulder propped on the bedroom door frame and watched her place her phone back on the table.

He crossed his arms, tried to focus on all the things that he had been looking forward to while he'd dressed.

Today's helicopter ride to Lisbon with Jamilla running through the itinerary in the seat next to him while he tried to distract her. The evening banquet with a consortium of dull European business leaders, the tedious conversation enlivened by the game of footsie he had planned to play with her under the table.

And all the memories of the last week which had made him whistle in the shower for the first time in his life.

Jamilla coming apart in his arms last night, her throaty cries spurring him on as he worked the spot with ruthless efficiency he knew would make her climax. The feel of her arms—strong and tight—around him, the scent of her hair—spicy and sweet—as they'd drifted into sleep. The vicious moment of panic when he'd woken up alone this morning, the bed beside him empty, only to relax when he'd heard her on the phone in the sitting room. The decision in the shower to tempt her back into bed before they left for the day—so he could feed the hunger that would not die. Not just for her, but for that soft smile, that sweet shyness beneath the efficiency, the eloquent compassion he'd spotted so many times in the past week—hell, the past three weeks.

But even as he tried to regain that easy balance, that heady feeling of anticipation…the words he'd just overheard made his stomach burn, taking him back to the child he'd been in Zafar, being led to the waiting helicopter by his mother's assistant. Crying as his father turned away from him to return to the palace without a backward glance.

And, worse, that sickening day six years later when his mother had screamed at him—in a fit of temper—the real reason his father had never replied to any of his letters…

A moment he'd spent the rest of his life determined to ignore, determined never to care about…never to let it matter to him.

'Even if I wanted to be with him long-term, which I don't, Dane isn't the man for me.'

The pain clamped around his ribs like a vice, making his breathing laboured and his heart hurt. Why was that? Why should he care what Jamilla thought of him, that she could never love him, when he didn't love her? This connection had only ever been about sex; they'd agreed upon that, right from the start. She'd wanted to keep their liaison a secret and he'd never had a problem with that…had he?

But, even as he tried to convince himself, the vice around his ribs tightened. He straightened away from the door, cleared his throat.

Jamilla swung around, her eyes widening as she spotted him in the doorway. 'Hi, Dane. You're dressed,' she said, the tell-tale blush on her cheeks. But he could see something in her eyes. Had she realised he'd heard her? Had she meant for him to hear?

He'd always found the way she flushed so easily every time she laid eyes on him a major turn-on. Now was no exception as the inevitable heat pooled in his groin. But his instant, unstoppable reaction only made the twist and burn in his gut more vicious. He ground his teeth to stop the turmoil of emotions from showing on his face. Or pouring out of his mouth.

Because that would make him weak. Something he had never been. Not since he was a little boy, writing those damn letters and kidding himself that one day his father would write back.

He strode across the room and cradled her cheek, vindicated by the warmth of her blush and the awareness that darkened her eyes, her response instant and unequivocal.

This was about hunger, not need. What the hell was he getting so worked up about anyway?

She *was* his. All his. In the only way he wanted.

'That can easily be remedied,' he said, keeping the ruthless desire at bay.

You're not that dumb kid any more, needing validation, needing acceptance.

'We don't have time.' She drew back but, instead of letting his hand fall, he cupped her neck, tugged her back.

'Sure we do—we've got twenty minutes,' he said, the strange feeling of loss turning the pain in his chest to a hollow ache. He bent to fasten his lips on the flutter of her pulse, determined to make her ache too, as he flicked open the buttons on her blouse with ruthless purpose. 'More than enough time to get us both off.'

Her breath caught, probably at the crude statement, but her body reacted instinctively, leaning into his caresses as her nipples hardened beneath his questing fingers. He scooped the swollen flesh out of her bra. The musky scent of her arousal turned his erection to iron, but did nothing to soothe the aching pain in his gut. And before he could stop himself the need he didn't want to feel, didn't even want to acknowledge, consumed him.

'Do you want me, Jamilla?' he asked, but he could already see she did, her passion at fever-pitch.

Snapping the hook on her bra, he captured one stiff peak with his mouth, then the other, suckled hard as she shuddered with reaction.

The need became frantic, desperate, clawing at his self-control and exposing that lonely, vulnerable part of himself he thought he'd destroyed long ago.

Just once more.

If he could have her just one more time it would be enough. That was all he wanted now. All he had ever wanted.

He pulled her round, bent her over the sitting room chair. Her breath came out in ragged pants as he lifted the pencil skirt, released the painful erection from his pants.

He didn't want to see her face, didn't want to drown in that look that had fooled him…and made him want more. When he could never have more. Should never need more.

His fingers found the slick bud of her clitoris. She jerked, wet and ready for him. He found the condom in his pocket, somehow managed to roll it on despite the frenzy churning inside him as he stroked her with ruthless determination.

At last, he edged the gusset of her panties to one side and placed the thick head of his erection at the tight entrance.

'Tell me again you want me,' he demanded as he held her breasts, poised to take her. Wild now, to control the pain that threatened to consume him. A pain he couldn't— wouldn't—acknowledge.

'I… I want you,' she groaned, sounding shocked, wary, confused, but as desperate as he.

He sank inside her in one brutal thrust, filling her to the hilt, feeling her stretch to accommodate him. She was already coming, the soft cries, the tight heat driving him mad—with lust and grief—as he began to move.

You're mine. You're mine. You're mine, his mind shouted as he rocked hard and deep, giving her all of himself. But even as the ruthless climax clawed at his self-control, promising untold pleasure, the pain of her rejection bit into his heart.

She didn't want him. However much he might want her.

As the orgasm slammed into him at last, he emptied himself into the void. And the hopes and dreams he hadn't even admitted existed died, leaving only the great gaping hole of loneliness behind.

CHAPTER FIFTEEN

JAMILLA SHUDDERED. DANE'S penis was still huge inside her. Her heart thundered so hard she could almost feel it shattering.

His fingers dug into her hips. 'Don't move,' he grunted.

She held still, struggling to get her breath back, aware of the tenderness in her body, and the elemental sadness in her heart.

Why had that felt like more than sex…so much more? When she knew it wasn't.

He softened at last, then pulled out of her. She gasped, her swollen flesh releasing him with difficulty.

She struggled to pull down her skirt, brutally aware of how she must look. Standing upright, she hooked her bra, began to frantically redo her buttons, the sting of tears threatening to well over her lids as she saw one button had been torn off in his frenzy to have her.

She felt as if she had survived a hurricane. Or had she? Because the shimmer of afterglow from the brutally intense orgasm was doing nothing to control the longing shattering her heart.

She wanted this to mean more than it did.

She gulped down the sob working its way up her throat and continued to button her blouse right up to the neck. 'I should have a shower,' she said, suddenly desperate to escape from him and the panicked direction of her own thoughts.

But as she turned to leave he grasped her wrist. 'Look at me,' he demanded.

Her gaze rose to his, scared she would see contempt, judgement. Or, worse, indifference.

But what she saw made the agony back up in her throat and swell to impossible proportions. Not contempt, not judgement but regret.

Why did that only make the sadness swell, the tears threaten to overflow?

'I'm sorry,' he said, and the lump in her throat threatened to choke her.

What was he apologising for? Could he see the yearning in her heart? Did he know she'd lost all perspective?

'What…what for?' she asked.

He continued to watch her, and she suspected he could see right through her desperate ploy to appear unmoved, unshattered, undevastated.

'When we get to Lisbon I won't come to your suite again,' was all he said, with a finality that pierced her heart.

She wanted to argue with him, to tell him how she felt about him. To tell him she loved him.

But what would be the point? This affair had only ever been about one thing for him. And now, after that last cataclysmic joining, he'd finished with her.

It hurt, but only because she'd allowed herself to become delusional.

So she nodded. 'Okay,' she said, then turned and walked into the bedroom they'd shared the night before, holding her head high and refusing to look back.

Even once.

Until she'd walked into the bathroom, locked the door, and her legs gave way beneath her.

She discovered later that afternoon that she wasn't pregnant. She should have been relieved, but somehow the empty space in her womb felt like another cruel trick.

She whispered the news to him on the Zafari royal jet en route to Portugal. The sadness engulfed her again when he showed no reaction, not even relief. He simply stared back at her then nodded.

Two days later, the morning after their final assignment in Lisbon—during which she had been far too aware of him keeping his distance—she arrived at his suite to bid him goodbye, only to discover he had caught an earlier flight home to Manhattan.

By the time she arrived back in Zafar the next day, the speculation about their grand love affair had become little more than a footnote in the press. But the gaping hole remained in her heart.

The good girl was gone for ever, but the woman who had replaced her was little more than a shadow. She needed to know, she decided, why he had cut her off so easily and so comprehensively. Why had she been so wrong about where they might be heading? Was this really about her, or about something that had happened before she'd ever known him, before she'd loved him?

It took her most of the day to pack up her belongings. Then she emailed her resignation to Orla and Karim.

Before waiting for a reply, she left the Palace of the Kings for the last time on her mare Sana, with a pack of supplies and a bundle of old letters in her saddlebags.

Letters she hoped would give her some insight into the mind of a man who had been tender and passionate and possessive, but determined never to need her, the way she had come to need him.

CHAPTER SIXTEEN

Why aren't you answering your phone? We need to talk.

DANE STARED AT the latest message from Karim, but as his thumb hovered over the delete button the ringtone sounded, startling his horse, Tucker.

'Hey, boy, cool it,' he said, calming the thoroughbred Kentucky quarter horse. Jumping down, he threw the reins over the corral fence, then stared at his phone some more, which was still playing the theme tune from *Game of Thrones,* which he used for Karim.

Talk to him, get it over with, then move on.

It had been over a week since he'd sneaked out of Lisbon on an early-morning flight. Over a week since he'd taken Jamilla as if he owned her, pounding into her, trying to brand her as his when she'd already rejected him. Over a week since his life had disintegrated. He couldn't sleep, couldn't eat and couldn't stop thinking about her.

He dreamt about her constantly. Imagined those moments: when she'd looked at him out of the corner of her eye, excitement and compassion making the amber sparkle; when he'd woken up with her soft butt pressed against his arousal, her spicy sultry scent surrounding him; when she'd cajoled, directed and nudged him into becoming a halfway decent prince; when she'd spoken about her jerk of a father with that lost look in her eyes;

when she'd danced the night away in his arms and made him see for the first time who she really was—a fiercely passionate, genuine, incredibly beautiful woman who could never be his.

Patting Tucker's rump, he walked round the horse, leapt over the corral fence, then clicked the phone's answer button before he could second-guess himself again.

Karim would have news of Jamilla. And he wanted to know how she was doing.

'Hey, bro,' he said, the relaxed tone not even convincing him. 'What's up?'

'Dane, where are you? I've been trying to contact you for nearly a week.' His brother's voice sounded strained.

'At the farm,' he said. 'What's wrong—is something up with Orla? Or Hasan?' he asked, suddenly realising his brother's desire to contact him might not actually be about him. Or Jamilla. Or the way he'd managed to screw up the one favour his brother had asked him in thirty years.

'Orla's good. Although she's not enjoying this pregnancy. At least the morning sickness has calmed down a bit and the doctors are not as worried about the hypertension at the moment. Hasan's good too, into everything and driving all three of us nuts,' his brother said, his voice softening in the way it always did when he referred to his wife and child.

'Okay, good to know,' Dane replied, not surprised by the swift spike of jealousy. His chest tightened, the emptiness still there from a week ago, when Jamilla had told him she'd had her period. Dumb, really, because an unplanned pregnancy would have been a disaster. Wouldn't it? He had lost her before he'd ever had her. And he knew why, because he was and always had been damaged goods. His old man had figured it out by the time he was five.

'So why so desperate to talk to me?' Dane asked, trying

to stop his mind going over those unpleasant thoughts all over again.

Karim and he were close enough, but it wasn't as if they spoke to each other constantly.

He heard Karim's sigh. 'Mostly, I just wanted to thank you properly, for doing the tour. I know it was way outside your comfort zone and I wanted you to know how much Orla and I appreciated you stepping in like that. And how impressed I was that you made such a success of it.'

'Are you serious?' Was his brother making fun of him? Because it was the last thing he needed. The whole experience had already messed with his head and his equilibrium. He didn't even know any more who he was, or who he wanted to be. All he knew was that he wasn't enough.

'Absolutely,' Karim replied, sounding genuine. 'Why wouldn't I be?'

'Because we both know I messed it up,' he shot back. The horse whinnied behind him and he lowered his voice and stepped away from the corral. The late summer sunshine warmed his skin, but the cold weight in his belly refused to budge. The weight that had been there ever since he'd walked out of the hotel, knowing that the woman in front of him was everything he wanted but couldn't have.

He'd been there before, as a boy. When he'd acted out so his mother would notice him—she hadn't—or sent increasingly desperate letters to his father, telling him the truth about his home life so he might step in and take him back to Zafar—and his father hadn't even bothered to open the damn letters.

He hated that kid.

'I jumped her when I had no right to touch her. Luckily for both of us, she figured it out though.' The words tumbled out, his voice breaking on the wave of misery he'd kept so carefully at bay for over a week.

'*Whoa*, Dane, take it easy.' His brother's deep calming

voice reminded him of their boyhood, when he had always been there to soothe the futile tears. 'Are you talking about Jamilla?'

'Yeah,' he said, humiliation joining the other emotions making the lead weight plunge. 'How is she?' he asked, because there wasn't much point in keeping the desire to know more about her a secret any longer. He'd already spilled his guts. 'Have you spoken to her since the tour ended?'

'No.' He could hear his brother swallowing. 'She resigned.'

'She…she what?' Why would she do that? Sick dread joined the misery. Had he done this too—ruined her career somehow?

'She quit,' Karim reiterated. 'And then disappeared. Orla hasn't been able to reach her in Zafar. Even Saed—our all-seeing household manager—has no idea where she went. We figured her disappearance probably had something to do with you—which was kind of the other reason I wanted to speak to you.' His brother paused, and Dane could hear the hesitation. But instead of sounding furious when he continued, all Karim sounded was concerned. 'What exactly happened between you two? Because you looked really good together in all the press photographs. When you were here in Kildare, seeing you with her… I thought maybe…maybe there was more there for you than just a convenient hook-up.'

There was no judgement in the observation. But somehow that made it worse.

He deserved judgement. Hell, he deserved a damn good horse-whipping. The kind of whipping his father had given Karim more than once. But had never given him.

He thrust his fingers through his hair. Damn, exactly how screwed-up was he that he'd rather get whipped than be ignored? Or rejected.

'It *was* more...' he said, blurting out the truth.

'Then why did you break up with her? And why did you keep the affair a secret?' His brother's pragmatic questions reverberated in his chest.

Because she didn't want me.

But the answer that he had told himself for more than a week—the answer that had given him a convenient get-out clause when he'd needed it—didn't seem so damn convenient any more. Because he could finally see it for what it was. An excuse, an easy out, a way of never facing the demons that had chased him for most of his life.

He wanted more from Jamilla than sex. He had done almost as soon as he'd touched her. Heck, the minute he'd laid eyes on her and seen the sharp intelligence and feisty spirit behind the mask of perfection. But he had been more than happy to accept those parameters, because he'd been too scared to ask for more. In case she rejected him. And when he'd heard what she'd said to Orla, he'd taken it at face value. He hadn't confronted her, hadn't told her how he felt. Because he hadn't wanted to risk the fallout if he laid his heart on the line and she kicked it to the kerb. He hadn't been straight with her. Hell, he hadn't even been straight with himself. And finally he knew the real answer to Karim's question.

'Because I'm a coward,' he said.

His brother let out a heavy sigh. 'You're not a coward, Dane. But it's not me you've got to convince. It's yourself. And Jamilla. If you want her back, that is?'

Yes, I do.

Karim's quietly spoken question had the dam breaking inside him, the need flooding through.

His brother was right. What was he doing hiding out and licking his wounds in upstate New York when he should be in Zafar, tracking down the woman he'd thrown away so carelessly?

If he put himself out there and she told him he wasn't enough it would hurt like hell, but what would hurt more was never knowing what they might have had.

Because he'd been too much of a coward to even ask.

CHAPTER SEVENTEEN

Dear Father

Mom wants me to ask you for money again. But I don't have to, because she never reads the letters I send you. I know you're mad at her. I'm mad at her too. We moved again last month. I put the new address on this envelope—so if you want to send me a letter you can. I've also got an email address, if you want to talk that way.

Could I come over to Zafar this summer? While Karim is there? I won't get in the way, I swear. You won't even probably know I'm there. I don't cry all the time like I used to. Perhaps I could help out in the stables. I love horses, even though we live in the city. And I haven't forgotten how to ride.

Do you still have the black Arabian with the white socks? I rode him a couple of times with Karim and I didn't fall off.

Please write back, Father.

I won't tell Mom you did.

Your son,

Dane

JAMILLA FOLDED THE old letter and sniffed loudly.

Reading Dane's letters to his father had been a mistake. Because she could feel the desperation of the boy in every word, the need to connect with a man who didn't want him.

It hurt to know that while she'd always had her mother—however broken, however sad—Dane had had no parent who cared for him.

Her head lifted at the sound of hoof beats from beyond the Bedouin tent. She reached for the pistol in her pack. Bandits were very rare in Zafar these days, but she was a woman alone in the desert and she wasn't taking any chances.

Wrapping her headscarf across her nose and mouth, she lifted the tent flap.

A rider approached over the dunes, on a black horse.

Reaction shimmered through her, followed by a twist of anxiety and panic, and the heavy weight of grief.

Dane?

What was he doing here? Had he come to reject her again? And how had he found her? Only her mother's family knew this spot, a place she had come often when she was a teenager, not long after her mother's death.

He pulled the powerful stallion to a stop in front of her, then jumped down in one fluid movement.

'Jamilla,' he said as he draped the horse's reins over the corral fence and strode towards her. 'What the hell are you doing out here alone?'

She lifted the pistol. 'I am well protected,' she said, even as she could feel her heart shattering all over again. She shouldn't have read his letters, because she could see the little boy who hid inside the man. The child she had come to know in the last few days, as she'd read about the neglect in his own words.

But this wasn't the boy; it was the man. The man who didn't want her. Couldn't love her. Would never want more from her than sex.

'How did you find me?' she asked.

And why?

Why had he come to Zafar? Why had he followed her here when he had discarded her so easily a week ago?

'Your mother's father was surprisingly cooperative when I spoke to him on the phone and he figured out who I was. Apparently the speculation about our secret romance reached the Zafari press too.'

So it was still a joke to him.

A fortifying anger stirred the anguish, making her stomach feel like a black hole—an anger she clung to now. 'Please leave. I do not want you here, nor do I need your protection.'

But as she turned to return into the tent he grasped her arm and tugged her back round to face him. 'Why did you resign?'

That piercing blue gaze, the gaze she saw in her sleep now, searched her face with an intensity that made her skin flare with sensation and her heart pummel her rib-cage.

She yanked her arm out of his grasp, suddenly furi-ous—with herself as much as him. How could she still respond so easily, yearn for him so much—a man who had made it very clear he felt nothing for her?

'Not that it's any of your business, but I resigned be-cause I needed a new challenge. Somewhere far from Zafar.' Where she would not be constantly dogged by the reminders of how she'd failed herself.

And even if the ambition to see and experience more in her life felt hollow now, and empty, it didn't mean she couldn't nurture it. She refused to be that sheltered woman who had concentrated on her career—and had fallen too easily for a pipedream.

The frown on his forehead and the doubtful expression in his eyes made it clear he didn't believe her. 'You're sure about that?' he asked. 'You're sure you're not just running again? From me?'

The accusation felt like a dart to her heart.

'I wasn't the one who ran,' she said, suddenly tired of the lies and evasions. 'I read the letters, the ones you wrote to your father,' she said, and saw him flinch. 'So I know you lied about them. You were a little boy who needed someone to show him he was valued, he mattered. I know what that feels like. I would have understood, if you'd trusted me.'

He stiffened, the guarded look, the wary tension in his body rejecting the truth even now. She wasn't having it, not any more. Hadn't they both run from the truth—that the rejections they'd suffered in childhood had made them both cowards? But she was through being a coward. He'd come all this way; he deserved to know how she really felt. No more evasions.

'I was falling in love with you. You made me feel valued, important, cherished. But you threw me away,' she finished, glad when she managed to keep her voice firm, level, despite the agony twisting her guts.

She blinked, letting the tear fall. She brushed it away with her fist. She'd given him all the power in their relationship, let him set all the terms. So who was really to blame for this crippling heartache?

'You need to go now.'

'Wait… No.' The words exploded out of Dane's chest.

He'd travelled through the night to get to Zafar, a place he'd always hated, tracked down Jamilla's family, had to phone her very disapproving grandfather. And then he'd taken his brother's stallion Azzam out before dawn to ride here.

When he'd seen her, standing proud and alone in the entrance of the Bedouin tent she'd seemed like a goddess to him. And he'd known he would do anything to undo the wrongs he'd done her. But the fear and panic which had assailed him ever since he'd finally acknowledged the truth had refused to abate. And he'd screwed up all over again.

I was falling in love with you.

Was.

He caught up with her again, gripped her upper arm, felt the muscles tense. But the zing of attraction was nowhere near as terrifying as the driving need.

'You said you didn't want me, didn't want anything long-term. On the phone that day. To Orla. I heard you...' The accusation burst out, but even he could hear how lame it sounded.

He'd known, from the way she looked at him, touched him, supported him, they could have had so much more.

'I didn't... I didn't know you heard me say that.' Her eyes darkened with a sadness that made his ribs contract. 'I was scared. My feelings were so strong and Orla said... She said she thought I was falling in love. She was right, of course. But why didn't you tell me what you'd overheard?'

He shook his head. 'I should have, but that would mean admitting how I felt. I guess.'

Her brows rose and understanding crossed her face. An understanding he was sure he didn't deserve. 'Is that why you took me with such...desperation? Before you broke things off with me?'

'No... Yes...' He swore and let go of her arm, then thrust his fingers through his sweaty hair. He had to make this right. But how? 'Everything got so mixed up in my head. I lost my mind for a moment. I wanted more but I was too scared to admit it. Even to myself. And hearing you say that to Orla...it made me feel like that damn kid again. Always on the outside looking in.'

He looked away, unable to meet her eyes while he said what he had to say. She deserved to hear the truth. 'I want to be the guy you see when you look at me. But there's stuff you need to know.' He heaved a sigh. Stared out at the blue of the oasis near the tent, reminding him of another time, the day she had found him at the Halu Oasis, and everything had seemed so simple. 'You're so smart. And I didn't even graduate high school,' he began, determined to tell her everything. Every damn inadequacy that had haunted him for so long.

'Dane, that's ridiculous. You've built a multi-million-dollar business from nothing.' He heard the incredulous tone and almost laughed. 'The fact you didn't graduate only makes that achievement more impressive.'

He turned back, making himself meet her gaze. The laugh got stuck in his throat because he knew the biggest hurdle was yet to come.

Absorbing the sheen of moisture still lingering in her eyes, he murmured, 'I might not be his.'

Her brow furrowed. 'I'm sorry?'

'I might not be of royal blood,' he said again. 'She told me once, when she was hammered and strung out—she'd taken lovers. Because he had, and she wanted to spite him. The timing meant Abdullah may have been my father. But she couldn't be sure.' The crippling inadequacy threatened to choke him, but he forced himself to continue. 'I was eleven, maybe twelve. I stopped writing the letters after that. And she couldn't make me. I'd invested this whole identity in being his son, in being Karim's brother. I locked it all away, convinced myself it didn't matter. But when I heard you say that to Orla... I don't know, it made sense. Why would you want me, when I'm more than likely not the guy you think I am?'

Jamilla pressed her fingers to her lips, holding back the sob queueing up in her throat. But the tears fell freely down her cheeks now. Because she could see the boy now, inside the man, a shining light shadowed by uncertainty, as clearly as the sunlight glimmering on the water. She'd hurt him with the lie she'd told Orla. A lie she'd told to protect herself. Perhaps it had been bad timing, a foolish misunderstanding, something she had never intended for him to overhear. But if she'd been honest with him sooner, and herself, and told him how she really felt, her lie would have had no power to hurt him.

Reaching out, she touched his cheek. The day-old stubble abraded her palm as his jaw tensed. 'Dane, you must know, it doesn't matter to me who your biological father is… Or isn't. It's you I love.'

He covered her hand, his eyes flaring with an intensity that stole her breath. Dragging her hand down, he pressed it to his chest, making her aware of the thumping beat of his heart. 'You love me? Still… Even after everything I've…'

'Yes, yes, yes.' She pulled her hand free, threw her arms around his neck to press her body against his and shower him with kisses. All the fear was gone in a heartbeat, to be replaced with that painful bubble of hope. 'You idiot,' she said, drawing back.

He wrapped his arms around her waist, lifted her off the ground and squeezed her so tightly she felt sure he would never let her go again. 'Thank God.'

He buried his head against her neck, kissed the sensitive skin beneath her chin, caressing the pulse point with his lips. But as he scooped her up, to march with her into the tent, she wriggled free.

'What's the deal?' he asked, looking wonderfully confused.

'Don't you have something you want to tell me first?' she asked, part sass, part determination. And part panic.

'Yeah, I guess I do.' Her confidence surged again when

his lips curled, but then, to her astonishment, he dropped to one knee.

'Dane, what are you…'

'Shh…' he said, clasping her hands in his and staring up at her, the humour gone, to be replaced with a focus so intense it made her ribs ache.

Even if Dane Jones wasn't a Khan by blood, he was—and always had been—every inch a prince.

'I absolutely adore you, Jamilla Omar Roussel. Your smarts, your sass, your beauty and your far too well-developed sense of what's right and what's wrong. And for all the sexy times you're only ever gonna get to have with me.'

Her face burned and he laughed, before standing up to tower over her and pull her into his arms.

'I'm head over heels for those blushes too,' he murmured, placing a kiss on her lips that managed to be both tender and tantalising in equal measure. And only made the blush more vivid. 'I want us to build a life together,' he continued. 'I want you to have my babies. But, more than that, I want to marry you, because I love you. So, so much.'

She sank into the kiss, as ravenous and joyous as him.

When they finally came up for air and he scooped her back up into his arms, she clung to his broad shoulders and pressed her face into his chest to stop her buoyant heart from bursting right out of her chest and flying off into the cosmos.

EPILOGUE

Four months later

'YOUR HIGHNESS, A package arrived this morning at the palace for you...but addressed to me. It had this letter inside.'

Dane glanced up from his desk to find Hakim—the young valet who always attended him when he and Jamilla returned to Zafar—standing in the doorway of his study holding a large envelope and a curious expression.

Dane's heart battered his ribcage, his breath becoming trapped in his lungs, but somehow he managed to close his laptop, get up from the desk and cross the room without losing his cool. 'Great, thanks, I've been expecting it,' he said, pasting an easy smile on his face and taking the envelope from Hakim.

The young man nodded, keeping the obvious questions he wanted to ask to himself. Then he excused himself to prepare Dane's outfit for tonight's official naming ceremony.

Dane had asked specifically that the Narabian clinic send a letter instead of an email, and that they post the results care of his valet, to his apartment in the palace in Zafar and not the brownstone he'd recently purchased in Manhattan—where he and Jamilla had been living for most of the last four months, ever since their whirlwind elopement.

It had made sense to get the results sent here, he told himself staunchly. They were due to be here for a week, finishing off their visit tonight attending the state ceremony to declare Karim and Orla's twin daughters—Rana and Amina—heirs to the Zafari throne. But as he held the heavy cream cardboard envelope in his hand he knew those weren't the real reasons for keeping the test on the downlow. Not even close.

He had made Karim swear not to mention the DNA test to anyone, when he'd asked him to provide a cheek swab four days ago to have couriered to the clinic. Karim had been unhappy about the secrecy, and mad as hell about the fact Dane was taking the test at all.

'You're my brother, Dane, no matter what some damn DNA sample says. You understand? If you think you're getting out of your royal duties now on a technicality— or shirking your responsibility to Hasan and the girls as their uncle—you can forget it.'

His heart thundered in his ears at the memory of Kasim's furious expression when he'd made the request. And the deep well of love for his brother that had spilled over in that moment.

He slid his thumb across the address of the fancy clinic on the back and his breathing eased a little.

Yeah, Karim wasn't wrong. No matter what was in here, they would still be brothers. Funny to think he'd spent so much of his life scared of finding out the truth about his heritage because he was terrified he'd lose that connection, without ever realising that what he shared with his brother went a great deal deeper than blood.

But it wasn't Karim's reaction he was concerned about. Not really.

It was Jamilla's.

He swallowed down the thick tide of dread in his throat. A dread that had been building for days, ever since she'd snuggled into his arms in their palace chambers after a tiring first day in Zafar spent getting acquainted with their new nieces and whispered, 'You were so wonderful with the babies, Dane. I think you'll make an amazing father...' But then she'd stiffened slightly and her voice had taken on a strangely tentative quality when she finally added, 'Some day.'

It hadn't been a question. After all, they'd spoken about having children before, when he'd first proposed to her. And she'd seemed keen. But her slight hesitation that night had bothered him ever since.

At first he'd convinced himself it was because she simply wasn't keen to start trying too soon. He got that; they deserved more quality time, just the two of them, before they settled into the rigours of parenthood. The twins were cute as hell but they were also a lot of work, and while Karim and Orla looked ecstatic with their new babies, and Hasan had turned into an endlessly fascinating toddler, his brother and sister-in-law also looked exhausted.

Then there was the problem of Jamilla's career—which she had only just started establishing in New York. He could understand why she'd be reluctant to start a family before she'd got the new diplomatic mission she was managing in Manhattan for the Zafar monarchy properly established. But then again—because it was being run by his super-smart and super-efficient wife—it was already a roaring success, organising a wealth of new educational and cultural exchanges and travel and tourism opportunities between their two nations.

Jamilla had never again mentioned what he'd told her in the desert that day, the stuff his mom had claimed about his parentage. She'd told him then that his biological inheritance didn't matter to her, and he'd believed her. Absolutely.

But that conversation a week ago had played over and over again in his head. Not least because holding Karim's tiny daughters in his arms had made the yearning in his chest that much worse.

What if Jamilla was having second thoughts? What if it did matter to her, even if only a little, that they didn't know for sure who he really was? Wasn't he robbing her of the chance to know who she'd really married?

Eventually, the damn questions had bugged him so much he'd decided the only way to get past them was to finally confront the truth. It was better to know—for her sake as well as his. If they were going to have kids, she had a right to know if they were of royal blood. They both did.

He flipped the envelope over, reached for the letter opener on his desk. But he couldn't seem to make his fingers stop trembling long enough to slit the paper open. And the long-ago fear roared back to life, like a fire-breathing dragon sitting under his breastbone, ready to burn his sense of identity, his sense of belonging right down to the ground all over again.

What the hell will you do if you don't get the answer you want, and it does make a difference to her after all, you dummy? Because no way in hell are you letting her go.

'Dane, what on earth are you doing hiding in here? Hakim is waiting for you to get changed.' Jamilla stood on the threshold of her husband's study, happy to have found him.

But the nerves that had been tying her stomach in knots for days cinched tight when his head lifted and she

saw the haunted look in his eyes she remembered from
the first time he had returned to the Palace of the Kings.

'What is it? What's wrong?' she said, rushing into
the room.

She hadn't seen that look for months now, even though
they'd returned to the palace several times since their
marriage. But the thought was quickly followed by panic.

Oh, God, had Orla told him what Jamilla had confided in her that morning? Surely she wouldn't have,
even though her friend had been fairly unsubtle about
her thoughts on the subject when the palace doctor had
confirmed the results of Jamilla's blood test.

*'Jamilla, you are joking? Dane absolutely adores you;
it's plain for everyone to see. And he's wonderful with
the twins and Hasan. You have to tell him; I think he'll
be overjoyed.'*

*'But I was going to tell him my suspicions a week
ago and...when I mentioned him being a father, he went
so still, I just... I couldn't. It's too soon, it's totally unplanned. I just need more time.'*

The choking panic closed around her throat again, but
then she noticed the envelope in his hands.

'Dane? What is that?'

'Busted.' He handed the large, official-looking envelope to her and she read the clinic address on the back.
'You want to open it for me?' he asked as she realised
what the envelope contained. 'Find out if I'm really a
Khan or not.'

She stared at his face, her heart breaking at the tense
look, the desperate attempt to appear nonchalant. She
knew how much this meant to him, even though it
shouldn't.

To her he would never just be someone's son, someone's brother, a Prince of Zafar by blood, or by shared

history, or both. To her he was all those things and so much more.

He was her husband, her lover, her soulmate, her best friend. The person who made her laugh, who made her happy, who frustrated and teased and challenged and provoked her. The man who could make her skin tingle and her heart race with a single look. The man who had finally shown her what unconditional love and approval felt like. And who, by doing so, had made her the best person she could be.

But, even knowing all that about Dane, she nodded. She couldn't tell him any of that; he had to believe it himself.

'Okay, I'll open it and, whatever is in it, we'll deal with it together,' she said. Maybe he needed to take this step, to finally release him from the fears of his past so he could become fully invested in his future. In their future.

His lips quirked and some of that haunted look faded. 'So fierce,' he murmured.

She nodded, tears stinging her eyes at the appreciation in his voice. 'But first I have something to tell you,' she added.

Something, she realised, she should have told him ten days ago, when her period had failed to appear. And a week ago, when she'd had that first positive home pregnancy test, before she'd chickened out. Apparently her husband wasn't the only one still pandering to the insecurities of the past.

But that ended now.

She placed the envelope on his desk, then reached up to press her palms to the tight muscles in his jaw. 'I had it confirmed by the Palace doctor this morning... I'm pregnant.'

His brows shot up his forehead, those pure blue eyes

widening. 'You're *what*?' his voice croaked out, his hands grasping her waist, holding on to her, the joy in his eyes banishing the last of that haunted look. For ever, she hoped.

She grinned. 'We're expecting a baby.' Her heart leapt into her throat at his stunned but ecstatic laugh.

It wasn't too soon. It could never be too soon. They were going to be parents, together. They both wanted this so much, and they would be good at it, so good, because they both knew far too much about how to be a bad parent.

'Oh. My. God.' His gaze dropped to her belly then shot back to her face. 'For real? *Already*?'

'Yes, for real. I'm not sure how it happened but...'

'Who cares?' he interrupted her. 'This is the best news ever.' Lifting her up, he spun her around. And when he finally dropped her back on her feet they were kissing, touching, loving each other, and she had totally resigned herself to being really late for the naming ceremony.

When they finally arrived in the palace courtyard—half an hour later—Jamilla was flushed and exhilarated and ready to face her future with courage and determination. While Dane stood beside her in his dress uniform, looking smugger than ever as they gave Karim and Orla their two pieces of exciting news.

In approximately seven and a half months' time she and Dane would be welcoming yet another brand-new member of the Zafar royal family—or, given the Khans' propensity for having twins, possibly two new members of the royal family.

And Dane was going to find it next to impossible to weasel out of his duties as a Prince of Zafar from then on because there was a ninety-nine point eight per cent probability that he was the current King's biological half-brother.

But in the end all four of them agreed only the first bit of news really mattered—because there was no way in hell Karim and Orla would have let Dane off his royal duties ever again now, whatever the result of his DNA test.

* * * * *

HIRED BY THE FORBIDDEN ITALIAN

CATHY WILLIAMS

MILLS & BOON

CHAPTER ONE

'I AM SORRY, Nicky, but I have no choice. Your *papa* cannot walk with that leg of his in a *gesso*, or whatever you want to call it. Your *mama* is in a state. She needs me.'

With a mountain of work to get through, a pile of reports to sign off and a delicate, monumental deal which had been months in the making nearing its long-awaited conclusion—not to mention a six-year-old daughter who was about to start her summer holidays—Niccolo Ferri had looked at his aunt two evenings before, as she'd stood there with her suitcase packed and the taxi driver all but blowing his horn in the circular courtyard of his London mansion, with something approaching horror.

Yes, his father *had* had a fall, foolishly swerving through the streets of Rome on a moped Niccolo had warned him not to get, but why on earth did that mean his aunt, here in London, suddenly needed to rush off in the guise of Florence Nightingale? To the best of his knowledge, his aunt had precisely zero medical qualifications.

He had telephoned his mother on a daily basis ever since his father had been sent flying off his moped three days previously, and Anna Ferri had certainly not sounded like a distraught woman in desperate need of her sister's help.

Indeed, she had rejected his offer to have round-the-clock nursing installed in their villa in Tuscany without bothering to hear him out.

So, what had changed in the space of twenty-four hours, necessitating his aunt's hasty and ill-timed departure?

'I need you here,' he had said. 'Annalise begins her summer holidays tomorrow and there's no way I'm going to be able to find someone to stand in at such short notice. I might be able to throw money at an agency, but I doubt they'll be able to conjure up a suitable candidate from thin air.'

'I would not dream of leaving you in the lurch, Nicky.' His aunt's words had oozed with a level of soothing piety that had had every antenna in his body quivering with suspicion. 'I have just the lady for you.'

He had conceded because he'd simply had no choice. He had huge respect and fondness for his aunt, his mother's only sister and a force of nature who had spent years travelling the world. She had descended every so often on their tiny eighth-floor flat, sometimes to stay for weeks at a stretch, bringing with her the tantalising scent of adventure, of possibilities of other lives lived in places that weren't poky flats in rundown estates.

As a child, Niccolo had watched his mother's face light up every time Evalina had wafted through that front door, had watched his father relax, laugh out loud, shed some of the concerns that seemed to dog his daily existence.

Where his parents had led a dutiful life, Evalina had

thrown herself into travel with the gusto of someone permanently hellbent on having a good time. She was outgoing, engaging, and with a streetwise sharpness that allowed her to wheedle her way into jobs wherever her wandering feet had happened to take her.

Of course, over time, the stars had faded from his eyes and he had realised that where his parents' lives were reduced and constricted through lack of money, his aunt, likewise, had ended up travelling down the same path even if the scenery on the way had been slightly different. He had watched his father work all the hours under the sun, yet, without the required university degree, never finding the voice to make a case for moving up at the family-owned garage where he worked, where kith and kin counted for far more than innate talent and unexploited brains.

Where the right accent got the plum jobs. As a hard-working immigrant, his father had slaved away for years until, three years previously, his heart had decided that the stress was just a little too much, and it had decided to warn him that a change of direction might be a good idea. The help Niccolo had offered the minute he'd started making serious money—always declined because of pride—had finally been accepted because the stakes had been so much higher.

And while his father had slaved away his mother had done her bit, cleaning other people's houses and, at one point, walking other people's dogs.

They were both humble and had never asked for much, and their reward? They had received precious little.

Were they in love? Yes. Were they happy? Yes—

they enjoyed one another's company and relished the small pleasures in life.

Was that enough for him?

A thousand times *no*.

And his aunt? So vivacious, so beautiful in her prime, independent and clever...

Yet eventually, in her late fifties, as her exciting nomadic life had drawn to its inevitable close, where had she been left? Without the degree? The diploma? Without any connections whatsoever?

Where had all that excitement led?

To a life without any sort of security, financial or otherwise.

Watching them all as he'd grown up, Niccolo had absorbed learning curves he hadn't even been consciously aware of.

Innately gifted academically, he had known what had to be done and he had worked. At eleven, he had been accepted on a scholarship to a prestigious boys' private school and he had seen, over the years, where power and wealth and privilege got a person in life. He had seen how people who had a mere fraction of the talent and sharpness of his own father had prospered because they had had the right education, the right background, found the right foothold, could hold their own and blag their way through situations with confidence.

Not always, of course, but often enough for him to have understood the importance of that ladder that led to those glass ceilings waiting to be broken. By him.

He had recognised that what money and power bought wasn't just the house and the holidays. Money and power bought freedom from insecurity, and that had been instructive because what he had seen in his own home had been insecurity. Love had been there, close family ties had been there, but as far as he was concerned they were blighted by the nagging worry about what tomorrow might bring.

He had determined from an early age that he was never going to have to worry about tomorrows.

He had been sought-after following his stellar career at Oxford, but he had chosen the least promising of the companies headhunting him, the one where he could make the biggest mark because it was failing the fastest, and he had spent three years turning it around. From day one, he had asked for shares and just a fraction of the salary he'd been offered. By the time he left, his shares were worth a fortune and he had then moved to diversify every penny he had made, dipping fingers into pies and taking risks in acquisitions that no one would have dared. But Niccolo had had the Midas touch. Everything had turned to gold, and with that gold he had been in the fortunate position to save his parents, and his aunt, from insecurity and those uncertain and frightening *tomorrows*.

And if he'd made one error of judgement…

He thought of his daughter now and sealed shut that door, because it opened onto memories he had conditioned himself not to revive.

Evalina had told him that she had 'just the lady' for him. Very nice, she had said, very reliable, someone she had met at her allotment. More importantly, she had confided, Annalise had met her a couple of weeks ago when they had been there on the weekend.

'Three Saturdays ago, when you were out with that dark-haired woman with the make-up and the *tette grandi*,' she had expanded, while Niccolo had absently recalled the big-breasted woman in question. Their early trip to the theatre had been followed by the expensive meal and relief when he had left with merely a peck on the cheek because somehow the thought of going where the evening should have taken them could not have been less appealing.

Now that his aunt had disappeared, he was relieved that she had not managed to leave him in quite the lurch he had feared. The lady's being a trusted friend from her allotment, and furthermore one his daughter had met, went some way to compensating, presumably, for a lack of formal qualifications.

He trusted his aunt's judgement implicitly. She had fortuitously slotted into his household when her wandering feet had started protesting at the constant travel five years ago, just when he had needed someone. Left with an infant following the premature death of his wife, Evalina had moved in and taken charge, relishing the joys of helping to raise Annalise, which had filled the void of never having had a child of her own.

He had been immeasurably grateful.

His life had been lived in the fast lane from the very moment he had married and he'd realised within six months that it had been a mistake. No time to press a rewind button and no pause to draw breath and take stock. Marriage…fatherhood…divorce rushed towards him in the space of two and a half years—a time of anguish, guilt and regret, the only shining light his daughter. And then, a mere eight months after his divorce, Caroline had died behind the wheel of her Porsche, which she had been driving, he had been informed at the inquest, far too fast and with far too much booze in her system. She hadn't stood a chance when she had lost control in torrential rain.

So, yes, he had been immeasurably grateful to his aunt for being there. Right time, right place and a rock in stormy waters.

So this lady she had recommended? It would work.

His aunt was in her sixties and he presumed that her friend would be of similar age and thus not constrained by a daily commute to work or the trials and tribulations of a young family. Doubtless, the enormous pay cheque to cover the four weeks his aunt would be away would also ease matters somewhat.

With that in mind, he checked his watch and ordered another drink, barely glancing in the direction of the neatly uniformed waiter who sprinted towards him to take the order.

In this elegant five-star wine bar and with his daughter spending the night at the house of one of her friends, he would interview the Baxter woman, explain what would be expected of her and make sure she knew that the bulk of her pay cheque would be safely deposited into her bank account just as soon as her satisfactory interview with him was completed.

He was wholly assured that whoever his aunt recommended would be more than adequate. Evalina adored Annalise and would never suggest anyone she didn't have absolute faith in. But still...

When it came to hard cash, it paid to never take chances. His aunt's allotment pal might be as cosy as a patchwork quilt and as wholesome as apple pie, but he still intended to lay down the law and make sure the woman knew that, friendship or no friendship, he would be keeping a firm eye on her and slip-ups would not be tolerated. When it came to his daughter, normal rules of engagement definitely did not apply.

He glanced at his watch again and frowned.

She had approximately five minutes to make it to the wine bar and be positioned opposite him at the table he had reserved. Unreliability before day one had even begun was not going to impress.

He anticipated being back in time to cover a couple of hours of correspondence before he hit the sack at his usual post-work time of a little after midnight, and with another glance at his Rolex he settled in front of his phone and began scrolling through his emails.

Sophie Baxter made it to the wine bar with only seconds to spare and at speed.

Yet another protracted call to the bank, followed by one from the estate agent asking about party wall agreement documents, which had thrown her for six because she hadn't had much of a clue where to begin hunting those down...

She had already spent so long dealing with all the chaos and despair of life after her parents had died, and yet here she was now because suddenly, in the space of just a couple of days, life had gone flying off in a direction she could never have anticipated.

Lovely Evalina, her neighbour at the allotment she had managed to land seven months ago through a friend of a friend of a friend of a friend, had contacted her with a surprising offer that could not have arrived at a more fortuitous moment.

A month in a house nannying her nephew's six-year-old daughter, Annalise, whom Sophie had met only a fortnight or so ago and thoroughly liked.

'I know it's probably very last-minute, my dear, but the pay will be excellent...'

She had asked about an interview—surely she wouldn't be hired sight unseen? Her experience when it came to nannying, she had worriedly pointed out, was negligible. A few months with a family in France, where she had learnt a bit of French and had had a lovely time looking after their two young kids. It had been something of a gap year, but she had no formal qualifications...

But Evalina had vaguely waved away the suggestion. Speed was of the essence, she said, and her recommendation would carry sufficient weight with Niccolo—that and the fact that Sophie had met his daughter and they got along. There was no time for anything to be arranged, she had elaborated, because she had to leave the country immediately to help her sister and brother-in-law. There had been an accident—lots of broken bits and pieces, she had hinted darkly, without going into detail. Probably, Sophie concluded, because she found it too painful, something with which she could more than sympathise.

Sophie was guiltily aware that she had veered away from asking too many questions because the money had appealed, along with the fact that having somewhere to live for a month would tide her over until the stuff with the house had been sorted. It had felt like a reprieve and, after a year of horror and sadness and pain, a reprieve had been too good to pass up.

So now here she was, having an interview for a job she had already been offered, meeting an employer with only a description to go on: *'A very nice, very dutiful father, who works all hours to keep a roof over their heads. The poor, poor man lost his wife some years ago. That is why it is so important that he has faith in the person looking after his beloved daughter.'*

Tragic, Sophie had thought. Evalina's words had brought home to her all those memories of the accident that had taken both her parents in one fell swoop. A rainy night, a truck travelling too fast in the opposite direction…and suddenly lives ended far too soon. Sophie felt her life had ended there too, a little over a year ago, and so it had, in a way, because everything that had followed on could never be called *a life*. She had lurched her way through an unfolding horror story of pain as, bit by bit, her life unravelled in slow motion and the foundations underneath her that had always felt so secure crumbled away. She had had to deal with woes that she knew her parents had kept from her, financial problems that must have been slowly eating away at them for years. They had sheltered her from finding out the extent of their debts, all undertaken to put her through private school, all targeted to giving her the best possible head start in life. And then, with everything collapsing around her like a house of cards, she had made the biggest mistake of her life and sought comfort from the wrong guy.

Just thinking about it made her shudder.

So, whilst nerves had kicked in now as she paused in front of the chi-chi wine bar in Mayfair, it was a relief after months of numbing despair, with each day promising to deliver nothing new, just more of the same—debts to be paid, bills she hadn't known existed to be settled, and a future so unsteady that she couldn't bring herself to examine it in detail.

For the first time in months, she could feel a tiny ray

of optimism trying to break through the dense storm clouds overhead and her nerves ratcheted up a couple of notches because she was *desperate* not to blow this opportunity.

She inhaled, exhaled, inhaled, exhaled, counted to ten and headed for the entrance of the wine bar.

Looking up from the report he had been reading, Niccolo saw the woman hovering in the doorway and drew in a sharp breath. She was arrestingly pretty yet he was surprised at how riveted he was by her blonde good looks because she was not at all the sort of woman he usually went for. He liked his women earthy, flamboyant, confident and on the same page as he was. Sexy, busty brunettes who didn't play coy games and never asked for more than he was willing to give.

His ex-wife, a refined Italian beauty with a pedigree as long as your arm, had charmed him with her softly spoken, coy, genteel cool. She had played hard to get, reaching out just so far before shyly pulling back. After four months and in a headlong rush of thwarted passion—partly driven, he had retrospectively concluded, by the fact that were he not so rich, she wouldn't have spared him a second glance—Niccolo had proposed.

Very quickly, he realised that with refinement came problems he just hadn't anticipated. The new Mrs Caroline Ferri of the impeccable lineage and the cut-glass accent—because she had been privately educated at a boarding school in the Shires—was agonisingly and, in the end, infuriatingly high maintenance. Her demands became imperious. She required constant attention and round-the-clock adulation. She had Annalise but parenthood was not something she relished. As the only child of cold, distant parents who resided in regal splendour in Italy, she lacked any desire to bond with her child because her own parents had never bonded with her.

Niccolo, driven by ambition though he was, understood the importance of family, and their lives veered off in different directions very quickly from that point.

The ending of their marriage had been in the making before it had really even begun, although he would always feel subliminal guilt about the way everything had unravelled—so quickly and so completely.

He was adept at learning lessons. Promise nothing and look for less when it came to women. In the end, it was all about fun and sex. The obvious worked. The woman hovering nervously by the door was the opposite of obvious.

Tall and willowy, with her hair scraped back into some kind of bun, she was clutching her backpack in front of her with the tenacity of someone warding off evil spirits.

But her face…perfectly heart-shaped with a small, straight nose and a full, inviting mouth. Her pink tongue flicked out, moistening her lips, and Niccolo was shocked at the sudden surge in his libido, which went from zero to ten in the space of seconds.

He fidgeted, returned to his phone and only raised his eyes again when he was aware of a shadow across the table.

In the space of time it took Sophie to approach the table where Niccolo was sprawled in a chair, staring at his mobile phone, she registered that this was not what she had been expecting.

By the time she was standing directly in front of him, her nerves had had time to multiply tenfold. She cleared her throat and shifted awkwardly. She felt like an idiot in this smart place. Her clothes were all wrong. Her capacious backpack was all wrong. She knew that she shouldn't be feeling like this. She had never been awed by expensive restaurants or flashy houses or idiotic, over-fast cars, but she felt awkward now, and she registered, subliminally, that it was the guy sitting in front of her who was encouraging that response.

Evalina had somehow managed to give the impression that her employer was a kindly, middle-aged, man—a devoted dad, a widower who had never quite got over the death of his wife. Details had been in scant supply, but Sophie had had no problem filling in all the gaps herself.

She had pictured a small, thin Italian gentleman who worked hard to make a good living. He would adjust his specs and they would have a comfortable conversation during which Sophie would do her utmost to reassure him that she would be a brilliant nanny for Annalise. She had done a lot of background research into things to do in London with young kids and all sorts of brochures were stuffed into her backpack, to be produced as evidence of her commitment.

This guy…

He looked as comfortable as a prowling shark in a tank full of minnows. He was younger than she had expected, mid-thirties perhaps, and his face was the perfect blend of beauty and power. Dark, dark eyes and raven-black hair cropped short so that nothing deflected from his harsh, stunningly perfect features. And where Evalina was slender and slight, her nephew was not. The opposite. He dwarfed the chair in which he was sitting.

In all respects, the man was breathtaking.

Apprehension threaded through her and her breathing quickened.

No, this was emphatically *not* what she had expected, and it certainly was not what she felt she could deal with at this moment in time. A too good-looking employer, free, single and unencumbered, who could get it into his head that his live-in nanny might be interested in some after-hours hanky-panky... Sophie wasn't vain, but she was realistic. She knew that her looks attracted attention just as much as she knew how much of a problem that could be. She'd learned how to ignore lascivious stares from men and protect herself, but she was still raw from her recent disastrous relationship and the last thing she knew she could emotionally handle would be a guy showing any kind of interest in her. At this moment in time, she just felt way too fragile to deal with anything like that.

She felt faint as she saw all of her hopes of some kind of breathing space fly through the window.

'Who are you?'

Sophie blinked. His voice matched his looks. Dark... exotic...strangely mesmerising.

'Sophie Baxter.' She held out her hand and wondered how she could phrase the beginning of her excuse for backing out of the arrangement his aunt had made. 'Your aunt? Evalina? She recommended me to you about the...er...vacancy for the nanny job to replace her now that she's had to return to Italy? I'm really sorry about your father, by the way. It must be worrying for you, stuck over here when you know he's been in an accident...'

'*You're* the woman my aunt has recommended?'

Sophie instantly felt her hackles rise. He sounded horrified.

'Sit.' He half rose, as though belatedly remembering that there was something called *common courtesy* and nodded to the chair opposite, and Sophie duly sat down, defences fully in place at his surprising reaction.

'Were you expecting someone else?' she asked politely, eyes reluctantly riveted to his dark face as he lounged back in the chair and looked at her with brooding intensity.

'You're younger than I expected,' Niccolo said flatly. 'When my aunt told me that one of her friends at the allotment would be perfect to stand in for her in her absence, I was expecting a woman of a similar age.'

'My apologies for being twenty-five,' Sophie replied coldly. 'I didn't realise there was an age threshold for the position. Evalina never mentioned that.'

Niccolo was working out that there was probably quite a bit his aunt had failed to mention, and not just to the blonde sitting in front of him with an expression that could freeze water—not that that had the slightest effect on him.

Up close, the woman was even more stunning than at a distance. Vanilla-coloured hair, eyes the most peculiar shade of blue, tall and slender. It seemed a catch-all description to describe her as a typical English rose, but this blue-eyed blonde had something he couldn't quite put his finger on, something that elevated her from the ranks of attractive blondes into something that had temporarily sent his libido into freefall.

Was it the unusual violet-blue of her eyes? Or the lushness of her lashes, dark in contrast to the white-blonde of her hair? Or the fullness of her mouth? Or maybe it was just because she was glaring at him, which wasn't the sort of reaction he was accustomed to getting from a woman.

At any rate, a twenty-five-year-old leggy blonde wasn't going to do and there was no point beating about the bush—although the prospect of putting work on hold indefinitely while he hunted down a suitable nanny didn't fill him with joy. He could, naturally, bring Annalise into his offices, arrange for his PA to keep an eye on her while he spent the day in back-to-back meetings, but how rewarding was that going to be for an energetic six-year-old who would want to be outside in the sunshine having some fun at the start of her summer holidays?

'Would you like something to eat?' He signalled to the waiter, who raced over, and he watched for a few seconds while she buried herself behind the oversized menu before emerging to shake her head.

'A cup of tea would be lovely.'

'A bottle of Chablis,' Niccolo drawled, 'and some tapas. Along with the cup of tea, of course.' He leant forward, hands on the table, and looked at her seriously for a few silent seconds. 'I apologise if you found my reaction rude,' he said.

'I get it. You thought that because I met your aunt at an allotment, I would be in my sixties, maybe without a partner and definitely without a nine-to-five job.'

Niccolo shrugged and laughed drily. He sat back,

dark eyes roving over her face, appreciating the symmetry of her features and working out just why it was that his aunt had failed to provide him with an in-depth description of the woman she had recommended.

Evalina, like his parents, wanted to see him remarried. One tragic mistake, they were fond of telling him, was no excuse to remain a confirmed bachelor for the rest of his life. Annalise needed a mother and he needed the love of a good woman. Their exuberant Italian enthusiasm alternately amused and frustrated him. Respect compelled him to avoid confrontations on the issue but, thus far, they had backed off from the actual business of *matchmaking*.

He felt a surge of irritation that he had now been put in the awkward position of having to deal with a situation he hadn't envisaged.

'It had crossed my mind,' he admitted and then added, after a moment's hesitation, 'I think my aunt may have been playing games with both of us.' Why not be perfectly honest? When it came to addressing most thorny issues, honesty was usually the best policy as far as he was concerned. This was particularly true when it came to his dealings with the opposite sex. He liked things to be crystal clear, all cards on the table, for the avoidance of misunderstandings. He watched her closely, noted her frown as she thought about what he had just said and then also noted her flashbulb moment of comprehension.

'I see. At least I think I do.' Sophie sighed, amused despite herself by Evalina's manoeuvring. 'Your aunt thinks you…need to settle down? Is that it?'

Tapas and wine arrived, along with a pot of tea. Niccolo half smiled as she absently bypassed the tea and sipped some wine from the glass that had been poured. He shrugged.

'I am the only child of a traditional Italian family and that family very much includes my aunt, who sees me as something of a surrogate son, especially as my parents live in Italy. They are all of the opinion that marriage is what we everyone should aspire to.'

'Perhaps the fact that you have a young child also has something to do with it.' This man's personal life was none of her business, but she was relieved he had cleared the air because she didn't want complications and it would seem that neither did he.

He knew nothing about her aside from the fact that she came recommended by his aunt as someone who could be trusted with his daughter. She had brought her own references from the family she had nannied for in the past. That was the sum total of what he needed to know because her private life was hers and hers alone. If he wanted more formal qualifications, then he would have to look somewhere else. She would lose the life-line she had been hoping for, but if the past year and a half had taught her anything it was that she could cope with whatever was thrown at her.

She knew nothing about him and had no intention of asking questions. Had he been happily married? Was he still in mourning for his late wife?

'Why me?' she heard herself ask, bluntly.

'Who knows? Maybe because you have a shared love of allotments.'

'I'm glad you've brought this out into the open. If I wasn't what you were expecting, then you weren't what I had expected either. If we're being honest, I can tell you that I looked at you and had already made up my mind that the job wasn't going to work out.'

'Sorry?'

He looked genuinely startled. Sophie grasped why. He was so good-looking, so crazily *sexy*, just so eminently *eligible* that he was probably accustomed to women seeking him out rather than shutting the door in his face.

Just for a moment—a very brief moment—Sophie enjoyed the thought of bringing him down a notch or two. Good-looking guys were always just a little too self-satisfied, and this one—far and away the most disconcertingly good-looking man she had ever met— would be more self-satisfied than most. Made sense.

'I… I'm recently out of a poor relationship with a guy I should never have gone near.' She didn't bother beating about the bush. 'I saw you and the last thing I felt I could deal with was the situation of sharing space with you and…'

Niccolo's face was moving swiftly from resignation at having to clear the air, to surprise that she hadn't reacted as expected, to downright stupefaction.

'You thought that I might turn out to be…*what*? Some kind of *sex pest*?'

'It's been known,' Sophie returned frankly.

'I can't believe I'm hearing this! I have *never*, repeat, *never* heard anything quite so outrageous in my life before!'

Sophie stood her ground and met his outraged midnight-dark eyes without flinching. She'd forgotten about the wine, and the plates of delicious tapas, and the pot of tea she had insisted on hadn't begun to register at all. She was consumed by his energy and immersed in a bubble where everyone and everything around her had morphed into white noise. She'd never felt the intensity of anyone's personality the way she was feeling this man's right now, and that alarmed and panicked her. And excited her. Although that was an emotion she stifled before it could take root and cause any damage.

Her heart was pounding.

'I should ask,' she said, breaking the electric silence but not the eye contact that held her spellbound, 'do you intend to employ me for the position or not? Because if not, then I'll make my way back home and won't waste either your time or mine any further.'

CHAPTER TWO

NICCOLO WAS BEGINNING to wonder how a straightforward path had managed to become so convoluted. Expectations of a homely, middle-aged spinster baking cakes with Annalise while he carried on with his hectic work life now seemed as ridiculous as believing in fairies at the bottom of the garden.

Should he have firmly but politely told the woman now looking stubbornly at him that the position was no longer on the table? No further explanations needed.

Rhetorical question because he knew the answer to that one: he should have. The minute he had clocked what his aunt was up to, he should have taken appropriate steps to ensure the situation was nipped in the bud.

He knew that neither Evalina, nor his parents, could fully understand just how bitter the lessons learnt during his marriage had been for him and all the more so because of the speed with which his life had raced out of control, veering over the side of the cliff before he had time to find a brake or a rudder or anything at all that could help control its devastating collapse. Nor would they ever understand how profoundly he had absorbed the ruinous path his parents had taken, content to work for nothing, to enjoy the simple pleasures of life without realising that simple pleasures were never enough. The day of reckoning would always come, and when it did, simple pleasures just didn't cut it. His father's day of reckoning, after years of working for a pittance in a company that had never been going to elevate him beyond a certain point, had come when he'd had a stroke. When he had had to retire from his job. What kind of future would they both have been facing had he, Niccolo, not had the wherewithal to rescue them? To give them the life he felt they deserved?

And his marriage? A fiasco. He had thought, against his better judgement, to find that elusive love and happiness his parents had been desperate for him to have. It had been a mistake, with his daughter the only good thing to emerge from the disaster. He could remember those endless times facing a ceaseless barrage of recrimination from his wife, the tug of war trying to balance work and play, with Caroline wanting *'fun and attention'* and viciously condemning when he failed to deliver. From the moment the ring had been put on her finger, life had changed for him.

Nothing was ever right, and living in a war zone had driven him to despair.

Silence had become his friend.

No one knew how deeply affected he had been, so, of course, any hint of compliance by hiring the woman should have been out of the question.

The last thing he needed was his aunt imagining that he had conceded to her Cupid tricks. That would be opening a Pandora's box.

On the other hand…

He was in a bind. He needed cover and he knew that

there were some things you couldn't throw money at and get the required happy outcome.

The woman knew his daughter.

Was it any wonder he had hesitated? Why he had fought the impulse to do what his head had immediately told him to do? Why he had done the sensible thing and broached the thorny and delicate matter of laying down ground rules should he decide that he was prepared to go on his aunt's recommendations?

However much he disapproved of the reasoning behind said recommendations?

The fact that his first glimpse of her had taken his breath away had nothing to do with any subsequent decisions. The opposite! It had been all the more imperative to make it clear that he was out of bounds.

Whatever response he had anticipated, it hadn't been the one he'd received.

Who the heck was doing the interviewing here?

'Well?'

Still reeling from the shock of someone actually daring to think the unthinkable, Niccolo scowled.

'I've been put in an awkward position,' he returned, reasserting authority at speed. 'Evalina has vanished and I need help. So, to answer your question, the offer remains on the table with, as we have both acknowledged, certain conditions and ground rules in place.' He paused and searched for a less contentious footing from which to start their relationship. She was going to be in charge of his daughter, and a brooding and resentful nanny was the last thing he needed.

His eyes roved lazily over her cool, determined face and for the first time he found himself dealing with a situation he couldn't really remember having encoun-

tered before—an attractive woman who didn't automatically seek to please him.

He didn't want to stare or make her feel uncomfortable in any way, but hell, she was just so…spellbinding.
The way she was dressed and the tightly pulled-back
hair advertised someone wanting to downplay her as-
sets, but nothing could quite extinguish her impact.

He looked away and shifted, annoyed with himself
for being unable to control instincts he should be able
to master.

'Tell me how you met my aunt,' he said abruptly,
slamming shut the door on an imagination that was
threatening to steer his responses. 'You seem, if you
don't mind me saying, somewhat young to be working
on an allotment.'

Sophie's heart was still pounding. He unsettled her
in ways she couldn't quite understand. He had been
open and honest with her, which had allowed her to be
open with him in return. They had cleared the air. A
little embarrassed, she wondered how she could have
gone down the road of issuing warnings. The more
she looked at him—and she couldn't seem to stop herself from looking—the more she realised that he was
probably the last man on the planet to give the nanny
a second glance.

The man oozed sinful sex appeal. He could snap
his fingers and have any woman down tools and race
towards him. Sophie knew that she was attractive
enough, just as she knew that there were far more beautiful women out there than her and he was a guy who
would have no problem getting any of them.

Had Scott, with his determined pursuit that had

spanned so many years, somehow given her an inflated idea of how appealing she was to the opposite sex?

She had grown up with boys looking at her, but this wasn't a boy. This was a man, and he would certainly not be interested in a twenty-five-year-old woman with scant experience who was unsophisticated when it came to playing urbane, come-hither games with men.

She reddened just thinking about how misplaced her apprehensions had been, but then immediately reminded herself that it was better to be safe than sorry. She'd learnt that the hard way and it was a lesson she wasn't going to forget any time soon.

'I… They're very hard to come by in London.' Sophie felt as though she was releasing state secrets, even though she knew, realistically, that he was just asking the sort of normal questions any prospective employer would be asking. He wanted to find out about her, and that made sense given the role she would be accepting. Her nerves were all over the place, though. She could feel his dark eyes on her in a way that was disturbing and physical.

Was she making a mistake taking this job on?

She thought about the money problems that had plagued her since her parents had so suddenly and unexpectedly died and breathed in deeply. She had barely been able to mourn because her life had been thrown into such turmoil. She reminded herself how grateful she had been for Evalina's offer because the money would help clear some of the crushing debts.

Faced with that, what were a few harmless questions?

'I… I was actually studying land management at university…when… I had to cut short my course to deal with a few issues. I had a base in London, knew it well and decided to put my name down for an allotment, but before I could actually do that I found out a friend of a friend's grandfather was giving his up and I managed to secure it. I... I love gardening, had hoped to be a landscape gardener one day. Maybe that swung things in my favour. So many people don't look after their allotments the way they should.' She looked away and swallowed. She could feel her eyes welling up and wanted the ground to open and swallow her whole.

The thrust of a handkerchief against her clenched fist on the table was a shock.

'I think I must be one of the last people left in the world who still sees the value of a handkerchief.' He smiled. 'Take it. It's pristine, I promise.'

Their eyes tangled and Sophie nodded shakily.

'My apologies,' she said gruffly and was relieved when he moved swiftly along, acknowledging her apology with a shrug of his broad shoulders.

'You say you had *hoped* to be a landscape gardener one day?'

'Life had other plans,' Sophie said warily.

'And you would rather I didn't delve any further?'

'That's correct.' She held his gaze and refused to be sucked into over-confiding. What had Evalina told him about her? Not much, Sophie guessed, considering she had managed to leave out the most important fact, which was that she wasn't one of her contemporaries. In fairness, there wasn't much Sophie had told Evalina. Her grief still felt too raw, her heartbreak too recent and her life in too much of a mess to detail, so she had kept the conversation light and bland and talked about plants and her love of them.

Sophie wondered whether Evalina would have

started having mischievous notions if she had known how complicated her life really was, how very far from the straightforward plant-loving girl she really was.

She had spent ages with Annalise when she had visited the allotments, showing her the vegetable plants she had started to put in, the flowering plants that would bloom in time. It had been soothing. It had made her feel peaceful, had reminded her of the way her mother had patiently shared her own love of gardening.

The money was important and the fact that she would have a roof over her head for a while was also important, but Sophie felt that she had formed a bond with the little girl, which had played a great part in her accepting Evalina's offer.

Niccolo looked at her guarded expression and for the first time felt the kick of curiosity.

A man? A broken heart? A broken heart that had made her issue her crazy warning to him? What had happened to have caused her to quit a course that could have advanced her career?

He was surprised at how powerful the impulse was to question her further about a personal life that was none of his business, because he had a marked lack of curiosity when it came to asking questions, possibly because he was so accustomed to women providing answers without much encouragement. The less you asked, the lighter things were, and he liked things light and breezy and uncomplicated.

'You have previously worked for a family as a nanny, I understand. My aunt mentioned something of the sort when she recommended you. I'm guessing this was before you embarked on your now abandoned university career?'

'I can provide references if you like.' She reached down to her backpack and pulled out a number of brochures. She casually rearranged the plates on the table, absently popping some kind of mini meat pastry into her mouth, making room for the paperwork.

Tendrils of hair were escaping the confines of all the clips she had used to tie it back.

Watching her, Niccolo distractedly thought that there was something fresh and genuine about her. Was that an illusion? He didn't go for the *butter wouldn't melt* types. He liked things straightforward and wasn't interested in the usual courting games that presumed a conclusion involving a bridal shop and a walk up an aisle.

He also didn't do cut-glass accents and boarding-school backgrounds. Having entered that world with his ex, he now stayed true to his own background. Definitely smoky singer in a club as opposed to soprano diva at an opera.

On all fronts, Sophie Baxter didn't make the grade, so why was he so compelled to look? What was it about her that stirred his imagination?

Whatever it was, it wasn't going to do, and it annoyed him that for once he was finding it difficult to rein in his responses.

She raised her eyes, true blue that almost veered into violet, and he shifted uncomfortably in the chair once again.

When she thrust a piece of paper towards him, he reluctantly took it and read a glowing recommendation from the family for whom she had nannied three years previously.

Oddly, and if he'd wanted any further reassurances about taking her on, he knew the family in question. He had done business with the guy only a handful of months previously. He was as solid, as respectable and as trustworthy as they came. Small world, but he knew only too well that it was a village when it came to people who were filthy rich.

'How did you find this family?'

Sophie hesitated. She thought of her darling parents, struggling without her knowing to maintain a façade, and all for her. To keep her at the expensive private school, to fund the university fees and the holidays and a lifestyle she could happily have done without.

Two people who had started out comfortably enough, she guessed, from weeks of scouring a million bank statements and a thousand receipts. Her father had been a partner at an accountancy firm and her mother had been a very happy housewife.

At some point within the past five years, things had gone horribly wrong. A poor investment had spread all sorts of toxic tentacles through their finances and, reading between the lines, Sophie had sensed the panic that must have overwhelmed her dad because he had thrown bad money after good in an attempt to staunch the haemorrhaging of cash. With a mortgage still on their house in London and bills to pay, she could only imagine how fearful he must have been.

The heady days when he had known the likes of Eric and Lina Buhler seemed like a lifetime ago now that she was sitting here, remembering those times of innocence.

She wasn't going to go down any roads of sharing

confidences, though. Niccolo had made it very clear that lines of demarcation between them had to be in place for this to work.

However much she found him disconcerting, she wasn't going to nervously impart any information that wasn't strictly necessary, and it wasn't necessary for him to know anything about her parents. He was free to assume what he wanted.

'They were recommended to me.' She lowered her eyes. 'I enjoy skiing and I wanted a bit of time out before uni. It seemed like a good idea and it was great fun. I loved it and I got along very well with the Buhlers. They are a lovely family. I haven't done any nannying since then, but I've met your daughter and we've clicked.' She nudged the brochures and pamphlets towards him and Niccolo duly scooped the top two up and perused them.

Museums…a Disney art exhibition…the zoo…lots of gardens… She'd done her due diligence and that impressed him because she obviously hadn't taken anything for granted simply because she came with his aunt's blessing. She was leaning towards him, her white-blonde hair escaping around her flushed cheeks, her violet eyes one hundred per cent focused on him, her lips slightly parted.

'Good.' He sat back and looked at her carefully. 'And will there be any impediment to your living with Annalise and me for the duration of your tenure? This is important to me because as much as I try, it's impossible to dictate my working hours. You'll need to be on hand to cover those times when I can't make it home… as early as I would like.' He paused, guiltily aware that far too often he worked late, and with his aunt there he had become too comfortable with long hours. In the wake of his failed marriage and after his wife had died, Niccolo had striven to work normal hours, but it was difficult running his sprawling empire between the strict hours of nine to five. He had all the money in the world but not enough time. Work was his fortress and it had been easy to sit behind those impregnable walls, controlling the direction of his life, but had he somehow become a less than effective father in the process? He adored his daughter, but was adoration enough? Things, he suspected, would have to change with a new woman on the scene. He would have to be physically present to keep an eye on proceedings.

'What sort of impediment?'

'Parents? A relative you may be looking after? Unresolved boyfriend issues? Cats? Dogs? Goldfish?'

'I...' She paused as she blindly sought the handkerchief she had rested on her lap. 'No, there won't be any impediment.'

Niccolo looked at her for a few moments, head tilted to one side, then he sat forward and briskly slapped both hands on the table. 'Right. Here's what is going to happen next. You'll get a contract from my PA, which you will be required to sign.' He named a weekly salary that he could hear took her breath away. 'That will be your basic pay,' he said. 'Purely covers nine to five. You start work earlier or end later and you will be compensated accordingly.' He paused. 'I hope you don't think that we got off on the wrong foot, Miss Baxter—'

'Sophie, please.' She tried a smile on for size.

'And of course, you must call me Niccolo.'

'And no, I don't think we got off on the wrong foot. Makes it easier, knowing that...'

'That there will be no unpleasant mixed messages? Agreed. Moving on... I will expect you on Monday at eight a.m. sharp. I have a series of meetings but I can push them back so I can show you the ropes.' He hesitated. 'I may work long hours, but let there be no mistake: my daughter is the centre of my life, and I am putting a great deal of faith in you that you won't let me down.'

'I won't.'

'Whether I am physically in the house or not, there will be a strict rule in place that there are no parties... or men sleeping over...'

'There won't be!'

'You'll be relinquishing your free movement for a few weeks,' he elaborated gently. 'Whatever situation you may have been through that's brought you here...' He found himself pausing, giving her time to jump in. She didn't. 'You're young and you might find it difficult having your wings temporarily cut to some degree, and I say to some degree because you will naturally have your time to do as you wish outside the house whenever I am at home. I intend to spend as much of the weekends as possible working from home.'

'Can I ask you something?'

'I'm all ears.' He made a magnanimous, sweeping gesture with one hand and relaxed back.

'Do you *ever* stop working?'

For the second time that evening, Niccolo was knocked for six.

His aunt nagged him about the hours he worked. So did his parents. He indulged them.

Beyond those privileged three, no one had ever

broached the subject, including the many women he had dated in the past. He'd never had to make a point of it. Perhaps they had all read invisible warnings he had projected and steered clear from a topic that would spell the end of any relationship.

He had emerged from a broken marriage where the hours he worked had become a bone of contention, always to be used whenever an attack was to be made.

He had no intention of returning to that place. Reproving dark eyes clashed with calm, serene violet ones.

'How I choose to spend my time is of no concern to you and has no bearing on this job,' he said coolly, and he was perversely even more furious when she shrugged.

'Of course, I understand,' Sophie murmured, dropping her eyes.

'What exactly is it that you understand?'

'I'll be paid to do a job and part of that job is never to ask any questions. You give orders and I obey them.'

'That's not quite the situation as I see it,' Niccolo inserted. 'Whatever questions you ask about your duties will be welcomed. Beyond that, everything is off limits.'

'Of course.'

'I'll expect regular briefings, but my plan, as I said, is to try and limit my working hours while my aunt is away.' He felt restless, edgy. It wasn't just that the woman wasn't what he had been expecting. There was something about her that unsettled him, that derailed his usual cool, clear thought processes and encouraged wayward thoughts.

'If I choose not to go out…er…when you're around,

would I be expected to…? I'm assuming that it would be okay for me to retire to my bedroom?'

'Of course. This is a business arrangement, Sophie. I don't expect you to hover in the background waiting for instructions when I'm in the house. I'll take over the minute I return home and you're then free to do whatever you want.'

He couldn't have given a more clear-cut answer and yet there was something that didn't feel quite as businesslike an arrangement as it should, and she wondered whether that was because she was so *aware* of him. He made every nerve in her body go into full alert mode, made the hairs on the back of her neck stand on end. In every way he was compelling, and she wondered how this arrangement, which had seemed such a godsend at the time, was actually going to work.

She couldn't possibly vacate the house every evening. She couldn't afford to go anywhere, for a start. She'd also, in the aftermath of her unravelling life, discovered just how unreliable good friends could be. When they'd thought she had money, when she'd been one of them, they'd been there, happy to socialise, keen to drag her out to whichever club was the flavour of the month, even if she would rather have stayed in. And when everything had come crashing down and life as she'd known it had become a thing of the past, they had sympathised, but honestly, where were they now?

Invites had dried up and she would have struggled to find the cash to go anyway. When you mixed with the rich crowd, they quickly lost patience, she had found, with anyone who couldn't keep up, and there was no way she could any more.

Only a handful of friends had stuck by her, for which she was grateful, but she knew that they tactfully avoided asking her to places that cost a lot, and there were only so many occasions when they wanted to entertain at home.

She had vacated one world and entered another and this new world did not accommodate lots of after-work activities. Even going solo to the movies would require thought because every penny saved was a penny towards paying off the bills that needed sorting.

So she would be confined to her bedroom, hesitant about venturing out when he was there because she didn't want to bump into him, though it was likely inevitable. How big was his house going to be, after all?

When she thought about that, her head felt woozy at the series of uncomfortable images suddenly crowding in, jostling for space.

She pictured him relaxed, in a pair of jeans and a T-shirt, barefoot and roaming at all hours of the day and night, turning her every waking moment into a cat-and-mouse game just to avoid the peculiar effect he had on her nervous system.

'There'll be no need for you to do anything of a household nature,' he belatedly added. 'I have someone who comes in daily for a couple of hours to clean and a dedicated chef on standby. Of course, my aunt would have nothing to do with anyone getting under her feet in the kitchen...'

Sophie smiled and relaxed when she thought about Evalina. 'I know. I don't think she appreciates anyone touching her homegrown produce on the allotment either. She's very competitive when it comes to what everyone else grows. My beans never seemed to be quite as good as hers, as she very kindly pointed out on one occasion. Not as long and definitely not as fat and juicy. She offered to bring a measuring tape to prove it.'

Niccolo burst out laughing. 'Evalina is never backward when it comes to speaking her mind.'

'Has she always been like that?'

'As far back as I can recall. Two sisters and they couldn't have been more different. My mother was the dutiful wife and Evalina was the nomad who travelled the world.'

'Yes, she's told me a lot about her adventures.' Curiosity crept stealthily through her, making a mockery of her vow to remain uninterested and detached. Ground rules, after all, had been laid down on both sides but the temptation to side-step them was too great. There was something about the depth of his eyes, the tug of the forbidden pulling her to go beyond the lines he had laid down. 'I'm an only child so I wouldn't know, but isn't it odd that sisters can be so different? How lovely that your mum was there for you while Evalina travelled. She must have wafted in and brought lots of excitement when she came.'

Niccolo hesitated. 'She did,' he admitted. 'My parents led a very…predictable life. Evalina brought the scent of adventure. To a young child like me, it was always a thrill having her around.'

'Annalise adores her.'

'She does.'

He wondered how they had made it to this topic. Her eyes were calm and interested but nothing about her manner suggested anything other than the sort of polite small talk that might happen at the tail end of a conversation.

He hadn't shut the conversation down, as he normally would have, because she wasn't trying to wheedle her way into his affections. She'd be living under his roof, he uneasily decided, so where was the harm in a bit of harmless chit-chat? They could hardly plan on spending the next few weeks in a state of freezing silence, interrupted only by exchanges about Annalise.

Even so...

This would not become a trend. He wasn't going to be settling down to cosy evenings in, chatting about this, that and nothing in particular, simply because she happened to be temporarily living with him.

He wasn't going to forget that she was there for a very specific reason.

He abruptly relegated that brief lapse to the history books. 'Naturally, you'll want to return to your home to see your parents in your free time. In which case, you can bring as much or as little as you think you'll need when you move in on Monday...'

Sophie reddened. For a few seconds, she appeared lost for words, struggling to find some kind of coherent response.

'I...no, I don't live with my parents.' She glanced away, as though waiting for him to pick up the thread of the conversation and move on to something else, but he didn't. His eyes bored with laser intensity into her as he waited for her to speak.

'I... Actually, my family home is in the process of being sold...so...'

'When?'

'When what?'

'When are you due to move out?'

'I... The new occupants will be moving in in a few weeks' time.' She rubbed her temples and appeared startled when he reached across the table and brushed her wrist with his finger.

'Are you all right, Sophie?'

'Of course!' She smiled brightly.

'If you've always lived in the family home then it would be upsetting to think of moving house.' He looked at her, expression shuttered, noting the way she couldn't meet his eyes. The smile was bright. The eyes were telling a different story.

'These things happen,' she said stiffly.

She finally looked at him and her violet eyes were defiant. Niccolo appreciated her stubborn refusal to pour her heart out. There was a story there, but she had no intention of telling it. She had her boundaries and, for a man who had his, that was something to be respected.

'They do,' he murmured smoothly and called for the bill. 'My driver can collect you on Monday along with whatever possessions you want to bring with you for the duration of your contract.'

'No! It's fine. I can always return if I need more stuff,' she expanded, evading his searching gaze.

'In that case...' Bill paid, Niccolo began rising to his feet and Sophie hurriedly followed suit, reaching down for her backpack and scooping up all the pamphlets and brochures still on the table. 'Like I said, my PA will be in touch with all the details, and I look

forward to seeing you next week.' He held out his
hand to shake hers and a jolt of electric charge shot
through him, as powerful as though he'd suddenly
been plugged into a live socket.

CHAPTER THREE

SOPHIE REALISED SEVERAL things very quickly the following Monday when she showed up for duty promptly at eight a.m. wheeling her suitcase behind her and burdened by an assortment of various other bags.

The first was that she wouldn't be popping back to the family home on a regular basis. Of course, she would return once every few days to check the post, but, since nearly all the companies she was dealing with now had her email address, physical bills through the door were scant. The truth was, the second she shut that front door behind her, turning around for one last look at the pretty Georgian edifice that had been the bedrock of her entire life, she had felt a sense of release.

With military efficiency, the contract Niccolo had mentioned had been in her message box within two hours of her leaving the wine bar, and the stipulated duration of her employment would be a month, on an eye-wateringly generous pay package.

A month away from being in the family home, with its sad reminders of better times and memories of how much love she had known within those walls, had seemed like manna from heaven.

Any uncertainties she had entertained over the

weekend about Niccolo and his peculiar, unwelcome effect on her had dissipated, and by the time she had lugged her case to the front door of his London mansion she had convinced herself that this month away would mark a turning point in her life.

On that optimistic note, she had been dismayed to find that her glib assumption that he couldn't possibly be as disturbing as she had originally thought was way off target.

When he had answered the door the breath left her body in a whoosh and she momentarily lost all power of speech.

He was taller than she'd recalled, sexier than she'd remembered, and as much of a challenge as she'd sincerely hoped he wouldn't be.

But she'd swallowed back her unwelcome response, allowed him to carry her cases and various bags in, somehow managing to reply when he'd asked her, with amusement, whether she hadn't found the journey on public transport a little tedious with so much stuff.

He had been scrupulously polite as he'd shown her to her room, a word which did no justice to the sweeping suite which would be her home from home for the next few weeks.

Thank goodness for Annalise, who had hopped along with them, an unwitting chaperone keeping nerves at bay and allowing her to have something else to focus on—though not even that little hand slipped into hers could distract from Niccolo's overwhelming presence.

It had been a relief when he had finally excused himself to leave for the office.

Annalise, a beautiful child with long dark hair, was

a joy. Having only seen her at the allotment when she had been there with Evalina, Sophie now relished the chance to get to know her better.

She had numerous activities lined up, but in the end it was a bright day, warm and cloud-free, and so they took a picnic to the allotment and spent much of the day there, peacefully weeding and planting and going through some of the gardening books Sophie stored in her little shed.

They brought out two deckchairs at lunchtime and chatted, and she was glad for the easy tranquillity, which soothed her troubled mind.

Annalise reminded Sophie of herself as a child: quiet, thoughtful, curious.

How had her mother's death, she wondered, affected the little girl? She would have been young at the time, but of course Evalina would have been there for her. And her father.

The minute Sophie began thinking about Niccolo, her mind went off at a tangent and it was next to impossible to rein it in.

And yet...for all that...for the first time in a very long time, she felt *alive*, capable of thoughts that weren't depressing and inward turned.

Even when she had been fool enough to be persuaded into a relationship with Scott, she hadn't felt so...alert, so stimulated...so aware that there was life happening out there still...

It puzzled her how one perfect stranger should have kickstarted such a fundamental change in her, but perhaps she'd lived for so many months dealing with everything on her own that just coming into contact with someone else, someone disassociated with what she was going through, accounted for her reaction.

That and the fact that the man is impossibly good-looking, a little voice whispered inside her head.

Disillusioned though she'd been after Scott, and determined as she had been to give men a wide berth for the foreseeable future, she was still, it would seem—against all odds—a woman capable of feeling things even if those things happened to be things she didn't want to feel.

Having convinced herself that the mansion he lived in was plenty big enough for them to co-exist without too much crossover—and besides, he would be hard at work until who knew what time of the night—she was taken aback when, after a day at the allotment and part of the afternoon at the park near by, she opened the door to find that her employer was not conveniently holed up wherever he worked. He greeted them, larger than life, emerging from one of the doors that led out of the spectacular highly polished marble hallway, where two small Picasso paintings sat alongside a more substantial Hockney.

'You're here.' Sophie walked slowly towards him while Annalise flew ahead before screeching to a stop as though suddenly aware that she shouldn't fling herself into her dad's arms but perhaps shake his hand instead.

From what Sophie had seen, there was certainly love and affection in abundance there, but it didn't seem to transmit into hugs and kisses.

Had those hugs and kisses been the domain of his wife—Annalise's mother?

Their eyes met over Annalise's dark head and Sophie blushed.

'I thought I'd return early as you're still finding your feet and we haven't had a chance to chat about the arrangements.' He ruffled his daughter's hair and smiled down at her before once again looking at Sophie, moving slowly towards her while Annalise fell into step alongside him.

'Good!' Sophie said brightly. She wondered whether he was checking up on her and thought that that was to be expected and a good thing, in a way.

'It's after five-thirty.' Still in his work clothes, he glanced at his Rolex then back to her. 'Why don't you go and freshen up? I will sort out my daughter's dinner and have some time with her, then I'll order some dinner for us and you can debrief me on how your day today has been, fill me in on anything you feel I should know.'

Sophie hovered. Dinner together? When she'd thought about their infrequent meetings to discuss Annalise, she'd imagined something more formal. Not requiring a suit, a briefcase and a PowerPoint presentation, but not a million miles off.

She opened her mouth to tell him that she would be more than happy to settle Annalise but then, looking at the rapt expression on the little girl's face, she realised that her father taking time out to spend with her was not an everyday occurrence. It was something to get excited about.

'You look like a rabbit caught in the headlights,' he murmured, standing directly in front of her now, and looking down into her upturned face. 'No need to panic. It won't be the Spanish Inquisition.'

'Of course not,' Sophie returned in the same bright voice, her expression glazed. 'But my feet haven't had a chance to really touch the ground, and of course I'm nervous at the thought that you might want to quiz me because you don't trust me.'

She started when he leaned close to her, close enough for her to feel his warm breath when he whispered, lazily, 'I trust you, Sophie. If I didn't, I would have had you followed. You come recommended by my aunt, though, and to do such a thing would have gone against the grain. So relax. We're going to be in one another's company for the next few weeks. You're going to have to learn not to look at me as though I might bite.'

He drew back but his dark eyes were still pinned to her face and he was smiling, eyebrows raised, his expression amused but watchful.

Was he playing games with her? No, he was being utterly serious. He really *would* have had her followed, and the thought of that sent a shiver down her spine.

He might be the perfect gentleman and together they might have worked out their boundary lines, but he was leaving her in no doubt that he called the shots.

She was pretty sure he would have checked up on her references. Had he also checked up on *her*? Unearthed her past? How much of her life was still private?

The questions pinged in her head for the next hour and a half as she roamed around her suite of rooms, too anxious to appreciate her luxurious surroundings.

Her massive bedroom overlooked an actual *garden* big enough for flowerbeds and a paved area with extensive seating. There was also a massive en suite bathroom and a sitting area with a television. It wasn't Evalina's—not unless he had had the wardrobes cleared of all her clothing—which meant that she would have her own quarters somewhere else. It was a four-storeyed house. It made her parents' place, which she had always considered big, look like a doll's house in comparison.

She'd spent most of her formative years mixing with the wealthy. Here she had a glimpse of how those people several hundred steps above actually lived.

She'd brought what she'd considered suitable and sufficient, provided she kept on top of the laundry. After a long bath, which felt like the very height of luxury because this place was like a hotel, and if she closed her eyes she could forget that her nagging problems were just a heartbeat away, she changed into jeans, a T-shirt and some espadrilles and headed down to the kitchen.

She'd barely had time since she'd arrived to explore the house because it had felt rude, but without Annalise next to her she opened a few doors and looked into a series of spectacular rooms.

In the hallways pale wood replaced the marble used in the wide entrance hall, and the rugs were silk and looked priceless, co-ordinating with the art on the walls, which also looked priceless. It was an uncluttered modern house that just escaped being minimalist.

She hesitated outside the kitchen door, which was ajar, and then pushed it open on a deep, steadying breath.

Niccolo looked up from where he was sitting at the kitchen table, laptop open in front of him, and half rose, nodding to the seat opposite him. She duly slid into it and rested her hands on the table.

'Glass of wine?' he offered, reaching for the bottle of red in front of him, and Sophie shook her head. 'Tell me about your day.'

'Hasn't Annalise told you what we did?'

'I'd like to hear your version.'

She smiled stiffly and relayed how they had spent the day, from beginning to end. She fidgeted under his steady, dark gaze, shying away and back to feeling as though she was in the witness box, being asked deceptively easy questions that might or might not be leading straight into quicksand. He had a watchful way about him that made her want to babble. It also made her want to defend herself, even though she didn't know what she should be defending herself against because he hadn't accused her of anything.

Eventually her voice tapered off, at which point he said, matter-of-factly, 'I didn't have you followed but I did do a few rudimentary checks on you...'

Sophie didn't say anything. Of course he had. It would have been an oversight of his not to have done so. Trusting his aunt was one thing but no one got to the top of the food chain by being a fool.

Still, she felt violated.

How much did he know about her? She'd always been a private person and events over the past year and a half had made her even more so. She had dealt with all the money issues, with all the emotional issues, on her own, and thinking that this sloe-eyed sexy stranger *knew* some of her history sent a ripple of alarm and panic racing through her.

Logic and reason had no part in her sudden tension and the overpowering temptation to tell him that her life was none of his business.

'Your parents…' Niccolo said quietly.

She wasn't looking at him.

'Why didn't you do your background checks before I came to the interview?' She looked at him with bitter, accusing eyes.

'I wanted to meet you first. I imagine you've had a tough time of things and I'm very sorry about your parents, Sophie.'

'It's none of your business.'

'Your background became my business when I agreed to hire you to look after my daughter.'

Sophie sighed and looked at him. 'They died in a car accident,' she said quietly. 'It was rainy. My dad lost control. They hadn't been drinking and it wasn't even really all that late at night either. It was just one of those things.' She hadn't spoken about this to anyone in a long time. She had held it all to herself while life carried on around her, amidst the sadness and the confusion. She'd thought it would be difficult to actually talk about what had happened, but now that she had begun, she could feel a sense of release sweeping over her.

'I was at uni. I had a career ahead of me and then just like that life came crashing down and I was drowning.'

She realised that this was now the second time in a matter of days that a man who was, really, a complete stranger had brought her close to crying. She wished she'd hung on to that handkerchief. There was a river of tears inside her and she knew that it was going to burst its banks and overflow, but suddenly she didn't care.

'I was very close to my parents. They were ripped away from me and I just couldn't really cope.' She held her head in her hands and stared down at the smooth surface of the table, not bothering to try and staunch the tears that had been a long time coming. She felt them leak out and then there he was. How had he moved so quickly to put his arms around her?

Suddenly, that physical contact seemed the most comforting thing in the world.

She was dampening his shirt. She also wanted to blow her nose. After a few seconds, she drew in a shuddering breath and sat back and said, prosaically, 'I'm sorry. Your shirt's wet.'

'It'll live to fight another day. I have another handkerchief.'

'A constant supply.'

'Like I said, old habits die hard. My father was a fan of handkerchiefs. Inherited trait. Tell me what happened, Sophie.'

She wanted to. It was the strangest thing. Had she bottled everything up for so long that all it took was a kind word from a stranger for the dam to burst?

She talked about her parents, remembering small details and smiling at the memories. She could sense some of the darkness leaving her. It felt good to let it all out of her system.

'You probably know that I have considerable money problems,' Sophie said in conclusion as she finally looked at him, in control of herself now. 'I suppose that would have been one of the first things any background check would have thrown up.' She sighed. 'It all came out in the wash. Poor investments, over-extension on the mortgage... They did everything within their power to keep me in the life I was accustomed to.' She pressed fingers over her eyes and rubbed them wearily. 'They didn't think to ask me whether any of that mattered or not.'

'And would it have?'

'No!' She laughed bitterly. 'Private school was fine. The classes were small and the surroundings were amazing, but the other kids… Some were great, but a lot were privileged and entitled and downright annoying.'

Niccolo smiled.

'I've met a fair few of the entitled and privileged in my time,' he admitted drily, 'and I must say I agree wholeheartedly with your sentiments.'

'I took this job for a lot of reasons,' Sophie told him truthfully. 'Of course, I really do like kids, and I really do like your daughter. She's…very special.'

'But you also need the money.'

'I'm not materialistic,' Sophie automatically protested, and he raised his eyebrows wryly.

'Have I levelled that accusation at you?'

Sophie shrugged. 'I've had to sell an awful lot of things to pay off all the debts that just kept coming on a daily basis.' She grimaced. 'I also had to sell the family home. It still had a mortgage but there should be sufficient money made from the sale to clear the majority of the debt. So yes, I took the job because I need the money. And being here for a month? It buys me a bit of breathing space while I decide what happens next now the house is sold and there's nothing left but memories to pack up.'

'Would you return to your studies?'

Sophie laughed without humour. 'I don't think that's on the cards. It's a luxury I can't run to. Maybe one day. No, for now I'm compiling a résumé to go into landscape gardening. It's something I would love to do and it's possible someone out there might be prepared to give me a chance.' She paused and looked at him without flinching. 'Working on the allotment will help. I've got an excellent idea of how harmonious spaces can be created with vegetables and fruits and plants built around office spaces so that people can work and simultaneously be calm and relaxed. I think I could put together some good ideas on how this concept could be turned into something really special.'

Another first. Talking about a plan for the future. She scooped up her hair with one hand and then absently began braiding it into one thick plait while she looked at him uncertainly.

'I suppose you're going to tell me that my services are no longer required...'

'Come again?'

'I realise I...must have come across as...as...something of an emotional train wreck and I can only think that that's a trait you might not want in an employee.'

'You lost your parents without warning and you've been dealing with the wreckage of what was left behind,' Niccolo said gently. 'So, do I consider you an emotional train wreck? No. I don't.' He looked at her steadily. 'In fact,' he continued pensively, 'it helps that you need the money. I sense you'll be prepared to go the extra mile when it comes to working more hours, and as an added incentive I will escalate your pay on a sliding scale. The later you work and the more demands I find I need to make of you, the more your pay will rise.'

'There's no need to do that. You're already paying me far more than I could get anywhere else.'

'I will also send someone to help you collate the

things you want to keep from your family home and I'll arrange the necessary storage.'

'I don't feel comfortable with that.'

'Why not?'

'Because…it's not part of the job. If I were to get a regular nanny job through a regular nanny agency, there's no employer who would do favours like that.'

'I can afford it and let's call it buying your loyalty and ensuring my trust in you isn't misplaced. I will arrange for half of the money to be transferred to your account tomorrow with the other half to follow when your stint is at an end. While you're here, you're to put everything pertaining to Annalise on expenses and I'll ensure you have a separate credit card for that purpose and a few hundred quid in petty cash.'

Sophie gasped, with a shade of discomfort. 'A few hundred pounds in petty cash? That's very generous.'

'Yet you look as though you're tempted to turn down the offer. I wouldn't get into a lather about it, Sophie. Anyone casting an eye over the accounts that cover the payroll for my many, many companies will find one thing in common: I pay well. Over the odds. Substantially so. I find that the fatter the pay cheque the more loyal the employee, and for me, loyalty is everything.'

'You like buying people,' Sophie mused, then reddened because the remark was inappropriate, given that he was her boss. He appeared to think about what she'd said, though, and when he spoke, softly, it was to concur.

'I find it works,' he murmured.

On a subconscious level, Niccolo acknowledged that that had been ingrained into the fabric of his life for a very long time. He had seen how his parents had lived their lives—dependent and in the service of those higher up the pecking order—and it was a life he had chosen to reject.

For Niccolo, that rejection meant rising and rising fast to a place where he was dependent on no one, a place where no one could ever call the shots and expect him to follow. He would never be a follower. The collapse of his marriage had taught him that the path he had chosen was just not compatible with the demands of any relationship that required exhaustive emotional input. Everything had imploded quickly with Caroline, all done and dusted in under four years, but had it stretched out for longer, would it have been any more successful? No.

Yet no one had ever pointed that out to him quite so bluntly. He was disconcerted to find himself suddenly and thankfully very briefly questioning that firmly held belief, the lodestar which had guided his life.

'Food.' He cut short the conversation and stood up. 'I can order something in.'

'I...' Was this going to be a habit? Sophie wondered. She was acutely conscious of the very personal information she had shared, even though the information had already been in his domain. She had embellished the bare bones, had released so many feelings, and something was telling her now that that kind of release was utterly inappropriate, given their situation.

It wasn't simply the fact that she was being paid by him to do a job. It was because he was a man who put money and what it could buy, including people, over and above everything else.

He might be a good listener, but it would be a mistake to be lulled into thinking that she could vent to him about what she had gone through. She couldn't. In fact, when she thought about that, about another intimate conversation, she felt a shiver of apprehension.

'You've been here a handful of minutes,' Niccolo said briskly. 'I don't expect you to scuttle up to your bedroom, hungry and disoriented because I don't want company. You needn't fear that you'll be compelled to dine with me whenever I'm here. In fact, my hours are so unpredictable that that would be impossible anyway.'

'Good.' Sophie smiled.

'Interesting response,' Niccolo said wryly. 'Are you usually this forthright? No, scratch that. I think I've already reached the conclusion that you are. Dinner? What do you want?'

'I don't mind. Thank you.'

'In which case,' Niccolo drawled, 'I'll see what's available here and wing it.'

He spun round and walked towards the fridge and peered inside.

Sophie wanted to drag her eyes away from him but she couldn't. The way he moved, fluid and economic, was arresting. She could almost *see* the flex of powerful muscles under the T-shirt and the faded jeans.

How on earth could she have actually poured her heart and soul out to him? The ease with which she had opened up baffled and scared her because she had been so determined never to trust a man again. At least not until she was strong enough to deal with it.

'You…er…cook?' she asked politely, breaking the silence and watching as he took stuff out of the fridge.

As with the rest of the impressive house, everything

in the kitchen seemed to be beyond expensive, from the metal and granite table where she was seated, to the pale, oversized tiles on the floor and the dull brushed chrome of the appliances. It was a marvel of grey and white that was both functional and aesthetically beautiful at the same time.

Niccolo turned to look at her for a few seconds.

It was a relief to have put some physical distance between them.

Back to business. He had laid his cards on the table, told her what his background checks had uncovered, and she had been open with him. No, he hadn't expected the conversation to be quite so emotional, although he should have predicted it, but he had risen to the occasion and she had quickly regained her self-control.

She clearly had no interest in shared meals and that suited him fine, even if it *was* a first for him.

She could be a distraction. Something about her got under his skin and he was very happy to take whatever steps were necessary to avoid dealing with that unexpected occurrence.

He would want to communicate with her often about Annalise, but he could easily do so in the relative formality of his home office.

Looking at her now, he caught himself thinking, once again, how very unusual her eyes were, then he snapped out of it and said with a self-deprecating shrug, 'I'm Italian. I grew up with my father at the stove. I used to stand on a chair, watching him make pasta.'

'That sounds wonderful.'

'I don't have time to do very much cooking these

days.' Niccolo wasn't looking at her. He was chopping tomatoes, smelling the herbs he had extracted from the fridge and thinking how long it had been since he had lifted a hand in the kitchen. And when it came to women...

Home-cooked meals at the kitchen table definitely weren't on the agenda.

He was always upfront about his lack of interest in anything remotely permanent, but just in case the message wasn't relayed in sufficiently loud and clear tones he made it a priority to give no encouragement.

His home was his space where he spent time with his family. He had a penthouse apartment in Mayfair, and that was where he spent time with whatever woman he happened to be seeing.

Hot nights and no sleepovers.

'That's a shame. I expect cooking for other people is a bit like gardening is for me. Something restful that takes the stress out of everyday life.'

'I find a chef can do that just as well.'

He expertly threw ingredients into a frying pan, smelling and seasoning as he went, flicking the pan with his hand so that the chopped vegetables somersaulted in the olive oil and butter.

'It'll be ten minutes.' Niccolo turned to her and for a few seconds their eyes tangled, and he drew in a sharp, unsteady breath.

She'd admitted to a lot, he realised, probably a lot more than either of them had expected. He had inadvertently opened a door to an outpouring of emotion that had been bottled up for months while she dealt with the material fallout from her parents' death.

So much revealed and yet...on one matter she had been conspicuously silent.

What about the guy who'd made her bitter enough to be cautious when she had first met him? Where did he figure in this whole scheme of things?

And suddenly there it was again...curiosity. The last thing he needed...

CHAPTER FOUR

'SHALL WE COUNT the number of floors?'

But that was never going to be possible. Neither she nor Annalise stood any chance of working out how many storeys made up the glass skyscraper that towered above them.

She looked down at the little girl's rapt expression and grinned. 'Are you looking forward to taking the lift to your dad's office, or are you scared? I'm scared. You have to promise to hold my hand and not let go.'

Actually, there was an element of truth in that remark. *Scared* might not be the right word but she was certainly nervous, and it wasn't because the lift would be whizzing them up to one of the offices in the building, but because of who would be waiting to greet them and take them both out to lunch.

After days of seeing Niccolo only in passing, he had unexpectedly arrived back to the house three hours ahead of schedule one day to find them in the kitchen, where Sophie was sitting at the table while, opposite her, Annalise worked at tracing a picture of a flower, her face scrunched up with concentration.

Sophie had looked up and there he'd been, looming

in the doorway, filling it and in the act of cuffing the sleeves of his white shirt.

Her throat had gone dry, and she'd been conscious of a slow burn that spread from the inside out, firing up nerve-endings she hadn't known even existed.

What had he been thinking? It had been a hot day and he had surprised her as she'd relaxed after a morning with her little charge at Kew Gardens followed by a picnic under a spreading tree, which had been absolutely idyllic.

She'd been wearing a pair of denim shorts and a T-shirt and no bra, her hair all over the place. She'd felt grubby and she'd *looked* grubby, and even though the dark eyes that had briefly rested on her flushed face had revealed nothing, she'd taken less than two seconds to fill in the blanks and speculate at what had been going through his head.

A kid in charge of a kid.

Since she'd started working for him, Sophie had more than once berated herself for ever imagining that she might find herself in the awkward position of having to fend off unwanted advances.

When she remembered how she had practically warned him off, she cringed with embarrassment.

Memories of Scott had been in charge of her response, but even so…how on earth could she ever have imagined that someone like Niccolo Ferri would ever be tempted to behave in an inappropriate way towards her?

He was the very essence of gentlemanly decency. He was scrupulously polite without being stand-offish with her. Because he rattled her didn't mean that he was the slightest bit interested in her aside from judging her ability to look after his daughter.

He was nothing like Scott.

From nowhere, that thought flitted through Sophie's head as she held Annalise's hand and they made their way into the impressive foyer of the skyscraper.

He was nothing like Scott and she wasn't nervous now because of how he might react to her, but because of how she would react to him...

She feared her own responses, which were wildly out of sync whenever she was in his presence. Her head kept telling her how she should behave but something wayward and disobedient kept letting the side down.

She didn't want any wayward anything letting down any sides.

She didn't care if it was all down to chemistry. She didn't care that it meant nothing in the great scheme of things. What she cared about was that she should be immune to him after her miserable time with Scott.

She'd let herself trust Scott. He'd pursued her in the past but something about him, something about the fact that he seemed a little too charming and a little too good-looking and a little too sincere, had turned her off.

Then her parents had died so suddenly and, with everything around her going to pieces, she had fallen onto his sympathetic shoulder, which he had magnanimously told her she could cry on.

She had been grateful for the distraction but then, bit by bit, she had started to notice the way he had wanted to take over her life. He had seen the mess her finances had been in, her fall from grace, and he had slyly reminded her of her newly acquired far lower status amongst the peer group she had grown up with.

He had become comfortable putting her down in front of them and, caught up in her own mix of sadness and confusion and misery, she had helplessly kept silent, gradually retreating from socialising, which hadn't been that difficult because friends had begun showing their true colours and retreating from her.

Maybe it had been his way of exacting some kind of revenge because she had ignored him in the past.

But gradually she had realised that that was just the person he was. His need to control was absolute and he was someone who preyed on the weak. He had issues and Sophie felt that she had escaped in the nick of time.

If anything, the experience had made her stronger and she had learnt from it, which was why, now, with butterflies in her tummy at the prospect of seeing Niccolo, she felt so irritated and frustrated with herself.

They took the lift up to his suite of offices, and Sophie wasn't sure what she had been expecting but she knew what she *should* have expected: luxury.

Still, she was unprepared for the *level* of luxury that confronted her when she emerged from the lift with Annalise attached to her like a little limpet, eyes wide and mouth open in awe.

She fiddled with the lanyard she had been given at the sprawling reception desk before they were ushered like royalty into the mirrored lift.

The expanse of pale wood seemed to go on for ever, broken by a clutch of sofas upholstered in vibrant yellow and clustered in a way that should have promoted an atmosphere of comfort and relaxation but instead made her feel a tad queasy because it was all so very elegant and picture perfect.

Beyond the furniture was a semi-circular mirrored desk, behind which two strikingly beautiful men seemed to be hard at work in front of oversized monitors.

It was a completely silent space. Beyond the foyer, the office meandered between clever glass partitions and long, low marble containers spilling over with plants. The desks were all occupied and there was the low buzz of conversation and an atmosphere of ferocious concentration and hard work.

Uninterrupted floor-to-ceiling glass drew the eye to the swirl of sky outside, and way down below, like a miniature Lego city, she could see the jagged contours of buildings and office blocks.

It was irresistible to a six-year-old. Annalise relinquished her hold of Sophie's hand, sprinting to the bank of open glass with Sophie following in hot pursuit, and they were both laughing when they were shown to Niccolo's private office space. It was up a short flight of steps, on either side of which the thin, pale railings were as delicate as a waterfall of crystal.

Nerves hit her as she saw him in his natural habitat, every inch the top dog in the cut-throat world of big money.

He wasn't formally dressed. Instead he wore charcoal trousers and a white shirt cuffed to the elbows, with no sign of a tie.

'I see Annalise has already taken herself off to see what's outside?' He half smiled and his eyes met hers over Annalise's head as he stooped down to his daughter's level to give her a brief hug. Then, as though thinking better of it, he scooped her up and carried her to the window so that she could peer outside—a bird's eye view from the top of the world.

'I couldn't stop her.'

'It's the first time she's been here.' Niccolo looked at Sophie, his expression concealed behind lush lashes.

He'd spent the past couple of days keeping their meetings brief. As distractions went, he wasn't usually open to any. Unfortunately, as distractions went, he was very much open to this particular one and he didn't like the feeling.

With all the women he dated, he knew the lie of the land. He wasn't interested in intellectual stimulation. He was interested in the business of enjoyment and so were they. He had never, to his knowledge, broken any woman's heart, and there were times when he'd seriously doubted he'd broken his ex-wife's.

He was generous to a fault when he was in a relationship. Except with his emotions. Work would always come for him, but he'd caught himself thinking about this particular woman at the most unexpected moments…during a high-level conference call…just before he switched off the light for bed…when he stopped for two seconds to gaze down absently at the view from his glass house…

Right now, she was dressed in an unalluring outfit of flowered overalls with a white T-shirt underneath and flat, tan sandals. She looked wholesome—free of make-up and extraordinarily pretty.

'You kept promising, but you were always too busy,' Annalise said, picking up the conversation after an exhaustive exploration of what the world looked like forty storeys up from every single window in Niccolo's office.

Sophie looked between them, noted the wistful look on Annalise's face and Niccolo's dark flush, and wondered how it was that he was so protective of his daughter, clearly loved her so much and yet, in some ways, was so incapable of complete engagement.

But the conversation was swept aside, carried along by Annalise, whose chatter was a buffer against any personal tangents. There were questions about everything. The eye-wateringly expensive restaurant on the thirty-first floor, with its sweeping panoramic views, was, for Annalise, *'The best place I've ever been to in my whole life...and could we come again...please...?'*

She had a photographic memory and spent some time listing every plant and flower Sophie had shown her, using their Latin names. She chatted breathlessly and with the enthusiasm of a child yearning for parental approval, and in fairness Niccolo did not stint when it came to that.

And yet...

Sophie was desperate to maintain the professionalism she knew she had to hang on to at all costs.

There was no room for curiosity, but he intrigued her, and she told herself that there was nothing wrong with that, in a way, because it was great at taking her mind off her problems. In his mansion, her frantic, depressing life seemed distant and manageable. Already bills had been cleared and what hadn't would be. There was light at the end of the tunnel and somehow, strangely, not surrounded by all the memories, she could feel her head clearing.

Her nights were becoming more peaceful, and bit by bit she felt she was finding a way to piece together her broken life so that it would once again make sense.

What was it about sharing space with a guy who got under her skin like an itch she needed to scratch that cleared her head?

After lunch she and Annalise headed back to the house, but not before Niccolo told her that he would want to chat to her after his daughter was in bed.

'I'll be late.' He had been distractedly looking at his computer as he'd spoken, propped up with his hands flat on his desk while, on the other side, Sophie could feel Annalise yawning, exhausted after the excitement of the day. When he'd glanced at her, she'd known that his mind was already somewhere else. He had had his window with them and now it was time for him to return to the business of making vast amounts of money.

'I'm in the final stages of an extremely sensitive deal and it's proving a mammoth task co-ordinating the participants to meet because they're from all over Europe.' He had smiled crookedly at her and her heart had flip-flopped madly, even though she had successfully maintained an interested but reasonably vague expression on her face. 'So, my timing is unpredictable.' He glanced at his watch and then back to her. 'Expect me back by eight-thirty, at the latest. Or is that too late for you?'

'I think I can keep my eyes open until then,' Sophie had returned politely.

'And I should have asked. Will I be interrupting any plans you might have made?'

She'd flushed because no, no plans had been made.

'I'll eat with Annalise,' she had said quickly.

'Don't be ridiculous.'

'It was a huge lunch.'

'You had an ornate salad,' he had responded drily. 'A

bird would find it hard to keep going on that for the remainder of the day. I'll bring something back with me.'

And that had been the end of the conversation.

Waiting for him now, in the kitchen, Sophie felt a revival of the curiosity that had bitten into her earlier on in the day.

He'd warned her he'd be late, so she'd expected his eight-thirty to be more along the lines of nine-fifteen, but in fact she heard the sound of the front door at a little before eight and instantly all thoughts flew out of her head and every muscle in her body tensed while her nervous system went into overdrive.

She was half standing when he strode into the kitchen, laden with various bags and bringing with him the mouth-watering aroma of Chinese food.

'I...' Her mind raced, her mouth went dry, and as always the responses she least wanted were the first to announce themselves. 'You look tired...'

'Say that again?' Niccolo stopped dead in his tracks and looked at her with his head tilted to one side. He slowly deposited the bags on the table, but his eyes were still on her and they remained there.

She looked flustered and he realised with a start that, aside from his aunt, no one usually made any kind of comments to him of that nature, and yet it was a simple enough observation and genuinely meant.

'It's been a long day,' he said eventually, breaking the silence, and sat opposite her at the kitchen table.

'But at least not as long as you'd thought. I was expecting you later.' She smiled. 'The food smells delicious.'

'You need to do it justice, so I hope you haven't eaten already...'

'Annalise ate just a little too early for me. I draw the line at five-thirty, but she could hardly keep her eyes open after all the high excitement of today. Shall I fetch some plates?'

'And two wine glasses. Join me.'

His dark eyes were thoughtful when they rested on her as she dutifully fetched the wine glasses and poured them both a glass while he began opening boxes, releasing divine aromas.

'We haven't really chatted in any great detail about how you're finding it working here, generally speaking,' he said, when she had finished bustling with the crockery and the cutlery and the glasses, notably uncomfortable at the prospect of once again having a meal with him.

Sophie glanced at him as she slowly took her place at the table. She had braided her long hair into a single plait and she absently flipped it over her shoulder and played with the end, twirling the fine, platinum blonde strands between her fingers.

'What do you mean?'

'Are you enjoying looking after Annalise? Forget about the money...are you satisfied with the work that's being asked of you?'

'Of course!' She sounded genuinely surprised at the question.

'I wouldn't want you to think that you're being asked to work too many hours, whatever you're being paid.'

'Why would you think that?' She sipped her wine and then followed his lead and began helping herself to some of the dishes in their fancy black and gold containers.

He piled into his food, drank a mouthful of wine and then proceeded to look at her over the rim of his glass. 'Because you've been nowhere since you got here, even when I've been back reasonably early in the evening— early enough for you to go out.'

Sophie stared at him. She drank some more of her wine and this time slightly more than a delicate sip. He knew his silence left no room to wriggle away from some sort of response.

'I… I'm planning on having the weekend at home to get through some more…er…clearance…'

'Maybe you could get a company to do that for you?'

'I can't. No.' She looked down and resumed eating, this time not looking at him. 'Well, I suppose I *could*,' she eventually conceded. 'I've cleared out all the bits I want to hang on to…'

'Then why don't you? Is it the cost?'

'No.' She smiled stiffly. 'Thanks to this job, I can afford it, but it seems a little wasteful to spend money for something to get done when I'm more than capable of doing it myself.'

'Thrifty.'

'I haven't had much choice. I don't suppose you'd understand.' She looked around her at the exquisite kitchen. 'Maybe *I* didn't really understand what it felt like to really have to count pennies but now I do and it's been a valuable lesson to not take anything for granted.' She half laughed and then grimaced. 'Not that you're in the slightest concerned by all of this but to get back to your question, I love being with your daughter. She's smart and very engaging. You aunt must miss being with her. How is she doing? How is your father?'

Never one to encourage girlish confidences and

outpourings of heartfelt emotion, to which there was no rational response, Niccolo strangely found himself hesitating, not quite wanting to shut down the conversation just yet. He was enjoying the array of emotions that flitted across her face and the way she half toyed with her hair even when she ate, expertly wielding the wooden chopsticks provided with the meal, and the translucent violet of her eyes when she looked at him.

'What makes you think I have no idea what it feels like to be broke?' he asked, pushing his empty plate to one side and relaxing back in his chair, which he angled away from the table so that he could extend his legs, loosely crossing them at the ankles.

His eyes drifted to her mouth and it was an effort to drag them away because there was a lot to appreciate there—full lips, perfectly formed…whose imagination wouldn't shift gear?

'Do you?'

Niccolo frowned because not only had his imagination wandered into no-man's-land, but so too had the conversation.

'You don't have to answer that if you don't want to. In fact…' She stood up, reaching out to sweep the plates together, along with the boxes in which far too much had been left.

'Where are you going?' he asked irritably.

'I thought I'd tidy this stuff away and head up.'

'We haven't finished talking.'

Sophie paused. He'd asked her whether she enjoyed her job, money aside. She'd answered him. He'd felt free to pry, and she'd got the message loud and clear, but the boot was clearly not going to be put on the other foot. He asked questions, he didn't answer them.

He'd elicited information from her she hadn't shared with anyone but her curiosity about *him* wasn't going to be satisfied, so what else was there to talk about?

She lowered her eyes and kept stubbornly quiet, and when she finally looked at him there was open amusement on his face, which made her bristle.

'You can speak your mind, Sophie,' he encouraged flatly. 'This is what this conversation is all about. It's important you don't feel as though you have to stay within these four walls even when I'm here and you're technically free to go out. You must have friends you want to meet up with?'

The question hung in the air, so that she gritted her teeth and made an effort to count to ten.

'I'm fine for the moment.'

There was sudden understanding in his eyes and that felt equally offensive. He was seeing straight into the very heart of her and she didn't like it.

'I don't ask you questions about your private life,' she said tersely and then reddened at what felt like an act of insubordination, but the words had left her mouth and she didn't want to claw them back with an apology. 'I respect the fact that you don't want to impart personal information about yourself.'

'I know what it feels like to have no money,' Niccolo said quietly. 'You grew up with money and now it's gone. I grew up with none and now I have it. Both of us have had our learning curves.'

'Were your parents happy?' She tilted her head to one side and met his eyes steadily. 'I'm guessing they are now as they're still together. I'm guessing you grew up in a tightly knit family unit because Evalina is immensely close to you and to her sister and presumably to her brother-in-law.'

'Happiness isn't the be all and end all when the chips are down. There's a lot of happiness to be found in the security that comes with having deep reserves of money, enough so that you become untouchable.'

'My parents were happy,' Sophie said wistfully. 'I think it pretty much *is* the be-all and end-all even when the chips are down. I just wish I could tell them that now...' So he had grown up in poverty, and she could picture him, fiercely ambitious, contemptuous of the sordid business of never having enough, putting the learning curves in place that would make him the man he was now. But was that the whole of his story? He professed to have no time for love, but what about his wife? Maybe that was where his disillusionment stemmed from. She thought that when you lost the person you loved you probably lost your faith in happiness, and yet he had his daughter. Did he blame a childhood of having nothing for the fact that he was emotionally out of reach, or was that just a way of not dealing with the real reason, which lay in love that had been lost? He aspired to be untouchable, but really, how reasonable was that when you had a child to consider? Was that why he seemed sometimes so awkward around Annalise?

Had he ever thought to replace his ex with someone else...someone who could be a mother to Annalise?

Speculation rattled around in her head, spreading tentacles everywhere, making her wonder about him, turning him into a three-dimensional man, complex and full of depths she could feel herself wanting badly to explore.

'But moving on…'

Sophie blinked, focusing on him, wondering if she had imagined that brief lapse when he had let her past whatever iron gates he had built around himself.

'Yes.' Her voice was brisk. 'It's late.'

'There's a reason I returned home earlier than expected.'

'Oh?' She hovered, unsure whether this was a prelude to a long conversation or a brief, winding-up remark.

'I said it's been problematic getting various people together for a deal I've spent the past eight months working on.' He pushed the plates to one side and abruptly sat forward, crowding her so that she drew back a little, eyes widening.

'You mentioned that,' Sophie said vaguely.

'To expand, there's a great deal of secrecy surrounding this arrangement. It involves a family business, and my takeover has to be presented as a fait accompli to ensure that there's no loss of confidence in their market share, which would happen were there to be months of speculation about a takeover. Public knowledge that they were ready to sell would also open the door to a possible hostile takeover, which they don't want. Everything has had to be handled delicately but I have finally found a solution to all parties being present at the same time and in the same place for the details to be finalised. You might think that it's unimportant for everyone to be physically present, given the speed and efficiency of the internet and the convenience of video calls.'

'That thought hadn't crossed my mind,' Sophie said politely. 'I'm just wondering where this is all going, although, of course, I'm very happy that your deal is now finalised. That must be…er…very rewarding for you.'

'Very rewarding, and extremely lucrative,' Niccolo added drily. 'I also had no plans to disperse the hundreds of employees who currently work at the various offshoots, which is the main reason the family decided that I was the buyer they wanted.'

'That's wonderful.'

'I know what it's like,' Niccolo mused, half under his breath, 'to live at the receiving end of a company that thinks it's acceptable to get rid of someone who's given a lifetime to them because they think he's outstayed his welcome…' He frowned, then continued without allowing room for interruption. 'At any rate, there has been insistence on the part of my client that everyone meets for the closure.' He shrugged eloquently. 'Call it an old-fashioned Italian thing…or a general mistrust on the part of an eighty-two-year-old in the workings of the internet…'

'Sometimes when you see people face to face you get a completely different opinion of them.'

'Possibly. At any rate, various family members, all of whom have shares in the company and are scattered in various parts of Europe, need to meet along with the discreet team of international lawyers I have put in place, and the financial and tax accountants who have done their job with admirable discretion over the months. Co-ordinating diaries has been a nightmare and more so when Evalina disappeared to Italy because there was no one to look after Annalise.'

'That's fine.'

'Say that again?'

Sophie thought of a few days without Niccolo around, during which she could work on getting her nervous system to a place where it didn't hive off on a dangerous tangent every single time he was around. A peaceful few days. She and Annalise could busy themselves during the day and have lovely, relaxed evenings, uninterrupted by her heartbeat picking up speed the closer to his possible arrival back at home.

She could devote her time to reminding herself just how disillusioned she was when it came to men. She could answer all those nagging emails she had tried hard to focus on before being ambushed by thoughts of her over-sexy employer.

'I'm more than happy to stay here with Annalise while you go abroad on business.' She smiled with warm reassurance. 'I hope I've proved that I'm one hundred per cent trustworthy and capable of looking after your daughter. You needn't fear that I'll be having wild parties at your house the second you board a plane!'

'No,' Niccolo murmured. 'I actually have no fears in that direction at all.'

'Good!' Sophie marvelled that he could simultaneously compliment her on her reliability and trustworthiness while in the same breath making her sound like a crashing bore with no social life.

'But I think you may have got hold of the wrong end of the stick…'

Sophie was still smiling, although there was a little thread of apprehension filtering through her as he continued.

'I won't be leaving my daughter behind with you. Far from it. You'll both be coming with me.' He paused, giving her time to digest what he'd just announced. 'You can consider it a mini-holiday of sorts. Yes, you'll be looking after Annalise, but you'll be on board my superyacht and there will be other people around for company.'

'On board...'

'My superyacht, which is currently moored off the coast of Sardinia. I'm surprised it didn't occur to me that it would be the perfect spot to host this very private gathering, far from the reach of any snooping eyes.' He delivered a smile of complete satisfaction. 'Don't look so alarmed, Sophie; all you need is your passport, some clothes for very hot weather and, of course, as many swimsuits as you can stuff into your suitcase. My yacht comes with several extremely pleasant swimming pools...'

CHAPTER FIVE

NOTHING, NOT EVEN mixing with the kids at her fee-paying school who had come from wealthy families, could have prepared Sophie for the assault on her senses at what life looked like when you moved in the world of the uber-rich.

With back-to-back meetings before a departure date that seemed dizzyingly soon, Sophie saw precious little of Niccolo over the next three days.

He had arranged for professionals to help with the final stages of the house clearance, which had been in limbo for the past couple of weeks.

He had texted her with just a day's notice.

Friday morning at nine. I would say that I can get cover for Annalise for the day, but I have a feeling that she might enjoy the bedlam.

She did, and so did Sophie when, at a little after five on Friday, she had looked at how much had been accomplished. Not everything, but there was hardly anything left to do, with the remainder of her personal belongings all delivered to Niccolo's house, where he had assured her they could remain until her contract was over.

And, as he had predicted, Annalise had enjoyed every second of the chaos of packing and clearing, and oddly it was an exercise that had hurt far less than Sophie had expected.

Had she been subconsciously putting off the final hurdle because of the pain she had anticipated? The memories she would have had to dust down and look at?

With Annalise there and the packing men in and out and an alarming but stimulating trip staring her in the face, she had dusted down those memories but then cherished them instead of being broken up by them.

It had been fun packing for Annalise.

'Have you ever been on your dad's yacht?' she had asked as they had sifted through the sizeable wardrobe of designer summer clothes, selecting some, discarding others.

Annalise had shrugged and said, without skipping a beat and without any hint of sadness, that she hadn't.

'He doesn't come on holiday with us,' she'd explained, standing up and showing Sophie a swimsuit with frills and a pattern of fish which she exclaimed was her favourite in the whole world. 'Aunty Eva and I go, and sometimes Daddy joins us, but he's always on his computer when he comes anyway.'

'And do you mind?' Sophie had asked casually, thinking of her own idyllic childhood with her doting parents.

'It's nice he's around more now. I liked going to see him in his office in the sky.' She had smiled and looked at Sophie with her big, dark, serious eyes. 'And it'll be nice on the boat, especially as there's a pool. Daddy has a house in the country and there's a pool there, but I only get to go with Aunty Eva for a week over summer and then Daddy comes for a week, but he prefers to be in London.'

Niccolo left ahead of them for his yacht to make sure everything was in place.

He had expanded on who would be there: the powerful Italian family, rooted in tradition, who would be able to confer as one in the same place, and six outsiders from legal and accounting professions, who would take care of all the nuts and bolts to secure the deal.

Sophie had semi-absorbed this information. She wouldn't be there to socialise. She would be there with her working hat on, whatever Niccolo might have implied to the contrary.

They would stay aboard the boat for four days while every small detail was finalised in between ensuring the clients relaxed and had some enjoyable downtime.

She decided that one sensible black swimsuit would suffice. She had several racier ones, but as she'd fished them out and looked at them they had reminded her of a time long gone and she had stuffed them in the bag of things to be donated to charity.

It was surprisingly exciting to think about having some time abroad, even if it would be of a very brief duration and even if she would be working while she was there.

She'd always loved the thrill of travelling and it was something she had foolishly never even thought about until it had been snatched away in the face of all her financial woes.

What had she expected?

The first-class flight over to Cagliari Airport, yes.

She didn't think that Niccolo would consider flying anything but First. She was still impressed, however, with just how pampered she had felt. First-class flights had always been out of her parents' league. Annalise, accustomed to nothing else, took it all for granted, amusing herself with some of the fun activity books they had bought together the day before.

What Sophie had definitely *not* expected was the limo to the airfield and then the helicopter waiting to whisk them off to his superyacht.

With the sun beating down, they had been ushered like royalty from plane to limo to a small field where a black helicopter was on standby.

Luggage had been dealt with by staff who had been virtually invisible, taking care of every single thing so that she and Annalise had nothing to do but look around and absorb the scenery.

From the air-conditioned comfort of the limo, Sophie had gazed at the coloured houses and buildings, tightly packed together in hues of reds and yellows and oranges, climbing neatly up the hill and descending to the sea, which glittered like a jewel, dotted with the bobbing white of small boats.

Annalise gasped and squealed, her excitement making Sophie smile.

She was cool inside the limo, but the bright blue skies outside made her feel hot.

She'd worn some white jeans and a loose pink top, and wished she'd had the foresight to wear a dress instead.

The views from the limo had been beautiful, but

from the buzzing helicopter the unfolding panorama was so much more spectacular.

Transported into the air and gazing down from giddy heights—while next to her Annalise clutched her hand for dear life, barely able to keep still—Sophie fell silent at the distant view of the sea, glittering and turquoise, unbelievably Technicolor-bright.

They swooped over coves nestled in steep, rocky enclaves that were lush with bushes and green with outcrops of trees.

A brief flight before the spectacle of vessels once more dotting the ocean blue preceded a sharp, giddy descent, and for a few seconds Sophie squeezed her eyes tightly shut, but not before she understood very clearly that in a sea of boats there was only one massive mothership, to which the helicopter was descending.

Niccolo wasn't the young upstart in the jungle. Niccolo was the roaring lion who sat at the top of the pecking order.

Just like that, nerves and wild anticipation replaced carefree excitement as the frantic swirl of the rotor blades stopped and the door was pushed open, and there he was, devastating in a pair of cream shorts and a faded striped T-shirt, barefoot and wearing dark sunglasses, which he immediately removed.

He moved towards them and stooped down as Annalise began running towards him before slowing to a more grown-up, sedate pace.

Sophie hovered and looked at him, and on cue he raised his dark eyes to hers above Annalise's head before vaulting upright and lifting his daughter up in one swoop that made her squeal with pleasure.

'Trip okay?' he asked, and Sophie nodded while every nerve in her body went into crazy overdrive.

How on earth could a guy look so sexy? He was the picture of bronzed, muscular beauty, his dark hair curling at the nape of his neck, his dark eyes lazy and penetrating and his wide, sensuous mouth promising untold pleasure.

The last thing Sophie wanted was to think of any kind of pleasure with the man who was employing her to look after his daughter.

'It was great. Annalise could barely contain her excitement.' She stroked Annalise's satin-smooth cheek and was rewarded with a dimpled smile as she rested her head against her father's shoulder, clearly overjoyed at this uncustomary display of physical affection.

They began walking away from the helicopter into the bowels of the superyacht, where Sophie stood completely still and gazed around her at a vision of ridiculous luxury.

Annalise had drawn back from her comfort zone and was doing the same, but hours of travel were taking their toll and she was yawning widely, eyes staying open with difficulty.

Leather and teak and glass dominated the space. Everything was pale.

'I'll show you to your rooms.' Niccolo began moving through the living area, chatting to her about the yacht as they headed deeper down a circular flight of stairs. 'Custom-built,' he said, 'with four decks and a top speed of twenty-one knots. There's enough space for everyone coming and the crew, including two chefs. If you need anything, then you just have to ask.'

'First thing I'll need is a satnav to work my way around this. It's absolutely *massive*.'

'Never been on a yacht before?'

'Never. I don't think many people have.' She didn't quite know where to look because it was all so magnificent. 'Where is everyone?'

'Due tomorrow evening. Complex arrangements delivering them all here in various stages. Tonight, there will just be the two of us. I would include my daughter in the equation, but she's already asleep on my shoulder.'

'I… I should stay with her.' Sophie's heart sped up. She thought about them dining together and then realised that with that one thought came a spiralling cyclone of more dangerous ones. 'She'll be confused if she wakes up and she doesn't know where she is.'

Niccolo frowned. 'I could get one of my staff to sit in the adjoining room, so someone is at hand if she wakes up and is disoriented.'

'But she won't *know* whoever it is.'

'Annalise is accustomed to a variety of different people on the scene,' Niccolo said wryly. 'Evalina lives with me and is at hand ninety per cent of the time, but there's still that ten per cent when she's not around and occasionally neither am I.'

They had begun strolling through the mega-yacht. Everything was pristine. There were seating areas in places where the view of the open ocean was uninterrupted, and they walked past an entire section that included more informal seating and a bar.

'What happens when you're not using all of this?' Sophie asked, knowing that she would return to their conversation about Annalise but too distracted by her surroundings to pursue anything at the moment.

He'd grown up without much and she was beginning to realise just how ambitious he would have been and probably still was, when it came to ensuring that a life of *being without* would never be his fate. More so, she suspected, because it wasn't just about himself but about his daughter as well, about ensuring *she* had everything he had not.

But what had been sacrificed?

She slanted disobedient eyes sideways to see that Annalise was fast asleep against him, mouth half open, her long, dark lashes fluttering in sleep while he held her effortlessly with one arm. Sophie shivered as she noted the flex of muscle in his forearm, the definition of sinew and the suggestion of leashed strength.

He was a magnificent blend of grace and power and she was so busy staring that she had to drag her brain back into gear when he said, with amusement, 'Am I about to get a telling off?'

Sophie smiled, relaxing at the teasing lightness in his voice. 'It seems a waste if it's just left here bobbing about on the water, waiting for you to pop in for a visit now and again to make sure the engine's still ticking over and there are no cobwebs on the decks.'

Niccolo burst out laughing then stifled his laughter as Annalise shifted against him, her eyes fluttering open for a few seconds.

'You have a colourful way with words, Sophie,' he whispered.

She realised she quite liked the way he said her name, as soft and sensory as the brush of a feather against her skin.

'Well, you have to admit that it's an awfully big toy for a rich guy.' She glanced sideways to the view of a lavender sky announcing the end of day. 'Do you have people on board all the time even when it's not being used?'

'If I said yes,' Niccolo drawled, with a thread of laughter still there in his voice, 'would I get a few brownie points for alleviating any unemployment problems in this part of the world?'

'No!'

'That's very harsh. Up this flight of stairs is the master suite and two adjoining rooms that have prime position with excellent views of the ocean from all angles. I have arranged for us to occupy these quarters.'

Suddenly the mega-yacht seemed to shrink to the size of a matchbox.

How private could bedrooms be on a yacht, however big the yacht was?

Big enough, she discovered seconds later, to accommodate a suite for Niccolo and mini-suites for her and Annalise, each with generously proportioned bathrooms. They were connected by a sitting area where they could all relax.

It was the last word in luxury and yet all that occupied Sophie's mind was the fact that Niccolo's room was directly opposite, and to make matters worse he inserted, casually, 'If you need anything, you just have to knock on my door, or...' he nodded to a small gadget on the wall by the thick glass window that looked out on a dazzling view of sea '...that will summon someone.' He nudged open one of the doors that led to the smaller of the rooms and gently deposited his daughter on the bed, which was beautifully made up with just the sort of brightly patterned linen that a child would love. 'For now, we will have dinner brought to us here. That way Annalise will have familiar faces around her if she wakes unexpectedly, although it's my experience that being on this size yacht on calm water is actually very conducive to sleep.'

Sophie, still playing with myriad images of him sleeping in his own quarters practically within touching distance, nodded vaguely and watched, eyes glazed, as he settled Annalise.

'You're hovering,' he pointed out, helpfully. 'Your luggage will already be in your bedroom. Why don't you unpack while I organise something for us to eat?'

He was already pulling out his mobile phone, which was probably the most efficient way of contacting his chief steward on a yacht the size of a small town.

'Go on,' he urged, looking at her with amusement, 'feel free to shower and change if you want. I'll wait here just in case Annalise wakes up. Then we can eat, and you can tell me how wasteful I am having a yacht this size and I can defend myself.'

He grinned, and just like that Sophie was swept away on a rush of something warm and uncomfortable and alarming. It was as though all those nebulous responses had finally coalesced into a pool of hot, naked attraction that made her heart leap with frenzied panic and brought a surge of hot colour to her cheeks.

He was teasing her. For a moment, she saw past that remote, powerful, charismatic stranger to someone utterly charming and insanely sexy.

And her body was reacting like the young, red-blooded woman she thought she had safely confined to deep freeze after all the business with Scott.

Dampness pooled between her legs and she had to resist the urge to squirm. Her breasts, pushing against her cotton bra, felt heavy, and her nipples were stiff and sensitive.

She was horrified because all she could think was, *I want them to be touched...played with...sucked...by this man.*

She almost put her hand to her mouth in shock.

'I'll unpack,' she said on a deep breath, 'but I'll leave the shower for later. And there's no need to justify why you own this lovely yacht.' Her brain had cranked back into gear and was shrieking that the only defence against this unwelcome attraction was to make sure she didn't lose sight of the fact that theirs was a working relationship.

He was her boss.

He gave the orders and she obeyed.

There was a little bit of socialising but that was to be expected. In short, there were lines that were not to be crossed and she was upset with herself for looking at those lines and then stepping over them.

She fled to the safety of her bedroom, keenly aware of him outside, metres away.

It was huge, with a double bed beautifully made up in deep burgundy linen, exquisitely soft to the touch. The carpet was thick and plush, and everything was fitted, seamlessly blending together in shades of pale wood, from the bedside cabinets to the generous bank of wardrobes nestled around a sleek dressing table. The bathroom was even bigger than the bedroom and she was briefly tempted to actually do as Niccolo had suggested and have a shower, but instead she unpacked quickly, more to give herself a bit of breathing space than because there was any need to actually hang anything up.

About to head outside, she paused to look in the mirror above the dressing table.

She looked flustered. Her cheeks were pink, and she placed both hands on them in an attempt to cool the heat. She had tied her hair back, but now she neatened it because she looked tousled when she wanted to look prim and professional. Her eyes were bright—too bright—and when she squinted at her reflection she felt she could detect the very slightest quiver in her body, as though she was plugged into a socket and was quietly vibrating, engine fired up and ready to go.

She gritted her teeth, hating herself for her lack of control, and pushed open the door to the outside living area to find Niccolo sprawled in one of the cream leather chairs, feet crossed at the ankles, the very picture of a billionaire at rest.

'I've ordered a selection of salads,' he announced, his dark eyes resting on her face, watching as she primly sat on the sofa facing him.

Not even the non-stop stress of constant travel, he mused, could detract from her delicate, captivating beauty. He didn't want to look but he couldn't seem to stop himself. She moved with the grace of a dancer, blushed like a virgin even as she tilted her head in absolute defiance if she disagreed with him…and was she aware of how sexy she looked when she inclined her head to one side and parted her lips and did a little frown as she thought about something he'd said?

Playing with fire had never felt so tempting. He enjoyed watching the flit of emotions skittering across her face, and he really liked the way she reacted when he dumped the work hat and wrongfooted her by talking to her as any man talking to a woman, without the business of anyone being in anyone's pay.

He couldn't remember experiencing anything like this before. When he thought of his wife and their brief courtship, he realised that what he'd felt then had certainly not been this strange playfulness that wanted to get a reaction. He thought of Caroline and remembered the formality and sophistication of those few months before he had proposed. They had been an elegant couple moving amongst their elegant crowd, cocooned by wealth and power, the very wealth and power he had striven for all of his life but which had somehow felt hollow and empty when he was married, as though something vital had been missing.

He surely couldn't recall this simple enjoyment of looking and musing and imagining. Was it because he knew that nothing would come of it? Or was it simply a case of a change being as good as a rest? Shy, ethereal blondes who didn't play games versus bold brunettes who held nothing back?

'Yummy.'

'Of course, if you'd rather something else…'

'A salad would be fine,' Sophie said politely.

'You can relax, Sophie,' Niccolo said with a disgruntled edge. 'Tell me how much more you have to do with your house. Has it been completely cleared?'

'Mostly.'

'And…how do you feel now? About that?' He was taking steps down that previously taboo road of encouraging an emotional response and he realised that this was becoming something of a habit as far as this woman was concerned. Curiosity was trumping common sense, but instead of being wary he felt invigorated. His palate had become jaded, and it was thrilling being unexpectedly presented with an opportunity to dust it down and take it for a walk. Who would be able to resist the temptation?

It would seem, he mused, that money didn't buy everything after all.

Sophie sighed. She thought of her family home quietly and efficiently being stripped of its soul as personal effects were boxed up or given to charity or sold to help clear debts.

Suddenly everything had happened faster than the speed of light, which, she now reflected, wasn't a bad thing. It had been easy to fall into the trap of struggling to find a way forward.

Why was it so tempting to pour her heart out to this guy?

'You can talk to me,' Niccolo urged softly.

'Stop being so persuasive,' she responded with helpless honesty and he smiled, long and slow, thrilling her to the core and killing off the bit of her that was so keen to keep distance between them. If he chose to breach the distance and close the gap, then it was just so hard not to yield.

'I'm normally not,' Niccolo admitted, and she frowned.

'What do you mean?' She gazed at him and then said, in a low voice, 'Ah, I understand. You don't want anyone trespassing and the best way to stop that is to never take down the *Keep Out* signs.'

'I'm not sure I would describe it like that...'

Sophie didn't say anything, but she wondered whether he was aware of the compliment he had just inadvertently paid her. Did he feel that it was different encouraging her to talk to him about stuff that mattered because she *worked* for him? Because she posed no threat when it came to emotional involvement?

In one fell swoop he had established the door that stood between them even though it felt as though he had opened it, allowing her to see what was inside.

'I feel,' she said truthfully, 'as though sorting the house out is something that's been a long time coming. I thought it would have been so huge that subconsciously I'd put it off even though, naturally, with people moving in, I would have had to focus and get on with it eventually, but somehow…'

'Somehow?'

'It's been good to have taken my time sorting through things…not being rushed into doing anything hasty…maybe getting rid of anything I might have later regretted getting rid of…'

'You're too young,' Niccolo murmured with heart-felt sincerity, 'to have had to cope with events that could have overwhelmed you. Is that when you made your mistake?'

'What are you talking about?'

Was he opening a can of worms?

She'd been through a tough time…so yes, he'd encouraged her to open up and he couldn't beat himself up over that because she was in charge of his daughter and it made sense that he get to know her on a more personal basis than an employee in his company. But asking her about her love life...about her sex life...was that a step too far?

Yet he wanted to cross whatever lines should or shouldn't be crossed. For the very first time in his life.

There was no way he would ever, *could* ever, *not* exert complete control over himself, over his decisions, but for the moment, relinquishing control felt like a good option. Everyone needed to take a break now and again and, as breaks went, they didn't come safer than this.

'The guy who broke your heart.'

Of course, he knew that she wasn't going to give him an answer, but he was still taken aback when she said, recovering fast from her confidences of only moments ago, 'You should tell me what my duties are while I'm on board your yacht. I know I'll be in charge of Annalise, but we won't be able to do our usual things and I'm guessing you'll want to make sure your deal-making isn't interrupted too much by the presence of your daughter.'

'Have you always been as private as you are?'

'Have you always found it hard to let yourself go?'

'In actual fact,' Niccolo murmured huskily, 'I'm exceedingly good at letting myself go, given the right circumstances...'

He looked at her with lazy, brooding eyes, skewering her to the chair and obliterating all thought from her head.

Of course she knew what he was saying!

Was he aiming to shock?

Did her reticence challenge him, somehow? She suspected that perhaps it did. Maybe he enjoyed rustling her feathers. He was a man who had everything, and sometimes people who had everything took pleasure in finding those small things they didn't have.

Like a nanny in his employ who reacted to everything he said without being able to help herself...a girl who had never quite learnt how to flirt, despite mixing in groups where that was the norm. A girl who, face it, had been slightly out of her depth at her expensive private school, too bookish and too shy, despite her looks, to cultivate the veneer of easy arrogance that so many of her peers had had.

Her parents had been too protective for her to really ever know what it felt like to be free to do exactly what she wanted without caring whether she disappointed them or not.

Did he find something amusing about the fact that she was at odds with her accent?

And yet, he had told her that his background was far from wealthy. Did he now surround himself with the sort of women a life of crazy money had opened up to him?

She lowered her eyes, her long lashes concealing her expression, but she could feel the heavy thudding of her heart at the graphic images his throwaway teasing rejoinder had kickstarted inside her.

'I've made you uncomfortable,' Niccolo said huskily. 'I apologise.'

'You enjoy making me uncomfortable.' Sophie looked at him, clear eyed, her violet gaze unwavering.

'Strangely,' he raised his eyebrows, his dark eyes locking with hers, 'I find you have a similar effect on me whether you enjoy it or not.'

The silence stretched and stretched until Sophie could almost hear it humming between them.

She licked her lips and this time the fire that was suddenly blazing between them was so hot that Niccolo could almost reach out and touch it.

Was she aware of it?

If *she* wasn't, then he certainly was, and suddenly it no longer felt like an amusing game.

What the hell was going on?

He breathed in sharply, but it was the deferential knock on the door that severed the connection.

Food. How long had someone been trying to get their attention?

He vaulted upright, relieved when the young lad bowed his way into the suite, taking far too long to explain what salads had been prepared and apologising profusely because he should have been there ten minutes ago, but he was a new member of the crew and had yet to fully familiarise himself with the layout of the yacht.

Niccolo allowed him to ramble on for a while because it was preferable to returning to violet eyes that seemed capable of doing all sorts of uninvited things to his peace of mind.

Eventually, he waved the boy out and quietly shut the door behind him before turning to Sophie.

'Help yourself.'

Everything was spread on a double-tiered chrome and glass trolley, including a bottle of wine, which Niccolo felt it prudent to steer clear of.

He helped himself to what was there and out of the corner of his eye noted every detail of her slender hands as she scooped salad onto a plate. The very fair, downy hair on them, the length of her fingers and the blunt practicality of her short nails. He could just about catch a glimpse of her blonde hair escaping around her face in untidy tendrils and he could hear her soft breathing as she concentrated on what she was putting on her plate.

He told her what she was expected to do, and he was aware of her answering, her voice low. How had he failed to realise just how pleasing it was to the ear?

Yes, she would make sure Annalise was entertained, but she was here to work and not play...

Were things back to normal?

He damn well hoped so.

Eyes carefully averted, Sophie heard herself relentlessly chattering her way through the meal. The salads were delicious. She ignored the wine, as did he, and instead washed everything down with bottled water.

His eyes were on her, lazy and assessing. She suspected he was probably bored witless with her non-stop twittering, but she was desperate to break a silence that seemed suddenly fraught.

As soon as she had eaten the last of what she thought was an acceptable amount of the fantastically prepared food, she politely pushed her plate to one side and began standing up.

Only then did she risk looking at him.

He too was rising to his feet—so tall, so aggressively masculine...and so close to her... Far too close, close enough to set her heart thumping a panicked tattoo, close enough for her to stumble back a few inches.

Close enough for her to see, with alarm, panic and

dark, forbidden excitement, her own dangerous desire mirrored in his lazy, brooding gaze.

After half an hour of ceaseless wittering, she could find no words to break the thick, electric silence. It wrapped around them until breathing became difficult.

'No,' she finally croaked. She realised that somehow they had closed the gap between them. She realised that *somehow* her hand was resting on the washboard hardness of his stomach. She could feel him breathing and it was as if they had suddenly become bonded, his energy flowing into her, energising her and terrifying her at the same time.

'No,' Niccolo echoed thickly. He stepped back, breaking the spell but not so much that she could tear her eyes away from him. The drag on her senses made her weak, weak with a fierce longing she hadn't known she possessed.

Loneliness, she thought wildly. Stress and loneliness, and there he had been, the last guy she could ever possibly go for, and all that stress and loneliness had found refuge in him because, whatever stupid attraction she felt, she was inherently safe.

'I'm tired. I need to go to sleep. I'll see you... *Annalise* and I will see you in the morning.' She knew that she was stumbling over her words.

Staring at him, she was ashamed that she wanted to see more of what she had seen before, more of that burning desire, but he stepped back as well and looked down for a few seconds, shielding his expression, and then when he lifted his eyes they were cool and controlled and she wondered whether she had imagined the past five intense, scorching minutes.

He didn't say anything, except to tell her that someone would collect the dishes within the next half an hour, then with a nod he was gone, and she sagged like a puppet, strings abruptly cut.

What had just happened? She didn't quite know, but she *did* know that it was not going to happen again.

CHAPTER SIX

NOT EVEN SIMMERING tension and a sickening sense of needing to be on guard at all times could detract from the magnificence of her surroundings.

The following day was a busy one, with Niccolo's clients arriving in stages, some by the very same helicopter that had transported her and Annalise to the yacht, others by speedboats, one of which was a dedicated speedboat that seemed to be stored somewhere within the vast hull of the yacht.

Because of the number of decks on the yacht, all of which overlooked the main entry point, Sophie and Annalise could keep a safe distance while they both watched the comings and goings, fascinated. There was a sense of urgency in the air, which even Annalise felt because she couldn't quite focus on any of the fun activities Sophie had planned for the day.

The sun was beautifully warm, even in the shade where they both lounged on sofas that perched by one of three outdoor pools, this one small but with a lovely jacuzzi to one side. They could hear the distant sound of voices carrying on the warm air up to where they sat.

They had been shown to the pool area first thing by one of the many members of staff, and several hours later that very same member of staff had been their self-appointed waiter in residence, bringing them drinks and lunch and hovering to make sure their every need was met with speed.

They had swum and done some arts and crafts, and for a couple of hours they had watched a bit of television and then eaten at the private dining area just off the pool area.

And Niccolo? It was a little after four in the afternoon and Sophie had not laid eyes on him yet. She had finally stopped glancing surreptitiously in all directions, like a spy in a B-rated movie, and was just beginning to relax, back at the pool, when she was alerted to Niccolo's presence by Annalise.

He was behind her and she froze for a few seconds, then turned around, her smile in place, the lectures she had given herself during the course of the day echoing in her ears.

The modest black swimsuit she wore suddenly felt like a thong bikini as she rose fluidly from the padded deckchair, swiftly wrapping her sarong around her waist while Niccolo was distracted by his daughter.

'Had a good day?' He glanced at her for a few seconds from the kneeling position he had adopted to look at his daughter's sketchpad, and then stood up to move to one of the chairs next to where Sophie had been sitting moments earlier.

Suddenly roused from her natural tiredness after having spent most of the day outside in the sun, Annalise was now bright-eyed and bushy-tailed and desperate to commandeer her father's attention.

Still in her swimsuit, she proceeded, for the next ten minutes, to proudly demonstrate her swimming prowess until, laughing, Niccolo stood up and started unbuttoning his loose white linen shirt.

Sitting ramrod-straight on the deckchair and hiding behind sunglasses, Sophie watched in fascinated horror at what looked like the beginnings of a striptease.

Off came the linen shirt and her mouth went dry at the sight of a body not even her wildest flights of imagination could have done justice to. Broad shoulders rippled with muscle. His nipples, flat and brown, were small discs accentuating his pecs. His stomach was flat, the perfect six-pack tapering to a narrow waist. He had just the right amount of body hair to advertise in no uncertain terms that he was all male...all glorious, unashamedly and outrageously sexy alpha male.

The shorts were now coming off. Sophie held her breath. Underneath, he was wearing swimming trunks, loose and silky and riding low. Made sense. He was on his yacht surrounded by the ocean. No better place to be prepared for getting wet.

She realised that she was still holding her breath and still gaping as he stepped into the pool. It wasn't big enough for fancy diving, but she suspected that if it had been he would have executed something pretty impressive.

He was beautiful. He moved with the grace of a panther and was compelling to look at. Thank goodness he was too busy swimming with Annalise, allowing her to clamber onto his shoulders so that she could splash with spluttering laughter into the water, to notice that he had become prime spectator fodder for Sophie.

She tore her avid gaze away with difficulty and was busily staring at a jumble of words in her book, pretending to read, when she became aware of his shadow looming over her.

'You didn't want to join us?'

Sophie looked up at him through her dark sunglasses and plastered a rictus smile on her face. Once in that forced position, her jaw began to ache, but she couldn't seem to assume a normal expression because she was too aware of him right there in front of her greedy gaze, all wet and lean and sinfully, sinfully sexy.

Annalise, wrapped in one of the oversized beach towels that had been brought for them, had plonked herself on the deckchair and was lying down, eyes closed, a little smile on her face.

'Sophie's been teaching me how to do handstands in the pool,' she said, without opening her eyes.

'Maybe she could teach me,' Niccolo said, his dark eyes not leaving Sophie's face for a single second. 'It's been a dream of mine…'

'Has it really?' Sophie said drily. She drew her knees up and wrapped her arms around them, and then stared out to sea.

The yacht had moved during the course of the day, although the sailing had been so smooth that she had barely noticed, and land was now a distant slither, a dark strip far off into the blue horizon. All around them, the ocean was still and dark, gently lapping the steep sides of the yacht.

'Where are all your…er…guests?'

'Busying themselves relaxing and then getting ready for a three-course meal,' Niccolo said as he sat on the chair next to her and laid back, mimicking his daughter, arms folded and legs lightly crossed at the ankles.

Sophie felt a little telltale tic at the side of her

mouth, a giveaway sign of the strain of keeping her eyes averted when her whole body was reminding her of how vitally aware she was of his presence inches away from her.

He was a burnished, healthy bronze, and alongside him she felt translucently pale.

'I've asked the lovely guy who's been taking care of us all day to bring us an early supper in the room.'

Niccolo opened his eyes to slits and slid them across to Sophie.

She'd been in his head off and on throughout the day. He'd found himself actively resisting the temptation to seek her out on the pretext of making sure she and Annalise were okay even though he knew they would be. He had given appropriate instructions to the head of staff to know that their every need would have been met.

He had held out because surely the magnitude of this deal overrode any inexplicable desire to see what his nanny and Annalise were up to?

But now...

He had taken one look at her in that swimsuit over which she had hastily flung a sarong and the libido he had sternly reprimanded the evening before had promptly decided to break free and run wild.

The sun was already beginning to turn her skin a pale gold and bleach her hair to an even more impossible shade of white-blonde, and those dark-lashed violet eyes, resting briefly on him as he'd made his appearance, had detonated a series of explosive images that had forcibly reminded him just how easy it was for her to wreak havoc with his prized self-control.

She'd hidden away behind some oversized sunglasses and that had been frustrating because he'd been desperate to read the expression on her face.

For the first time in his life, Niccolo had reluctantly been forced to acknowledge that he was interested in a woman who didn't seem disposed to return the favour.

Did she fancy him? He was sure she did. He'd read it in her eyes the evening before, had felt that swift intake of breath and noted the way she had moved towards him, their combined heat suddenly turning the space between them into a furnace until he'd broken the connection.

Thankfully, she had stepped back at the same time, as keen as he had been to move away from a potentially awkward situation.

That said…

Niccolo realised that he'd grown to take it as a given that a woman, in receipt of any show of positive encouragement from him, would pursue him even if he'd had a change of mind.

Since when, he thought wryly, had he become such a spoiled brat when it came to the opposite sex? Had he reached a place where he stamped his feet if a woman he happened to fancy decided to give him the cold shoulder? In this case, the cold shoulder was *precisely* what was needed!

He should have been breathing a sigh of heartfelt relief that he wasn't in the position of having to deflect unwanted attention! Or worse…sack his aunt's friend for inappropriate behaviour.

Far from breathing any sighs of relief, however, Niccolo was frowning, already deciding that he would make sure whoever was at hand to wait on them the following day was not a young, red-blooded guy who would not be able to resist Sophie's obvious appeal.

'There's no need,' he drawled now, 'to be cooped up in your quarters with Annalise for the duration of the night. Every single member of my staff has been vetted and the majority are permanent employees on this yacht as well as at my villa in Costa Smeralda. I know several who would be delighted to help out with Annalise so that you have a bit more freedom of movement while you're here.'

'I'm not here to have freedom of movement,' Sophie said, turning to him with some consternation. 'I'm here to look after Annalise. That's my job.'

Niccolo didn't reply. Instead he lazily reached down to where he had tossed the shorts he'd worn over his swimming trunks and pulled out his mobile phone to make a quick call. Within minutes, a young woman, introduced as Julia, was on deck with them. She was smartly uniformed with dark hair tied back and a pleasant, friendly face.

Niccolo told her what he wanted, and Sophie listened in mounting dismay as she heard him instruct the young woman to take over.

Annalise was flagging and seemed content enough to head off with Julia, who, it transpired, she had actually met some while back when she and Evalina had gone to Niccolo's villa for a holiday.

'She might show you something special if you're good...' he said as he smiled at his daughter.

'What?' Annalise had sprung to her feet, eyes immediately bright.

'You'll see. Word of warning, though...' He was still

smiling, and Annalise had moved to stand to attention in front of him, hands behind her back. 'Fifteen minutes of play there and then it's dinner for you and bed. It's been a long day.'

'Will you...?' She hesitated. 'Would you listen to me read for a bit? I've started a new book with Sophie...'

Keeping to the background, Sophie smiled and gave her small charge an encouraging nod and a thumbs-up sign. She'd forgotten that this was something they had chatted about a couple of days ago. Having observed his hesitancy in being hands-on, which seemed so strangely at odds with his keen sense of protectiveness for his daughter, she had figured it was a good idea to help encourage more time together to help rebuild their bond.

Just thinking along those lines calmed her, enabled her to shove to one side the intrusion of physical responses she didn't want.

'She's doing brilliantly with her reading,' Sophie added warmly. 'She's started a book I can remember reading when I was her age. You're enjoying it, aren't you, Annalise?'

Annalise was nodding with enthusiasm while Sophie wondered how she would spend the remainder of the evening if Julia was going to take over night duties.

The yacht was so large that there was no end to places she could explore, but of course the last thing Niccolo would want would be for her to keep popping up like an annoying jack-in-the-box wherever he happened to be with his clients.

He answered her question before she had had time to mull it over in depth by saying, sotto voce as he headed off with Annalise grasping his hand just in case he chose to wander off, 'I would very much like you to join us for dinner tonight, Sophie. There will be a total of fourteen people and it'll all be very informal, so…' he looked at her wryly '…no need to worry about not having the right thing to wear. A pair of shorts and a T-shirt will do the trick.'

'But…'

'Drinks at six-thirty and dinner to be served at seven-thirty.'

'But won't you want to discuss business…to work?'

'Today has been very successful on the "discussing business" front.' Niccolo shot her a slow, curling smile that made her think that he could read every objection racing to the surface in her head and would be keen to discuss each and every one of them. 'So it's all about relaxing this evening. It won't be a late one. The head of the clan likes his early nights. I'll knock on your door at six-fifteen. Doesn't give you a huge amount of time to play with but, like I said, there's no dress code, so just wear the first thing that comes to hand.'

And that was the end of the conversation.

In a hurried daze, Sophie took the opportunity to grab some clothes while Annalise was being shown whatever surprise she had been promised. Then she raced through a shower, using the facilities by the pool, where everything was at hand, including towels and shampoos and scented body wash, all in a space that was as luxurious as the most expensive scented spa. It was preferable to jostling for space in her quarters, where Niccolo would be bonding and Julia would be hovering, waiting to take over.

She had five minutes to kill before a knock on the door signalled Niccolo's arrival.

Sophie immediately tensed, breathed in deeply and pulled open the door.

She had put on a navy-blue button-down dress with a pattern of tiny white flowers and cap sleeves. It was figure-hugging to the waist and then flared to just above the knee. And she had left her hair loose, for once, a tangle of curls that reached almost to her waist.

Nothing could have prepared Niccolo for the assault to his senses brought on by the sight of her. He sucked in a sharp, shaky breath and for a few seconds his mind went completely blank.

He had such a sudden, powerful urge to reach out and touch this sweetly forbidden fruit that he shoved his hands deep into the pockets of his loose grey linen trousers.

'You're ready,' he said gruffly. 'Most women I've met find it impossible to get their act together in under two hours.'

'And even more women would be insulted at that sweeping generalisation.' Sophie half turned to gather a small string bag then spun round to see him grinning as he backed towards the door to nudge it open with his shoulder before stepping aside to let her precede him out.

'None of the ones I've ever dated.' He was still grinning, his dark eyes sliding appreciatively over her as she looked ahead, chin tilted, mouth pursed in righteous indignation. He wanted nothing more than to kiss it back into a smile.

He gave up trying to fight an urge that felt too powerful for him. Sometimes, he thought, it might actually be a good thing to release some of that rigidly held self-control which defined his behaviour.

It had certainly worked when it came to Annalise, he now thought. Hadn't it? He'd never been so relaxed around his daughter before. He'd stopped being the father whose job it was to provide and protect and allowed himself to be the father who also had fun. Or at least he was getting there.

Sophie muttered something but he didn't quite catch it. 'What?'

She followed as he led them through the yacht and the myriad nooks and crannies for sitting and relaxing and socialising and eating, all a marvel of sophisticated leather and glass and metal combinations interspersed with rugs and expensive artefacts.

'I *meant* that I'd bet every one of those women you dated could get ready in under fifteen minutes if they had to,' Sophie said tartly.

'Then why do I always end up looking at my watch whenever I arrange to meet them somewhere?'

'I hear that nothing beats a fashionably late entrance.'

'Do you use that gimmick when it comes to impressing a man?'

Instead of her hackles rising, and maybe it was the effects of a day spent lazing in the sun by a pool with someone waiting on her hand and foot, but she couldn't get annoyed. She said on a groan, 'Are you about to invade my private life again?'

'I wouldn't dream of it,' Niccolo murmured.

'Wouldn't you?' she returned drily, breath hitching in her throat as she glanced across at him.

'You've already warned me off asking questions you don't want to answer—'

'And you often obey when people warn you not to do something? You never, *ever* just ignore them and power ahead regardless?'

'I'm very much liking this new-style Sophie,' Niccolo said in a low, amused voice which managed to be serious enough for Sophie to feel a tingle of delicious danger thread through her. 'Can I see a bit more of her? She's a lot more intriguing than the one who's on guard all the time.'

Sophie became aware of the low murmur of voices ahead of them, but strangely she wished they could carry on talking. His sexy drawl was sending pleasurable shivers through her and she was sick of being on the defensive around him.

'I'm on guard for a reason,' Sophie murmured, half to herself, thinking about Scott and the way she had walked through a door she should never, ever have walked through because, for a moment in time, she had been so vulnerable after her parents' death.

'Tell me...'

But it was the wrong time and the wrong place, Niccolo knew, for this conversation and it was one he would return to.

She intrigued him and he had given up trying to either analyse or justify his reactions.

Ahead of them, duty called. This was what he was about. Duty and work first. This was what he had spent his entire adult life striving for and his entire teenage life aiming to achieve...financial security on such a scale that he became untouchable.

For once, duty felt onerous, but for the next three hours he complied, even though his eyes kept straying and his thoughts kept playing around with all sorts of contraband scenarios.

She circulated with grace and ease, comfortable chatting to whomever she happened to be with. No one would ever guess that this was a woman who had been through a year and a half of trauma and was only on this yacht at all because circumstances had forced her hand, because she had needed the money on offer.

Was it a background at private school that had accomplished that? No, he surmised. She was simply someone who didn't put herself ahead of the crowd, despite the way she looked. She was happy to listen, and a good listener was usually excellent when it came to putting people at ease.

His ex-wife had had a tendency to dominate proceedings. All eyes had to be focused on her. She had been raised to expect adulation, and the women he had dated since then? Lush, raven-haired beauties who knew how to flirt but would have been at sea amidst this sort of crowd, where the gentle ebb and flow of conversation they would have found too highbrow and probably boring as hell.

But Sophie…

Niccolo found himself itching to pick up the conversation where they had left off and he did, the moment the last of the guests had retired to their various cabins.

'As bad as you imagined it was going to be?'

They had left the table at a little after eleven. Now, walking slowly through the yacht, Sophie felt a lazy sense of contentment.

'I never thought it was going to be an ordeal,' Sophie returned. 'I'm accustomed to…well, entertaining, I guess. Cocktail-party small talk. Mixing and mingling with people you know you're not likely to see very much of again. My dad…' Her breath caught in her throat and she swallowed hard. 'My parents used to do quite a bit of entertaining back in the day, and they always encouraged me to take part.'

'Proud of you, no doubt,' Niccolo mused, 'and for good reason.'

Sophie blushed and kept her eyes averted, but she was too alert to his presence alongside her to be aware of anything else, including the hushed elegance of her surroundings. 'I made small talk.' She shrugged. 'It's not exactly the same as winning the Nobel Peace Prize or finding a cure for cancer.'

Niccolo burst out laughing. 'Join me on the upper deck,' he urged. He looked down at her, his dark eyes warm and amused, and Sophie blushed even more. 'It's not that late. A nightcap? Before the coach turns back into a pumpkin and Cinderella has to flee the ball?'

His soft laugh felt like a challenge and Sophie thought that there was surely no harm in chatting to him for another half an hour or so. She was all wound up after a night of socialising, which was something she hadn't done in a very long time. Was it selfish to want to feel normal again? Was it wrong to want to indulge in the heady and perfectly natural glow of having a conversation with a handsome guy? It was hardly as though anything was going to go anywhere, but she felt as if she'd spent so long with the weight of the world on her shoulders, feeling weary and old before her time.

'Maybe a quick nightcap,' she said in a rush, before she had time to change her mind.

'You won't regret it. There's nothing quite as spectacular as the view of an ocean at night when you're in the middle of it.'

He led the way. The stillness around them felt impossibly intimate and Sophie gasped when they emerged out onto the upper deck and the balmy night air, salty and aromatic, wrapped itself around her.

Above, the sky was velvety black, studded with infinite stars. She moved to stand by the railing and breathed in the night air. Into the distance, the ocean was as dark as a vast inkwell, softly rising and falling, breathing gently all around them.

And the silence was so profound that she could hear the smallest sound of the ocean lapping against the hull of his massive yacht.

Niccolo moved to stand right next to her, hands also on the railings, both of them staring out to sea.

'You're right,' Sophie said into the silence, her voice hushed and awed, 'it *is* spectacular. Out here…it's an amazing feeling being adrift on the ocean.'

Niccolo didn't say anything. He looked sidelong at her, appreciating the tilt of her head and the way her eyes were half closed as she absorbed her surroundings. He angled his body round so that he was now leaning against the railing, elbows over the side, and he continued to stare at her for a few more seconds, before saying casually, 'So you were going to tell me why you're on guard all the time…'

'Was I?' But she wasn't on guard now. She was ridiculously relaxed and just a little bit pleasantly heady

after a couple of glasses of champagne and fine food
and pleasant company. She turned to face him.

The breeze, still close and warm even at this time of
the evening, blew her fine hair this way and that and
the summer dress billowed ever so slightly, and Niccolo
discovered what it felt like to have trouble breathing.

To have trouble getting his thoughts straight.

'You were,' he said in a strangled voice. He couldn't
peel his eyes from her delicate face, upturned as she
gazed at him. The ache in his groin was so uncomfortable he had to adjust his stance, and just like that he
thought about no longer fighting this inexplicable urge
he had to let desire call the shots.

If she pushed him away, if she managed to cling on
to enough sanity for the two of them, then so be it. He
would back off at a rate of knots, and in fact, maybe it
would be a *good* thing if she told him to get lost.

He stared down at her, then he reached out and
stroked the side of her face with his knuckle. Her skin
was satin-smooth and he felt her breathe in sharply
and still.

'Niccolo…'

'Tell me to stop, Sophie, and I'll stop. Immediately.
No questions asked.' His voice was unsteady, his craving reaching fever-pitch as she started to breathe rapidly, and soft temptation drifted in the air between
them. 'This will never be mentioned again, but, Sophie… I want you. I want to make love to you.'

CHAPTER SEVEN

TERRIBLE IDEA. The words rang through Sophie's head, strident and imperious and demanding she call a halt to this.

He was her boss! And she was sworn off men! She'd made a promise to herself that she wouldn't dip her toes into matters of the heart until she had sorted herself out…and when she did, *if* she ever did, then she would use cool judgement to ensure she never made another mistake again. She would never allow another Scott to worm his way into her life.

But her feverish mind was playing second fiddle to her even more feverish body and she knew that her breathing had become sluggish, and her eyes remained treacherously riveted to his dark, unbearably handsome face.

She reached out to gently push him back, to create some desperately needed space between their bodies, but found her hand remained on his stomach, and after a couple of seconds he covered her hand with his and then stroked it, rolling his finger over her knuckles, which elicited a soft moan from her.

Sophie closed her eyes and tiptoed up, inviting his kiss. Still, the touch of his lips against hers sent a rush of blood to her head and she almost swayed. She reached to clutch his shirt and took a step towards him, eyes still closed, not breaking their contact, just loving the feel of his tongue against hers, wet and hungry.

She was close enough to feel the prominent bulge in his shorts and moaned again.

The air was warm and sultry and the stillness of the dark night around them seemed to lock them into a bubble where the only sounds were the telltale noises of two people craving more.

And how long would they have remained there, locked in their embrace?

Would they have somehow found themselves making out like a couple of horny teenagers by the side of the pool?

At what point would one of them have woken up to the madness of what they were doing?

Neither had the chance because they were interrupted by a soft cough from somewhere behind them.

It was so soft that for a few seconds Sophie wasn't sure whether she'd heard anything at all, but then suddenly Niccolo was drawing back and she heard him swear in Italian under his breath before spinning round to face the elderly couple now stepping out of the shadows.

Sophie blinked.

Vincenzo de Luca and his lovely, charming wife, Maria. Vincenzo was the head of the Italian family selling to Niccolo. Sophie had spent ages chatting to both of them and one of their sons.

The couple were as family-oriented as Sophie's own parents had been, bursting with pride at the achievements of their boys and eager to show her pictures of their grandchildren.

Their stay on the yacht, just long enough to fine tune the final details of the deal—which she had shrewdly interpreted as making sure that Niccolo was the real deal...an honourable man who treated his staff well and was considerate to all members of the de Luca clan and not simply the ones that held the pens to sign the deeds—would be followed by a huge family holiday in Tuscany.

They couldn't wait.

And now here they were, smiling broadly and moving towards them, and Sophie's heart sank so fast she was surprised she didn't keel over from the impact.

Vincenzo said something to Niccolo in very fast Italian and, picking up minute signs of embarrassment, she noted Niccolo's passing flush before he drew her towards him, hand curled round her waist, just as Maria said, with a little whisper of delight to Sophie, 'I told my Vincenzo when we went to bed that the two of you were in love. I am a *mamma* and a *nonna* and I can see these things.'

Framed by a halo of moonlight, Sophie could see the sparkle in her dark eyes.

Around her waist, Niccolo's hand felt heavy and deeply intimate.

They had decided to venture to the top deck to see what the view was like, they explained. It was such a lovely evening it felt a shame to let it go to waste.

Sophie's smile had frozen into something she fancied might look reasonably terrifying, and she did her best to relax.

They'd been caught *in flagrante delicto*... Except

they hadn't been committing an offence. They had been wrapped around one another on the verge of making love and she knew, in a heartbeat, that Niccolo's arm around her was the gesture of a man acquiescing to a pretence that was necessary. For him, the deal would risk being scuppered because the de Lucas were traditional enough to reconsider what they were on the verge of signing if they got it into their heads that their knight in shining armour was a bounder.

And for her?

She knew how much this deal meant to Niccolo and she cared that he got it. And more than that, she had really liked the elderly couple.

She saw the warm pleasure on their faces to learn that she and Niccolo were an item and, with an inward sigh of resignation, she nestled a bit closer to Niccolo, playing along with the fiction.

Relief and a certain apprehension filled Niccolo. He had expected her to stiffen against him, not move closer. He had banked on their weird body language being misinterpreted under cover of darkness. The very second he had become aware of the presence of his clients on the deck with them, he had foreseen an awkward situation between himself and Sophie, but here she was, nudging her ballet-dancer-graceful body against his side, laughing and chatting without a care in the world.

It was doing the trick, he thought, but what might be the price for this particular gambit?

Something spontaneous was fast turning into a situation where damage limitation might be needed.

He'd thrown the rulebook out of the window the second he'd met this woman. There hadn't been the usual predictable path that always invariably led to the bedroom. A path where certain ground rules were laid down and parameters put in place.

Yes, he'd confided in her, much to his surprise, but had that been enough to fill her in on the lie of the land? Had she got the big picture? That he was a man who wasn't in it for the long term?

That hand looped through his…was it a sign of something Sophie felt she might lay claim to? Emotion? Involvement?

She was young and vulnerable and had been through a tough time. If she was searching for someone, might she think that that someone could be him? This game of pretence, generated by Vincenzo and Maria's ill-timed interruption, risked becoming a prelude to all sorts of possibilities which he knew to be out of reach.

He gently detached himself as soon as the group began heading away from the deck and stepped even further away from her to bid goodnight to Vincenzo and Maria, giving them a warm reminder that should they want anything at all they only had to ring the bell inside their suite.

'I should thank you,' he said once they were alone, swerving towards the stunted staircase that spiralled down towards the expansive area where their bedrooms were located.

Sophie didn't pretend to misunderstand. He had paused on the staircase, his hand on the steel banister, to look at her seriously.

She hadn't missed the way he had pulled back from her just as soon as he could.

Had he thought that she might be getting ideas into her head?

'It seemed appropriate,' Sophie said, half smiling although her voice was a shade cooler now. 'You're on the brink of signing your big deal and I know, from having spent the evening with the de Lucas, that they might be the sort of uber-traditional couple to disapprove of you having a romp in the sack with the nanny for a bit of fun—'

'I wouldn't have been quite so basic about it,' Niccolo interrupted.

'It's the truth, isn't it? Aside from that, Niccolo, I happen to really like them. They interrupted us in the middle of something and it would have been awkward and shocking for them were I to try and distance myself from you. It would have reflected badly on both of us.'

She met his dark eyes without flinching and continued, unhurried and calm, which was very much the opposite of what she was feeling inside.

'Just in case you might have got it into your head that that phoney display of affection was in any way *real*, I feel I should set you straight.' It was the last place for a confidence to be shared but the timing felt right. She barely hesitated before carrying on. 'I'll tell you about Scott. In a nutshell, we were in the same social circle for years. You could almost say we grew up together. When my parents were killed and the magnitude of their debts began unravelling, so-called friends were suddenly thin on the ground.' She tilted her head to one side, hoping to read what he was thinking, but his fabulous dark eyes were veiled as he looked at her. 'I couldn't keep up with their lifestyle any longer and I was too busy trying to deal with what life had thrown at me to worry about my disappearing social life. But while everyone else melted away, Scott stuck around.

He was a shoulder to cry on and I… I gave in. He was persuasive. He was charming. I also discovered that he was abusive and controlling. He enjoyed making me feel like nothing. He watched every move I made and did his utmost to wrest the few friends I had left away from me. I didn't know what was going on and I was just so worn down from dealing with all the stuff that had happened that I suppose I let things run on for a lot longer than I ever would have in other circumstances. But when he decided that yelling wasn't doing the trick and maybe a smack or two might get through to me more effectively I finally got it together to chuck him out.'

Sophie skipped over the fear and the confusion and then the dismay and disappointment she had felt in herself that she had allowed someone to take over her life and put her in a place where nothing had seemed manageable at all any more.

She didn't explain how terrifying it had felt at the time to have placed her trust in a guy who had used it to try and take over her life. It had been a bit like watching a tornado, only to blink and find that the tornado was upon you and you were at risk of losing everything, including your sanity.

'So,' she said briskly, 'there's no need to be afraid that five minutes pretending to have more than what we actually have is going to go to my head. Believe me, I'm not looking for anything from anyone.' Her voice was hard. 'I was attracted to you and the wine and the moonlight and the atmosphere led us to make a mistake.'

Niccolo raked his fingers through his hair. He was shaken to the core. The thought of any man hitting any woman made him feel physically sick, and the fact that the woman in question was Sophie made him see red.

She was so open and outspoken and funny…

He balled his hands into fists. If the scumbag had been standing in front of him right now, Niccolo didn't know what he would have done. Delivering a nice, long, cold dip in the midnight ocean would have seemed a very good idea.

'Sophie, I'm so sorry.'

'There's nothing to be sorry about,' Sophie said. 'And I didn't tell you about Scott to garner your sympathy. I just wanted you to know that I'm not interested in anything at all.'

'Come to my room,' he murmured. 'This conversation can't stop here.'

'I don't want to come to your room, Niccolo.'

'Why? Are you afraid?'

'I suppose I am, really,' she said with a crooked smile.

'Of what?'

He looked so genuinely shocked that this time Sophie's smile was heartfelt.

'Not you, Niccolo. Don't be an idiot.' Something flashed through her head, as fast as quicksilver: she could never, ever fear anything from this man because, however commitment-phobic he was, there was a deep core of honour running through him. Underneath the harsh exterior, he was *kind*, although she wasn't sure he would want her to bring that to his notice.

Comprehension dawned on his beautiful face. 'You're afraid you might succumb? Give in?'

'Something like that.'

'And would that be such a bad thing?'

'I swore I would never get involved with another man again. Not for a long, long time. Once bitten, twice shy.'

'I am not your ex-lover. In fact, if you ever fancy letting me have his full name, he would find out just how long and how powerful my reach is. I would make sure he spent the remainder of his useless life grovelling on the street for coins.'

'I think Scott just needs therapy,' Sophie said. 'Anyway. Enough of him. I just wish I could warn whoever happens to come after me that he's trouble.'

'Come back to my room.'

'I don't want...complications...' She heard the hesitancy in her voice with alarm. She was riveted by the shadows and the angles of his face, thrown into stark relief by the darkness outside and the intermittent lighting inside.

'Trust me, that's the last thing I want,' Niccolo said gruffly. 'But I feel a need to...to hold you. I want to hold you close, breathe you in, feel your softness against me.'

Sophie laughed and felt a whoosh of inappropriate tenderness steal into her.

'I never saw you for a poet, Niccolo.'

'I'm a man of many surprises. I know you're scared but I won't hurt you. We're on the same page, though perhaps for different reasons. Neither of us wants complications. You've been through hell...maybe it's time you allowed yourself some enjoyment.'

'I'm already enjoying myself...being here...' But his words were enticing. She hadn't enjoyed herself for a long, long time. Was this what she needed? As well as wanted? She was still young. Did she just need to have some fun?

He could be dangerous…something inside was telling her that. But he had laid his cards on the table and however thrillingly, excitingly *dangerous* he seemed, like a huge, burning fire, dazzling in its beauty yet perilous if you got too close, she knew what she wanted in her forever guy, and it wasn't commitment issues.

He was dangerous if he stole your heart, but her heart wasn't up for grabs and enjoyment—pure, undistilled enjoyment—was dizzyingly enticing.

'Besides,' she was peering into an abyss and it made her shiver, 'I look after Annalise…'

'You do,' Niccolo murmured, 'although I'm struggling to see where that fits into the picture. Naturally, we won't be all over one another in public. Nothing will change in connection with you looking after my daughter. I have always protected her, the best I can, from my private life, and nothing will change on that front. And if for the rest of the trip the de Lucas see what they expect to see, then that wouldn't be a problem.'

'You mean, on the face of things, you're still my boss and nothing else? At least insofar as Annalise is concerned, but it's okay for Vincenzo and his family to believe that we're an item?'

'We're adults. Two adults who want one another and are both honest enough to admit it. Neither of us anticipated this, even if my aunt may have…' For a few seconds, Niccolo couldn't help but smile at the thought of Evalina, who had accurately predicted a spark but had certainly been wildly over-optimistic when it came to longer-term predictions. How could she have known that both he and Sophie had their hearts locked away for very different reasons? But here they were and the thought of sleeping with the woman looking up at him with a little frown, chewing over a decision that was, in the great scheme of things, not exactly world-shattering, filled him with a heady sense of euphoria.

'Annalise will be sound asleep, and she knows where I am if she needs to find me. But, trust me, she won't.'

'And I'll return to my room afterwards?'

'I don't tend to spend nights with anyone,' Niccolo admitted. 'That's not how I'm built.'

They were walking now, slowly, Sophie trailing her hand along the smooth walnut of the banister that separated a sumptuous sitting area from a space that was clearly designed for conferences and work, with a long table, upright chairs and USB ports everywhere.

The smell of the ocean filled the air, tangy and salty. Romance all around them, a bubble waiting to be burst, but who cared? This was a magical setting and if she gave in to the magic then it wouldn't be the end of the world, would it?

'You've *never* spent the night with a woman? Apart from your…wife?'

'Don't sound so shocked.' Niccolo was amused by her reaction. 'I have a daughter, and the last thing an impressionable child needs to see is a revolving door filled with women.'

'Revolving door?' Sophie asked with saccharine sarcasm. 'I'm not sure that's something you should be bragging about.'

Niccolo grinned and looked across to her appreciatively, anticipation fizzing inside him.

She wasn't a turn-on because of the way she

looked—although no one with eyes in their head could deny that she was sensational…no, she was a turn-on because of who she was, her personality, her absolute willingness to say what was on her mind without thinking that she might offend him.

She didn't obey the usual rules that seemed to keep everyone who dealt with him in check, and he was finding that he liked that.

Annalise was out for the count when they checked in on her.

'It's the ocean air and the hot sun,' Niccolo said as he closed the door to his daughter's cabin. 'Tomorrow, the sea beckons. She'll enjoy swimming in it. It's quite different from a pool.'

Their eyes met and there was a question in his as they stood in the quiet of the spacious living area.

'I should confess that there's no revolving door when it comes to women,' he said seriously. He reached out and curled his finger into a strand of blonde hair and then stroked the side of her face and watched as she caught her breath, nostrils slightly flaring and a soft pink creeping into her cheeks. 'I've made sure to be very selective when it comes to the women I've dated in the past. I may not want commitment, but neither am I the sort of guy who would pick up someone on a Tuesday and replace her on a Friday. I treat women with respect and honesty. They know where they stand with me.'

'I believe you,' Sophie said simply, and he smiled.

'Sure?'

'One hundred per cent. I may not…' She looked away with difficulty, but she was so aware of his finger resting on the side of her face, lightly brushing, that she could scarcely breathe at all. 'I may not be looking for a relationship either, but there's no way I would even contemplate…doing anything with you unless I knew that you were a good guy. I made a huge mistake with Scott, but I was in a bad place,' she continued, speaking her mind aloud, mulling over the surprising realisation that she had spoken more to Niccolo than she had to anyone else about what life had been for her over the past year and a half.

'You were vulnerable,' Niccolo said softly, 'and it was your bad luck that someone was waiting in the wings to take advantage of that, but there are always lessons to be learnt from miserable experiences. You're made stronger by what you went through, not weaker.'

'Thank you.' She smiled wryly. 'You're a philosopher as well as everything else.'

'Everything else?' he teased. His dark eyes were lazy and unflinching. 'You need to be sure that you want to do this, Sophie. Are you?'

Sophie felt a second of giddiness, as though she was looking down a vertiginous drop into a black hole, then she made her mind up and took his hand in hers and kissed it.

'Never more sure of anything in my life.'

The next few minutes passed in a daze. Was this the same Sophie who had been so racked with anxiety and so full of sorrow only weeks before?

How could she be discovering what recovery felt like with this man? In these circumstances?

Was that what made it feel right? Being here?

His suite was bigger than the one she shared with Annalise, a sprawling affair with two outside rooms and a massive bathroom, which she glimpsed as he nudged open the door to his bedroom with his foot. He hadn't switched on any lights. There was no need because moonlight streamed in through the thick panes of glass, carried on a refreshing breeze. Overhead, a fan lazily circled, the only sound in the bedroom aside from the sound of their breathing.

Sophie drew in a sharp breath as he traced the outline of her small breasts pushing against the soft cotton of her blue summer dress.

Very gently he began to ease the dress off, the cotton slippery against her arms, against her ribcage, dropping until it was gathered at her waist, and then he stood back and looked, and in response she unhooked her bra from behind and tossed it on the floor without her hungry eyes ever leaving his face.

Her nipples stiffened as cool air hit them and she tilted her head back and sighed as he swept her off her feet and deposited her on the king-sized bed, from which advantageous position she could look at him through half-closed eyes as he began stripping off.

He was truly a thing of beauty. Moonlight, she thought wryly, became him.

He dumped his shirt on the floor then stepped out of his shorts and her eyes widened. She propped herself up on both elbows and shamelessly stared, and Niccolo grinned back at her.

'I like the reaction.'

He moved towards her, pausing to flip open his wallet and rifle through it, then he joined her on the bed, big and muscular, his nakedness sending a tsunami of want and longing racing through her in a tidal surge.

'Now I get to look.' He tugged the dress all the way

off and her briefs were scooped along for the ride as she wriggled free.

She knew that she should have been feeling shy and confused and maybe just a little bit hesitant.

She really wasn't this kind of girl. She'd never had a one-night stand in her life. In fairness, she'd never felt this wild, intense level of *lust* in her life before either. She revelled in her nakedness. His dark eyes, roving over her, made her less inhibited, not more, and she wasn't going to pretend that she wasn't as turned on as he was.

Maybe it was months of sickening anxiety, but she felt a tremendous sense of release as he settled on the mattress alongside her and pushed her hair back to lightly kiss her forehead, her temple, the side of her mouth, his every gesture curiously gentle and tender.

'You're beautiful,' he murmured, half smiling.

'So are you,' Sophie told him truthfully, and he smiled more.

'Your honesty never fails to surprise me. I don't think any woman has ever told me that I'm beautiful.'

He covered her breast with his hand and rolled the pad of his thumb over her nipple, and Sophie's eyes fluttered. She moved and moaned and then gasped when he took her nipple into his mouth and did something wonderful, tugging and sucking at the same time until she couldn't keep still.

One hand curled into his dark hair, even as she arched up so as to intensify the pleasure of his tongue lathing her stiffened nipple while the other hand skittered over his back, tracing muscle and sinew.

His arousal throbbed against her and she parted her

legs, feeling the wetness between them, craving more than just his mouth on her breast.

She wanted to feel him moving inside her right this very minute, but he was taking his time.

He moved from one breast to the next, paying the same level of attention to the second as he had to the first, caressing one nipple with his fingers, teasing and tugging while his mouth drove her crazy as he suckled the other.

She was panting as he nuzzled the underside of her small breasts before trailing his tongue lazily along her stomach, pausing only to dip into her belly button before sinking between her thighs. Sophie gave a little squeak of shock but then the pleasure that washed over her as his tongue found the groove between her legs closed her mind down completely.

Sensation replaced thought. He teased her core with his tongue and kept his hands on her inner thighs, keeping them apart as he continued to explore. When he dipped two fingers into her she groaned, and felt the slow build of an orgasm.

She didn't want to come like this.

She wanted him *in* her, filling her up, but that tongue was devastating. She moved against his mouth, loving the twin sensations of her core being stimulated while inside her his fingers were equally erotic, driving her relentlessly to heights she had never dreamt possible.

She drew her knees up and her orgasm, as she spasmed and shuddered against his mouth, was as intense as a runaway train barrelling into her. On and on it went, wave upon wave until she was utterly spent.

She lay like a rag doll for a few seconds, but as she drowsily looked at him, once again drinking in his beauty and power, she could feel her sated body begin to stir again.

She stretched and smiled, looking at him with slanted, contented eyes.

Niccolo stared back at her. He could still taste her on his tongue. He was so turned on that he had to drag his thoughts into safer territory, but that was impossible when she was looking at him the way she was now. Her eyes were dark and amused and satisfied all at the same time and it fuelled a heat in him that made his mouth go dry.

For a few seconds, staring at her with the deep, dark night skies outside and the distant whisper of the ocean, he felt a stab of pure confusion, a feeling of being suddenly out of his depth, then the feeling was gone and he smiled back at her, in charge again.

'Enjoyed that, did you?' he asked in a husky undertone.

'No complaints.' Sophie sighed. She pushed herself up and then knelt so that they were facing one another, and she ran her hands over his shoulders, then along his forearms, curving around to stroke his ribcage and circle his small brown nipples.

'I can't believe I'm being…this person,' she confessed, dipping to kiss his shoulder and then tilting her head to look him straight in the eyes.

'What person is this?'

He manoeuvred them so that they were once again lying down but this time facing one another, their bodies lightly touching.

'You make me feel…a little reckless and very confident about my body.'

'You're a beautiful woman with a body to match. Where's the lack of confidence coming from?'

Sophie laughed a little under her breath. Yes, she knew she was attractive enough but that wasn't a sure-fire path to the sort of extrovert self-assurance most of her peers had possessed. She had missed some of the signposts along the way and had ended up the sort of girl who was happy enough to socialise but given half a chance had always been happier with her head in a book or lazing in the gardens of a National Trust house.

This man somehow made her aware of a side to her she had hitherto ignored.

'Who knows…?' She laughed away the sudden serious moment as she began touching him, emboldened because she could see and feel how turned on he was.

This time, their lovemaking was long and slow. She had hurtled over the edge and now he built her back up again, back to a place where her body was humming and on fire.

He paused only to make sure he was protected, and then when he at last sank into her she was already so turned on that she climaxed on his first deep thrust and felt a burst of pleasure when he climaxed soon after, arching back, wildly and beautifully out of control.

How much time had passed? It could have been a hundred years. Sophie was energised and felt really alive for the first time in her adult life.

She realised she had no idea what happened next in this scenario, although what she *did* know was that he was a man who never spent a night with a woman; she began edging her way towards the side of the bed, but he stilled her before she could clamber off.

'We're here on this yacht,' he murmured, sitting up in one fluid motion and cupping the nape of her neck as he looked at her with a little smile, 'in the middle of the ocean, and Vincenzo and his family now think we're an item. I wouldn't want to disappoint...'

Sophie was mesmerised by his smile. Yes, here they were, and this was a world away from real life. Reality was a plane flight and several taxis away...

'Just while we're here...' She reached out to stroke his face and was powerless to do anything but obey her body for the very short while they would be on his yacht.

'Just while we're here,' Niccolo agreed. 'I may not have the rule book when it comes to predicting the future, but one thing I do know is that nothing lasts for ever. When we return to London, this will be a dream easily forgotten. You'll be with me for a couple more weeks and then you can return to your life with a lot more peace of mind that your financial woes are ebbing away.' He smiled crookedly.

Sophie looked at him for a few seconds. To jump or not to jump...

She had learnt lessons from Scott, the biggest being that when it came to longevity, she would take her time and go safely, go with the guy who would be her rock.

But she had learnt other lessons along the way... lessons from having to deal with the sudden death of both her parents. Life was short, and tomorrow was, after all, another day easily dealt with...

CHAPTER EIGHT

NICCOLO'S CLIENTS STAYED a further two days, during which time Sophie emerged from the shadows of being Annalise's nanny. She had envisaged, before arriving on his amazing superyacht, that she and Annalise would amuse themselves wherever the action happened *not* to be. Certainly, on day one, reclining on the upper deck, she had happily concluded that that would become the routine over the next four days. While big money was made and deals were finalised over fine wine and fine food, she and Annalise would be out of sight, although not out of mind, because she had, of course, factored in the fact that Niccolo would spend some quality time with his daughter and when he did she, Sophie, would busy herself reading or relaxing in one of the many secluded areas on the yacht. It was certainly big enough for her to find a spot where she could be on her own.

There were a multitude of decks, after all, and no less than three swimming pools!

That had been the plan.

Plans, she discovered, changed. Secret desires, she discovered, changed too. Lusting undercover was quite different when the forbidden became accepted. Over the next couple of days, whilst she occupied Annalise in the mornings, enjoying the run of the yacht, including the child-friendly space which had anything and everything designed to amuse a kid, she was invited to spend time mixing with the guests in the afternoon and in the evenings. It had also become routine for Julia to take over childminding duties from six onwards.

Sophie was guiltily conscious of those lines that had been blurred but she was too wrapped up in a haze of unimaginable excitement to pay much attention.

Whatever Vincenzo's assumptions about their relationship, Niccolo made sure to limit public displays of affection, and so there was a heightened sense of awareness of one another as they socialised under the hot, starry nights, dining informally on exquisite tapas served by his various chefs, with the ocean lazily lapping the sides of the massive yacht.

She would catch his eye and know that he had been looking at her, and even if he wasn't anywhere near her she would feel his dark, brooding gaze as powerful as a physical caress.

And the sex…

Mind-blowing. It was as if her body had finally realised what it was meant to do, as if her femininity had, at last, been wakened, reminding her that she was still a vibrant young woman, still *alive*.

Strangely, she knew that this person who had emerged in the least likely of circumstances would have thrilled her parents. They would not have wanted her to spend the remainder of her youth wallowing in grief. They would have wanted this adventure for her and knowing that gave her tremendous peace of mind.

She had thrown herself headlong into a situation

with a predetermined outcome and she was loving every illicit second of it. Eyes wide open, she was doing what she had never, in a million years, thought she was capable of doing…

She was enjoying a relationship that was going nowhere with a man. Love…commitment…any notion of longevity was absent from what they had and, for someone who had always been conscientious to a fault, good at making sensible decisions, this represented a huge diversion from the norm.

With the last of the guests now gone, Sophie stared out at a blue horizon and slowly accepted that London was a mere two days away, once Niccolo had finalised the last touches to his deal and communicated with various departments within his sprawling organisation on the business of briefing the press.

Today, for the first time, she and Annalise would not be spending the day together because Niccolo was taking her out for lunch.

'Where?' she'd asked, wondering whether she'd missed some other five-star restaurant nestled in an obscure corner of his fabulous yacht. She didn't think anything could surpass the pleasure of eating perfect food under blue skies, with the salty ocean breeze all around and a horizon that stretched limitlessly into a fine strip of navy where sky and sea seemed to become one.

'It's a surprise,' he had drawled. 'The code is casual dress. Let's refine that…the code is swimwear until such time as it becomes birthday suit…'

So now here she was, and she gave a little yelp when she felt him dip behind her to kiss her shoulder.

She turned around, standing as she did so, and her

heart gave that familiar flip-flop and all the thoughts she'd been having skittered through her head and disappeared like water running down a plughole.

'I'm liking the dress code,' Niccolo murmured, holding her at arm's length and inspecting. 'Bright colours suit you.'

'It's the first time I've worn anything bright in a long time,' Sophie admitted. She glanced down at the swirls of orange and yellows in her long, flowing skirt and the pale blue of her sleeveless top. In the canvas bag, one of many beachwear accessories available on the yacht for anyone who might need them, was her black one-piece, her towel and the usual array of suncreams and sunglasses.

Niccolo nodded. She confided easily. Little confidences told with a certain hesitancy which he actually liked and had certainly become accustomed to.

She didn't demand his undivided attention and he figured that that was why she managed to get it so easily because he certainly hadn't been able to keep his eyes off her over the past couple of days, when their relationship had gone from platonic to sexual with the speed of a supersonic rocket.

'Make sure you've got a lot of sunblock.' He tucked some strands of blonde hair behind her ears. 'You're so fair you'll end up looking like a lobster if you're not careful.'

Sophie burst out laughing. 'I appreciate the concern. Not to worry, I've packed enough sunblock to open a small shop.'

Just for a second, Niccolo stilled and frowned, disconcerted by a certain protectiveness that had swept over him and even more taken aback by the shift in atmosphere from sexual banter and teasing to something more unsettlingly...*familiar*. Since when did he do familiar? He had spent years mastering the art of conducting affairs without *familiar* ever becoming part of the package. Maybe it was just his imagination, but he wasn't about to take any chances.

Have I said something wrong? Sophie wondered.

She'd noted the way he had pulled back, a shadow of withdrawal that had been glaringly obvious to her, and after a few seconds of confusion she rallied fast because of course she knew exactly why the mood had shifted.

A line had been crossed.

The way he had touched her just then, the look in his eyes...there had been amusement and indulgence that had made her squirm with pleasure but had clearly had the opposite effect on him. This was just a bit of time out for him, she thought, whereas for her it was...

Well, what was it?

The voice in her head was more insistent now than it had been previously, and her heart began to beat at a rapid tempo. She cared for him. How had that happened? This was more than just a sexual craving for her. Somewhere along the line, the force of his personality, his intelligence and wit, curious kindness and generosity of spirit had pierced through her defences and got her feeling things she had no right to feel.

Had he sensed that?

Sophie felt a prickly, heated rush of blood to her head as the mortifying possibility that he had sensed something she herself had only now begun to figure out took shape.

And he'd retreated faster than a speeding bullet.

He had made it clear what he wanted from this...liaison. She had agreed because at the time it had seemed a simple equation: fun and adventure with no price to pay afterwards. Months of pent-up misery and anxiety had fuelled a response in her that had been easy to categorise. Very quickly, Sophie knew that she had to make certain decisions. She could retreat or else she could enjoy what they had, knowing that she would be heartbroken when it ended.

Whoever said that life was simple?

She wanted to pack as many memories as she could into the next couple of days, enough to keep her warm at night and to remind her of what it felt like to be *alive* after months of living the life of a zombie. Scott had broken through her misery, but his presence had been toxic.

Niccolo, on the other hand, inappropriate as he was when it came to any sort of forever guy, had somehow managed to go a long way to healing her.

She reckoned that might be just about the last thing he would want to hear, only slightly ahead of *I'd really like what we have to continue*...or *maybe we could see where this takes us...*

'I got sunburned once,' She carried on the conversation, her voice light and unbothered. 'When I was ten. We went to Majorca on holiday and I forgot about the sunblock and, believe me, it's a mistake I'll never make again. How is Annalise? We had breakfast together and I left a few bits and pieces with her to do if she gets bored.'

She began walking away, ignoring any awkwardness and shutting down the thoughts swirling in her head. She felt him fall into step alongside her but she didn't look at him.

'Although,' she continued gaily, 'how on earth could anyone get bored on this yacht? Sun...sea... I guess all that's missing is the sand! She might feel something of an anti-climax when we get back to London, but I have lots of things in store that Annalise and I can do together.' She glanced sideways at him to see that he was staring ahead but no longer frowning.

'That's very diligent of you.' He was smiling when he said that and she relaxed fractionally, eager to pick up the thread and run with it.

'I'm a very diligent person.' There was a smile in her voice now as well. 'It's something to do with dealing with plants,' she confided. 'You can't hurry them along. You have to be patient and wait to see the results of all the effort you put in.' She launched into describing some of the projects she had worked on before her university career had abruptly ended and was still chatting as they made their way down a stunted stairwell to a part of the yacht she had not even glimpsed in passing.

She fell silent. Somehow she had expected...she didn't quite know what. Certainly not a boat within a boat. Belatedly she spotted two of the crew waiting in the wings, and in a daze she was ushered into the speedboat, along with two hampers and a Louis Vuitton canvas bag.

Only as the streamlined boat slid out from the bowels of the superyacht did she turn to Niccolo with an awestruck expression.

'Really?' she asked, and he burst out laughing as he steered the boat away from its mothership, picking up confident speed across the open ocean.

'It's an indulgence, I admit,' he shouted over the powerful roar of the motor, and for a while Sophie just stayed completely silent and watched the blur of scenery whipping past her as she held her face away from the spray of sea flicking up as the boat shot through the water.

There was nothing to see and yet there was everything to see. Sea and sky and the pure vastness of nature took her breath away. She'd always been way too careful to enjoy going fast in anything, from a car to the one time she had been persuaded by Scott into riding pillion on his motorbike, but this...

She'd tied her hair back and she could already feel it unravelling, whipped around by the force of the wind against her face.

The speed was an aphrodisiac...not to mention the sight of him, all bronzed, with his shirt unbuttoned and his shorts emphasising the length of his muscular legs.

She gasped as the speedboat began to slow and then the deep navy blue of the ocean gradually gave way to paler, lighter blues, then streaks of bright turquoise blending with dazzling clear green, lapping the shores of a completely deserted cove.

With a tangle of trees and shrubs and bush rising against a steep hill at the back, the cove was clearly accessible only by boat and they seemed to be the only visitors.

'An indulgence...' Sophie said as he killed the engine and expertly anchored the speedboat so that it was just a case of slipping over the side into warm, shallow, stupidly transparent water.

'Haven't done anything with it for too long,' he admitted, helping her out and to the beach and then proceeding, in stages, to transport the hampers to dry land.

Sophie smiled and said teasingly, as she looked all around her, taking everything in, 'That's the problem with toys. Sooner or later they get chucked to one side.'

Niccolo grinned and saluted. 'Yes, ma'am. That's told me.'

He pulled her towards him, and just like that all the doubts that had earlier crowded into her head disappeared and she cleaved her body against his with delight.

He smelled salty.

'This is all ours for the day,' he murmured.

'How do you know? Anyone might decide that this is the perfect spot for a picnic...'

'Oh, any billionaire worth his salt wouldn't dream of intruding on another billionaire's territory. They'd spot my speedboat and head for another private cove...'

He pushed his fingers into her hair, undid what remained of the thick plait and then spread it across her shoulders. Then he turned his attention to the tiny buttons on her top, taking his time.

'Braless.' He groaned. 'You have no idea how much I've been thinking of touching you.' He inched her back and then broke free to delve into the canvas bag, from which he extracted an enormous towel to spread on the ground.

It felt thrilling and wicked to be doing this, Sophie thought, already wet.

He had positioned the towel under a cluster of trees, avoiding direct sunlight. While she lay on the towel to look at him—half naked because she had finished what he had started and had removed her top—she watched as he stripped off, revealing his glorious body in slow motion, bit by gradual bit until she could barely contain her rising excitement.

She propped herself up on her elbows and blushed as he stood over her, towering, his burnished torso roughened with dark hair and his arousal proclaiming that he was as turned on as she was.

He took himself in one hand and idly stroked, and her whole body went up in flames.

Lovemaking in the intimacy of a dark cabin was so different from this…with the warm sun beating down on them and the sea and the icing-sugar-white sand all around.

As his dark eyes skewered her to the spot, Sophie followed his lead…pushing her hands under the soft, tissue-paper-thin skirt and then pressing her fingers against herself until a burst of sensation began spreading through her.

Niccolo smiled. He didn't step towards her. Instead he half nodded, urging her on, and she stroked until she felt the slow, urgent build of her climax.

This was shameless, wanton…but oh, so shockingly erotic. She came in a surge of pleasure, her body quivering and arching against her fingers. In her most intimate moment, this man had seen her and it felt right, somehow.

'Your turn,' she murmured as he sank down next to her on the oversized towel.

He grinned and nibbled the side of her mouth while simultaneously relieving her of her skirt and underwear, out of which she helpfully wriggled without separating from his small kisses. 'You look like a sexy, ruffled little angel. I like it. A lot. And I have more important things to do right now than worry about my own needs...'

'What have you got to do?' Sophie pouted. She was still warm and tingly as her body gradually began to calm.

By way of response, Niccolo reached across her to her bag, extracted the sunblock and informed her that it was time for him to make sure she was fully protected against the damaging effects of the sun.

'Don't be fooled,' he warned piously as he slapped some cream on the palm of his hand, 'by the fact that we're lying in partial shade. This sun is ferocious. The last thing I want is for you to have to experience a bout of nasty sunburn. Now, where would you like me to start? Front or back?'

It was a luxurious experience. His hands were cool and slippery, and he paid minute attention to every square inch of her body. He rolled his hands over her breasts, cupping them and massaging the cream onto her, then along her waist and over her stomach, and then came her thighs, on the outside...and on the inside, and she whimpered, eyes closed, as he smoothed his hands over the sensitive skin of her inner thighs, nudging her wetness along the way, teasing her just so much but no more.

It was a lazy, sensuous experience and it was clear he was beyond aroused, but instead of taking things further he finished his very thorough job of applying the suncream. Once it was dry, he suggested they should take a dip in the sea.

'Sensible of you to get waterproof sunblock,' he announced, vaulting upright while she hurriedly followed suit, although he stopped her before she could slip into

her swimsuit. 'You won't need that. You're fully protected from those harmful UV rays…'

'I had no idea you had a degree in medicine,' Sophie returned, turned on and amused and completely
in the moment.

'I'm a man of many talents…' Niccolo grinned wolf-
ishly at her and then casually reached to circle her nipples with his fingers until she was breathing quickly,
mouth parted, nostrils flaring just enough to tell him
how turned on she could be by the merest touch.

The sea was warm, the water so clear that she could
see her nakedness distorted in it, moving this way and
that as they swam out, he with long, sure strokes, she
following behind and catching up when he stopped to
lie on his back, floating.

She joined him in gazing up into the bluest of skies
and wondered whether this was the sort of perfection
that could be bottled. If it could, then she would make
a fortune.

To one side, the speedboat bobbed gently, and as
he had said to her there was no one else around. They
could have been marooned on a desert island.

She was overwhelmed by a feeling of utter peace and
contentment and her thoughts were drifting too sleepily
in time to the small ebbs of current under her to focus
on anything much bigger than *I'm happy*.

'Penny for them,' Niccolo murmured from next to
her.

'I'm offended you think that my thoughts come that
cheap,' she said, her smile evident in her voice. Their
bodies were touching ever so slightly and each passing touch, with the warm water slapping against them,
turned her on. Even through the haze of intense hap-

piness washing over her, Sophie was astute enough to realise that giving him any kind of unedited version of what was *actually* going through her head would be a horrendous mistake. 'I'm thinking that it's a shame the sea back home is way too cold to do anything like this. I could float along and just fall asleep right here. Penny for yours.'

With his own question thrown back at him, Niccolo found himself actually considering what she had asked. What was he thinking?

And just for a second, he was alarmed by the disconcerting realisation that he was thinking that he didn't want this to end. In a life spent in the fast lane, where decisions were made that changed lives and finding time out was always something that had to be worked at, this was relaxation at its most perfect, and he didn't want it to end.

It was a ridiculous thought, of course. Hadn't he lived with a first-hand vision of how life panned out for people who didn't throw everything into work?

Evalina, touring the world until she was a little too old for the luxury of being a nomad, would have ended up in a pitiful, low-paid job had it not been for him.

His parents, irrespective of their love for one another, had similarly failed to realise the vital importance of putting work first and had ended up vulnerable to the consequences, which had been miserable.

He had built his life on the very simple acceptance of certain unquestionable facts.

You worked hard, you accumulated wealth, and you gained freedom from anyone to have a say over the direction of your life.

So this fleeting notion that relaxing as he was doing right now could possibly have any kind of place in his high-octane life was, frankly, foolish.

But it still unsettled him that he could even think like that.

'I'm thinking,' he drawled, 'that this has been a very successful trip work wise and, as an end to my very satisfying closure on the de Luca deal, a couple of hours here couldn't be better.'

Sophie felt a cool trickle run through her because that was as direct a reminder she could get that what they were enjoying had its limits, boundaries beyond which it would not be allowed to run.

'And,' she pointed out, stung by the fact that she had become way too involved with someone who just wanted a playmate for a few days, 'it's also been great for you and Annalise.'

'Meaning?'

He flipped over, treading water for a few seconds, while his eyes met hers, cool and questioning, and that cold trickle got a tiny bit colder.

But they were lovers and why shouldn't she say what was on her mind? He was only allowed so many ground rules!

It was a mischievous thought but, once lodged in her head, it stubbornly refused to budge.

They were in a bubble where he was no longer her employer and she was no longer his employee. She could revert back to being tactful and discreet when they returned to the UK, just as she would revert back to being the woman who no longer had the pleasure of touching the man she never wanted to stop touching.

'You're not really that interested in hearing what I have to say, are you?' She looked at him for a couple of seconds and then forked off, back towards shore, swimming as fast as she could and aware that he was easily gaining on her without much effort.

But she made it back to the beach and stood up, heading straight for one of the towels in the big canvas bag and wrapping it around herself.

When she turned, it was to see that he had slung a towel round his waist and was moving to the one on the ground, beckoning her to accompany him, his expression no longer cool and remote.

'I'm not used to people being as forthright with me as you are,' Niccolo told her quietly, which, for a moment, rendered her a little speechless because she had expected him to move into defence mode, prepared to guard his precious ivory tower whatever the cost. 'You want to talk to me about Annalise, and of course I want to hear what you have to say. So tell me and don't think that you have to hold back.'

Sophie hazarded a small smile. 'When I first arrived,' she said boldly, 'I would say that the interactions between the two of you were incredibly formal.' She ignored his developing frown and the dark flush spreading across his high cheekbones. He looked *uncomfortable* and her heart went out to him. Ivory towers had definite drawbacks, and not having the privilege of people daring to confront you had to be one of those drawbacks. Perhaps even his aunt and his parents would not go where she was now determined to tread, but then they would be in his life for ever, whereas she was a temporary fixture, soon to be dispatched.

'Formal...like how?'

'I could see how much you love your daughter, Niccolo,' she said gently. 'And it's obvious how hard you work to give her the sort of life you never had, but sometimes I almost got the feeling that you might feel more comfortable if she just saluted you as a greeting instead of running towards you for a hug.'

She watched as he raked his fingers through his hair, and her keen eyes noted that there was just the slightest tremble there, although his expression remained composed and pensive.

'Now,' she said on a deep breath, 'you just seem so much more relaxed around her and I can tell she feels it as well. She lights up when you come into the room. I don't think she really knows that, and you probably don't either, but I see it because I'm perched on the outside and sometimes it's easier to spot stuff as a spectator.'

'I've...yes... I've known it as well...' His voice was gruff. 'I've seen the way Annalise feels more comfortable around me.' He shot her a crooked smile. 'Maybe you have something to do with that.' He shrugged.

'I don't think so,' Sophie returned thoughtfully, then she paused, before adding, 'I won't be around for much longer, so you have to promise me that it's a closeness that's going to last, to get stronger, even.'

Not going to be around for much longer...

Those words penetrated Niccolo's consciousness and he felt a gut-level dismay, which he slammed a lid on fast.

'Scout's honour,' he drawled, putting a full stop under any further heart-to-heart, touchy feely conversation. 'And now…let's park that topic because I can think of a hundred more things I'd rather do…'

'A hundred?'

'Okay, maybe just the one…'

'And what might that be?'

'Lunch, of course.' He grinned and then chuckled. 'What else were you thinking?'

CHAPTER NINE

TWENTY-FOUR HOURS LATER, as she watched him play in the pool with Annalise, Sophie was thinking that time was running out.

The deal had all been concluded three days earlier. It had hit the headlines two days ago and Niccolo had spent time on various calls, some of which were with the financial press, who were asking for details of how he saw the company moving forward.

She knew that because, for once, he had not retired to his dedicated office aboard the yacht to do business but instead had sat at the low glass table on the middle deck where she and Annalise had been spending the day, watching them and joining in when time permitted, only breaking off to take calls, answer emails and communicate with all the people who seemed desperate to have air time with him.

Now there was no further reason for them to remain on the gently floating yacht. Reality was a heartbeat away and it was beckoning.

She didn't want it to. When she thought about the cut and dried business of returning to London, where this moment in time would be forgotten, she felt physically sick.

She had embarked on this brief affair and if there had been a certain apprehension that the water she was stepping into might prove a little deeper than she wanted, she had not expected to find herself in water so deep that she was in danger of drowning.

Stepping back from the past year and a half, she felt she could disentangle all the threads that had wrapped themselves around her in a frightening stranglehold.

She could mourn the loss of her parents and see that although the loss would always be a part of her, the sun would still keep rising and setting and life would still be there, waiting to be lived, which was what her parents would have wanted for her.

And it helped that the fabulous sums of money she was being paid, plus the sale of the family home, actually meant that she no longer had to panic about her finances.

She also knew now that Scott, the guy who had loomed so large and caused her so much grief, had been merely a blip on her confused horizons.

Not because Niccolo had been a pleasant distraction, supplanting those depressing memories with more uplifting ones. Not because he had shown her that she was still capable of having fun, had taken her to a place where she had been able to glimpse sunshine through the dark clouds, but because he had filled her entire world with sunshine. She had been roused, like Sleeping Beauty, except she knew it wasn't going to last.

And it scared her to imagine what life was going to be without him as a physical presence in it.

She was beginning to think that despite what she had told herself about lessons learnt, she was fundamentally a girl who had grown up with the love of parents who had set a shining example of what a happy life should look like. Her faith in love was too strong to be destroyed by one bad experience. Niccolo had shown her that. Unfortunately, he was the wrong guy for her.

As though sensing that her thoughts were on him, he turned to look at her, shielding his eyes from the glare of the sun, and grinned.

'Care to join the fun?' he called and Sophie, also shading her eyes, smiled back at him.

In front of his daughter, he remained her boss and she was the responsible nanny.

Annalise was oblivious to any undercurrents.

'The fun's happening right here, thank you!' She tapped the book which she had not been reading for the past twenty minutes because her mind had been going round and round in circles. 'If I don't finish this before we head back, then I'll never finish it!' she carolled, almost kicking herself for bringing to his attention the inevitability of their imminent departure.

Yet it was a subject that had to be raised and she was already prepping herself to be nonchalant when it was.

She couldn't see his expression when he laughed a response and she actually did force herself to read and to try and relax for the next couple of hours. Annalise, who had endeared every member of staff to her, had her favourite dinner prepared for her by the chef, and then she insisted on going with Julia to the bit of the boat with a glass bottom which gave her a view under the water, even though Sophie laughingly told her that there wouldn't be much to see at night.

Suddenly, the silence left by Annalise's disappearance, the lack of comforting background childish chatter, felt awkward.

Was it because of all the thoughts that had been wreaking havoc in her head? The fact that she was getting to the point where she *needed* him to tell her when they would be leaving if only to give her the chance to work through her emotions as best she could?

The easy familiarity between them failed to reach the mark as he towelled himself dry and strolled towards her, a dark, silhouetted shape in a sky that was already turning from orange to midnight blue.

'You're tense,' Niccolo drawled, dropping into the chair next to her and staring out at the rapidly darkening horizon. 'Why? Anything going on with your house that I should know about?'

'My house?'

'The sale.' He slanted dark eyes across to her questioningly. 'You said the valuators came to process what furniture was left that you wanted to auction. Did it all go okay?'

'I'd forgotten about that,' Sophie confessed. 'But I haven't heard from them so I'm guessing there were no problems. They'll email me with the amount I can expect.' She sighed. 'It'll all go towards paying off the people my dad owed money to.'

'Tell me,' Niccolo said casually, 'how much money you have left to pay off those pesky people...'

Sophie laughed.

He was funny. It was something that hadn't been apparent when they had first met, when she had written him off as another rich, arrogant guy who thought he could rule the world and everyone in it with a snap of his fingers.

He had a dry, witty sense of humour that never failed to make her smile.

She told him, and then, for the first time, really thanked him for the very generous salary he was paying her.

'You have no idea what it feels like to have some of that financial burden lifted off my shoulders,' she said quietly.

'I know what it's like to have very little. I can only imagine how much worse it has been for you because there was a time when you thought you had a great deal. And you still haven't told me why you're so tense.' His voice dropped to a husky murmur. 'Is that your way of letting me know that a back massage wouldn't go amiss?'

Except, for once, the dark, exciting promise of desires fulfilled between the sheets failed to evoke that complete emptying of her head as it had done before.

'I suppose,' Sophie said, opting for a bit of a half-truth, 'I can't help but think about the fact that my family home is now empty of everything that made it a family home…and some other family will be living in it, filling it up with different memories, rubbing mine out along the way.'

'I'm not sure that's how it works, Sophie.'

'What do you mean?'

'You know what they say about doors shutting and others opening.'

'I'm not as good as you when it comes to moving on,' she ventured a little tautly, then, just in case he got the idea that this was a statement that was leading to something else, something she quite frankly wanted to avoid, she hurried on without pausing for breath. 'When you've talked about your family home, you've always implied that it was a relief when you left it and a relief when you'd made enough money to move your parents out…to make sure you could set them up in style back in Italy.'

'I've said that to you?' Niccolo frowned and shifted so that he was looking at her. 'When?'

'What do you mean *when*?'

'I just don't recall… Well, yes, I do remember telling you a bit about my family…but—'

'Don't worry about it.' Sophie picked up the edge in her voice and wondered whether he did as well. Why, she wondered, did he have to act as though those little morsels of confidences were somehow a crime against humanity?

She knew why. Of course she did.

For most people, sharing was something that was a bonding experience. It was something they did when they actually gave a damn about what the other person thought.

Niccolo had shared stuff in soundbites, and she figured that it was because he'd wanted to give her just enough explanation for her to understand the man he was, a man who had nothing inside to give and was not interested in any sort of relationship that demanded more than what was on offer.

No wonder he was aghast at the thought that he might have told her anything that had been close to his heart.

It would be tough for anything to be close to a heart that wasn't actually there!

'I wasn't,' he said irritably, 'worried about anything. Perhaps my experiences of the place I grew up in aren't rooted in sentimentality.'

'You can be so…*cold*, Niccolo.'

'Show me a successful man who enjoys hugging trees and cries when he sees a pleasant sunset.'

Against her will, Sophie laughed and then told him off for making her laugh, but in a way she was pleased because the atmosphere had been veering into dangerous territory and she had wanted to find a way of pulling back, of reminding herself that she was in it for the moment, to enjoy what remained and not let despair at what would never be tarnish the present.

He pulled her towards him, nearly causing her to topple in her chair, and she laughed again.

'Annalise might come back,' she whispered.

'Julia will settle her. We're here…the stars are in the sky and the ocean is stirring around us. What could be more romantic?'

He kissed her. Long and slow, barely giving her time to surface for air. His tongue moved against hers and Sophie felt dampness between her legs, aching for the sort of release only he was capable of affording her.

'I'm hungry for you…' he whispered hotly into her ear. 'You've been driving me crazy sitting on that lounger pretending to read when you'd rather look at me.'

'You're so full of yourself, Niccolo.'

'Tell me you don't like it.'

'Your ego is as big as your yacht…' But she was laughing softly again and capturing his face between her hands so that she could pepper his cheeks with small, fluttering kisses.

'My yacht's not that big. There are bigger…'

They didn't make love. Both were too aware that they were out in the open and not in a deserted cove on a deserted strip of white sand.

But he pulled her to sit between his legs on the long, wooden deckchair with its deeply padded cushions. She had her back to his stomach and they were both gazing up at a star-studded sky. The breeze was soft and silky and smelled of the salty ocean.

Sophie closed her eyes and let her mind drift off, but not into any dangerous places because she didn't want to ruin the atmosphere.

The silence should have felt odd, but it didn't. It was warm and familiar, and when he spoke, his voice low and pensive, she wasn't surprised that he was speaking from the heart.

He hated heart-to-hearts. He hated opening up. He saw it as a form of weakness because strength was in moving forward, and only looked back if looking back served a purpose.

'I think,' he mused softly, his chin resting on the crown of her head before he sat back and nestled her into the crook of his neck, 'that I was always a little apprehensive that my marriage had blotted my copybook when it came to Annalise. I think perhaps that's why I've always unconsciously held back when I was around her. That and a very healthy mistrust of my ability to handle an infant without dropping her...'

Why had he just said that?

Was it some kind of fatal combination of stars in the sky and the absolute stillness of the night all around them?

How could he relentlessly remind himself of the restrictions of this passing liaison only to ambush his own good intentions by doing the very one thing he had sworn to himself he would avoid doing?

It felt as though he was very good at talking the talk when there was some distance between them, but in a situation like this, with his arms around her, feeling her heartbeat and smelling her flowery, clean aroma, she had a way of bewitching him into confiding.

'I don't think there's a single new parent who isn't afraid of accidentally dropping their baby,' she said lazily. 'Why do you think your marriage affected your relationship with Annalise?'

'I have no idea how we've ended up having this conversation.' Niccolo knew exactly how they'd ended up having this conversation. The woman had cast a spell over him! He was amused, though, rather than rattled. His hands drifted underneath her loose, sleeveless vest to cup her small breasts pushing against her swimsuit. He rubbed the pads of his thumbs over her nipples and felt them stiffen through the Lycra. More than anything he wanted to shove both hands underneath that Lycra and feel the coolness of her skin. Even more than that, he wanted to nuzzle that softness, suckle on the taut bulge of her nipples, lick and tease them until she moved against him, out of control and begging to be taken over the edge.

He couldn't wait to get her to bed.

It was astonishing to think how much she still drove him nuts with desire and how much the thought of her still popped into his head when he was least expecting it.

'We've ended up having this conversation because you raised it. Strangely, it does sometimes help to talk about stuff.'

'Never in my experience.'

'You still haven't answered my question.' Sophie

clearly wasn't about to let him off the hook. 'Shall I tell you what I think?'

'Not necessary because I'm already regretting having raised the subject in the first place.'

'I think you've been scared that because you failed at your marriage you would fail at parenthood. So even though you adore your daughter, it's felt safer to keep your distance instead of throwing yourself wholeheartedly into the whole bonding thing. Know what else I think?'

'You think too much.'

'I think it's a whole lot easier to hide behind a wall than it is to engage.'

'I engage.' Niccolo slid his hand along her thigh, underneath the flimsy sarong, and Sophie watched the bulge of that hand as it moved closer and closer to nudge the wetness between her legs.

'I'm not talking about sex...' Her voice was an unsteady rasp as he slipped his fingers under the swimsuit, and then slid one finger along her dampened crease.

Nothing fast, nothing urgent...just a steady tempo that first cleared her mind and then catapulted her body towards the inevitable build-up, the heated flush of a spiralling sensation that started low in her pelvis and then invaded every part of her until she could scarcely breathe.

There was no way they would be interrupted, but she knew that even if a member of staff was idiotic enough to interrupt them, nothing would be visible. They would just see the two of them lying together on a deckchair, staring out at the ocean, wreathed in only the silvery slant of a half-moon.

She clutched the arms of the deckchair and closed her eyes as she came on a long, low shudder of utter pleasure, her body rocking gently into his as she orgasmed against his questing finger.

She had to fight to control a moan as he withdrew his finger and whispered against her hair, 'There. That was me punishing you for thinking too much. Did you enjoy the punishment? I'm guessing that you might have…'

He very neatly straightened the dishevelled sarong and then swore silently under his breath at the vibration of his mobile on the table next to the deckchair.

Sophie immediately gathered herself and sat up.

Work. Sure to be. And between Niccolo and work there could be no blurry lines. Not according to the role she was playing, the girl who was in it for fun and happy to walk away by mutual agreement.

He slid his long legs over the side and walked towards the railing as he answered the phone. He leant against the railing, his back to her, his body language relaxed as he stared out to the dark swells of the ocean, but that body language imperceptibly changed as he carried on talking, about who knew what because she couldn't hear a thing. There was no inflection in his voice that could give her a hint, but something felt weird.

She wondered whether something had gone wrong with the deal but she doubted it. Everything had been signed off and Niccolo, she knew, would have been scrupulous about the details.

He was that kind of guy.

She dragged her eyes away and, sitting upright on the deckchair, she drew her knees up, wrapped her arms around them and rested her chin on them, looking out at the same dark panorama he was looking out upon.

Out of the corner of her eye she couldn't help but watch him, though, and she tensed as he finally straightened and turned, hesitating just fractionally before walking slowly towards her.

When he sat down, his face, all shadows and angles in the diminished light, was serious.

'That was Evalina.'

'What's wrong?' Panic made her lean forward as he sat heavily at the end of the deckchair. 'Is your father all right? Is it bad news?'

'His recuperation has been nothing short of miraculous,' Niccolo assured her, 'to the extent that he and my mother have decided that a cruise somewhere to aid his speedy recovery would be an excellent idea.'

'A cruise? Are they planning on coming to the yacht? Here?'

She squinted into the darkness and looked around, and Niccolo, watching her closely, wondered whether she expected to see his parents lurking with a couple of suitcases behind the teak bar or emerging from under some cushions.

'This isn't quite what they have in mind,' he told her, with a small smile. 'Their idea of a cruise involves many more people around them on a boat five times the size.'

'That's good, isn't it?'

'It's very good. It also means that Evalina will be back in London by tomorrow evening.'

So what happens now?

Niccolo realised that that was a question he had been putting off answering since he had completed his deal.

But now it was a question that demanded an answer.

He didn't want her to go. Was that selfish? It certainly hadn't been part of their deal. Their deal had involved them returning to normality and leaving this wild nonsense behind when they left the yacht. But then again, in that scenario, the abrupt appearance of his aunt had not featured.

When he thought of her leaving, walking away…he felt a sense of loss and emptiness that had never been part of any scenario and he had no time for that.

Niccolo was uncomfortable with the assault of disturbing feelings and emotions that had no place in the cool and collected life he had built for himself, and he was silent for a few seconds, frowning darkly.

Sophie could feel every muscle in her body straining with sudden tension.

He was frowning. Of course he was. Did he imagine that he had been abruptly stuck in the awkward position of having to remind her of the laws they had laid down at the start of this situation?

She had just given herself to him in the most intimate way imaginable and now everything had suddenly changed.

She could feel it.

She blamed herself for being badly prepared for the inevitable, for being a coward and kidding herself that the bubble they were in was something that would pop but not just yet, and so why think too hard about it?

He, certainly, wasn't torn because she hadn't heard

him launch into any speeches about continuing what they had, and just the thought of him mentally trying to work out how to tell her that their time was up without her making a fuss was enough to bring her out in a humiliating cold sweat. Maybe he thought that she might be clingy…might want things to carry on. He was rich, he was good-looking and he had the charm of the devil. Those were attributes that would keep many women hanging on for dear life until he prised them away from him and scarpered. Oh, God.

'That's wonderful.' Sophie tried to inject some warmth into her voice but her heart was breaking in two, even though she knew that she was successfully replicating something of a smile. 'Wonderful that your dad is well enough to contemplate going away. It'll do him a world of good. Both your parents. Do you know how long they'll be gone for?'

'How…long?'

'A month? Longer? Where will they be going? My parents always planned on going on a cruise, but they never got there. Perhaps somewhere along the line, they realised that they would have to count their pennies. I know in the couple of years before…before…well… there were a lot more staycations…' She was babbling, words pouring out of her while her brain furiously computed the road that lay ahead and the direction her life would now be taking her.

'And,' she continued into the lengthening, awkward silence, 'it's brilliant that Evalina will be returning. Annalise will be over the moon.'

'You think?' Niccolo murmured, still frowning and ill at ease in himself. 'She seems to have become very accustomed to having you around…'

'There won't be any point in my staying on, Niccolo,' Sophie said briskly. 'Annalise has got accustomed to me, of course, but there's no job for me with Evalina returning. Of course, I'll see Annalise at the allotment...' Her voice faded away and the smile felt forced. Her jaw was beginning to ache.

'You'll be wondering about the financial side of things, I imagine...'

Was that all he could think about?

Sophie was relieved and offended at the same time. Relieved that he hadn't seen through her over-bright voice yet offended that, after everything between them, he could actually think that she was mercenary enough to focus on the money when...when her world felt as though it was collapsing.

'Of course not. I've already been more than generously paid for looking after your daughter. I'm not concerned that I won't have an extra fortnight to earn a bit more.'

'I'm not asking you to leave, Sophie,' Niccolo said gruffly.

He looked at her.

Of course, they were ships passing in the night. This was never going to last beyond their brief time on the yacht. They both knew that. He had been very clear on that point and yet he was taken aback at the alacrity with which she was already, it seemed, mentally packing her bags ready for departure.

More than taken aback.

'What are you asking, in that case?'

For once, faced with a direct question, Niccolo found that he couldn't come up with an equally direct answer.

'My house is big,' he prevaricated, annoyed with himself for not taking the way out that had been handed to him, for not liking the fact that she was just serenely adhering to the ground rules he had laid down. 'Annalise might benefit from your staying on for the allotted time you were hired for. It's hardly your fault that my parents have decided to disappear on a cruise, leaving my aunt no choice but to return to London.'

'I don't think,' Sophie said carefully, 'that my staying on would be a good idea.'

'Why not? Of course, far be it from me to stop you from leaving, but I'm curious.'

'If I were to hang around for the remainder of my time…well, yes, of course things would revert back to where they were before we came here.' Her eyes on him were clear and direct. 'We've been very discreet in front of Annalise but she's a child. If Evalina were around… well, she's astute and it's not beyond the realms of possibility that she would suspect something. And what if she does? Bearing in mind that there's a chance she might have had some matchmaking in her sights?'

'I admit that hadn't occurred to me.'

Niccolo scowled.

So what if she got a whiff that he and Sophie were somehow involved? Would it really be the end of the world?

In fact, would it be so horrific if they continued what had been started? They were both adults! And if Evalina caught on, then she was an adult as well and more than capable of dealing with the fact that he and Sophie were having a fling.

Yes, the very idea went against what they had both signed up to, but all things in life were organic.

If you didn't adapt to change, you got left behind. Life in the fast lane had taught him that. He had come from nothing and had had to work hard and think fast to make things happen the way he wanted them to.

'We could always just let nature take its course,' he drawled in a soft, lazy undertone.

Sophie stiffened. She knew exactly what he was saying and in some ways she wasn't that surprised.

The fling he'd wanted, conducted away from the reality of daily life and with a time limit he could wrap around it so that he could parcel it neatly away when it was over, hadn't reached a natural conclusion as far as he was concerned.

When Sophie thought about it she wondered whether they hadn't already overstayed their time on the yacht, because why else was there any need to be here if the deal was done?

Had he subconsciously prolonged their time here because he'd known that, once they left and returned to London, they would have to walk away from what they'd started?

Maybe that and the fact that possibly for the first time he was moving from being a father to being *a dad*, with all the subtle rewards that brought.

At any rate, those dark, assessing eyes left her in no doubt that he would be very happy for them to carry on sleeping together until such time as he got bored and decided to call it a day.

He would play with her and then discard her and his life would move on. Had Evalina really thought that she might be the one to change that? Ha!

She'd stuck her head in the sand like an ostrich

while she'd been here. She'd held off thinking about the inevitable because enjoying the present had been too seductive.

Well, Fate was giving her a choice and she intended to make the right one.

'I don't think so, Niccolo.' She smiled. 'And you don't have to worry about the fact that I won't be in the job for the length of time I thought I would be. My finances, for the first time in ages, are actually looking pretty healthy and I finally feel I can get things together and see a way forward.' Now her smile was warm and genuine. She would never tell him how she really felt about him, but she *would* tell him *this*. 'You've been more than generous, Niccolo. You'll never know how much I appreciate being given the chance to look after Annalise even though you must have had some doubts about someone who came with practically zero experience of childminding. In a lot of ways, you've helped me so much more than you'll ever know.'

She stood, began collecting her things—bits and pieces that she shoved into the canvas bag she had brought with her to the pool.

There was a chill in the air, and the sea, dark and flat, suddenly struck her as full of foreboding rather than deep with mystery and promise.

She shivered, and when their eyes met she knew that they were both thinking the same thing...

They had made love for the last time.

CHAPTER TEN

NICCOLO SWIVELLED HIS chair at such an angle that he could stare out of the floor-to-ceiling pane of glass that offered the sort of view of London that people usually had to pay to get.

Right now, there was little to see aside from grey skies and the sort of persistent, fine drizzle that would have plunged even the most optimistic person into a slough of despond.

It was a far cry from the wall-to-wall blue skies and sunshine he had enjoyed a fortnight ago when...

Niccolo gave up trying to shut the door on thoughts that had plagued him ever since he had returned to London to pick up where he had left off before his life had decided to do its own thing and take him on a magical mystery tour of places he had never gone before.

This shouldn't be happening because he shouldn't be thinking about a woman who had always been destined to be nothing more than a fleeting visitor in his well-oiled, well-run life. He had never expected to have any sort of fling with Sophie Baxter but, once he had abandoned his half-hearted attempts at resistance and brought her into his bed, guidelines had been laid down, had been agreed. No promises of anything more than a few days of fun.

It was what he did.

It was the man he was.

He had learned lessons from his childhood. Those lessons had been cemented into him, had roots so deep in his soul that not even his marriage could survive the tenacity of their hold on him.

Looking back on Caroline Ferri, so exotic, so refined, so impossibly glamorous, he could see the cracks that had been there, waiting to open up.

Mistakes were always so easy to spot with the benefit of hindsight. He should have known that exotic, refined and impossibly glamorous would eventually equal high-maintenance.

He should have known that any man who worked hard to earn the sort of money that could give him absolute personal freedom—a man like him—would have found the shrill demands of a high-maintenance woman impossible to deal with.

He had been foolish, but even so...that disastrous union had embedded in him the rock-solid conviction that he just wasn't cut out for the sort of sacrifices that had to be made for a relationship to stay the course.

That was something he had happily accepted.

He had his daughter. She would be the recipient of every single luxury extreme wealth could buy.

She would never be patronised by people who thought they were superior to her because they happened to have more in their bank accounts.

She would never feel angry on his behalf because he had not made the most of what he had been born with, because he had found himself in a position where other people called the shots over the direction of his life.

Oh, no.

Work had come first. It had been the engine that had fired up his life for as long as he could remember.

Women were fun and he was very happy to shower them with gifts, but none of them were there to stay the course, and within those boundary lines he had never known anything but pure contentment with the life choices he had made.

Until Sophie Baxter had arrived on the scene.

When had he started questioning the things that had been the cornerstones of his life?

When had he started looking at his relationship with his daughter and seeing that it wasn't enough to ensure that there was nothing she lacked that money could buy?

He was very glad he had, but even so, how was it that he had not noticed the way those firmly held convictions about how he ran his life had begun to unravel, as if a thread had been gently pulled until every weave in the fabric became unstable?

He and Sophie had become lovers and she had made him feel like a horny teenager. She had lain in his arms and he had been loath for her to leave the warmth of his bed. She had smiled at him and he had felt as if there was nothing in the world that wasn't possible.

Nothing.

Not even the chance to love.

Staring out of his office window now, Niccolo closed his eyes and breathed in deeply, steadying his runaway thoughts.

She'd left. She hadn't tried to find any reasons to

stay. She'd turned down his offer to hang on to what they had. She had been polite and gentle and firm, and he only now recognised his reaction to her departure for what it had been.

Love.

She'd carved a path through the walls he had built around himself and managed to get right down to the very foundations where, brick by brick, she had somehow dismantled all his defences and he hadn't seen it coming.

He'd been so intent on making sure she got the message that there could be nothing between them but a brief, flickering flame to be snuffed out the second they returned to reality that he had missed all the signs of his own heart disobeying the rules his head had always laid down.

And now here he was. Wondering where she was and what she was doing.

Instead of leaving at the same time, he had remained on his yacht for a further two days, discreetly allowing her time to pack her things and leave. The perfect, thoughtful gentleman.

Was that why he had done that? Or had he subconsciously realised that it would have hurt too much to spend those final hours in her company knowing that she wouldn't be around for much longer?

He cursed under his breath and vaulted out of his chair, moving to the sheet of glass that separated him, cocooned in his magnificent, expensive ivory tower, from the rest of humanity far down below.

How could he have ever accepted that it was normal to remove himself from the things in life that really mattered? Or believed that happiness lay in isolation?

That the challenges of meaningful interaction could or should be sidelined?

And where did this onslaught of introspection leave him now?

At a little after seven in the evening, there was a miserable air of dreariness to the wet, grey vista below.

Most of his employees had already left to begin their weekend.

He had absently mulled over the possibility of digging into his metaphorical little black book and finding himself some amusing company but had ditched that idea as fast as it had appeared in his head.

As he had been doing since returning to London, he would stay at home, spend time with Annalise and dodge his aunt's sneaky attempts to find out what he had thought of Sophie.

And what else?

Think of Sophie?

Wonder what she was up to? Had she decided, after the fling she assured him was a one-off because she wasn't that type of girl, to spread her wings and see what else was out there? Would she be spending her Friday evening in a nightclub somewhere while he remained in his ivory tower, brooding?

She was so damned spectacular that she wouldn't be short of admirers if she decided that there was more to life than allotments.

More importantly, Niccolo thought grimly, could he live with himself if he allowed her to walk away without telling her how he felt?

The very notion of sharing his innermost feelings with someone else was so alien to his mental make-up that he almost shook his head in an attempt to clear it.

The very notion, furthermore, of chasing a woman who had walked away from him was even more alien to his mental make-up.

Those were both very valid reasons for putting the whole sorry episode behind him and moving on, and yet, even as he thought that, he found he was moving towards the leather sofa on which he had earlier dumped his lightweight jacket.

He had the address of the house she had sold, and with that information he would be able to get in touch with the estate agent who had sold it. Whatever security checks they had, he was confident he would be able to bypass them to find out where she had moved. She would be renting somewhere. He had ensured she'd been paid enough to make it possible for her to rent a pretty decent place.

He could have got his PA to do the leg work, but doing it himself felt right, felt like just part of the road he had to travel to reach her, to unburden himself. To tell her what he felt. To open up for the first time in his life, even though opening up would leave him vulnerable.

Thankfully, finding out where she was turned out to be a piece of cake because she was in the very house waiting to be handed over to new owners.

Having discovered this, he headed down to the underground car park and straight to his Porsche, zapping it open on the move and easing out of the slot without giving himself too much time to think about what he was doing. This was a journey with no turning back.

So it was highly likely that she would slam the door in his face.

They'd had some pretty amazing sex, and on reflection he swore there were times when he had sensed *something* in her, something that had alerted him to an attraction that was a lot more than skin deep.

But had he been wrong?

If she'd been interested, wouldn't she have jumped at the chance to continue their relationship once they'd returned to London?

Should he phone to warn her that he would be coming to see her? Would the element of surprise work in his favour?

For the first time in his life, Niccolo really had no idea where he stood and was facing a situation the outcome of which was a complete mystery.

It was unnerving to say the least.

But the alternative was even more unnerving. He had been accused of many things in his life before but never of a lack of courage...

Sophie had no idea why she was still here, in the now almost completely empty family home.

Everything that she wanted to keep had been put into storage and the rest had been given to charity or sold to help pay bills.

Thanks to her brief period of employment and the money she had managed to retrieve from the sale of the house once most of the outstanding debts had been cleared, she was in the black, no longer swimming against the current.

Yet here she was, locked into some kind of apathy, which meant that she still hadn't moved, sleeping in a sleeping bag, caretaking a house that would soon no longer be hers.

It felt peaceful. It felt as though this last remnant of

her past was now fortifying her for taking the next step forward and moving on...

Without Niccolo.

She'd left with Annalise a fortnight ago, while he had remained on the yacht to finalise some business in peace and quiet, because peace and quiet would become relics of another age the second he stepped foot into his offices in London.

He'd been politely smiling when he'd told her that, but she wasn't born yesterday. She'd turned down his offer to prolong their little roll in the hay and he'd shrugged it off, but had then been eager to see the back of her. He might have paid lip service in telling her that there was no need for her to rush away because his aunt was back, but actions spoke louder than words and he was clearly keen for her to leave.

He'd said that sleeping together would change nothing and she'd agreed. She would have fun—and God knew, she was due a little—and he would have fun. Two adults having fun, no strings attached, and when the fun was over, they would both revert to the working relationship that had brought them together on his yacht in the first place.

How simple it had sounded at the time.

She wasn't expecting anyone to ring her doorbell. Not at a little after seven in the evening. Her communications had increasingly revolved around her bank manager and his attempts to help with sorting out all the various debts that had been uncovered following the death of her parents.

No one actually came knocking on her door any more and she padded to open it with mild curiosity, assuming it was a cold caller and already mentally rehearsing how she would tell whoever it was that she wasn't interested in whatever they happened to be trying to flog.

The last person she was expecting was Niccolo.

She'd tried so hard to erase him from her head and yet he had continued to invade every corner of her mind, and so, as she stood looking at that tall, striking, dominant and all too familiar figure, she had to blink and wonder whether her feverish thoughts were so all consuming that she was imagining someone who wasn't really there.

But then he spoke, and her eyes widened and her heart raced and her mouth fell open.

'Can I come in?'

'What are you doing here?' She was struggling to breathe and for a few seconds she wondered whether she might be having a panic attack.

'I've come to…to talk to you, Sophie.'

Staring at her, drinking in the face that had haunted his every waking moment since they had parted company, Niccolo was finding it hard to think straight.

Had he done the right thing in coming here, after all?

He refused to allow self-doubt to establish a foothold even though the look of barely concealed horror on her face was less than welcoming.

Courage was saying what you felt had to be said, he grimly reminded himself. It wasn't about backing away. He'd never backed away from anything in his life before and he wasn't going to start now.

On the other hand, he'd never been in this situation before, had he?

'What about, Niccolo?' Violet eyes narrowed warily on him. 'What do we have to talk about?'

'Nothing I can tell you standing outside your house.' He watched as she hesitated, and took considerable comfort from that. 'Why are you still here?' He peered around her to the now empty property.

'That's none of your business.' Sophie sighed and reluctantly fell back. 'You can come in,' she said quietly, 'but you shouldn't be here, Niccolo. I no longer work for you and I can't imagine what we have to talk about.'

Niccolo swept past her at speed just in case she decided to change her mind. A baring of his soul was going to be painful enough without him being reduced to doing so outside a locked front door.

Buying some time, he gazed around him at the loneliness of a house deprived of everything that made it a home. There was nothing inside and the bare walls told a story of gradual financial decline. He expected she noticed it as well. The paint was tired, the wallpaper in the room he could see through one of the doors was faded and the floorboards were worn and broken at the edges. Doubtless all covered up when the place had been dressed to impress.

'I'm going to be moving out the day after tomorrow,' she said with a hint of defiance. 'Rentals are hard to get hold of in London.'

Niccolo focused on her. There was nowhere to sit.

'There's no furniture.'

'Sold or stored,' Sophie muttered, looking down but still feeling the impact of him on her, strong and tangible and wreaking havoc with her fragile peace of mind. She looked around her and managed to completely avoid looking at him in the process.

'Where are you sleeping?'

'On the floor.'

'Why?'

She shrugged, ashamed to even think that he might see into her head and work out that leaving him had somehow managed to paralyse her.

'It's hard,' she muttered vaguely. When she raised her eyes it was to find that he had edged closer to her, close enough to mesmerise.

'There's nowhere for us to sit.'

'I hadn't expected any visitors.'

She froze as he reached out to take her hand, and memories shot out of nowhere, memories of those cool fingers touching her, exploring her body. They had held hands on their trip to that deserted cove, when he had whipped her off his yacht onto his speedboat. He had held her hand on the beach and they had walked and talked and she'd felt on top of the world.

Now he led her out of the hallway into the sitting room, then sat on the floor and invited her to do the same.

'You're in your suit.' She hovered and shoved her hands into the pockets of her dungarees.

'I've come straight from work. What I have to say… I didn't want to put it off.'

'What?' A stab of anxiety replaced the panic-attack feeling. 'Are you okay? Is Annalise? Evalina?'

'I'm not great, Sophie.'

'What do you mean?' She urgently leaned forward while her head filled with worst-case scenarios involving terminal illnesses.

He leaned against the wall, drew his knees up and let his hands dangle loosely between them.

'You're scaring me, Niccolo,' she whispered, dropping to sit facing him.

'Am I?'

'Are you ill? Stop playing these word games. I can't stand it.'

'It's taken a lot to come here today and yet I had no choice. Ever since you left me—'

'I didn't *leave* you, Niccolo. I... I...we agreed...that things would stop when we left the yacht and life went back to normal...and Evalina returned a little earlier than expected and so...there was no longer any need for me to stay on.'

'But I wanted you to.' His dark eyes held hers. She refused to yield to a thread of something in his voice that sounded a lot like *hurt*.

'You can't always get what you want.'

'You walked away from me and left me time to realise how much I missed you.'

'Is that what you've come to say?'

He missed her.

Translated, she knew what that meant. He missed her warm, pliable body in bed with him. To Sophie, it sounded very much like a repeat of what he'd asked of her on his yacht. Would she hang around for a bit longer...be his lover for just a bit longer...just until he got bored?

For the man who could have it all, not getting this one thing had been too much for him to handle. Well, that was tough because she was going to give him the same answer now as she had given him then.

'No.'

Not knowing what to do with that unexpected response, Sophie tilted her head to one side and remained silent. Her legs were crossed, yoga style, and she fiddled her fingers restlessly on her lap, unable to drag her eyes away from his sombre, dark-eyed gaze.

'I not only realised I missed you,' Niccolo flushed darkly, his voice so low that she had to lean forward to pick up what he was saying, 'but also realised that somehow, and I don't know how, you managed to get under my skin to the extent that I couldn't deal with the gaping hole you left in my life when you disappeared.' He raised his hand in a gesture to wave aside any interruptions.

Actually, Sophie had no intention of interrupting anything. She was struggling to join the dots, but beneath the surface his expression was telling her everything her mind was bravely trying to ignore.

There was a soft tenderness there that pulled at her heart strings.

'I never planned on sleeping with you. When I saw you for the first time...' He smiled crookedly and looked down, those amazing, lush lashes concealing his expression just for an instant, before he returned his penetrating gaze to her face. 'I immediately realised that my aunt was up to something when she'd decided to send you along for the job. I figured she'd finally decided to start meddling in my private life because she's never been backward in telling me what she thought about it.'

'I was cautious as well,' Sophie reminded him. 'I'd been through enough and had sworn off men, especially good-looking ones with racy private lives.'

'I know. Truth is, my marriage left me with the deep-rooted conviction that love wasn't for me.'

'Love?' Her heart sped up and she could feel a prickle of perspiration film her body.

'You left, and missing you was just the tip of the iceberg. I fell in love with you, Sophie, and I was too blind to recognise any of the symptoms. My goalposts were firmly in place and it never occurred to me that they were capable of being shifted.'

'You fell…*in love*…with *me*?' She plucked at the braid in which she had tied her hair. 'Please don't tease me, Niccolo. You can't get me back into bed by telling me what you think I want to hear.'

'You admit that you want to hear it?'

Sophie blushed, feeling as though she'd been caught in some kind of trap.

'No…' She thought about what he'd just said and her heart did a few more somersaults. Did she want him to stop? Of course, she wasn't going to fall for any smooth talk and casual lies, but his words were like nectar. 'Maybe…' she fudged.

'Which bit do you want me to repeat? The bit where I tell you how hard and fast I fell for you? Or the bit where I say that I've been a blind fool for not seeing what was in front of me?' His voice was soft and serious and thoughtful. 'I can't live without you, Sophie, and what I'd really like is for you to give me a chance, a chance for us to build a family.'

Which bits did she want him to repeat?

All of them. For ever and in slow motion. Because happiness could not have felt more perfect.

'Really?' was what she said, and he smiled.

'Really. And to prove I'm not stringing you along,

which, incidentally, I would never do, I'm going to do something I always swore I would never do again. I'm going to ask you to marry me. So, Sophie, will you wear my ring and spend the rest of your life by my side? Because if you don't then I have no idea what I'll do.'

'Give me a while to think about it…' Sophie smiled. Cloud nine was feeling good. 'I've thought. Yes. Yes, I will. Because I love you now and for ever.'

* * * * *

COMING SOON!

We really hope you enjoyed reading this book.
If you're looking for more romance, be sure to
head to the shops when new books are
available on

Thursday 12th
May

MILLS & BOON®

Coming next month

THE SECRET SHE KEPT IN BOLLYWOOD
Tara Pammi

It was nothing but sheer madness.

Her brothers were behind a closed door not a few hundred feet away. Her daughter…one she couldn't claim, one she couldn't hold and touch and love openly, not in this lifetime, was also behind that same door. The very thought threatened to bring Anya to her knees again.

And she was dragging a stranger—a man who'd shown her only kindness—along with her into all this crazy. This reckless woman wasn't her.

But if she didn't do this, if she didn't take what he offered, if she didn't grasp this thing between them and hold on to it, it felt like she'd stay on her knees, raging at a fate she couldn't change, forever… And Anya refused to be that woman anymore.

It was as if she was walking through one of those fantastical daydreams she still had sometimes when her anxiety became too much. The one where she just spun herself into an alternate world because in actual reality she was nothing but a coward.

Now, those realities were merging, and the possibility that she could be more than her grief and guilt and loss was the only thing that kept her standing upright. It took her a minute to find an empty suite, to turn the knob and then lock it behind them.

Silence and almost total darkness cloaked them. A sliver of light from the bathroom showed that it was another expansive suite, and they were standing in the entryway. Anya pressed herself against the door with the man facing her. The commanding bridge of his nose that seemed to slash through his face with perfect symmetry, the square jaw and the broad shoulders…the faint outline of his strong, masculine features guided her. But those eyes…wide and penetrating, full of an aching pain and naked desire that could span the width of an ocean…she couldn't see those properly anymore. Without meeting those eyes, she could pretend this was a simple case of lust.

Simon, she said in her mind, tasting his name there first…so tall and broad that even standing at five-ten, she felt so utterly encompassed by him.

Simon with the kind eyes and the tight mouth and a fleck of gray at his temples. And a banked desire he'd been determined to not let drive him.

But despite that obvious struggle, he was here with her. Ready to give her whatever she wanted from him.

What did she want? How far was she going to take this temporary madness?

Continue reading
THE SECRET SHE KEPT IN BOLLYWOOD
Tara Pammi

Available next month
www.millsandboon.co.uk

MILLS & BOON

THE HEART OF ROMANCE

A ROMANCE FOR EVERY READER

MODERN

Prepare to be swept off your feet by sophisticated, sexy and seductive heroes, in some of the world's most glamourous and roma locations, where power and passion collide.

HISTORICAL

Escape with historical heroes from time gone by. Whether your passic for wicked Regency Rakes, muscled Vikings or rugged Highlanders, a the romance of the past.

MEDICAL

Set your pulse racing with dedicated, delectable doctors in the high-p sure world of medicine, where emotions run high and passion, comfc love are the best medicine.

True Love

Celebrate true love with tender stories of heartfelt romance, from th rush of falling in love to the joy a new baby can bring, and a focus o emotional heart of a relationship.

Desire

Indulge in secrets and scandal, intense drama and plenty of sizzling action with powerful and passionate heroes who have it all: wealth, s good looks…everything but the right woman.

HEROES

Experience all the excitement of a gripping thriller, with an intense mance at its heart. Resourceful, true-to-life women and strong, fearl face danger and desire - a killer combination!

LET'S TALK
Romance

For exclusive extracts, competitions
and special offers, find us online:

- facebook.com/millsandboon
- @MillsandBoon
- @MillsandBoonUK

Get in touch on 01413 063232

For all the latest titles coming soon, visit
millsandboon.co.uk/nextmonth

JOIN US ON SOCIAL MEDIA!

Stay up to date with our latest releases, author news and gossip, special offers and discounts, and all the behind-the-scenes action from Mills & Boon...

 millsandboon

 millsandboonuk

 millsandboon

might just be true love...

MILLS & BOON
HEROES
At Your Service

Experience all the excitement of a gripping thriller, with an intense romance at its heart. Resourceful, true-to-life women and strong, fearless men face danger and desire - a killer combination!